For the girls who hide and the fate that finds them.

ONE

STORY

My love story began when it ended. With a savage kiss and a confession whispered in the dark that wasn't meant for me.

I was walking the corridors of Crowne Hall when I was grabbed, pulled into a dark room. Moments later I was shoved into the center of the room. Ms. Abigail Crowne's "must be *exactly* 180 degrees" white tea fell off my sterling silver tray with a crash and shatter.

The smell of salt air floated in the darkness, white cloth draped over one-of-a-kind furniture, and gold frames glinted along the walls. I knew this room—it was designated for only select, trusted servants. This place, though shoved away and forgotten in the no-man's land between Ms. Abigail and her sister Gemma's wing, held millions' worth of treasures.

The antique room.

The door slammed shut behind me, and I jumped, spinning to find the shadow of a tall man only inches from me.

"Excuse me—" I started, but then the mystery man seized my face, his mouth on mine, and words left me. Thoughts left me. All I knew were his lips—unyielding yet soft. *So* soft. Searching and commanding and consuming.

I wasn't ever one to kiss strangers in dark rooms.

I wasn't ever one to kiss, *period*. I'd come close...once, but in the end that boy made it clear he'd wanted only one thing.

This was what people talked about in fairy tales. It was the *pop*. It was *fire*. Something I didn't know existed, a tether in my soul, came loose, and latched on to him. The silver tea tray fell from my hands with a clang to the floor, and I grasped my mystery kisser, trying to give him all that he was searching for.

He slammed me against the wall with a rattle, fingers tangling in my spirally, curly hair. He tasted like lollipops and whiskey.

Who was he? A guard? A cook? No one ever gave me a second look, save West, but his attention proved worse than none.

I dressed conservatively, not even showing my collarbone. Even though I could look other servant staff in the eye, I *never* raised my eyes. I couldn't have people knowing anything about me, because then they would ask questions, like why I was here, why I didn't have any family, why I dressed so conservatively.

Questions opened up doors to the past, and taking one look back meant disappearing into a darkness so black it consumed me.

My mystery kisser slanted his mouth, diving deeper,

and I sighed into him, getting lost in whoever he was, letting questions vanish.

We broke on a breath, his forehead pressed to mine. A glimmer of the dying sunset sparkled on the iron-blue ocean between us. My eyes had adjusted to the dark and I could almost make him out. Messy blond hair, sharp, angular features.

No.

It can't be. He wasn't supposed to be in this part of Crowne Hall.

Each Crowne had their own wing, and they stuck to them like someone had demarcated the lines with lava.

"You came," he said.

Alarm rang my heart like a bell. I know that voice. I didn't want to believe it, but I hadn't *come* anywhere. Of course it made more sense that I would be mistaken for someone, than that I had a secret admirer.

No one admired Story Hale.

I wasn't the girl you looked at; I was the girl behind the girl.

"I always wondered what you'd kiss like now." He dragged a closed fist down my cheek. "It's so much better than my imagination." The groan strangling his voice nearly toppled me. I still had some small hope that maybe this man wasn't the person every sign pointed at.

But then my eyes adjusted, and I knew for certain.

Blue stared back—the notorious steely blue reserved for almost all Crownes. A color as vivid and cutting as the ocean on a stormy day at Crowne Beach.

I should've stopped then. Looked away. *Run* away.

There's a rule at Crowne Hall: *no* servants can look the Crownes in the eyes—ever. It was one I'd obeyed religiously.

Yet I couldn't avert my gaze. There was a look in his eyes I'd only ever dreamed of receiving.

Grayson Crowne, playboy prince, heir to Crowne Industries, was staring back at me. It wasn't to knock books out of my hands and laugh like in high school. It wasn't to kick over my bucket of soapy water while I cleaned his floors. Gray Crowne was looking at me like he *wanted* me.

"You're so goddamn perfect, you know that?"

He pressed me against the wall, abs and chest flat with mine, hips sharp. Every rigid and sculpted piece of him pressed deeper and deeper into me, until even lungfuls of air brought him inside me. He smelled expensive and heady and unobtainable.

"Do you know what I want from you now?" He grew hard on my hip, and suddenly I couldn't speak. I swallowed and shook my head.

"Honesty. Bloody, raw, jagged truth."

Alarm bells rang louder than a tornado siren, blaring in my gut. I knew I should pull away, but with him so close, and his breath hot on my lips, I couldn't.

I wanted that too. Oh my God, I didn't know how much I wanted that until he said it.

I had no right.

I was an effigy of dishonesty. Lies never left my lips, but I made damn sure no one got close enough so the truth didn't either.

His lips went to my neck; then he paused. "Did you change?" I thought for certain I was done for, found out, dead. My heart pounded faster than a jackrabbit, louder than a drum. Then Grayson pulled aside the lace of my high-collared blouse. "What is this? Fuck. I like it. I get harder not seeing all of you."

He sucked on my neck, hard. So hard I saw stars. I knew

he would leave a bruise, and a sick part of me wanted that. I dug my fingers into his side.

This moment didn't belong to me, but I was going to steal it anyway.

"Tell me something. A secret. Anything. Something no one else knows."

"Sometimes I watch you," I whispered. "I know you don't see me, and you don't think anyone is watching."

Brief moments when Grayson Crowne was just Grayson.

Moments where I gave in to the insanity growing inside me.

A pause stretched long enough to be counted by the crash of waves outside. Then a distorted, jagged sound fell from his lips and reverberated against my neck. My knees weakened.

"Tell me more."

I don't know what came over me. I wanted to tell him everything, give him everything, be everything for him. It was a darkness, a need I'd never known before.

"I want you to bite me harder."

The tiny shred of sanity left was screaming at me to *shut the fuck up*. My escape door kept shrinking with each confession. When this inevitably ended, when the lights came back on, there would be no way out.

But he smiled against my flesh before he bit the skin at my neck, and that was all I could think about. All I cared to think about.

"Fuck," he groaned. "Where has this side of you been? More," he demanded.

"You're my first...first..." The word I struggled to say was *kiss,* but he fisted the material at my thighs, and my words left me. "I—I can't do it here. Not like this."

Not again.

He dropped my dress, hands coming beside my head. "More."

"Tell me something," I dared to ask. I'd dreamed of kissing Grayson Crowne...but never had I dared to dream I could ask for admittance into his soul.

Another long, weighted pause, then he whispered, "I'm a virgin too, Lottie."

Lottie? Was he talking about who I thought he was? Wait—too?

Oh no. He thinks I'm a virgin. But *of course* he does. *You're my first...*

"Wait, that's not—" Then his lips were on mine again, and I couldn't think.

The Grayson Crowne was whispering secrets and kissing me, and he'd just confessed he was a *virgin* to me. What was worse, I was kissing him back. I was kissing him back even after knowing those secrets weren't for me—these lips weren't mine.

It made me want them more.

I'd grown up in the basement of this palatial home, and I knew soul-deep the difference between me and him: those who were born with the right to have, and those with the right to want.

With his lips on me, I didn't care. I clawed at his shoulders, willing it to be different.

"More," I breathed into his kiss.

His grin stretched against my lips. "I like that word from your mouth." His tongue swept my lips, hot, demanding.

Then all at once, like a douse of scorching fire, the lights turned on. The bright-yellow light burned. I knew the moment it hit Gray, when he realized I wasn't the person he'd meant to kiss. I couldn't begin to describe the

emotions that swam across his face. Anger, of course. Shock. Disgust.

They cut old scars anew. One time, I'd let myself believe I could fall in love with a prince. I still haven't recovered from the cuts those glass slippers made when they shattered.

"Gray?" At the voice, he tore his eyes from mine. I blinked out of my foggy pain, following his line of sight.

A silhouette was illumined in the doorway, and it took only a second to recognize her. Charlotte "Lottie" du Lac. She looked kind of like me, if there was a better, billionaire heiress version of me.

My eyes were stony hazel, and hers were a warm dark chocolate. She was slightly taller, but the extra inch slimmed her waist and made her legs go on for miles. Her chestnut skin glowed from within, and I was lucky if I got a day without a blemish. Today our hair was similar...but where my curls were without direction, pulled back to get out of my face, hers were piled high, beautiful and natural.

Gray did a double take, turning from her then back to me, who was trying to huddle and disappear into the shadows.

Charlotte sighed. "I don't know why I believed you." She rubbed a hand across her forehead. "This is cruel, even for you."

With that Charlotte turned and left, red-soled heels clacking down the hallway.

"Charlotte, wait—" Gray started, then paused, eyes finding mine once more. The heat, the gentle desire, was extinguished. In its place was nothing save coldness. He looked down the hall, as if torn between chasing her and smashing me beneath his shoe.

He chose me.

In one swift motion, he speared my curls, yanking me toward him by my hair. "I don't know who the fuck sent you, but you'll regret this. Speak a word of what you heard and die, Snitch."

He dropped me so hard and fast I had to throw my hand out to keep from banging into the wall. I sucked in air.

"Don't go anywhere." He shot me a searing look, before turning his sights where Lottie had been.

"I have to!" I blurted. Grayson's eyes narrowed like I'd just spat in his face. "I mean, Ms. Abigail needs me."

I'd been kidnapped into a dream and forgot about reality. I was his sister's girl. I'd spent years trying to get that position and only *barely* achieved it. It was coveted. I'd started out as a servant in the kitchen and worked my way up. There were only two positions higher than working directly with a Crowne, one of which my uncle held.

I'd finally gotten my own room. I'd have vacation time, a higher salary. Tonight was Abigail's sister's birthday party, and she needed me to get dressed. If I didn't show up...

Displeasure iced his beautiful features. I wondered if what had happened really *was* a dream.

"I'm your sister's girl," I said weakly.

A cruel smile speared his pretty pink lips. "You're *my* girl now."

Leaving me with that, Gray left, chasing after Lottie.

TWO

STORY

I stumbled back against the wall, barely keeping myself from falling. I touched my lips, trying to rid the taste of him, the feel of him. That moment wasn't meant for me. The pounding in my chest wasn't meant for me. What I'd just learned spun around and skipped in my head like a scratchy record.

What I'd just *told him*.

What he'd just told *me*.

The whoosh and crash of waves filled the air like loud breaths. I never would have guessed Gray Crowne was a virgin—*no one* would. Every day a new tabloid printed him on the cover with a different girl. I still wasn't sure I'd heard right.

"I'm such an idiot." I exhaled, rubbing my hands over my face.

Sometimes I watched Grayson Crowne when he wasn't

looking, so I know he is cruel, unforgiving, and I have no reason to like him.

Oh, except for that one big, unavoidable reason.

I can't stop.

I'm not certain when my crush started, and I don't know what witch I pissed off in a past life to be afflicted, but it's there. In my heart. Scraping at the walls like a caged animal. My uncle always said I was the smartest person he knew, but when it came to boys, I was a damn fool. I can't say he's wrong.

I dragged my hands across my face. This room smelled sweet and ancient, like some magic perfume, and it was getting in my head. I relived his bruising touch and gentle words. *You're so goddamn perfect.*

Heat seared my gut.

I tore my hands away from my face, staring out the window at a nearly black sky.

That memory is a dangerous drug.

Salty night summer air drifted in through the open window. The sound of crashing waves drew me to it as well as the promise of getting away from the memory of Grayson's hands and lips on me.

I wove through clothed antiques worth more than I'd made in all the years I'd worked here and groaned out the window. Grayson Crowne was going to think I was like every other psycho girl sending him used panties, when in reality, I want *nothing* to do with him or anyone like him.

I had hoped to go my whole life without ever being seen by Grayson Crowne. I'd spent years working my way up to Abigail's girl. I was all but entirely screwed for missing her dressing.

All my life at Crowne Hall I'd lived by a code: don't be seen. I dressed conservatively so no one paid me any atten-

tion. It was the only way to survive. In one stupid, foolish night, I'd made my worst nightmare a reality.

Now he *knew*.

Now *I* knew, forever, what he tasted like.

I dropped my head onto the sill with a sigh just as Abigail Crowne ran out onto the sandy grass below, falling down. I lifted my head, leaning out the window, trying to get a better look. Tonight was her sister Gemma's birthday, and Abigail had a notoriously bad relationship with Gemma. I wouldn't put it past Abigail to start something.

A few seconds later, a very tall man approached her. He looked familiar, but who was he? I squinted as if that would help.

"I thought I told you not to fucking move."

I spun around, breath seized. Grayson stood in the doorway, the yellow light behind him making him bolder, greater. He'd been so quiet I hadn't even heard the door open.

"I didn't—"

"I definitely didn't leave you by the window, but if you're planning on throwing yourself out..." He waved a hand.

My lips parted at the cold words.

He hadn't spoken with any heat before, and he didn't now. Whatever sweetness, empathy, or even anger I'd glimpsed before, was gone. There were no emotions at all. Nothing. This was the Grayson Crowne I knew. Apathetic and entitled, smiles that barely veiled his boredom, edged laughter usually at someone else's expense.

I raised my shoulders slightly. "That isn't what I was doing."

He rolled his rose petal lips. "Too bad."

I fought the urge to bite my nail, instead digging into the

windowsill beside me. His blue eyes seemed to glow brighter in the dark.

Grayson Crowne was more than gorgeous; he was divine. There was a reason girls fell at his feet. He had more Instagram accounts devoted to him than could be counted, his Twitter stans ruled supreme, and it wasn't uncommon for people to tattoo his name for attention.

Grayson Crowne was infamous, notorious; he had the world begging for just a look—and he knew it.

The Crowne family's iconic rose gold hair fell wild over his eyes, straight but reckless, like him. The only thing marring his perfect features was a slightly crooked nose, from one too many fights. Considering the Crowne's on-retainer plastic surgeon, it said more about his personality than it did his bank account.

Maybe it was a warning that he, too, was unhinged, because of all the people to piss off, Grayson Crowne was the worst.

"What are you going to do to me?" I finally asked.

He tilted his head, lids heavy and bored. "Are you one of those chicks that gets off on punishment?"

I opened and closed my mouth before finally managing a very witty and eloquent: "I—huh?"

He took a step toward me, and I wanted to step back, but I was already flush against the window. "You must have heard what I do to the servants who make eye contact with me."

I quickly looked at the floor, shock and fear fighting to pound the drum in my chest. Almost ten years I'd lived in Crowne Hall and I'd never *once* looked a Crowne in the eyes. What made me think I could look *Gray* in his?

He was the worst of them all.

The cruelest.

Maybe even more so than his mother, Tansy. One time a guard accidentally caught Gray's eyes while saving him from a crazed fan. The next day he was just...gone. No one knows what happened to him, but people have theories. Some even think he was deported—even though he was a United States citizen.

Another torturous moment passed, and I knew he'd stepped even closer to me, because his bright-white sneakers came into view. Sneakers I knew cost more than a mortgage payment, that he would wear once then toss.

"Go get your shit out of whatever dark hole you're living in," he said.

Shocked, I snapped my head up, catching his eyes once again. He arched a dark-blond brow, and I quickly looked away.

What the hell is wrong with me?

"Why?" I finally squeaked.

Would I be like the guard? A ghost story the servants told each other?

When Gray finally spoke, every nightmare I imagined paled. "You're coming to my wing."

His wing? *No one* was allowed in his wing, not even maids or cooks or his freaking friends. It was the most heavily guarded place in this palace.

Remember to breathe. In. Out. In. Out.

"I'm Ms. Abigail's girl..." I finally managed. "I need to stay in the wing with the other girls."

He grasped my chin, dragging my eyes to his. Another illicit icy-blue flash before I closed mine tight.

"Not anymore."

Eyes closed, Gray was somehow *more* present. His soft touch and seductive scent heightened. Gray smelled expensive and unattainable, something someone like me

shouldn't be close enough to know, like touching the *Mona Lisa.*

"She'll be mad," I said with closed eyes.

His thumb dug into my chin. "I don't give a fuck."

Silence dug and scraped as I weighed my limited options.

Then his breath warmed my lips.

I stopped breathing. My lungs stopped working.

"We can just pretend this night never happened," I attempted. "You pretend you didn't hear me, and I'll pretend I didn't hear you."

That was the absolute worst thing to say, I realized too late. We hadn't acknowledged *what* I'd learned in the dark, and that had been my nebulous armor. But then I spoke, and his grasp on my chin turned vicious, deep, cutting.

"Should we?" he asked, so deathly calm and quiet. "I don't know, Snitch. How the fuck am I going to pretend I didn't hear your psychotic little love confession? Gonna have to start sleeping with one eye open now."

I closed my eyes tighter like that could protect me.

He dropped me with violent force.

"Pandora doesn't go back in the box. You have ten minutes."

What if I say no? pricked my tongue, but I didn't dare ask.

Grayson and I are the same age; we'd lived in the same house for years, and even attended the same school for a while, but I doubt he remembers me at all, or even knows my name. Because I'm someone who has to close my eyes to keep from seeing his, and he's someone who shines so bright it demands everyone's stare.

I swallowed, then nodded, turning on my heel toward

the servants' quarters, when his sultry voice drifted over my shoulders.

"You have no idea what you did tonight. But you will, soon."

The servants' quarters were on the west end of Crowne Hall, and, like most of Crowne Point, were something out of *Downton Abbey*. They had been my home since late freshman year of high school, when my mother died. Each room had phones with a mainline to the Crownes we served, but we might as well have used bells on strings. Ms. Barn was head of the girls, and my uncle, Mr. Hale, was head of the boys.

Gray might not have known who I was, but he definitely knew my uncle. If there was any servant the Crownes knew, it was Woodson Hale. He'd lived at Crowne Hall longer than Grayson had been alive, and he had cleaned up more messes for them than a fucking Roomba. He was one of the few servants the Crownes respected.

I sighed when I got to my bedroom. The wallpaper was peeling from the beach humidity. My bed was a twin, there was no closet, so I had to make do with a dresser smaller than most, and I had only one slightly crooked window above the bed.

But it was mine.

Or...it had been.

"Where have you been?" Ms. Barn's baritone voice startled me into a rigid spine. "I covered for you when Ms. Abigail called down, but I will *not* do that again—where are you going?" She broke off, seeing my paltry personal items shoved in my hands.

"Mr. Crowne has requested I stay with him."

Her jaw tightened.

I adjusted my grip, barely stopping my notebook from toppling down from my mountain of things.

"You don't have to do that, Story," she said after a moment. "The Crownes are a lot of things, but they aren't *that* kind of employer. They don't spoil their own fruit. Whatever he requested, I'll work it out. Stay here. I'll talk with Mrs. Crowne."

"It's not like that," I mumbled.

At least, I hope it isn't.

I rubbed my uniform-issued black leather flats on the cement floor. I sensed if I told her the truth, I would be in even more shit, so I told her an abridged version.

"I looked him in the eyes."

She sucked in a breath. "Story..."

My eyes wandered to the side, miserable, ashamed. The moon had risen outside my crooked, peeling window.

Ms. Barn didn't try to stop me when I left.

I paused outside a black wood door, my uncle's room. My uncle was like a father—actually, more of a father than my real father had ever been. He'd taken me in when my mother had finally succumbed to her demons. He'd always had dreams for me, even if I wasn't able to make them come true. College, an MFA, out of Crowne Point, a better life than he'd led, than my parents had led.

My hand raised in a knock.

What would I tell him?

I *can't* get fired. His health had been declining recently, and I'm the only one who looks after him. He's someone who spent his whole life looking after others, so he doesn't know how to look after himself. I force him to eat meals. I force him to go to the doctor. Without me, he'll have no one.

Crowne Hall isn't exactly somewhere you can just stop by and visit.

He was also the only person in this mansion with a shred of sympathy left for Grayson. No matter how cruel or wicked Grayson got, my uncle's understanding was unfailing. He always said Grayson Crowne was a nice boy who was forced to grow thorns to survive.

I dropped my hand.

He always said the key to surviving this job—to surviving Crowne Hall—was to keep your dignity. I think I'm about to test that.

The pitter-patter of my black flats tapping against black marble floors was the only sound as I walked to Grayson's wing. Crowne Hall was deathly quiet—odd, considering there should've been a party going on, the one I should have helped Abigail get ready for.

I held my items tighter against my body.

The closer I got to Grayson's wing, the darker it got.

Outside, Crowne Hall was known for its dark spires and shingles, a black castle that could be seen from anyplace in our town of Crowne Point. It was more than a mansion; it was a palace stuck in time. Inside? It was like something out of a Poe poem. Floral molding cut into pearly white walls, inky black railings and doors, with a peppering of gold trim.

Just outside Grayson's wing, I stopped.

Two scary-looking men in charcoal suits flanked either side of the arched doorway. They didn't so much as glance in my direction. Whereas Abigail had one constantly changing guard, Grayson was always flanked by a group of security.

I took a slow step, watching them.

When they didn't stop me, I scurried past them, looking

over my shoulder to double-check they weren't about to take me.

They hadn't moved a millimeter.

That didn't calm me. No one got past them without Grayson's say-so, not even maids.

Grayson was waiting for me.

I walked slowly down the hallway, soaking in my surroundings. I'd never been to Grayson's wing. In fact, none of my friends and coworkers had. The only person who'd been here, whom he *allowed* here, was my uncle. He made my uncle clean the entire fucking thing.

And yet my uncle still defends him.

Grayson's wing was long and winding, the architecture ornate, but it was so...empty. No pictures. No paintings. Nothing on the tables and no blankets on the chairs. Somehow my small bedroom felt more filled than this.

I finally reached his bedroom at the end of the winding wing. If I kept walking, I could go through a gilded door, taking steps down to Grayson's *own* personal beach. I'd never heard of anyone going there, not even my uncle. Instead, I turned and faced black-and-gold double doors, so huge I had to tilt my head back to see the top.

We servants had *one* question we were allowed to ask the Crownes, one thing we could say to them. One.

You called?

Should I knock on his door and act like I was any other servant coming because he rang?

I looked back down the long, dark hallway, contemplating running back and trying to disappear among the cooks, when a *crreak* startled me. I took a sharp step back, my personal items falling from my grasp.

Grayson Crowne was sandwiched in the doorway, leaning against one unopened door. Shirtless.

Carved.

The paparazzi photos don't do him justice.

I quickly scrambled to gather all my things, holding them tight to my chest.

"Let me go back to Abigail," I said, trying again. "I'm nothing. I'm nobody—"

"Get inside," he said, cutting me off.

He didn't move from the doorway as I scurried inside, and I brushed his bare golden chest with my shoulder. I swallowed, trying to get my heart under control.

Once inside, I stopped between the arms of two black leather couches. For a second, I forgot to be afraid.

This was Grayson Crowne's bedroom.

No one save close family and my uncle had ever been inside. It was the stuff of legends. Tumblr and Pinterest overflowed with the imagination of his fans, how they assumed a boy like Grayson lived.

And those pictures...all wrong.

Black and wood, iron and gold. I was reminded of Shelley and Poe, Byron and Brontë, all my favorites. My eyes wandered from the empty walls and emptier room, just like the hallway had been, nothing save bare necessities.

Everyone imagined Grayson as a prince living in a castle with warmth and laughter, friends and family. In reality, this place is dark, haunted, hollow, the only light from the chandelier.

"Get on your knees, Snitch."

I jumped when Grayson spoke. His command didn't hold any heat or lasciviousness; his words were burdened, bored, *annoyed,* as if scolding a toddler, like I was a chore. *Don't forget to remind the servant of her place.*

I fell to my knees a second later.

A boy I once knew, Grim, told me if I was ever

kidnapped to keep my eyes shut, because there was only one reason they'd let you see them, and it wasn't good.

This was Gray Crowne's bedroom. It's not a fairy tale, Gray isn't a prince, and I can't think of any good reason someone like *me* is being allowed to see what many prettier, richer, more powerful women have never seen before.

"What are you going to do to me?" I whispered.

"Tell me who sent you and I might let you live."

Out of the corner of my eye, I could see Gray still in the doorway. As a servant, you got good at watching the Crownes without actually looking at them. One leg was propped behind the other, one hand up. Maybe looking at his nails? I wasn't sure.

I could never be sure.

Watching a Crowne was like looking at an old, blurry Polaroid...you never saw the whole picture. Were never allowed to.

"No one sent me," I said quickly.

He laughed caustically. "The Carmichaels? The Blacks? Maybe some rag looking for a good story?"

"It was no one, I swear! It was just me. It was an accident."

I had a half second before I realized I was looking at him, when I saw he was *smiling*. He should've been angry at me, maybe even sad, but he just had that smile. The infamous *Grayson Crowne smile*, with the crooked petal lips that said nothing in the world could touch him, not even losing his chance at love.

Then it clicked *why* I could see those lips.

I quickly looked at the floor.

"No one..." He trailed off, a humorless bite to his words. "So interesting you found me at that exact moment, then. I

guess it's *fate*." He practically drenched the last word in acid and chucked it at my face.

I knew he didn't believe me, and I had no idea how to convince him, or what that meant for me.

He bent down, knees nearly touching my nose. I wasn't sure if it was the sound of waves I heard or the blood rising in my ears.

"What are you going to do to me?" I whispered.

He grasped my chin and slowly lifted my head, until our gazes collided like a car crash.

"I'll give you what you want then," he said, lip hooked. "A night with Grayson Crowne."

THREE

STORY

A laugh bubbled and burst out of me while I waited for Grayson to drop the other shoe.

When Grayson stood up, saying nothing, silence spread like storm clouds. I kept waiting for him to talk, to tell me he was fucking with me.

Opposite me, out the window that rose two stories and cut across most of the room, iron-blue waves rippled molten white in the moonlight. One after the other, they dissolved into the black sea, like the humor inside me dissolving into dread.

"Wait, you're serious?" I shook my head. "I won't do it."

"If no one sent you—"

"No one sent me," I interrupted. "No one!"

"Well, if no one sent you," he continued, boredom in his voice replaced with annoyance, "then how can the girl who *watches me when I'm not looking*"—he mocked my breathy voice—"not want my cock?"

Shame ran as if injected by a hot needle through my veins. Before this night, my crush was easy to ignore. Oh, Grayson Crowne is objectively handsome. Only a liar would say otherwise. That beating in my chest when he walks by? Anger. Anger at the way he treats me and my coworkers.

It was easy to tell yourself what you're feeling is nothing, because someone like Grayson is never going to look at you. You don't have to worry about the nasty, horned whys of how you could like someone like *him*.

It would never come true.

He would never look back.

"Don't you want it to be special?" I attempted.

All he did was laugh.

"I can be of way more use to you than just sex. I won't even be good at it..."

He laughed. "That, I believe."

He walked around me, each step lighting a jolt of electricity in my heart. Patterns from the iron-paned glass wall guarding stairs to the second floor darkened the already nearly black wood at my knees in crisscross shadows. I focused on them, not Grayson.

But then he stopped behind me, and only seconds later vicious hands fisted my hair, pulling my head back so I was forced to stare into his burning gray-blue eyes.

"Let's give whoever sent you a nice story," he growled into my neck. "So you can go back and tell them how you dropped your panties faster than a whore on prom night. How you begged me to fuck you. How much of a fucking slut you are."

I should hate this, but his cruel, crude words burned on my flesh and vibrated inside my bones.

"No one is going to believe me if I talk, anyway," I whispered.

My breath caught, and he dropped me without a word.

I stared at the floor, scalp burning. I know he was trying to call my bluff, to get me to say I *had* been sent, and my heart broke a little bit for him. For someone who couldn't believe in anything other than sabotage. I was a casualty of *fate*, as he'd said. I grasped at straws, something else to change his mind.

"I"—I swallowed—"I, um, don't you like Lottie?" I croaked. "Why would you ruin that with me?"

In that dark room, his feelings for her had been so earnest, so real. What had happened in the few hours between that dark room and now to make him do such a drastic one-eighty?

"The only thing you're ruining tonight are my sheets."

I swallowed all the air in the room at the image.

"But—"

"I think I've let you talk enough. Stand up."

I slowly stood. Grayson regarded me with little less than disgust. Everything about him dripped disinterest, like this was just another boring night.

"Are you some kind of burn victim?" He rubbed his eye, exhaling. "Never mind. I don't fucking care." Grayson paused, a finger below his eye resting on his cheekbone, his glare sharp.

"I don't remember saying you could look at me," he said softly. Too soft.

I sucked in a breath and stared at his chest.

"You want me to sleep with you and I can't look you in the eyes?" I'd learned to swallow indignity, shame, hurt...but even I had limits.

Grayson walked to me, forcing me to step back, back

until I was flush against the glass-paneled wall. I thought he was going to shove himself against me, but he stopped with just an inch of space between us.

His laugh settled in my stomach. "You're not sleeping with me, Snitch."

Snitch. That fucking name again. I wasn't a snitch. I hadn't told anyone anything. I'd only overheard something I shouldn't have.

"What if I say no?"

The Crownes were cruel, but abuse was limited to our morale and dignity, unlike many other employers in their caste who saw a disenfranchised girl as an easy target.

"You have this discount-bin nun look going, but I see you, Snitch. You're just like every other fangirl who sent *the* Grayson Crowne their dirty panties. And like them, you shiver." He curled a spiral of my hair between his fingers.

I tried to hold back a shiver and lost.

I wanted to tell him I wasn't like every other girl—Grayson *Crowne* was my least favorite thing about him—but we weren't shrouded by darkness anymore. I was back to being Story, the unknown maid, and he was back to being Grayson Crowne, the infamous prince, and that was all we could ever be.

I'd seen what happens when the prince chooses someone like me over the princess.

"Say no, Snitch." He tugged on that strand of hair, leaning forward until his mocking whisper burned my neck. "Tell me to stop."

Still with that inch of space between us, his other hand trailed the curve of my waist and I arched into his touch. He noticed. I couldn't lift my eyes to see if he smiled, but I saw the way his jaw twitched, imagined his plump pink lips curling.

Say no. Say no. Say no.

In the dark room he'd kissed me with passion, his fingers bruising. Now his touch was a lazy, bored torment, like the annoyed way he spoke to me. He didn't want me. This night would only end with my heart stomped and bloody.

So why couldn't I fucking say *no*?

His lips found my neck and my gut somersaulted.

"Would you really..." I grasped for anything, something.

I couldn't go through it again. A magical night followed by a nightmare. Giving up a piece of myself to someone who thought they deserved to smash it.

"Would you really take my virginity this way?"

The lie fell from my lips, and he froze.

FOUR

GRAY

"So tell me to stop," I said.

Snitch wouldn't look at me, wouldn't talk, her light breathing the only sound. From this angle, her eyelashes were too fucking long, eclipsing her full hazelnut cheeks.

"All you have to do is say no, Snitch," I repeated.

She licked pouty lips, and her kiss slammed back into me. The husky way she'd whispered *please* stuck on a loop inside my chest.

I can't. Fucking. Stop. Thinking about kissing her. Couldn't get the memory of her breath off my lips. How she'd gripped me. *Begged* me.

But that memory should've been Lottie, and for that, I hated her.

"You can't, can you?" I asked, voice rougher than I'd intended.

Snitch tugged her lower lip between her teeth, and her walnut-size eyes met mine. Fuck, she had a problem with

that. For a moment, I let her. They were the most intense shade of hazel I'd ever seen, a stony, mossy green that reminded me of forest floors. In them I saw need blazing back at me that said she'd let me do anything to her.

Still, I stepped off. As far as I was concerned, silence meant no. I ran a hand through my hair, tangling it in the way my mother hated, yet had landed me on the front of many magazines.

"You of all people should know how important this night is," she said. "Otherwise you wouldn't have waited. I don't know why you want to waste it on me, but I'm...I'm not going to lose it with someone who doesn't love me." She looked away this time, eyes glittering.

Important? I flexed my fingers in and out of a fist. What fucking fairy tale was this girl living in?

"If it's so important, then why would I fuck you?" I countered. "You're shit. You're nothing. This night? It means nothing."

A wrinkle formed between her brows and she tugged on the sleeves of her ridiculous dress. Who dresses like that? Floor length, with a collar up to the neck, and long sleeves. She was like a fucking nun.

"In your world, virginity is something you lose on a prom night." I trailed my finger along the lace at her throat, pulling at the collar at her neck, simultaneously bringing air to her breasts and choking her. "Let's be clear, the things I've seen, the things I've done, would wreck you."

My lips were at her cheek, breath ghosting the flesh, when I saw it—the mark, the bruise forming on her neck from my lips.

I want you to bite me harder.

I should've known then it wasn't Lottie I was kissing.

Lottie would never ask for that. But I wanted it to be her. Maybe that was why I ignored the signs.

Now *Snitch* had my mark on her.

I dropped her, taking furious steps away, putting a shit ton of space between us. Until I didn't smell fucking lemons, until I could barely see the mark. The back of my thighs slammed into the edge of a desk, rattling it against the wall.

I lifted myself up on the desk, opening the drawer in front of me, exposing a stash of weed, rolling papers, and loose suckers.

With an arm propped on a leg, I rolled a joint on my knee.

"My game of chicken obviously fucking worked." I licked the paper, watching Snitch. She stared at the floor. "You have two options. Tell me who sent you, or jail."

"No one sent me!" She lifted her head, eyes earnest. "I live here, I work here, this is my *home*."

"Hasn't stopped your kind in the past," I gritted.

"My *kind*," she breathed. "Are we really so little to you?"

We're accused of not treating our servants like people, and I won't deny it, but it goes both ways. To them we're pieces of diamond that they want to take a chisel to. I'd lost count of how many maids or cooks or guards we've had to let go, or even press charges against, because they'd tried to sell a story or steal an heirloom from that very fucking room.

I rooted around the drawer, looking for a lighter. After a moment I found it, lighting the joint.

I sucked in smoke, then blew it out. "So jail, then."

"You're not really giving me an option."

I trailed my ring finger along my other hand, thinking of

the first idea I'd had. "Do you know how easy it would be to make your life hell? I wouldn't have to lift a finger."

Her nostrils flared. "Are you threatening me?"

I smiled. "I was giving you an option, Snitch."

Through the smoke her mossy eyes found me, searching and seeking. Fuck. Those eyes. There was a reason we had our servants look away. Grandfather said it was because training them that way is one more step of corporate security. An intrinsic threat of don't look at us, don't look for our secrets.

Mother said it was because they need to learn who we are and who *they* are.

I think it's because the eyes are the windows to the soul.

Maybe they'd learn our real secret—we didn't have any souls.

Coldness filled my veins again. The kiss, the outfit—Snitch was like every other chick I'd met, pure manipulator.

"You really have some kind of death wish," I said.

She quickly averted her gaze.

"If you weren't there for me, then you were trying to snatch something priceless."

I don't believe in fate. Fate is the bedtime story people without power tell themselves so they can fall asleep.

"I don't know how else to say it. No one sent me. I'm Ms. Abigail's girl. I was on the way to bring her tea. *You* grabbed *me*."

"Are you saying I meant to grab you?" The idea would have been laughable if I wasn't so fucking pissed. "I must have missed the moment when you said, *Hey, you've got the wrong fucking person.*"

"No...no...I just..." She rolled her lips.

Our reflections shadowed the glass wall that separated the living room from the rest of my wing. I realized this was

the first time I'd had someone here other than Woodsy or Mom or Grandpa in, shit...ever. At least since Dad had died.

"I didn't know who you were at first," she said softly. "When you kissed me, I didn't know it was you. I should've stopped it anyway, because it's not like someone would be looking for me." She broke off on a self-deprecating laugh.

And that laugh *sucked me in*. That single shred of honesty, where in my world, no one would ever admit even the slightest chance they could be unwanted.

I leaned forward, elbows digging into my knees.

"But then...I realized who you were, who you thought I was, and I really should've stopped kissing you. I know that was wrong. I knew it was wrong in the moment."

It was like heroin listening to her, watching her.

A Crowne is never wrong; everyone else is simply mistaken.

My grandfather's advice echoed in my head, one of the many pieces of wisdom he'd imparted.

"I didn't stop because..." Snitch took a deep breath, and I leaned even more, trying to swallow every drop. Every slight pout of uncertainty on her lips, the small dip in her brow.

"I knew I would never get this moment ever again. So I stole it." Then she lifted her head, brown-green eyes furious in their earnestness. "But I stole it for *me*. No one else."

Every moment, experience, interaction in my life had taught me honesty wasn't something people actually *had*; it was a word used to manipulate. So why the fuck did my gut believe her?

"Listen, uh..." I hopped off the table. "My harem is full, so good luck."

I stole it for me.

I don't know why the fuck that was twisting me up so much.

I hated her.

Wanted to crush the part inside me that kept reacting.

Wanted to fucking crush her and bury my cock in her at the same fucking time. Shit.

Fuck.

I stole it for me.

That shouldn't affect me. It shouldn't make me twist on the desk in discomfort. She'd pretty much admitted to everything I expected and loathed in a person. However, no one ever wanted to keep the pieces they took from me for themselves.

"What do you mean?" she asked.

"I mean get the fuck out." My voice edged, apathy and humor waning the longer I was with her.

I'd learned never to let anyone see what I felt; even anger was a win.

But she was like poison ivy. Crawling inside, hot, flashing back to hours before when her lips were on mine, her hands clawing at me. A twisted part wanted to scratch the itch.

And her honesty. What was with that? No one ever talked to me like that.

If I never see her again, it would be too early.

"Like back to Ms. Abigail?" she asked.

"I'd suggest leaving Crowne Point entirely, if you ever want to work again," I said. "Maybe try someplace in...fuck, I don't know, maybe Portugal?" I suggested, trying to think of somewhere Crowne Industries didn't have a foothold.

There aren't many.

"Portugal?" she gasped. "But..." Panic strangled her voice, and she looked left and right. "I can't leave. My unc

—" She quickly backtracked. "I mean, this is my job. It's where I live. I have nowhere to go."

"You'll manage." I picked up a black-and-gold rotary phone that connected me to my security. "Yeah, we're done. Come and get—"

Snitch had it out of my hands before I'd seen her move, slamming the phone back against the receiver.

The balls on her.

I *liked* it.

"You wanna die, Snitch?" I growled.

"I can..." She drew her lip between her teeth, and instantly I thought about lemon, what she'd tasted like. Why the hell did she taste like lemons? Not sour, but sweet, Meyer lemons. The ones my mom put in everything when they came in season.

Venom sliced through my veins, hating her, hating myself, for having the knowledge.

"I can help you get Charlotte back!" Her eyes grew *so* wide with the idea, like the eyes of plushie dolls you got for kids.

Earlier, when I'd finally caught Lottie, she'd played it cool like anyone of her status would, but I knew I'd ruined whatever chance I had.

Lottie was like me. Trust wasn't something we gave easily, if ever.

One of the many reasons I liked her.

I paused as temptation stretched its inky tendrils.

The morbid reality was I didn't need to win Lottie back. She was already engaged to me; she just didn't know it yet. It was a merger my grandfather and hers had been working longer than I wanted to fucking think about.

The moment I learned about it, I forced my mother and

grandfather to let me tell her. They gave me a year, until the end of this summer, to do my "pedestrian proposal."

This wedding would happen whether Lottie wanted it or not. If Lottie doesn't choose me willingly, then her father would threaten her down the aisle.

Despite who everyone thinks I am, I won't fucking marry someone whose veil hides their tears.

"That's cute," I said, voice rough. "Thinking I give enough of a shit to chase her."

I went to pick up the phone, and she pressed her hands harder on mine, pinning it down, digging into my skin with little nails I couldn't help picturing digging into my back.

"I know you like her," she said. "You can't take back what you said in that room."

I quirked my neck to the side, a rush of anger I couldn't fucking tamp down washing over me.

"You're right about one thing..." I lifted my hands in the air, pretending to surrender. Like I expected, Snitch lifted hers off the phone, and I snatched her wrist, ripping her to me.

"But it isn't that I can't take back what I said. *You* can't take back what you heard, Snitch."

Her eyes widened and she yanked at her wrist. "Let me help."

I laughed. "The only way you can help is by getting the fuck out of my life. Or cleaning my shirts," I added absently. "Maybe both."

"That's not true I..." She tugged her lower lip between her teeth. Once again that fucking kiss slammed into me.

More.

She was so greedy, so fucking eager.

"Maids talk!" she exclaimed. "I'm a secret weapon. I can figure out what she likes and doesn't like. What she wants."

Her eyes met mine again, brows drooping at my face, misunderstanding my tight jaw and glare. Good. She doesn't need to fucking know I can't stop thinking about that kiss.

She keeps looking at me. And I keep liking it.

Fucking bad sign.

"Seems like a lot of work when I could just get you out of my life for good right now." My voice was too rough.

Lottie and I had been childhood sweethearts, and though people like us don't get to choose who we end up with, I always wondered what it would be like to end up with her.

But it was never like this. With her hating me. With a deadline. With a fucking servant as my last hope—a servant whose kiss I can't stop replaying in my goddamn head.

"It isn't just because I need to stay," she said softly. "I broke something priceless. I stole something that didn't belong to me. Let me help get it back. I don't expect you to believe me, but...I can't live with myself if it ends this way."

The earnestness in her eyes, the way her brows drooped in what looked like shame, once again had me believing her. *Shame.*

When was the last time I'd seen someone *ashamed*?

I loosened my grip, eyes sharp. "I guess I've done crazier things."

"I'll fix it. I promise."

She exhaled, and I yanked her closer. "Oh, but one thing, Snitch. What happens if you fail?"

She swallowed. "I'll leave. I'll leave Crowne Point."

"Nah...that's not good enough anymore."

"I'll leave New York?"

"I'm starting to like my original plan of shipping you the fuck out of the country and never seeing you again."

Never think about that goddamn kiss. Wonder about what she tasted like elsewhere.

Yeah. Great fucking plan.

"If I fail..." She drew her lower lip between her teeth, then sighed, resigned. "I'll be insurance. I'll give you my virginity."

The suggestion stopped me in my tracks.

I raked my gaze over her, picturing it. Her curly hair out of the bun she kept it in. How far down her back did it go? What did she look like under all those clothes? I'd cover her in bruises. Have her begging me for more, like she'd done in the antique room.

Shit.

I dropped her wrist and stepped back.

Bad idea.

Terrible.

But...I dragged a thumb across my lip, thinking. My virginity had always been a fucking anchor, another piece of me everyone wants to steal and sell. But with her? No one would get that piece.

Because I'd own her.

I exhaled. "I guess someone like you has nothing else to offer." Her eyes flashed, but before she could say anything, I cut her off. "Sure, whatever, Snitch. I'll take the cherry no one else wants."

FIVE

STORY

I woke to the sound of muffled voices. I rubbed my head, not quite registering where I was at first. It was like a bad dream. Above me, a three-tiered chandelier glittered in the hazy yellow morning light. Its tapered crystals both modern and gothic.

Then it hit me.

The kiss.

Our deal.

I was insurance to a plan I wasn't sure I could pull off. Maids talked, yeah, but I'd never tried to use gossip as leverage before. If I failed...

What would sex with Grayson Crowne be like?

The things I've seen, the things I've done, would wreck you.

I rolled my head, meeting the messy black sheets of Grayson's empty bed. When I'd gone to sleep, Grayson had put me next to his bed like a goddamn dog—no, worse. Dogs

had beds. He'd made it clear I didn't deserve that. He wanted it ingrained in me that my being in his room wasn't a privilege—it was a punishment.

At least the carpet was plush.

"Who's that next to your bed?" a steady, deep voice drifted inside. I sat up. I knew that voice—everyone knew that voice—and a blanket fell off me. I fingered the silken threads warily. I'd gone to sleep without any blanket. It was like everything else in Gray's wing—silky black, decadent.

Had Grayson given me a blanket?

"Nobody," Gray replied, and a booming laugh followed, pulling me back into reality.

Beryl Crowne, grandfather and patriarch to the Crowne family, was just outside the room. Just his name made me freeze up. Beryl rarely came home, but today...today was the *Swan Swell*.

Shit.

The Swan Swell was famous in Crowne Point. It happened every year, usually a week before their famous Fourth of July party. It was a time when the native swans flooded the sandy white beaches. It also happened to be Abigail Crowne's favorite time of year. She would never forgive me once today passed and I wasn't back in time to help her get ready. So what did that mean for me? What happened when Gray was finished with me?

Would I still have a job here?

Unlikely, I thought glumly.

I stood up, trying to see where the voices were coming from. Grayson's wing was huge. Abigail's entire wing could fit in his bedroom. I mean, just his *bedroom* was two floors. I guess that's what you get for being the favorite heir.

I peered over the iron balcony, down to the bottom floor. The double doors were open, and through them I could see

Beryl Crowne in his iconic three-piece suit, glimpse flashes of his silvering hair.

"So long as the du Lac girl doesn't see..." Beryl Crowne rubbed a hand through his moussed hair. "Your sister is a shitshow. We already have one marriage on the rocks; we don't need yours."

Marry? He was going to *marry* Charlotte? And Abigail was getting married? There was only one wedding I knew of, Gemma's. She'd been engaged for as long as I'd been at Crowne Hall.

Beryl continued. "You know how they get about the mistresses. Delicate matters to be worked out with the prenup."

He talked about mistresses like it was a fucking car or a house.

Beryl Crowne looked my way, and I ducked down. It was one thing for Beryl Crowne to see me when I was asleep, another to make eye contact. To the outside world, Beryl Crowne was famous for trying to cure diseases.

In here, we knew better. Beryl was the boogieman that went bump in the night, the reason people disappeared.

I slowly tiptoed down the spiral staircase, staying crouched.

"Right, yeah," Grayson said.

I could see only one of his shoulders, but I still knew his face by his tone. He *was* famous for it. A deadly disinterest in his blue eyes and chiseled lips that made millions of girls do insane things in hopes of sparking *some* kind of attention.

"But I have to say, if you want to fuck a maid, fuck a maid, Grayson. A mistress is not an excuse to lower the bar; even your father knew that."

"I won't have a fucking mistress," Grayson snapped.

I tripped, making a clang on the metal staircase, and grasped the railing.

Had they been talking about me?

I waited, sweat beading my neck, hoping they hadn't heard.

They started talking again, lowly, and I only caught *end of summer*. I quickly ran down the rest of the way, hiding under the table Grayson had sat atop the night before.

If you want to fuck a maid...

I framed my face in my hands, staring at the floor, trying to work out how so many things could've gone so horribly wrong in less than twenty-four hours.

I've only ever wanted one thing: live my life unnoticed. I was content to live here as a servant like my uncle, maybe even eventually become the headmistress. I wasn't brazen enough to dream. I had them...everyone has dreams. I just wasn't naïve enough to expect mine to come true.

I used to want to be a poet. I would share myself with the world like the women before me who were forced to hide under pseudonyms because their gender or race precluded them from being seen.

Now I don't believe in fairy tales or happily ever afters.

Not anymore.

I hadn't realized Beryl said goodbye until the door closed. I lifted my head out of my hands, finding the room empty. No sign of Grayson.

"You're overhearing all kinds of secrets."

I jumped, hitting my head on the underside of the table. Rubbing my head, I came out, and my mouth went dry; my brain short-circuited. Grayson wore no shirt, black sweat-pants hung indecently low on his sharp hip bones, and his sneakers were untied, like he'd thrown everything on in a hurry. Morning light illumined everything that shadows had

subdued the night before. Hell, everyone with access to the internet had seen Grayson Crowne shirtless, but this was the difference between seeing a marble sculpture in picture and in person.

Grayson Crowne was divine.

And he was looking at me like I was a bug stuck on his windshield.

"Come here, Snitch," he said.

I fiddled with the material of my dress, what I'd overheard weighing on me. He was supposed to marry Charlotte, and I'd messed it up.

I'd messed everything up.

"I had no idea," I said. "Does anyone else know about you and Miss Charlotte? You're marrying her..."

I really had broken the one thing more valuable than anything in the world.

"I promise I'll fix it," was all I said.

The silence was thorny. I pulled at the black threads of my skirt, stretching until light peeked through.

"Do you think I'm going to talk to you, open up, because you weaseled your way into a secret that wasn't meant for you?" Grayson asked. "That we somehow *share* something?"

"No, I just—"

Suddenly my chin was between his fingers. "First day of training. When I say come, you come." Grayson dropped my chin. "Kneel."

Kneel?

I'd learned a few things living here. Crownes aren't your average, everyday entitled rich person. Like their last name, they ruled. This town, the people inside it, the *world*. They demand perfection. They expect fealty.

Swallowing my indignation, I dropped to my knees.

Grayson spoke after a moment, voice low. "That's a good look on you, Snitch."

I rolled my lips, indignity burning its way up like heartburn.

"You think you know me so well, Snitch? It's been less than a fucking day. You don't know shit."

"I know you pretty well," I mused. "Your favorite food is steak. You have a mild allergy to strawberries. You're a Crowne, and my job is to serve you."

"Congrats, you know what every chick with a magazine subscription knows."

Sometimes I watch him when no one else is looking, so I know his favorite food really isn't steak. I don't know why he lies, but he does.

But I'm not going to tell him that.

"What is it you like about me, Snitch?" he asked, voice deceptively soft. "Do you think I'm broken, a bad boy you can fix?"

I wasn't sure how much I should say. How pathetic I should be. To admit that I knew what he was and *still* couldn't stop the fluttering in my heart.

"You know what I hate more than a snitch? Girls so pathetic they dream up scenarios where guys like me would give them a second look."

"I never wanted you to look back," I said quietly.

Silence weighed heavy as stone. I thought for sure Grayson was going to punish me for talking back, but he just disappeared out of my line of sight to the other side of the room, leaving me kneeling.

My knees were starting to ache and bruise against his hard floor, and I wished he'd at least let me kneel on a fucking rug. There were enough of them around, plush and soft.

I knew he returned when a packet of papers came flying at my face.

"What is this?" I asked, flipping through the pages, scanning.

Story Hale, hereby referred to as Party...

———

"A *contract?*" I lifted my head.

He gave me his trademark bored gaze. "Did you think I was just going to take your word?"

"This is weird," I blurted.

"It's standard."

"Maybe for people like you..." I flipped through the pages. It even outlined what would happen if I failed and didn't go through with my end of the bargain—*damages*. I sucked in a breath at the monetary amount. That was a lot of zeroes. I counted nine. It was nothing to Grayson, but to me? There was even a clause about how the damages could revert to my next of kin.

The contract stipulated two months. *Two months.*

It all at once seemed like purgatory and not enough time. The clock was ticking. Two months? Why such an arbitrary timeline? I had to somehow fix what I'd broken in two months, and I had no idea where to start.

"For these two months you'll be my pet. Follow me around. Sleep on my floor." He paused long enough to shoot me a wicked smile. "Sit on my lap."

I averted my gaze, staring at my clothed knees, wrinkly from having slept in them. I'd brought pajamas but hadn't been given time, or a place, to change. Is this how my two months would be? My bladder ached with needing to pee.

Would I have to ask him to do that too?

I swallowed. "I won't do any of that."

"Not yet. I'll have to train you, like any good pet."

"And if I don't?" I tested, tugging the thick fabric at my knees.

"I'm sure there's someone who would worry about you, or...someone who you might worry about." He let his words linger, and my eyes widened at the threat.

Uncle.

Grayson didn't know about my relation to Woodson Hale, and I'd like to keep it that way, but Uncle cleaned Grayson's room every day, usually in the mornings. It was already midmorning. What time did he clean today? I *had* to get out of this room before Uncle came to clean. I looked around, landing on a clock.

The time read ten fifty in the morning.

"No," I said quickly. "I don't have anyone. It's just me."

He arched a brow, and I wondered if I'd spoken too quickly. "Then I guess it's you I'll have to torture."

I threw the papers beside me.

"This is a weird rich-people thing. We should seal it with a secret."

It fell from my lips before I could take it back. It wasn't like Grayson would even realize what I'd given him, the piece of myself he now held.

It was his turn to frown, or a Grayson frown—a slight pout. "What?"

"It's something I used to do with...never mind." My knees were starting to fall asleep, so I shifted, putting the weight on one. "You tell me a secret, I tell you a secret, and we seal our deal."

"You want more of my fucking secrets?" he growled.

I waved my hands frantically. "No, I guess I already know yours. Technically you *do* know one of mine..."

His jaw clenched, muscle twerking, so I added, "But I'll tell you another. Um...I once changed Ms. Abigail's no-fat creamer with fatty creamer when she was being particularly awful. It was better than stabbing her in her sleep."

Silence passed, and I shifted again, trying to put less weight on my knees.

"Is this high school?" he finally asked. "Do you think I give a shit about teenage girl gossip?"

I worked my mouth to the side, thinking. I knew my deepest, darkest secret, but if I told him, it would ruin everything, ruin the lie I'd built my survival on.

I wish I'd waited. I wish...he'd let me wait. I wish he'd called me back afterward. I wish I hadn't been so weak to wish for him to call me back.

So I searched in my heart for the only other color of ink staining it.

"I have a good one," I said after a minute.

"Do you?"

"Yes." I smiled, ignoring his sarcasm. "When my mom died, I wasn't sad, I was relieved. I've never told anyone that because, well..." I picked at my cuticle. "I loved her," I added. "I just wasn't sad when she died."

Grayson folded his arms, giving me nothing. I quickly looked away. God, what was wrong with me? Do. Not. Look. A. Crowne. In. The. Eye.

Did I need to tattoo it?

I shifted with insecurity.

He walked by me, heading to a desk. A second later, a green pen and notebook flew at me, faster than the papers had.

"Write them down," he said.

I hesitated.

I didn't want to have to stare at the words, like looking yourself in the mirror after you've done something horrible.

He pushed the contract to me with his shoe. "If you'd like to reconsider."

I quickly scribbled the words inside the notebook. Eyes on the floor, I handed the notebook up to him, but he pushed it back to me.

"Hold it up, by your face."

I hesitated again, then held it up. Green ink bled through the back of the page.

"Smile," he said.

"Smile?" I allowed myself to look up, to see he had his phone out.

I did as he said, and he snapped a photo of me.

Fear at Grayson having photographic evidence of one of my deepest secrets nearly eclipsed everything, so I almost didn't hear the door *crreak* behind us as my next biggest nightmare approached.

"Mr. Grayson," a firm, weathered voice called out. One I knew very well. The voice that had told me bedtime stories and taught me poetry.

"Over here, Woodsy," he said, but his eyes were still on me.

Woodsy, as in, Woodson Hale, my *uncle*.

Oh my God, oh my *God*.

Shit, shit, where do I hide? Where do I go? How do I get out of this?

"I have to go," I blurted. "I need to use the bathroom."

Grayson tucked his phone in his back pocket. "Do you not realize what you just did?"

My heart lurched into my throat. I could hear my uncle advancing through the bedroom, his soft footfalls like a mouse leaving footprints in dust.

"You have proof of one of my darkest secrets..."

He shook his head, that wicked smile on his pink lips. "You're mine until I say you're not. You stand when I tell you to stand. You kneel for as long as I say kneel. I get to play with you for months."

I lifted my eyes to Grayson's deep, cutting blue eyes, heart throbbing at the promise in them.

The threat.

He quirked his head. "All my pets died. Will you survive?"

"Mr. Grayson—" My uncle stopped abruptly.

No, *no*.

My uncle, the man who'd taken me in when I had no one, who'd practically raised me, who'd worked as a servant his whole life and said the key to surviving it was keeping your dignity, had just found me on my knees before Grayson Crowne.

SIX

STORY

My uncle came to an abrupt stop, eyes landing on me, crouched and shamed before Grayson Crowne's feet. Sewage filled my veins, and this time I looked at my knees, because I couldn't bear to see my uncle's face.

He'd become a blurry Polaroid. His small frame—in a light suit as always—and curly gray hair, cropped close to his dark skin, just out of focus.

What had I become to him? My mother, maybe.

My uncle tried to warn me before he'd brought me in, but I had nowhere to go. My mom was dead. To my dad's side of the family, I didn't exist. My uncle was the only living member left.

A moment passed. I could feel my uncle watching me, and then he asked the only question he could: "Mr. Grayson...you called?"

Not *Why do you have a servant on her knees? What are you doing with my niece?*

Those were questions *I* would have to deal with, and his unasked questions burned into ruinous answers the longer he watched, the longer I didn't stand up.

"You should start with the bed. Strip it."

"Of course, sir."

More shame swamped me. Grayson didn't make it sound like we'd slept together, but he didn't *not* either.

Grayson placed an untied sneaker beneath my nose. "Tie my shoe."

"What?" I jerked my head up, meeting his stony blue eyes. "You can't be serious."

Grayson swiped a measured hand over his forehead, pushing messy blond hair from his brow, his glare pinned on me. I was once again hit with how devastatingly handsome he was, the kind of looks that ruin.

"When I say jump," he said.

I bit the tip of my tongue, anger flooding my chest as I leaned forward, and my fingers shook on the laces. That was when I finally met my uncle's eyes, as I tied Grayson's shoe.

Shame drenched my soul in oil.

I wanted to tell him I was sorry. I was doing this *for us*. So I could stay, so I could be near him. I was doing this because of him. There was more to this than met the eye. I'd stolen something priceless and I had to give it back. He would understand that. He'd instilled me with that value, one my mother conveniently left out.

In the end I looked away.

I tied the final lace, and Grayson pulled his foot back so quickly I nearly stumbled.

"Woodsy?" Grayson asked when he realized my uncle was still there.

Ever the composed one, my uncle straightened his spine

and turned from me to Gray. "Mr. Grayson, I will finish my job tomorrow."

"Sure, whatever."

A spark of surprise shocked my spine. *Sure, whatever* to a servant who'd basically just said he didn't feel like cleaning. I knew they had a unique relationship, but if I ever said that to Abigail, I'd be kicked out faster than I could blink.

I listened to my uncle's retreating footsteps as nausea grew like a weighted balloon inside me. I hadn't realized how much I'd depended on the hope I could keep my shame internal and secret until now.

I couldn't do this.

I couldn't fucking do it.

What was I thinking?

Grayson gripped my chin. "Do you know what today is?"

"T-The Swan Swell," I stammered.

"Time to test that big ear of yours."

SEVEN

STORY

All my years at Crowne Point I'd never been to a Swan Swell party at the Hall. It happened every year and was one of their more extravagant events. A little-known dirty secret: while we have a native swan population, more beautiful swans were imported to swim in the fountains, and silver and white glitter was brushed on their feathers so they shimmered in the air. Women spent the whole year designing their bespoke feathered white dresses.

And everyone looked bored.

At least, those surrounding Grayson Crowne.

"Let's go, Gray." A girl with heavy lashes and heavier lips wove her arm around Grayson's batting her eyelashes.

"I called dibs tonight." Another girl wove her arm around his free one.

Grayson shook them both off without a word or glance, reaching into his back pocket for a cigarette. Still, they

lingered at his side, watching him with gleaming eyes. They all did. Grayson had a quorum of people who hung on his every movement, just waiting for an order.

I recognized them, the way I recognized all Grayson's friends who visited the Hall, but I wasn't certain of their names, couldn't match them to faces. They were all beautiful, made to be on magazines and in movies.

I knew two of the boys specifically. They had the same impeccable features and bored, entitled air of Grayson, but more subdued. Nothing could match Grayson. I'd seen them the most and knew them to be Alaric and Geoff, but I just didn't know who was who.

I should be getting information about Charlotte, but Grayson wouldn't let me leave his side.

Not like anyone would notice me.

I might as well be one of the fountains to these people.

And what *about* Lottie? What about everything I'd been through the past fucking twenty-four hours? She was only just across the fountain, watching Grayson. Charlotte "Lottie" du Lac was a fairy tale princess, with a crown of braids and a dress of flowing white feathers.

I knew the look she wore because I'd worn it myself. It was uncertainty born of heartbreak. She cared about him. I was certain she did.

Gray either was oblivious or didn't care. Impossible to tell. It looked like he wanted to be anywhere else. With his head down and his suit jacket folded to the forearm, tie discarded, the top few buttons on his black dress shirt undone, he was something out of *The Great Gatsby*.

"She's staring at you," I whispered quietly. "Just go to her."

No one noticed me lean forward; no one noticed me period. If Grayson heard me, he didn't acknowledge it.

The models and influencers took selfies; they played a game of rock-paper-scissors for who would go home with Grayson, then posted a video of that game. Grayson just kept staring out at the inky ocean, as if he weren't even here.

"Get the fuck out of here," Gray said suddenly.

And like that everyone stood up and left. Gray decreed it, so it happened.

"Save some for the rest of us Playboy Gray," Alaric-or-Geoff said, chucking a gold leaf truffle at a swan as he walked away. It narrowly missed the swan's head, but still caused it to flutter nervously.

Curiosity grew in my gut. Was I the only one who knew the truth? No, that's impossible. But his grandpa thought he was fucking me. If he was anything like his sister Abigail, I would bet his mother didn't know. Was I the *only one* who knew Grayson Crowne was a virgin? I thought…I thought I'd just stumbled into a secret that wasn't meant for me.

No, I was certain he'd told his friends.

Gray eyed me from behind his lit cigarette as a swan feathered its wings behind him in the fountain. I quickly looked away.

I was getting caught *way* too often.

All the Crownes were here. Gemma Crowne was with her mother Tansy, but Grandpa Beryl Crowne was surprisingly absent. This was one of the few events he attended, usually for his granddaughter, Abigail—*Abigail.*

My eyes spotted the only woman dressed in black.

"What are you going to tell Abigail?" I asked. "If she sees us together?"

Is there anything you can say to salvage my job?

"Tick tock, Snitch," he said, ignoring me. "Do you think you're here to fucking party?"

"If you want me to find useful information, then you

have to let me go. I'm not going to find anything stuck next to you all night. There are no maids up here. They don't come to the party." I could hardly believe I was talking to Grayson Crowne this way, but really, I was supposed to get something out of the maids, and there *were no maids* up here. There never were. Parties were designated for servers and guards.

His eyes slimmed. "So you can find the nearest reporter?"

I sighed. "What good would that do me? I *want* to stay here." Another glare. "Do you trust anyone, Grayson?" My eyes popped with my own gasp. "I mean, Mr. Crowne."

If I didn't know better, I'd swear he smiled slightly.

"Not in the habit of trusting snitches, no."

"Lottie has been watching you all night. Just go up and tell her the truth. She likes you. I'm certain of it."

I pointed at Lottie, and he followed my finger. Of course, for the first time all night, Lottie was with another man. She laughed, touching his shoulder.

My gut dropped.

"Do you know what a Crowne's job is, Snitch?" he asked, after a moment, still watching Lottie. His jaw twitched, eyes narrowing.

Something with pharmaceuticals...or maybe food? Hotels, I think also. I see the Crowne label on *everything*.

"Get married. Do you know how fucking lucky it is that I actually like the person I want to marry? That for a moment, she liked me back? Do you know what you did?" He paused. "You took that from me."

"This is a lot of work for someone you only *like*..."

I covered my mouth, but it was too late. His hand froze with the cigarette at his pouty lips, and the muscles in his forearm tensed, veins rigid in his hand.

What is *wrong* with me?

What happened to blending in? When did I become a megaphone again?

"There you go again, sounding fucking stupid." He inhaled, then blew out smoke. "You think this is a lot of work for me?"

He took a step, nothing but broken blades of grass between us. I focused on his black sneakers, not the hammering in my heart or how my lips dried. But his black sneakers. Because only Grayson Crowne could get away with that at one of the biggest black-tie functions of the year.

He gripped my chin, dragging me back to him, once again forcing my eyes shut. "I see something I like, I take it."

A champagne bottle popped, and I jumped. Grayson dug his fingers harder into my chin as melodious laughter followed, mingling with that of my heart trying to break out of my chest.

Pound. Pound. Pound.

"I don't like anything about you." He rubbed my lip. "And yet I still own you."

No. No he doesn't.

Does he?

He pushed his thumb into my mouth, pressing my tongue down. Tingles erupted along my skin, hot and cold.

"Because you have nothing," he said. "You think wanting something is hard work."

Then, with his thumb still pressing on my tongue, he put his cigarette out on my shirt. My chest bottomed out. Utterly mixed up and lost in the pleasurable feel of him against my tongue and the acrid smell of burned fabric and ashes.

"You really shouldn't be worried about Abigail right

now, Snitch." He slid his thumb from my tongue, roughly wiping the spit off against my cheek. "When I get back, you better have some useful information about the girl I *like*."

I rubbed my lip, stuck on Gray as he talked with his sister. I don't know what's going on with me. Gray is a briar. Each layer you pick at, you cut and bleed.

But I can't stop wondering what's at the center. What if there's something beautiful?

Or maybe I'll just continue to bleed.

My eyes locked with Abigail's.

I should've looked away.

I know I should've.

But I couldn't.

I saw surprise on her face, confusion, then anger. Could she see the humiliation on mine? It was almost like Grayson *knew* she could see us. He stepped directly in our line of sight, blocking her. For a stupid moment, I felt something. It fed into that part of me that kept grabbing at his thorns. Maybe he stepped there on purpose. Maybe he was trying to keep me for himself.

I shouldn't want that.

And yet...

I shook out of it, making sure to walk away before she looked back in my direction. I'd just looked *Abigail Crowne* in her eyes. Somehow I was more of a servant than I'd ever been before, shackled to Grayson Crowne, and yet the lines had never been blurrier.

I wandered from the beach back into the Hall. I had to find something to give Gray, something that would fix what

I broke, or in two months I would give him everything. But I wouldn't find it up in the light and sparkle.

Crowne Hall had many secret doors that led to a labyrinthine underbelly. Maids and servants and cooks and servers worked under the house, while people like Grayson stayed up here.

I pushed open one of the many "secret" doors and slammed face-first into someone coming out. Whatever he was carrying fell to the ground in a crash of broken porcelain and smashed food. The man bent down and started to clean it up. He had closely cropped white curls, a light-gray suit, and only slightly weathered hazelnut skin.

"Uncle?" I asked, surprised. Uncle immediately stood up, turning on his heel to go back down the winding stairs.

"Uncle," I whispered, running after him. "Uncle, wait. Talk to me."

"They are expecting these items; you know how it goes. Crowne comfort above all else."

"Wait, stop, let me explain."

I wasn't sure *how* I would explain, but still.

We wound and wound down the staircase until I could faintly hear the sound of the *real* servant party. Someone yelling *Shots!* with pop music.

"Uncle!" I grabbed his arm.

We stopped at the bottom of the stairs, light melting in from the hallway.

"I have nothing to say to you, Storybook," he said.

My face caved in in anguish. Storybook. A name has so much power, doesn't it? Like a name given by a mother who didn't really believe in fairy tales, but loved to scam the princess out of her pumpkin and the prince out of his castle.

"Please, just—"

He spun on me. "What the hell are you doing? You were almost out of here!"

I sucked in a breath. My uncle never swore.

"Leaving was your plan. I never wanted to go."

"I'm not going to be here forever, and then what?" he asked. "What will you do when you have no old man to care for?"

"I'll become head of girls, like Ms. Barn."

His brows caved.

I slowly removed my grip, saying softly, "Just let me explain what you saw."

He paused. "I've lived here longer than you've been alive. Do you really think I don't know? What was my one rule I said you had to follow when you came to stay with me?"

I looked down. "Don't look them in the eyes."

"I know you. I know you're dreaming of happily ever afters."

"I'm not! Grayson Crowne is horrible. He sees nothing in me. He hates me."

My uncle clicked his tongue. "But what do *you* see in him?"

My uncle always saw through me. What did I see in Grayson? Why did my heart flutter for someone so *cruel*?

I saw...me.

Someone buried and buoyed in secrets. I saw glimpses of loneliness beneath a thick mask.

"He doesn't know who I am," I said, throat thick. "He doesn't know who you are. I'm fixing it. Everything will go back to normal."

He looked at my wrinkled, slept-in dress. Unwashed hair. Unwashed face. I'd barely had a chance to pee. Hadn't

eaten anything. His eyes landed on the cigarette stain. I slapped a hand over it.

"Are you living with dignity, Storybook?

"Yes," I lied.

He took a deep, rocky breath. "I'm afraid you've learned nothing I've taught you."

I countered, "You always taught me I could be on my knees, could have a plate of food thrown at my chest. They could call me names, forget my name, and just treat me like dirt, but I would still be worthy of respect."

He just stared at my dress. "But *you* have to believe that."

A tinkling of bells chimed through the hallway. They always reminded me of Christmas, but down here they were ominous portents.

"I didn't teach you to hide. This won't end well for you." Uncle disappeared in the tinkling of the bells.

I rubbed my chest. Grayson Crowne had kicked over my bucket more times than I could count. Abigail had thrown her tea at me. Gemma and Tansy probably didn't even know I existed.

All that time I thought I'd known who I was. Story.

Sure, I wasn't normally this person, not really. Timid. Shy. Growing up, my mother used to say I was a megaphone because I was loud, and everyone had to know what I was feeling.

I became this person to survive.

First, with Mom. Then, when I moved to Crowne Hall. Piece by piece I hid parts of myself. Hide my body. Hide my soul. *Hide.* Because they can't take what they can't find.

I don't know how Uncle does it, stays himself while others throw food on him.

Maybe I've been hiding so long I'm starting to disappear.

I haven't been living with dignity. I've been living with its dark twin, shame. Because even though I've got a cigarette stain on my shirt from how little Grayson sees in me, I know if im not careful, it will burn through to my heart.

EIGHT

STORY

Crowne Hall was the last remaining bastion of old Crowne Point. Like the family itself, it stood out amid the blue and white beachy shops and houses of the town. Once upon a time, the town shops had been black like the Hall, but the new wealthy felt that was a bit too gothic for a New York beach town.

Down in the servants' quarters, they hadn't bothered updating it like the rest of the house. Hundreds of maids, valets, and chauffeurs were crammed into a small, dank room, the only light from a dusty chandelier. They played cards or did shots on centuries-old wood tables. Anything else while they waited to be called. This was what the Swan Swell party had always meant to me.

"New game." A servant with red hair, Andrew, slammed his hands on a table. "Every time a Crowne calls us up for something they could've easily solved themselves, do a shot."

"I don't feel like getting alcohol poisoning tonight, so..."

One of them, a girl with dark-brown hair, sat up when she saw me and rushed over. "Story!"

I didn't have friends, but Ellie was the closest thing. We'd worked together in the kitchens, and though she hadn't moved up with me, we'd remained close-ish.

"Where have you been?"

"I, um," I rubbed my forehead, no idea where to start with an explanation.

"Your bedroom was cleaned out when I went to say good night. There are rumors spreading about you and *Grayson Crowne*," she whispered. "Stephanie swears she saw you go into his wing."

"I did," Stephanie said. "So either you're fucking him or you're lying. You're a code-breaking slut."

I glared, and she shrugged. There are two types of servants. The lifers, and the rest. Lifers watch each other's back. We cover for one another, a family without blood. Because we live by a code. It's us vs them, and you don't cross the line.

"*I'm* fucking Grayson Crowne? That makes as much sense as you being on time for a fucking shift."

Stephanie flipped me the bird.

The servants had set up their own spread of food, nothing like upstairs, but I quickly grabbed a piece of pizza, not sure when I'd get the chance to eat again.

"Which one of these chicks is Lottie's girl?" I asked Ellie, shoving the pizza into my mouth. She raised a brow, and I shrugged, having no way to explain it. But Ellie was Ellie, and she trusted me, so she pointed to a small brunette on her phone.

I plopped down next to her on the worn plaid couch. "Uh, hey."

She didn't look up from her phone. "What?"

"So..." I said. "I need info on Charlotte du Lac."

Her brows popped, interest piqued, and she lowered her phone, looking me up and down. After a second or two, she said, "You're the one fucking Grayson."

"T-That's—" I broke off as the mainline phone to the Crownes started ringing and everyone shouted:

Shot, shot, shot, shot!

"No!" I shouted over them.

She rolled her eyes. "Whatever, you know how it works. Pay up."

I narrowed my eyes. "One week's wages."

"Two."

"One and a half."

She arched a brow, then said, "Fine."

"I need something Lottie loves. Something no one else knows."

The brunette furrowed her brow, thinking; then a slow smile speared her lips. "Lemon cakes."

"Charlotte du Lac...loves...lemon cakes," I told Grayson, out of breath from running to find him—scared that if I didn't get to him soon, he'd think I was up to something.

He didn't look up from his phone.

Twinkling lights glimmered above us, and the black ocean glittered at his back. Behind me, a gold-flecked white chocolate fountain streamed like water. The party was getting late, easy to tell by the feathery fans every woman held. They'd lost their haughty edge, now mirroring their owner's tipsiness, flitting and floating like butterflies.

What would it be like to be one of them? The women dressed in white? The swans?

Seen.

After a minute of silence, I said, "That's what I learned."

Slowly, as if with great effort, Grayson put his phone in his breast pocket. "That's your great plan? Lemon cakes?"

I made a fist.

I paid nearly *two weeks' wages* for that information.

"No one knows she loves them," I added.

"Maybe because it's not worth finding out." He exhaled and shook his head. "It's my fault. I enabled...this." He cast a disinterested hand in my direction, then moved to leave.

I grabbed his arm.

"*Everything* is worth finding out. How are you going to convince her you love her when you don't even care enough to learn her favorite food?"

A wrinkle formed between Grayson's perfectly smooth golden brows. For a moment it was like he was looking at me—Story. For once, his stony blue gaze wasn't cutting or bored. It was open...soft, almost.

Then it wandered to my grip on his arm, and I dropped him, folding my arms, as if that would hide what I'd done.

"So..." he said, still eyeing where my hands had been. "Lemon cakes."

Unsurprisingly, it was easy for Grayson Crowne to conjure lemon cakes. Less than an hour later and fresh from the kitchen, we were on our way to woo Lottie du Lac. I followed Gray like a puppy out of Crowne Hall and back

onto the beach. No one noticed me; all eyes were on Grayson, and I was back to being invisible.

This I could do. *This* I was used to. Blending in was as second nature to me as breathing.

I'd barely stepped off the stone steps and onto the sandy grass when someone shouldered me—that I was also used to. About to stumble, I was steadied instead.

It all happened in less than a second. Grayson's firm hand, steadying my shoulder. His slight squeeze, as if making sure I was good to stand. Then his reach beyond me and his yank on the collar of the guy who'd grabbed me, tugging him back.

"Are you blind?" Grayson growled.

The tendril of possession weaving fire in his voice sent goose bumps up my spine. It was like in the antique room, and it lit the thing in my soul on fire, the one I need to rip out.

The guy blinked. "Dude, what?" He was one of the boys from earlier—Alaric or Geoff, I still wasn't sure. This boy had dirty blond hair, clear brown eye, and a sharp square jaw.

In one hand Gray held Lottie's lemon cakes; his other held Alaric-or-Geoff by the back of his suit collar.

Gray's jaw flexed. "Look where you're going, dumbass." He shoved him forward, making him stumble like I had. Alaric-or-Geoff walked a few paces away, situating himself on a stone wall that wrapped around the terrace. He pulled out a cigarette, eyeing me with a wrinkled brow.

When I looked away, I found Grayson watching me. This time his eyes burned; they smoldered and crackled.

"Grayson?"

The moment snapped in two. Grayson looked away, and I turned to find Lottie du Lac. Her two best friends,

Aundi and Pipa, flanked her. If Lottie was a princess, the same couldn't be said for her friends. They were like every mean girl stereotype in existence.

Lottie looked between us. "Were you asking for me?"

"Yeah."

Lottie looked at me again, and I quickly stared at the floor. Did she recognize me from the night before? It was unusual, though not entirely rare, for a non-Crowne to look us in the eye. We were instructed never to look back.

Lottie's soft, melodic voice continued. "If this is about last night..."

"It's not," Grayson said almost immediately.

"Oh shit, what went down last night?" Alaric-or-Geoff asked from his perch on the wall. He pretended to jerked off into the air toward Lottie, and Aundi shoved him.

"Shut up, Alaric," Aundi said.

Alaric. The blond one is Alaric. I made a mental note as he fell backward into Mrs. Crowne's favorite lilacs, laughing.

Grayson shifted the box he was holding, decorated in a sparkling white bow and feathers. Inside sat four lemon cakes with the cursive letter *L*.

Lottie rolled her softly glossed lips together, as if not wanting to ask her next question. "Who did I see you with last night?"

I stared at the grass like it would grow holes.

"Some random. Meant nothing."

I wished I could scarify his words on the part of my heart that wouldn't won't stop fluttering. The part of my soul that kept trying to sneak peeks into his.

This is the girl he's going to be with. This is his future wife.

I'm just a thief.

None of this is for me.

Grayson thrust the box out without emotion. "Here, this was lying around, and I heard you liked them."

Lying around?

I wanted to shout out, strangle him. *Tell her how much trouble you went to to get that damn box.* How much you *care.* Stop *lying.*

"They're lemon—" Grayson started, only to be broken off by Lottie's scream.

I looked up just in time to see her drop the box. In the distance, *pop pop pop.* The fireworks going off early. At the same moment, screams sounded. I followed them to smoke rising above the trimmed green hedges of Tansy Crowne's beloved garden maze.

"What the fuck, Gray?" Aundi snapped. "Are you trying to kill her?"

Just like that, fire forgotten.

"She's allergic to lemon. Just smelling it can put her into anaphylaxis."

"He didn't know," Lottie said, sounding scared. "He couldn't."

"He's Grayson fucking Crowne. He knows everything," Aundi said.

Alaric started laughing.

"Not funny," Pipa said. "Are you okay?"

"Right," Alaric laughed. "It was fucking hilarious."

"I think they used fake lemon," Lottie said, voice still shaken. "Gray?" She looked at him, eyes wide. Hurt. "You didn't know I'm allergic, right?"

"You're *allergic* to lemon," Gray repeated, but the venom icing his tongue was meant for me.

Fuck.

NINE

STORY

"I didn't know," I said for what must have been the umpteenth time. "I really didn't know."

Anger rolled off Gray and turned into terror inside me.

I'd followed his silent fury until we were just inside the gardens. He didn't say a word after Lottie rushed off with her friends. The sprawling maze flanked us on both sides. The party had ended early due to the fire, and it was eerily silent, only the smell of wet smoke mingling in the dark.

"I promise," I said. "I was told she loves lemon cakes."

I'd paid nearly two weeks' wages for that information. What the *hell* was that girl thinking? How could she not know her own employer's allergy? Unless...was it on purpose?

Gray pounded down the cobblestone, and I jogged to keep up. Beside us a pond that stretched over a mile glittered black in the night. Tansy Crowne fancied herself Marie Antoinette—no, that wasn't right. Tansy Crowne

would be insulted at that comparison. Versailles was a parking lot compared to Tansy Crowne's garden.

Gray took a harsh right into a path of thick, silky flowers. I stopped. You *don't* walk into Tansy Crowne's garden, not unless there is a clear footpath.

Grayson grabbed my wrist, yanking my body to his. His hair had fallen wild over his eyes, but they shined through. Burning.

"Where are you taking me?"

A salt breeze blew and petals floated down, around and between us.

"Lesson number two in training," he growled. "Follow your fucking master."

Gray was walking so fast I had to jog to keep up with him, but I also tried to soak in as much as I could. This floral tunnel wasn't known to servants. We shared all the secrets we found.

And it was beautiful.

Flowers surrounded us on all sides. The smell of smoke from the maze was strong, mixing with the heady scent of roses and lily and orchid. In autumn the flowers above us would fall and their leaves would change to brilliant ambers.

My foot caught and I jerked, lurching forward, the ground rushing to me. I threw my hands out to brace my fall, but seconds before impact, I was yanked back up with twice as much force.

Grayson held me by the collar, lips twisted in annoyance.

"Thank—you!" I finished on a yelp as Gray tugged me

by the collar down the flower tunnel, all but dragging me on my heels. I still didn't know where we were going. Part of me wondered if he was going to murder me.

Then we stopped.

I rubbed my neck, staring at...a shack? It looked like an old gardener's shack.

I eyed Grayson, wondering if he really *was* going to murder me.

"What are—" I broke off, stopping myself from asking, *What are you going to do to me?* Because how many times in the past twenty-four hours had I wondered what this boy was going to do to me, let alone asked? I stared at this shack, determination steeling my spine.

"I don't care. Make me kneel. Make me tie your shoes. You can't hurt me." I swallowed. "I know my place."

Intrigue flickered in his eyes; then he smiled.

He pushed the door open.

———

Outside was a shack.

Inside...inside was insane.

Music thrummed low. The walls were dark and glittered like diamonds. The ceiling dripped crystals. I tilted my head back. There must have been thousands of crystals, because you couldn't see anything but them.

"You sure about that, Snitch?" Gray's low voice heated my ear, his hand ghosting my lower back. Before my goose bumps had even left my skin, he was standing tall and walking across the room, already talking to some guy.

This was somewhere I couldn't blend in.

I stuck out like a sore fucking thumb.

All eyes were on me. Each step I took was a scratch on

the record. I couldn't hear what they were saying, but their lips moved with their eyes. Everywhere I looked, I found a new set of glowing orbs.

I had no clue where I was. I knew by the outside it was small, only fitting maybe fifteen people, but because it was dark inside, it seemed big. Vast.

Alarm rushed and pounded with the blood in my ears when I realized I was the only servant here.

They didn't even have a bartender.

"Surprised to see you here, Sis," Gray said.

In the center of the room, Gemma Crowne and a few others were seated around a softly glowing circular table. She pulled cards and chips from a metal box, but the chips were unmarked.

What were they playing for?

"Ha ha," Gemma said sarcastically, glaring at Gray. "I thought you weren't coming tonight?"

Gray shrugged. "Plans changed."

Grayson took a seat at the table just as I spotted someone. She had changed out of her glittery white tulle dress into jeans and a sweater more expensive than anything I owned.

Charlotte.

Everyone had changed. Only Grayson was still in his suit pants and dress shirt. Because unlike them, he'd traded a valet for me.

Charlotte was laughing with her friends, totally oblivious to me. I knew I should either stay put or follow Gray... but I crossed the short distance to her. Sweat beaded my neck, like tiny pinpricks.

Aundi and Pipa stopped talking once I reached them, glares furrowed on me. Charlotte stopped talking a second after them, slowly turning around at their glares, confusion

marring her smile.

It must have been my imagination. The room didn't go quiet. The music didn't get lower.

They waited for me to talk first. I wasn't someone who could just come up to someone like *them*.

But I could fix it, right here. Grayson was being so fucking stupid. I just had to tell her everything. Every little piece of what happened. Then she could take him back, and pull me out of this hell I couldn't stop myself from diving deeper into, the place that was starting to whisper *more*. The place that wanted to *take* instead of give back what I'd stolen.

"It was my fault," I said. "I told him the lemon cakes were your favorite. He was trying to do something nice for you. I had no idea you were allergic."

A moment passed.

Lottie's pretty, perfectly plucked brows caved. "Who are you?"

"Snitch," Grayson called out behind me. "Come."

Still, I stared into Lottie's wide brown eyes. *Tell her* what happened last night. I'm the one who stole your moment.

"Snitch."

Venom threaded his impassive tone, so subtle it barely stung.

I dropped my shoulders, going to Grayson.

He had a lollipop between his lips, and his blue eyes were harder than granite.

"Is she your buy-in?" Gemma asked. "I could use a new maid. I just had to let one go. So unfocused."

My head shot up, eyes wide on her. I *must* have misheard, because they wouldn't bet with people.

So casually Gemma asked it, too, like I wasn't a person.

That maid she had to let go? The unfocused one? She was fifty with fucking cancer.

He shook his hand in the air, and I let out a breath I didn't realize I was holding.

For a brief moment I thought the most I was going to be punished for my mistake was being made to feel like dirt.

How naïve.

When you look at a Crowne, they ruin your life.

When you cross a Crowne...they make sure you wish you'd never been born.

"You don't want this one," he said. "She's defective. She'll fatten your drinks and think about stabbing you in your sleep."

My mouth dropped open. My *secret*. He'd shared it without any hesitation.

"Then why is she here?"

Gray seemed to consider that, rubbing his bottom lip. "Who wants a night with a virgin?"

TEN

STORY

"Ugh, really, Gray?" Gemma threw her head back, then stood up, grabbing a bottle of tequila. "It's going to be that kind of night? I'm out."

She poured the golden liquor into three shots before taking them all herself. I stepped back, but I was like glitter trying to disappear into dust. An antelope hiding among lions.

Grayson Crowne, the lying playboy betting the virginity of a lying virgin. It might've been funny if I wasn't the lying virgin about to lose her fake virginity.

I don't know when the first tug came, when the first hand grabbed me, but soon I couldn't differentiate between all the paws.

"She's dressed like a fuckin' nun," someone said. A grab on my wrist, another on my hip, shoved from one person to the next, down the line. I tried to cover myself, but too many people were grabbing at me.

"And not a hot one," another said, and I was shoved forward, then sucked back into the grabbing hands.

Through it all Gray watched, blue eyes hazy in his smoke, icy and unfeeling.

"I don't know..." A new voice, another hand. "It's *kind of* hot."

Gray exhaled a musky, twirling tendril of smoke.

"We should get to see the merch first."

Some distant part of my brain told me to stand up for myself, but I couldn't remember the last time I'd done that. I wasn't sure if I even remembered how.

I was drowning. My voice gone, my breath gone, sinking into hands and smoke...

Gray grabbed my wrist, pulling me from them, still with his joint in one hand. I twirled until I fell to his lap.

I immediately froze.

I'm on Grayson Crowne's lap.

He reached for his cards, arms wrapped around me, keeping me pinned. The action jostled me, pressed me deeper into him. I sucked in nothing; I had no air left to swallow.

"Do they let you rip open the plastic and eat the steak before you buy it?" Gray maneuvered to hold his cards in one hand, his joint with the other. "Sit down, fuckheads."

Everyone slowly did as he said, and I could see the calculations in their heads. I wasn't a person, I was a *thing*, like a car or a house. How much was I worth betting?

Turns out, I was worth a company, a rare car, a house, and an *island*. I might've felt special if I wasn't so terrified.

The game started. I should've been focused on who was winning, who was going to get a *night with me*, but I couldn't stop focusing on the tiniest of things. The warmth suffusing off Grayson's chest, seeping into my back. His breath heating

my neck. How each time he called, he leaned forward and wrapped me tight in his biceps, and his lips grazed my neck. Their softness was a shock to my skin, hair rising to meet them.

He hadn't ceased caging me, even after everyone had calmed down and stopped looking at me like meat. Gray was tall, built like a swimmer. His knuckles were calloused, and his arms were thick. I felt oddly—wrongly—safe.

I shifted, an ache growing between my thighs.

I rolled my hips, trying to extinguish the ache, and it only made the throbbing *worse*. I shifted again, then again, trying to fix it.

"Chill," Grayson said, making me jump, lips at my ear as he played a hand.

"You're *gambling me* and telling me to chill..." I couldn't contain my incredulous laugh.

Suddenly there was a blunt against my lips. "Shut the fuck up, Snitch." He picked up his cards, holding the blunt against my lips. Waiting for me. I shifted on his thigh, trying to get back to a comfortable position.

Grayson gripped my thigh, keeping me still. "You're making me lose my focus. When I lose focus, I lose. Do you want that, Snitch?"

When I did nothing, his stony gaze connected with mine, a question in them. To extinguish that and whatever was happening to me, I inhaled.

It wasn't my first time smoking. Not by a long shot. But as the smoke filled my lungs, my eyes locked with Charlotte's.

Everything short-circuited. Smoke seared my throat. Tears blurred the room.

I couldn't cough hard enough.

Lottie didn't look happy. Her friends? Even less happy.

"This is a bad idea," I coughed.

Gray put the blunt back in his mouth, and my stomach did another pancake, thinking about how it had just been in mine. It stuck out of the corner of his lips.

"Nervous?" He arched a brow, a playful curve to his pink lips.

I blinked out of the hazy delirium I lost myself in whenever Gray shone his light on me.

"Charlotte looks upset," I said.

He froze with the hand he was about to play.

Then kept going.

"You should tell her the truth," I continued. "If you want her back. Tell her the truth."

"You really like stirring the fucking pot."

"It's called honesty."

He laughed. "Right. You're the biggest liar here."

"The more you lie the more you push her away," I said. "She thinks you don't like her."

Maybe it was the weed lowering my inhibitions.

"I want your pussy, Snitch. Not your psychoanalysis." With one hand still holding the cards, his other came between my thighs.

Deep. Breath.

He's fucking with me. I know he's fucking with me. He wants a reaction. I struggled not to give it to him. I'd always been too sensitive, and even with the material of my skirt as a shield, it wasn't enough. It was too thin, and I wished I'd worn something thicker.

Grayson Crowne's birthright was to own and possess, and it bled into the weight of his hand, the casual way he held me.

"I've been thinking about how to punish you for that

stunt you pulled." He lifted his leg, spreading my thighs around his knee.

I swallowed a breath. "This isn't my punishment?"

"Maybe I want you to beg me while I gamble your body. I haven't decided." He exhaled hot smoke, blurring the poker table, the glittery room.

My belly did a wicked twist at his words, feeding at the heat that was burning me to ash in his lap.

Don't. React.

That's what he wants. All of this is a game. He wants me to fall apart in his lap so he can laugh when I do. I stayed stock-still, saying the words over and over in my head.

"I'll never beg you." My words were jagged and rocky, and I swear Grayson smiled against my neck.

"I've been thinking we should put your virginity to the test." His lips vibrated against my skin. "It's always the quiet, modest ones that are the freakiest."

I know he was just saying it to get to me, and what sucked, is it *did*. Somehow, my virginity was still the most special thing about me, even though I'd lost it years ago. The reason these guys were willing to bet houses and cars and companies.

"I remember the way you begged. How you whispered *more*."

He was growing hard beneath my ass, but when he spoke, his words were laced with no emotion.

I tried to focus on the cards flying across the table. On his long fingers dealing the cards. But I couldn't fight the deep, needful ache inside me. It was consuming me, and he was going to humiliate me.

I had to fight back.

"So says the loudmouth playboy *virgin* with a hard-on," I whispered, words too breathy for my liking.

He tensed.

Then picked up his cards.

When he spoke, his voice was rougher. Meaner. "I don't believe for a minute you haven't had a cock inside this pussy." He gripped me harder, and my lips parted on a hollow breath. I couldn't lift my head to determine if anyone could see what was happening. I stared at the table, vision blurring, as humiliation coursed through my veins.

I almost caved. Just to sate the need growing untamed inside me. Instead I tried to subtly shift against his thigh, I wasn't sure if to relieve the throbbing or encourage it.

He laughed, dealing the next hand. "Does the idea of being sold get you wet? If you ruin my jeans I'm going to be pissed, Snitch."

I fought everything in my body to grip his thigh and give in. Instead I pressed back against his erection.

"If you come on my back, I'll send you the dry-cleaning bill," I whispered back.

Gray froze, then slammed his knee between my thighs in a harsh, violent thrust. I gasped, gripping his thigh. It was still a game to him...but I was falling apart.

I didn't realize the rule I needed to make until it was already broken: don't come with Grayson Crowne. I was too hot, my thoughts disappearing into the throbbing ache between my thighs, tingles sprouting with my goose bumps.

My head fell against his shoulder. Gray played, reaping in piles of coins like I wasn't there. His lips fanned my cheek as he leaned forward, hot and drugging.

"If she really loves you, she won't care you're a virgin," I whispered, maybe a truth in the moment, or one last-ditch effort to hide before disappearing into him.

His tense was so subtle I wouldn't have noticed if I wasn't literally melting into his body.

"Are you coming right now?" he hissed.

Maybe he didn't mean to really get me off; maybe I'd taken the game too far.

He'd grown rock hard. Iron. *What would sex with Grayson Crowne be like?* The thought popped into my head. Intense. *Too* intense. You don't put on a mask as thick as Grayson's unless you have something really untamable to hide.

"Fuck, you are." His palm tightened possessively between my thighs. There was a surprised edge, a strangle in his voice I might have believed meant something if not for the words that immediately came from his lips next.

"Want to know something cute, guys?" Gray said. "This servant has a thing for me. She's been saving her V-card for me. Which one of you wants to take it instead? I'm raising the pot. All in."

What!?

The words shocked me out of the sweet, hazy place I'd been. I scrambled to pull the chips back from the center.

"What are you doing? You have a *two* and a *three*."

Grayson pulled me back against his chest by the palm still between my thighs. All the oxygen in the room disappeared.

His breath feathered my neck. "Scared, Snitch?"

It took all I had not to shake. It came down to this hand. It was either him, or go home with some creep named Khalid.

"Are you wondering if they saw you come?" Grayson's fingers played over the thin cotton barrier, dangerously light, like he was holding some part of himself back. "Stay fucking still or I'll answer that question for everyone."

This was what my uncle meant when he said dignity in the face of indignity. Would I really go home with Khalid?

Would I *let* myself go home with him?

Khalid was about to lay down his card when a gold coin landed on the table.

Everything stopped.

Unlike the other coins, this one had markings. It was beautiful, almost looking like lace. I don't know what the markings meant, but the coin made Gray freeze.

"What the hell are you doing?" Gray looked up at whoever threw the coin. "Why would you use that on her?"

"You have to honor it."

My heart stopped. I didn't need to look to know who it was. I knew by the low, smooth timbre of the voice. I hadn't heard it in years, but I could never forget the boy who took my virginity.

West du Lac.

———

Instead of letting me go, Gray tightened the cage, palm spreading to fan across my entire abdomen, pulling me tighter against his chest. Briefly, stupidly, I wondered if he could feel the butterflies bounce in my stomach.

West arched a brow. "Are you challenging? Over a servant?"

The room went quiet.

West du Lac was tall—taller than Gray even—with broad shoulders and a square jaw. With fluffy brown hair and warm brown eyes, he was like everyone else here dressed in casually expensive clothes, however there was one key difference: his eyes were kind.

I'd fallen for them once.

"Is that any stranger than you using a fucking coin on one?" Gray asked.

West shrugged. "In the mood for something Gray Crowne wants."

Grayson laughed, but he was tenser than steel beneath me.

Lottie's brown eyes sparkled in the dark. I didn't know what any of this meant, why they had coins, and why everyone was watching so tensely; and the last person I wanted to go with was West du Lac, but I knew the look in Lottie's eyes.

I turned to my shoulder so I could whisper. "Lottie is watching. It's fine. I'm fine."

Gray cursed so low only I heard—and then shoved me off so I fell to my hands and knees.

I knew then that Gray could feel my butterflies, because he seemed determined to rip their wings off anytime they fluttered.

I stared at my shadow in the shiny floor. I could feel everyone looking at me, their laughs sinking into my back, when West knelt in front of me and gave me his hand.

Everything in me wanted to shove his hand away and spit in his face.

Lottie had moved to sit next to Gray, and his hand was over the chair, his other pushing a loose braid behind her ear.

I blinked at my shadow in the floor, lids suddenly on fire. Why did my chest ache?

"Angel?" West extended his hand farther.

"Don't call me that," I muttered.

But I took West's hand, because it was either that or stay on the floor.

Outside of the shack a few swans lingered on the beach. It was chilly, night air smelling more of cold sand and trees than salt. I shivered, and West handed me his jacket.

I stared at it.

He shook it at me. "Just take it."

"No."

We stared at one another.

What did he want from me? The past thirty minutes had been like this, both of us on the verge of saying something.

I'd cried for weeks when West ghosted me, because he didn't just ghost me, he *ghosted* me. He went from being my only real friend to nothing, acted like I didn't exist the next morning.

Then, one Christmas party, I overheard some socialites talking about how West couldn't stop bragging about how he got *some maid to give up her V-card to him*. I stopped crying, but I didn't stop hurting, and I could never really heal.

"So," West finally said, "you're letting Grayson Crowne bet your virginity?" He lifted his brows like he wanted *me* to acknowledge why that was wrong.

I pinched my lips together.

So that was the game we were playing.

"Why not, Mr. du Lac?" I blinked, feigning innocence. "It's not like someone's going to come out and say they've already had sex with me. That would be just too degrading."

His stare hardened.

I realized a long time ago the problem with us. Westley du Lac and I were two people who never should've crossed paths, should never have spoken to one another, and, somehow, we fell in love. Or at least, I had.

He sighed, then came to my side, draping the jacket over my shoulders. "Angel, that's not—"

Before West could finish, I was yanked from him, the jacket torn off my body, tossed to the dirt.

Grayson.

"West."

"Gray."

A staring match. A swan hissed.

"Some of your water polo frat buddies were looking for you," Gray said. "Something about running out of roofies? Not sure. It's hard to hear over all the high-fiving."

West glared. "I don't play water polo, and I'm not in a frat."

Gray frowned. "Huh...I don't know why I thought you did. Maybe it's that 'I just got fucked in the ass by Uncle Sam and loved it' smile you have."

Another tense second, then West said, "Let her go. I paid. Are you really going to challenge?"

"I let you walk away with her. Didn't say I was going to let you keep her." His grip on my arm tightened. "I'm sorry if you didn't get the memo, but she's mine."

My gut flipped like earlier, but worse. It dripped lower. It stayed. It throbbed. I liked him saying *she's mine*. I was trying to rip out the weeds growing inside me, but each time he spoke, it was like they were encased in steel.

He held out his palm, revealing three gold coins. "You've held on for so long, du Lac. Gave it up for what?"

Another moment.

West looked over his shoulder, catching my eyes. "Let me know if you need anything."

Gray grabbed my arm, thrusting me against his back so I slammed against his muscles with a thud. I couldn't see

West anymore, couldn't see anything but Gray's black dress shirt.

His grip on me tightened. "She's fine, Captain America."

Fabric filled my nose and mouth; his smell invaded my nostrils.

He let me go and I sucked in lungfuls of air.

"Why the fuck did West du Lac want you?" Grayson rounded on me.

"I don't know," I lied. "I have no idea why he cares so much." *That* part wasn't really a lie.

He scoffed. "Don't lie to me. You plotting or something? Telling him your sad little story?"

"Are you mad at *me*?" I asked, pointing at my chest, filled with indignation for bursting. "I'd love to hear the twisted Crowne logic that lets you think you can be mad at *me*."

I couldn't be subservient. I couldn't. I was so sick of rich boys who thought they could use me however they wanted.

Grayson made a face. "Twisted Crowne—"

"You *gambled* me!" The words came out a yell before I could temper myself. "You made me...in front of everyone... I don't care what you do to me anymore. I'm not going anywhere with you. I'm done."

Maybe to someone like Gray what just happened was normal, but I wasn't used to being fucking gambled.

Gray took less than a second to reach me with great, *angry* strides, swallowing the dark beach between us.

"It wasn't a gamble," he growled. "I was never going to lose, Snitch. I don't lose. I don't *share*. Your body is mine, and when you inevitably fail at this stupid plan, you'll know that without a doubt."

ELEVEN

GRAY

Hours later, Story is asleep on my floor and I can't sleep. Which wouldn't be news, except for the reason *why* I can't sleep. There's a need. A possession. Growing inside me like a weed. I didn't like them touching her. I don't like anyone even *looking* at her. The more time I spend, the more I realize one kiss isn't enough, and if we do it again, it won't ever be enough.

Which means it can never happen again.

I'd nearly ripped West's head off just for taking her. He used a family coin on her. What the fuck? You only got one family coin.

There was something about this girl that was creeping into my veins.

It was easy to mistake her as Lottie at first, but now the differences were so fucking stark. If Lottie was a diamond, Snitch was the metal you cast it in.

Outside the swans still hissed with the waves, but

tomorrow only a few would linger. The clock was ticking, and still all I can think about is the girl sleeping below my bed.

The way she wears her nun clothes, or how her eyes get big when she's angry. Fuck...when she's angry.

Twisted Crowne logic.

I like it when she's honest. I like it when she's brutal. I like it when she talks back.

It took every ounce of willpower not to get hard when she was on my lap, and in the end I failed, even when I got so high I almost didn't see straight. Because when she *came*.

Fuck.

When she came.

I slid my hand beneath my satin pants, grasping my cock, a fucking traitor already hard at the thought of her. It was nothing. Story was heroin, pure and simple. A traitorous high not to be trusted. A black sludge I would rip out of my veins no matter the cost.

It wasn't that I liked the feel of her in my lap.

Thighs spread on mine.

Ass against my cock.

Her small, throaty whimper only I had heard.

Fuck.

I gripped harder. The chandelier above my bed glittered in the moonlight and blurred. I hadn't wanted to yank her mouth to mine when her head fell to my shoulder. *Fucking Snitch, fuck, I hate her.* I tugged faster, harder, punishing her. Punishing myself.

Almost there.

I groaned. "Fucking lemons."

"I'm sorry," Snitch's small, raspy voice called in the dark.

I jumped, freezing.

"Jesus fuck." Heart hammering, I rubbed my forehead. After another breath, I rolled over, head throbbing with adrenaline. Snitch stared up at me, eyes wide and annoyingly cute. She was like a rabbit cuddling against a lion. "You're *awake?*"

It was three in the morning.

"I'm sorry," she said again. "I *really* didn't know about the lemons."

She thought I was thinking about Lottie.

Lottie, the chick I've been chasing since I was a kid.

Lottie, the only one who never cared I was a Crowne.

Lottie, the reason Snitch is asleep on my floor.

"Neither did I," was all I said.

Because how the fuck did I not know Lottie was allergic to lemons? Sure, Lottie and I had grown apart over the years...but aren't allergies something you're born with?

"Why are you awake?" I asked.

She shrugged. "I don't really sleep." She stretched, then rubbed her shoulder. I briefly wondered if sleeping on the floor was hurting her. Snitch had no mattress, no pillow, but I'd given her a blanket.

"Looking for more leverage, Snitch?"

She yawned. "It's the middle of the night. Can we just have a cease-fire. Truce."

"Truce?"

"I'll be Story and you be Gray."

I glared.

Everything said not to trust her, but when she stared up with wide eyes, stifling a yawn, my chest tugged to tell her the truth.

No, I don't.

She yawned again at the same time her stomach

growled, and she slammed her hands across it, like it would cover the sound.

I wondered when the last time she ate was. I hadn't even fucking thought about it. Had she been feeding herself?

"Fine. Whatever. Truce."

Her eyebrows shot into her head. "To be honest, after what happened...I thought you were going to, like, basti-nado me."

Bastinado.

Only Snitch would use a word like that. I smiled, because in the dark she couldn't see.

Only Snitch? The fuck is wrong with me?

I rubbed my eye until I saw white.

"You have another chance to fix what you fucked tomorrow—or today, I guess. Another day, another party. If you fuck it up again..." I raked my gaze over her body, a brief part of me wanting her *to* fuck it up. I shook my head and rolled back onto my back, staring up at my chandelier.

A few more minutes passed, Snitch tossing and turning. I opened my mouth to tell her to get up on the bed, but stopped. What the fuck was happening to me? Snitch was a means to an end.

Nothing more.

Snitch finally settled down, and for a second I thought she'd fallen asleep; then her quiet, husky voice drifted into the dark.

"I don't know how you can...do...the things you do to me...and also be with Lottie."

"What things have I done to you, Snitch? I remember *you* getting off on my leg." I shifted, adjusting my dick.

"That was...I...you started it."

"But you finished."

Snitch inhaled sharply, and I drew my lip between my teeth, trying to stop another fucking smile.

"You're twisting everything," she finally said.

I closed my eyes. I could fall asleep to her voice. Like good, clean whiskey. Smoky and sweet. The kind I used to steal from my dad.

"Whatever things I do to you don't concern her."

She scoffed. "I guess Playboy Gray is *somewhat* accurate."

I opened my eyes and rolled over, glaring down at her. "Am I supposed to be faithful to the idea of someone? Lottie is probably fucking someone as we speak."

I grimaced and rolled back.

"She's not my girlfriend." I exhaled. "We aren't together. Lottie has no idea she's getting married, much less to me."

"That's horrible." I could picture her open mouth, her wide eyes.

"That's how things work in our world."

Wedding days are funerals, the only difference is the women wear white veils to hide their running mascara.

Of course, it isn't completely ancient. We all have the *option* to say no—and lose everything. Our inheritance. Our family. Our social circle.

"Just tell her the truth," Snitch said fervently. "It was all a mistake. Or tell her I did it on purpose, that I knew you were going to be there and wanted to kiss *the* Grayson Crowne. I'll say it's true."

I shifted, a muscle in my back straining. Why would she do that?

"It won't do any good."

"But why—"

"Why not?" I cut her off before she could press. Fuck,

Snitch really didn't know when to let things go. She had no sense of self-preservation. It was annoyingly endearing. Everyone around me was too afraid to ask me real questions. They asked questions only if they were certain of the answer, sure it would make me smile.

Not Snitch.

Snitch asked because she didn't know.

I craned my head to the side, catching her hazel gaze. "Because I'm *Playboy Gray*, and you're just another girl I convinced to lie for me." She looked away, and I looked back at the ceiling, stretching my arms. "I've loved Lottie from afar for years. She's always made it clear she never returned my affection. She..."

She never wanted anything to do with who I was perceived to be, the Crowne family, and what it meant to be in it.

Can't say I blame her.

I cleared my throat. "I spent all year courting her, Snitch, convincing her I wasn't who she thought I was, for that one moment in the antique room."

All, in hopes that maybe I'd do the impossible and marry a girl who wants to marry me too.

I rubbed my head. *Fuck.* This wasn't like me. I didn't talk to anyone. The closest I ever got was with Woodsy.

A Crowne bends, it breaks.

"I didn't think I would ever hear you say the word *love*," she whispered.

"If you tell anyone—"

"I won't. And even if I did, no one would believe me."

My brow knitted at her easy acceptance. Another ghostly silence spread between us, and I figured she'd started to drift to sleep, when she spoke.

"I'm sorry. I'll try harder. Tomorrow—*err*, today. I'll

learn everything about Charlotte du Lac! I won't stop until I've fixed it. I promise. I know you don't know me very well, and what you do know isn't great. But I will fix it. I don't steal what doesn't belong to me. I don't rip apart people's love. I *don't do that*."

A whisper of a smile ghosted my lips. Even if I couldn't see her, I could see the look on her face. The determination pinching her plump lips.

"Truce over, Snitch. Go to sleep."

I must've eventually fallen asleep, because soon light blared against my lids. Groggy, I lifted my head. *Always* groggy. None of us Crownes slept well. My grandfather didn't sleep, liked to compare himself to Teddy Roosevelt too much. My mother and my sister Gemma used pills. I don't know what Abigail did; maybe she slept with her demons like me.

I shook the hair out of my eyes and got out of bed.

"Ouch!" Snitch yelped, rubbing her thigh.

I lifted my foot back instantly.

"Sorry. Not used to having guests," I said.

Not used to having people, period.

She shot me a look. I could tell she didn't believe I hadn't done it on purpose, but I didn't care enough to tell her. I waited for her to look at me, or look at me then look away, but she only glared at the floor. Her lips were a soft heart in the dawn light, begging to be kissed, sucked, bruised.

I jumped out of bed, putting distance between us. Snitch really was poison ivy. Itchy, painful, annoying, impossible to ignore until you rip it out at the roots.

"Umm...Gray," she called. "I mean, Mr. Crowne."

I paused at the stairs. "Yeah?"

"Umm...if I'm going to stay with you...I need to shower, and stuff."

It happened in a flash, before I had a second to fight back. Snitch *naked*, and then I was hard, fucking rigid. I shifted, swallowing, rubbing my right eye until I saw white, trying to rid the image of Snitch. What did she look like underneath all those clothes?

I can't decide if it's a good thing that she dresses like an Amish nun, if seeing what's beneath those clothes would drive me crazier, or stop my wondering.

"There are four-and-a-half bathrooms in my wing," I said, voice rough. "You can use one. Never use mine; it's the north one."

I picked up my pace, taking the open stairs two at a time.

"Wait!" she called after me. "Which one *can* I use?"

I took a detour into my office and slammed the door shut behind me. I didn't move. My heart pounded, and I felt like I'd just run from the fucking cops. My cock was hard as a rock. I couldn't stop getting hard around this girl. I banged my head against the door, willing my cock to go down.

The shower turned on, water spraying. It sounded close, like she'd chosen the one just down the hall, and I went rigid at the thought of her, water running down her body. I had only the barest idea of what she looked like. Her clothes were so damn bulky and shapeless, but I knew what she felt like against my chest, how her thighs spread between mine.

But how did her hips curve?

I didn't move from my spot. Listening to the water spraying. My cock pressed against my sweats, a wet spot darkening the fabric. Since she came on my thigh, I couldn't

get the thought of her pussy out of my damn head. Now I was picturing it—*her*—naked, wet.

Water dripping down her gingerbread skin.

Between her thighs.

Fuck it.

It's like porn. It doesn't mean shit if I jack off to her. I slid my hand beneath my pants, grasping hot, rigid flesh, determined to finish what I'd started earlier. Get it out of my system.

I stroked myself to the spray of the shower, the image of her like a siren calling to me. Her skin is so fucking soft. The kind for kissing and sucking and biting. She hides so much of it. I bet it's soft everywhere. I groaned, the doorknob digging into my back.

Bite me harder.

Fuck—that hickey I gave her is faded. I want to mark her again. Cover her in bruises. Between her thighs. On her cunt.

My grip tightened. I tugged.

Hear her gasp when I sink my teeth and tongue into her.

Feel her nails dig into me.

Her—oh—*shit.*

I banged my head against the door, coming with a groan as my orgasm ripped its way out of my body.

I breathed in and out, sweat beading my throat and chest. Holy shit. I can't remember the last time I came that hard or fast from jerking off.

I lifted my hand at the sticky mess.

Or the last time I came on my hand.

I don't know what it is about her. Everything was the opposite of what I should want. She looked a little bit like

Lottie, but she was *nothing* like Lottie. Lottie was quiet, reserved. Contrary to her outfit, this girl was a blaring siren.

I know despite whatever we talked about last night, Snitch was still like every other girl out there, someone who only knew *the* Grayson Crowne. Whether it was my money, my name, or what they printed in the magazines, whatever she'd fallen for was a mirage. And like them, she'd eventually seek to take.

I cleaned up and decided on a very fucking cold shower. Maybe by the time I was done her hair would be dry. The thought of wet curls dripping around her heart-shaped face, soaking into her clothes—*fuck*.

I shook my head.

Ice-cold shower.

I pushed the door open to my master bath; then everything in my head short circuited.

Snitch *naked*.

Well, fuck.

Question answered.

Our eyes locked in the same instant she screamed.

TWELVE

STORY

I scrambled for a towel, out of my mind with embarrassment, but Grayson didn't make any move. He just watched me.

"You said I could use any but the north one!" I said, shielding my body with the plush silver towel.

"This is the north one," Grayson said, an utterly addictive grit roughening his voice, like smooth whiskey.

I mentally did my never-eat-soggy-waffles and...*shit*.

This bathroom *was* nice, but I just figured it was Grayson's wing, so everything must be nice. The bath was bigger than most hot tubs and overlooked the ocean. In the shower, I imagined putting my elbows on the thin edge and staring out at the dark-blue waves.

Grayson studied my body without shame. Goose bumps pebbled my skin and slid into my throat as I watched him get hard beneath his gray sweats. A long, thick, tapered outline growing more and more defined. My eyes darted

from it, to his eyes, back to it. His just-slept-in hair was even sexier, messier, matching the look in his eyes.

"Grayson?" Mrs. Tansy Crowne's voice cut into the moment. "Grayson, are you here?"

My head snapped to her voice. Tansy *fucking Crowne* was out there, and I was naked with her favorite child.

"Sec," he called back, voice hard, eyes still locked on me.

I couldn't read the look in his eyes; it was dark and muddled. A quiet Grayson was a dangerous Grayson. Quiet Grayson had led me to the secret gambling den where I spent a night thinking he was going to bet me. Where I came so hard I saw stars...

"What are you doing?" I said low, so Tansy couldn't hear.

My eyes kept bouncing back to his hard cock. He didn't make me come yesterday because he cared. He did it to humiliate me. He wasn't actually *into* me. I was shit to him. Charlotte was the girl in his dreams. I was the girl ruining them.

The butterflies in my stomach would just have to listen.

Gray held out his hand. "Give me my towel."

I clutched it harder against my body. "What?"

He had no emotion in his voice, nothing. All fire, everything, was gone.

"I said, give me my fucking towel. I gave you one rule and you broke it. Which I'm starting to think is your deal."

All the emotion and intensity that had clouded Gray's face was gone. He was back to his normal half smile quirking his cheek.

I knew he was doing this to humiliate me.

To punish me for being in his bathroom.

But I wouldn't give him my reaction. I took a breath,

then stood. I undid the towel, holding tight for a fraction of a second before dropping it to the floor. I kicked it into the corner. His eyes blazed; then he turned on his heel, shutting the bathroom door behind him.

GRAY

I stared at the door.

My imagination was weak fucking drink. The hair she kept up fell to her back, curls a careless halo around her face. She looked untamed. Divine. Water dripped down her curves like she was a seventeenth-century oil painting. Her breasts were full, the perfect size for my hands, begging to be bruised and bitten.

When my eyes dropped between her thighs, that was the moment I knew I was fucked.

A freshly shaved pussy. *God fucking dammit.* It was like a nun just ripped off her habit, revealing a sex kitten. Snitch was a paradox inside a contradiction. A strong jaw holding too-soft lips. Sex wrapped inside purity.

"Grayson?" my mother called, and I realized she'd been talking. "Did you hear what I said?"

I blinked, finding my mother holding her neck softly with her right hand.

"No. Sorry."

"I said, did you see the latest stunt your sister pulled last night?"

Are you coming right now?

"I was a bit preoccupied."

"Well, Abigail destroyed my beautiful maze."

"Ah." So that was why it was on fucking fire.

"Honestly, I've been up all night," Mom continued. "Your poor sister struggles so much with emotions she can't control. You know how your cousin Emmaline went on that retreat? She came back so much more...refined. I think it might be good for Abigail."

Emmaline was all but fucking lobotomized. Our cousins looked at Rosemary Kennedy and thought, *Well done.*

This isn't unusual behavior, my mother threatening one of my sisters in my presence. It's a dance we do. She threatens them, and then I give up something so she doesn't go through with it. Usually we're more passive, we dance around it.

Gemma was caught with a gardener again, she might do better if we restrict her access to her own wing...oh, it's such a shame how you keep ending up on those covers, Grayson.

Today I don't feel like fucking dancing. "What is it you want, Mother?"

She made a sound in her throat like I'd just insulted her very core. "To talk with my son."

But she didn't say anything else, and she didn't leave.

I guess we were fucking dancing.

"Something on your mind, Mom?

"If you really want to know...the house is atwitter with gossip."

"Isn't it always?"

She rubbed her jugular. "A Cinderella story, some are calling it—don't give me that look, Grayson. I don't know what else to call it, either, when you've stolen your sister's girl and stowed her away in your wing."

I looked out the window. "Don't call it anything."

It was an overcast day. The beach colored in muted

shades of gray from the steel ocean to the smoky sky and ash sand.

She scoffed musically. "You've always been such a smart boy."

Wait for it...

"So I'm certain I don't need to worry. You're smart, Grayson, so you must have seen something I couldn't see in her. I know you wouldn't..." She took a big breath. "Jeopardize something that's decades in the making—"

"Mom," I cut her off, looking back.

"Hmm?" She gave me a wide-eyed, innocent smile, which, if you knew Tansy Crowne, you know is nothing more than a smoke screen.

I knew what my mother wanted; she wants me to say I was letting Snitch go. I was sending her back.

But I still pictured all the places I'd give her bruises.

The arch of her ankle. The inside of her thigh. Her naked pussy, her naked lips—

I scraped at my nail with another. "I'm not done with her yet."

For an instant, Mother's perfect mask dropped. Then she smiled sweetly and said, "Well, I should go say good morning to your sister, then."

I ground my jaw. "I'm not done *yet*. I'm not jeopardizing shit. Lottie doesn't even know about the marriage."

"Your grandfather has taken a particular interest in the bastards lately," she continued softly. "They go on vacation with him like you used to."

I snorted.

Vacation.

Funny word for child labor.

"Worried I'm falling out of favor?"

There are only five people who wear the Crowne last

name, but when my dad died, suddenly things like bastards became relevant.

Without me, this whole thing crumbles. My mother, who needs me to keep her world spinning. My sisters, who have no idea the threats she hangs over their heads behind closed doors. My grandfather...well, he honestly *would* replace me with a fucking bastard.

Mom *tsked* like what I'd said was ridiculous, placing a palm on my cheek. "That's impossible." With her palm still on my cheek, she glanced at the door. "I'm just so happy you'll have a real marriage. A happy one."

Unlike hers, she meant.

But Lottie wasn't just the girl I'd loved since I was a child; she was the only choice for Grayson Crowne, the heir. The only choice for my mother, my sisters, my grandfather.

I stepped back, pulling a sucker from my pocket—a nervous habit of mine I'd had since I was a kid shadowing Grandpa. The minute the hard candy hit my tongue, I paused.

Lemon. Why did the flavor have to be *lemon*?

"Charlotte du Lac is a lovely girl," she said, eyes shrewd.

"Yeah," I said. "She is."

THIRTEEN

STORY

When I came out, Grayson Crowne was gone. I was alone in his bedroom. Alone...for the first time since the ordeal began. A chilly, salty breeze blew through sheer curtains, feathering goose bumps along my arms.

I'd waited a good hour before I left the bathroom. I put on my clothes *immediately* after Grayson left, but I didn't want to risk a Tansy interaction. I only heard bits and pieces of the conversation. Muffled words like *holidays* and *grand-father* that, honestly, could mean anything. Their grandfather always comes for the holidays, and the pomp and circumstance rivaled any real royalty.

Every Crowne came for the holidays.

Every single one.

Great-aunts, first cousins twice removed, bastards. We servants have a term for it, when all the Crownes gather—a Corrosion of Crownes. I think Christmas at Crowne Hall might be a bigger deal than at Santa's.

I chewed my lip, standing in the middle of the room. I wasn't someone who snooped, but with Grayson the urge was *strong*. Still, I wouldn't want anyone going through my stuff, no matter the circumstance. So I sat on the couch with a view of the ocean.

And fiddled.

Now that I'd been here for a few days, I noticed the little things that I hadn't before, his *Graysonisms*. Like he had an entire drawer filled with lollipops. All his pens were green, not just the one he'd had me write my secrets with.

I wondered what I would learn if I managed to stay the full two months.

My stomach growled for the umpteenth time that morning as another strong breeze blew, knocking pens and a notebook from the lollipop desk near the open window. I got off the couch to pick them up. The notebook had butter-flied open, and I paused on the page. Before I could read anything, the notebook slammed shut.

I sucked in a breath, looking up into the eyes of Grayson.

"The fuck are you doing?" he growled.

"I—"

"I leave you alone for two minutes and you start snooping?"

"No—" I tried again, only to be cut off.

"Looking for something good to sell to some trash magazine?"

"I wasn't snooping!" I finally snapped. "It *fell*."

He blinked, the anger in his face disappearing into shock, settling into suspicion.

"Sure," he scoffed, getting to his feet.

"Do you write everything in green?" I asked, standing to my own.

He paused, then tossed the notebook and pens into the desk amid the loose lollipops.

"You're fucking nosy."

"I'm basically captive," I muttered. "What else do I have to do?"

A small smile broke his lips, but he quickly rolled his mouth, squashing it.

"Pablo Neruda used the color green because he said it was the color of hope," I mused.

He paused. "And?"

"Do you like Pablo Neruda?"

Another long moment.

"I don't know who the fuck that is." A cold look iced his face. Blank. I was starting to wonder if that bored contempt was a mask. Beginning to wonder what else this lonely boy was hiding from the world.

"Liar," I said.

His eyes popped just as I slammed a hand over my mouth. I was also beginning to wonder if I had a fucking death wish. His hands engulfed mine in a death grip, prying them away from my face.

"Do you really have a death wish, Snitch?" he echoed my thoughts.

"I don't know why I keep breaking the rules," I admitted. "I never once looked another Crowne in the eye, never once raised my eyes, never once spoke out of turn...until you."

"Lucky me," he gritted. "First you impersonate the love of my life, then you, I don't know? Did you think I'd finally fuck you if you stood there desperate and naked?"

My eyes grew. "That wasn't what I was doing—I would never—"

He laughed. "In case you haven't figured it out, Snitch, I've had enough pathetic girls for a lifetime."

My cheeks flamed. "Yeah, and you haven't *fucked* any of them."

His eyes flashed, the grip on my wrists becoming a vise.

Oh my God.

I was going insane.

I tried to backtrack. "I just...you have girls lining up around the block to be in your bed. And you're not bad at it...I mean...from what I can tell."

Grayson couldn't be afraid; he couldn't be *ashamed,* could he? There's no way he knows shame like I do. It doesn't burn him...does it? Does he throw fuel on the fire even when water is readily available?

"Are you ashamed?" I hedged, apparently suicidal.

"Yes," he said. "And now you're the only one who knows, the only one I can trust." His voice was pleading, but his eyes gleamed sharp and mocking. "Is that what you wanted to hear, Snitch? That you're special?"

He pulled my arms above my head, backed me up with the force of his grip on my wrists, until I slammed into the wall beside the open ocean window.

Grayson pressed his body into mine, molding us together, then dragged his hands down my body. I kept my arms in the air. I couldn't move. His touch was tender, almost *loving,* as if memorizing my curves through the fabric.

"Until recently, no one was worthy enough to have my cock inside them."

He left no section of me unexplored. My hips, my ribs, even the curve of my elbow. I couldn't breathe when his lips came to the underside of my jaw.

"You're not worthy, Snitch," he said. "You're expendable."

I swallowed air at his cruel, crude words. Heat and *shame* rushed through my body, inescapable partners.

He stepped back, unaffected. "We have a party to attend. Didn't you say you'd learn everything about the girl I actually fucking want?"

FOURTEEN

STORY

Things I've learned about Charlotte du Lac in my tenure with Grayson Crowne: she likes orchids, butterflies, and the novel *Emma*. She hates spiders, the color red, and mean girls. Ironic, considering who her friends are.

I was a Charlotte du Lac encyclopedia, and my head buzzed with what I'd learned. It was easier, better I focus on Charlotte, than what had just happened with Grayson.

"She *really* likes orchids," I whispered to Gray. "And truffles…"

"I already knew that," he said. "You're supposed to tell me shit I don't know."

Downstairs his mother held another party, this one outside on the terrace. By the looks of the world-class cellist and the informally dressed guests, it was a casual brunch fundraiser.

"What about you, Snitch?" Gray asked, whisking a glass

of champagne off a server. He wasn't looking at me, eyes zeroed across the golden stone, where Lottie du Lac was.

Like everyone here, she was dressed down, in a simple skirt and collared sweatshirt, but she looked elegant. Her dark-brown hair was piled in silky curls atop her head. The right side was pressed down with elegant braids, gold circles intertwined in them.

"I don't know..." I touched my wild, curly hair insecurely. "I've never received flowers. I don't like getting things that die, and I don't like sweets." *Unless I'm tasting them from your lips.* "I like peanuts and boring stuff like that —oh! Lottie likes surprises."

"No shit," he said. "I'm starting to wonder what your fucking purpose is."

A server wove amid the small crowd, carrying chocolate truffles shaped like cellos. Lottie reached for one, but he didn't see her, walking away to the other side of the terrace.

Gray pulled a server aside, whispering something I couldn't hear, eyes still locked on Lottie. A few seconds later, Lottie was surrounded by servers with truffles of all kinds.

She threw her head back on a laugh.

Gray couldn't stop watching her, and I couldn't stop watching Gray.

Grayson wore a black leather jacket, white T-shirt, dark jeans, and white sneakers. But like everyone else at this party, it somehow looked both casual and unaffordable. Maybe it was the way the leather shone, or the silky way his T-shirt clung to his pecs and abs.

"Did you know her favorite music is metal?"

He gave me a suspicious look. "No it isn't."

"Ha!" I pointed excitedly. "Finally something else Grayson Crowne doesn't know about Lottie du Lac."

I smiled a full-toothed smile, because I was so pleased with myself. Some emotion clouded his eyes. My smile dropped, suddenly nervous.

Insecure.

Grayson hasn't stopped chewing on suckers, whatever he and his mom talked about clearly bothering him, but his face hadn't changed, a total mask. I was starting to see through that, though.

"Did you know that love has the same side effects as cocaine?" I said. "It's addictive. And butterflies in your stomach are real; they're caused by adrenaline."

His jaw tightened. "I don't remember subscribing to Useless Facts Daily."

My stomach rumbled. I'd barely eaten since I'd been with Grayson. I'd only managed to snack here and there on scraps I'd found at parties. It wasn't sustainable. I knew that. I'd have to find a way to *eat*.

Grayson gazed at me with a strange look in his eyes, but it vanished. "Go find me something useful. I'm starting to rethink this deal we made."

He walked off, weaving through Grecian columns. I left the opulent terrace to look for information—*and* something to eat. The only thing being served were pastries, though. I don't want a fucking pastry. I want a plate of spaghetti.

Still, I snuck some truffles off the table anyway.

Across the way I spotted closely cropped silver curls and a light-gray suit. It was so hard to find time to talk to Uncle. I'd been swept away in Gray. I went to follow him, but a shoulder slammed into my back and I stumbled forward, barely catching myself on the thick ridges of the Grecian column.

"Oh, excuse me!"

Soft hands steadied me, pulling me back up, and I

found the dark-brown eyes of Lottie du Lac. I quickly looked at the stony ground.

She lifted her hands. "You don't have to look down. I'm not a Crowne."

"We don't look anyone in the eyes, Ms. du Lac."

A moment passed; then she said, "You're Grayson's...?"

"Maid," I supplied.

Silence. As if she was weighing my answer. Determining its authenticity.

I waited, curious of its weight too.

"You're the one who brought me lemon cakes—"

"I didn't know you were allergic, I swear," I interrupted. *Shit.* Who was I to interrupt her? I waited, muscles tensed, for her to reply.

She exhaled. "No one does...except my girl, and my best friends. It's an imperfection."

Once again silence engulfed us. I couldn't leave, though. Training told me to stay. A servant never left unless they're dismissed, or the other person leaves first. So I stayed, and stared at the floor.

"So..." Lottie eventually said. "I know how maids talk."

I wasn't sure where this was going, so I stayed quiet. Lottie continued.

"It's been so long since I really talked with him. My knowledge of him is a decade old. He's probably not still excited over the first iPhone."

I lifted my head, finally meeting her eyes. "Probably not."

She smiled a little, her right cheek quirking. "Do you know we've been going on dates for over a year? Our parents, or some proxy, is always there. It's like we're still in the Victorian era. We had scheduled one night alone but..." She looked away and sniffed. "Something got in the way."

Me.

I got in the way.

This was weird. I was talking to Lottie as if I only cleaned Grayson's bed, but I slept next to it. Only before this party, he'd touched me...really touched me.

But it was just to humiliate me.

This morning, though, when he'd seen me naked, for a moment his stony blue gaze was possessive and filled with fire.

But no...it was just to humiliate.

All this was nothing. It all *meant nothing.*

"You ever notice how often he has suckers in his mouth?" I said, swallowing. "He has a sweet tooth."

Her eyes bugged. "He does?"

I thought she was upset that I knew so much, so I said, "It's my job. I'm practically a Crowne encyclopedia."

It wasn't a total lie.

"When we were kids, I used to give him my suckers. He always had to work when everyone else was playing. I didn't think that was fair."

I couldn't look away from Lottie, as the realization swamped me. The suckers Grayson chewed at daily, the drawer he kept. She had no idea the extent of his love for her, did she?

Her eyes lifted over my shoulder at the moment Grayson's voice echoed over it. "Lottie, I've been looking for you."

"I was talking to your maid," she said.

"My maid?" He echoed my lie with the same suspicious lilt Lottie had had. We hadn't exactly gone over my cover story. "I hope she wasn't bothering you."

"Not at all."

I was literally stuck between them, but again, I couldn't move. I couldn't step aside.

"I'd like to show you something," Grayson said.

I watched them walk away, a tug in my gut. Grayson is meant for someone like Charlotte, someone with money, someone happy and light. Not someone darkened by the past, by baggage.

My stomach rumbled again, and I turned to *finally* go get a real meal when I was stopped by Ellie. She held a plate of food, and gestured for me to take it.

I stifled a laugh. "Ellie, have you lost your mind? I can't eat up here."

"This isn't from me." She looked around, looking more freaked out than me.

"What—"

"Just *eat it.*" She shoved the plate hard at me and I took the white and gold leaf porcelain just so it didn't drop to the floor.

"You should leave," she continued. "Don't hang out around the servant areas for a while. Stop asking us questions. Everyone is starting to think you broke the code."

The *code*, the us-versus-them mentality that made us more of a family than the actual family we serve. Protect each other at all costs, and never, ever abandon ship. Maids who came here looking to work for Grayson never lasted long. How could they? We worked for tyrants. You need a strong family to withstand torture.

I took a minute to pull myself out of the Grayson Crowne bubble that had consumed me and looked around. Several were watching me, eyes hard.

"I didn't," I said vehemently. "I—" What could I say to her?

Gray Crowne is a virgin who mistook me for someone else?

Yeah, that would go over well.

"I have no choice," I finally said.

"I believe you. Most everyone believes you. But...some people are starting to listen to the rumors."

I picked at the food. My first real meal...and it wasn't bad. It wasn't even servant food. It was the kind of stuff we made for the Crownes and their friends, meat with names I couldn't pronounce and green beans you said in French.

Suddenly my appetite was gone.

I was so worried about whether I would *have* a job, I never considered whether my job would welcome me back.

I always assumed my family would be there, waiting for me.

I had about another half second to feel hurt and worry before I was shoved in the chest. The plate flew from my hands, shattering to the marble floor, and I fell with it.

I stared up at my assaulters.

Aundi and Pipa, dressed to the nines, folded their arms, looking at me like I was a bug.

FIFTEEN

GRAY

Lottie smiled at the orchid I'd finagled for her. "This is much better than lemon cakes. I, um, I got you something."

I arched a brow as she maneuvered to hold the orchid and reach into her over-the-shoulder purse. She pulled out a...cake pop?

"It's the best I could do on such short notice." She held out the rose gold frosted orb. "It's also not really a gift, because I just took it off of one of the tables so..." She trailed off on a wrinkled brow, gaze drifting away.

I snatched it from her grip, leaning forward with a grin. "How does Lottie du Lac know I have a thing for sweets?"

She blushed. Shit, I like that. It was hard to get a girl like Lottie to blush. Too much fucking training.

"I don't, I just...thought you might like it."

I turned it over.

"I'll think of you now when I see it." She lifted the

orchid for emphasis, chewing her lower lip. "I'll put it next to my bed."

Was she flirting with me?

"Is your bed still covered in Beanie Babies?"

Her eyes found mine, bright and crinkled with a close-mouthed smile. Of course it was close-mouthed. Girls like Lottie were taught young never to smile with teeth.

I pictured Snitch with her rare full-toothed smiles, when her pink tongue pushed against the top two teeth. One I'd just gotten graced with earlier, because she'd found me something new about the girl in front of me, the one who should have my full fucking attention.

"You remember that?" Lottie asked, cheeks full with her smile.

"Yeah," I said, voice rough. "I remember."

She looked back at the velvety purple petals. "You were always such a Prince Charming. You remembered the littlest things. Did my *homework—*"

I cut her off on a barking laugh. "Whoa, that wasn't supposed to leave your bedroom. You're gonna ruin my rep, Lottie. What's gonna happen when people find out Grayson Crowne was doing a girl's homework for a chance between her legs? I'll sound like fucking Newt."

She rolled her eyes but smiled. "That's not why you did it."

I shrugged. *Maybe not.*

Her dark-brown gaze found mine again. "You're Prince Charming, Grayson. I don't know why you pretend to be a rogue."

She looked like she wanted to say more, but silence swallowed us.

So I took the plunge.

"It's always been you, Lottie," I said. "You're it for me."

116 MARY CATHERINE GEBHARD

Her brow furrowed, and I saw the part of her struggling with what I'd just said. Upset?

Fuck.

It was so hard to tell what these girls felt—well, any of us born into this life...really. Lottie was like my sister—not Abigail. Abigail apparently burned that part of her DNA— the dishonesty, the mask that wove its way into our blood. My older sister, Gemma.

"*You* left *me*, Grayson!" she said, upset, but still never raising her voice. After a deep exhale, she followed with, "Do you remember that day at Rosey?"

I groaned. "How could I forget?"

A small smile broke through her frown. "I always thought it was sweet."

And that right there is why Charlotte du Lac is different.

"The next day I went back to our spot in the book stacks and you'd brought someone else. You were with another girl."

I rubbed the back of my neck. I was a teenager, embarrassed. I had no fucking clue she was there. I didn't do it to hurt her.

I did it to prove something to myself.

She exhaled. "So I left after I saw you with whoever she was in that dark room. Can you blame me? After what you did?"

I couldn't.

"I thought you might come after me, try and win me back...but you chose other girls, then other women. For over a decade. Then when you did court me, for a year you won me over, only to make me relive that horrible moment."

Suddenly all of this seemed so fucking stupid.

The orchid.

Snitch.

Thinking I could win back Lottie.

From her point of view, I was trash. And I couldn't say she was wrong. Lottie had the clearest view of me.

I dragged a hand down my face.

"I'm not mad at you, Grayson," she said softly. "I knew who you were when I considered dating you. You made it perfectly clear all these years."

But *some* kind of emotion weighed her words. Caused her to swallow heavily and turn her attention back to the orchid.

I couldn't know for certain. The stupid mask was too opaque.

Was she sad? Was she...relieved?

"Why did you want to meet me?"

Her eyes met mine, big, but a few shades darker than Snitch's, and without the green.

Why the fuck am I thinking about Snitch?

She opened her mouth like she was going to say something, then changed her mind. "My father told me I might have a wedding to look forward to."

"Ah."

That's why she's so fucking sad. She knows she has to marry someone she hates.

Awkwardness bloomed. I dragged two hands through my hair as the cellist started up a faster, more urgent song. The low chords vibrated in the air...and I found myself looking around for a distraction.

For a girl with walnut eyes and a soul-deep stare.

"Ask me something." I turned to Lottie. "Anything, even if it upsets me."

She looked at me like I was insane. "I'm not going to ask you something that upsets you."

I *was* going insane. I was here with the girl I'd been chasing for half my life, and I couldn't get the nun out of my head.

"Would you, maybe..." Lottie trailed off. "Would you, maybe, like to be my date to your Fourth party?"

I looked back at her. "Lottie, do you even like me?"

I knew that look on her face. Gemma had worn it for over a decade. Forced to interact with a boy you hate, because your parents want something his parents have. Forced to pretend.

She looked back at the orchid.

Another drag of my hands through my hair, and I looked away from this fucking train wreck, when through the arching entrances of the terrace, I saw Lottie's friends, Aundi and Pipa.

At their feet, Snitch.

"I guess," Lottie said suddenly. "If I were to be honest. The kind of honesty that gets us in trouble. The kind our parents tell us not to use—"

"Lottie," I said, already backing away. "I'll talk to you later. We'll fix this. You don't have to marry me."

"Oh." Her brows knitted. "Um, okay..."

SIXTEEN

STORY

Around us, servants attended to the rich, but they watched me. A few had looks of concern, those that had actually been willing to talk to me about Lottie.

The others watched with hard, unfeeling eyes.

Instinctively I knew whatever was about to happen was because of Lottie's girl.

"Did you think we were just going to let you get away with it?" Aundi asked.

"People like you have tried to take advantage of Lottie for years," Pipa said. "They see innocent and they think no one is watching."

"I didn't know," I said. "I really didn't know she was allergic."

If I thought anyone might help me, the shreds of that hope scattered in the wind the moment Aundi bent over, nose almost level with mine. "We're watching."

"I don't know what the fuck you're doing with Grayson

Crowne," Pipa added. "But whatever it is, we're pretty sure it's why you gave her that cake."

I could see a glimpse of the terrace, of low light and guests laughing, but no one was looking my way. And why would they? The party was out there, and Aundi and Pipa all but blocked me.

Not like they would have done anything, if they *had* seen me.

"What do we do with lying, social-climbing, whores?" Pipa asked.

A cruel smile lifted Aundi's lips. "Expose them."

Aundi tore the satin buttons at my back, ripping them open, exposing me from neck to spine. Buttons flew and bounced along the marble floor. I grasped the front of my shirt to keep it from falling open, and she shoved a handful of mini cakes into my hair. Chocolate and vanilla frosting smushed into my curls, raspberry jelly melting down my forehead. I stared at the marble, willing this to end. The cellist still played. A deep, vibrating song.

Beyond her I saw Ellie and a few others exchange a look, then gather closer to us. A hope climbed like a weed in my chest. We lived by a code: fuck with one, fuck with us all. We might not have the privilege to be as brazen as Pipa and Aundi, but we did get our revenge.

Pipa took a bottle of champagne to pour on my head, and I closed my eyes. To stop the burning and count the seconds until this was over.

But then nothing happened, and a shattering crash sounded. Had the servants come to my rescue?

"Grayson—" Pipa started.

"Shut up."

Grayson's bitter, freezing voice sent a shock wave of silence through the room.

I opened my eyes, sucking in a breath. His eyes were on mine, asking questions in a language I hadn't learned to read. Jelly dripped into my eyebrow, and humiliation tore seams in the fabric of my soul. I looked away, finding Ellie's questioning eyes and the questions of every server watching, every server who'd been about to act for me.

Why was Grayson Crowne stopping this? Why was *the* Grayson Crowne helping me, a servant?

Then Grayson did something I never would have expected. He bent down, obscuring the view of the other servers as he extended his hand.

My eyes flashed behind him, where servers watched, their warmth dissipating into ice.

"What are you doing?" I whispered.

His glare sharpened, and I knew if I didn't take his hand, my torture would be a thousand times worse than champagne in my eyes. I placed my hand in his big soft one, and he yanked me up.

"You know," he said, still holding my hand. "I really fucking hate people touching my shit."

He eyed Pipa and Aundi, cold and callous, a king talking to his servants.

"Grayson." Charlotte jogged in and looked between me and her friends. "What happened? Aundi? Pipa?"

Grayson still hadn't let go of my hand, the warmth bled through my wrist, and my heartbeat couldn't be controlled. His grip was tight but not painful. His hand completely engulfed mine, and the veins on his hand throbbed.

I had no answers for Ellie, for the rest who watched us.

"If anyone so much as looks in her direction..." Grayson continued, ignoring Charlotte. He dragged his ring finger across his bottom lip, thinking about it. "You're dead."

He dragged me out of the room by the wrist.

SEVENTEEN

STORY

Grayson dragged me out of the Hall and inside a small stone shack. Then he dropped me and shook out his hand. I grasped my torn shirt, examining our surroundings. I'd never noticed it before. Inside smelled like salt and stone and moss, and foggy sunlight broke through the ceiling.

I held my shirt up tighter, and Grayson tossed his jacket at me, hitting me in the face. I caught it with scrambling hands. I slid one arm into his jacket. He threw me a glance, then with a frustrated noise yanked my arms into the sleeves.

"What are you doing?" I whispered. "Why aren't you with Lottie? Why did you save me?"

"I didn't save you." Bitterness tinged his tongue as he tightened the jacket around my shoulders. "I don't like people taking my car for a joyride, either."

He'd chosen me over Lottie. Again.

Each time he showed me a scrap of affection something

inside me grew. Something bad. Something that shouldn't be.

He buttoned the jacket up so much more carefully than the fury in his eyes would have me expect.

I chewed my lip and he froze, eyes locked on the action. The air ignited.

"You're mine now. Anyone who bothers you answers to me."

My heart pounded like a drum.

My mouth dried, and I licked my lips.

His words felt ancient and primeval. I wanted so badly to ask what they meant to him.

So instead I asked, "What is this place?"

"Dovecote. Some bullshit medieval thing my great-great-grandmother built to try and play at being a real queen."

I studied him, a question lurking in my gut. This place was easy to miss. Ivy crawled over the outside. It was on the east end of the Hall, the more historic part of Crowne Hall, where some of the old stone walls still stood.

"Why did you bring me here?"

"Too many assholes inside." His fingers tightened on his jacket.

"Friends," I corrected sardonically.

"Yeah," he said without any humor. "In this world, those are friends."

I lifted my head, tilting my neck back to look into his blue eyes. *Friends*...They don't know his favorite food. They don't know he's a virgin. What the hell *do* they know? Does *anyone* know the real Grayson Crowne?

"I always thought loneliness was the most addicting drug," I whispered.

His eyes pinched at the corners, and I just wanted to lift

the weight from his shoulders. So I pressed my palm to his cheek. He didn't stop me.

Maybe it was this place.

Seconds passed and Gray gave me nothing. Awkwardness and insecurity bled into my body. I was about to drop my hand when he pulled me closer by the jacket.

Barely.

Just a tiny fraction of an inch.

"What do you know about Pablo Neruda?" he asked, the sudden change in subject jarring.

"He's a poet."

His eyes dug into me, forcing the real answer out.

My palm slid from his cheek to his shoulder, and again he didn't stop me. I was touching Grayson Crowne, holding on to him, as he held me close by the jacket.

"My uncle read me his poem 'I Do Not Love You'... and I became obsessed after that. I actually wanted to be a poet for a while..." I trailed off, feeling naked, wishing I could take it back. I cleared my throat. "You use that pen because of him, right?"

His jaw quirked, silence pressed, and I waited for a lie.

"Someone once told me the story. I guess it stuck."

His eyes were so raw, stripped. I knew there was more to it, but I didn't push. He still held the lapels of the jacket, *his* jacket. It was like the very dust in the air had stilled for us.

"I know what it's like to have the world on your shoulders and have no one see the weight."

And with that, the moment splintered.

He cleared his throat, dropped me, and stepped back. Whatever I'd seen was gone.

"What could someone like you know about my fucking life? If you tell anyone I gave you my jacket—"

I curled my fingers, palm lingering in the air where I'd held him. "Even if I did tell, no one would believe me."

EIGHTEEN

GRAY

Later that night I tried to sleep, but Snitch's stomach wouldn't stop fucking grumbling. I stared at the ceiling as another round of monster growls started up.

"You still haven't fucking eaten?" I asked.

"When would I have?" her husky voice snapped back. "When I was being assaulted with cake, or when I was being gambled, or with all my *free time* in between?"

I moved my jaw.

Touché.

I hopped off the bed and went downstairs to grab the black-and-gold rotary phone that dialed the servants. After placing an order, a few minutes later there was a knock on my door. Woodsy appeared with a tray.

"Late, sir," he said.

I shrugged, taking the tray. "Sorry to wake you."

I all but dropped the tray in her lap. She sat up, eyeing the silver-capped food with suspicion.

"What is this?"

"Scraps." I hopped back on the bed. "Eat up."

"Omaghaaa," she moaned. "This is amazing. I *love* Italian." My entire body froze at that noise, rigid. Suddenly all I could imagine were the different ways I could make her moan. I slowly looked at her. Snitch had a little bit of red sauce dripping from her lips.

Fuck.

I shifted, hard again.

She spotted me watching and quickly swallowed, wiping her mouth.

"Eat your food quietly. This isn't a fucking slop house."

When she thought I wasn't looking, she rolled her eyes.

Fucking rolled her eyes.

I bit the inside of my cheek to stop from smiling.

"Where did you first read Neruda?" she asked, shoving a huge bite of spaghetti into her mouth.

Woodsy. He gave me my first green pen on a particularly shit day. Told me to write out anything I couldn't control, because green is the color of hope, and maybe fate would hear my hopes.

"School."

As I waited for Snitch to eat, a weird warmth spread in my chest at knowing she was fed. That I was keeping her fed.

"I'm finished. Thank you."

"Next time don't wait until you're starving. If you need food, if you need to shower, if you need more nun clothes, if you need a damn horse, if you need *anything*, tell me."

She frowned. "I can't look you in the eyes, but you want me to tell you when I need tampons or something? Yeah, okay. I'm the servant, Mr. Crowne, not you. I fetch, I obey—

it's completely against everything in my marrow to ask you for things."

She stared at her fingers.

I gripped her chin. "You're the servant, and I'm giving you an order. When you need something, you tell me. Okay?"

"Okay." Her raspy submission went straight to my cock.

I let her go, sparing a glance. "Why *are* you dressed like that?"

Snitch in pajamas was somehow *more* covered than Snitch in the day. A long-sleeved nightgown that went past her knees and covered her collarbone. If it wasn't for this morning, I'd think there were scars or tattoos covering her body.

"In this world, someone like me, it's better to blend in than stand out."

I laughed. "You did a shit job of that."

First she'd caught my attention; then she'd caught the attention of Lottie's friends.

Her eyes flashed. "I was in seven out of eight of your classes at Crowne Point High. I'm willing to bet you don't remember me in any of them."

My brow raised, interested. "You went to CPH?"

"I've lived here since I was fourteen. I've served you at all your breakfasts and dinners, placed your Christmas presents under the tree, shined the frame on Mr. Charles Crowne's portrait and waxed the floors after you scuffed them. You knocked my books out of my hand and kicked my soap bucket over more times than I can count."

I dragged my hands through my blond hair.

She chewed her lip. "This has been my home for the almost a decade."

"It's *my* home—"

"Not really," she shouted. Fucking *yelled*. It was enough to shut me up. Snitch didn't yell. "You might live above us, but you live in a house, not a home. You have no love or laughter. You interact with cruelty. We're like ghosts to you. We live here, it's our home, but if you notice us, you exorcise us."

I sat up, twisting my legs off the bed, elbows on my knees, until I was leaning off, closer to Snitch. Her honesty was so fucking addicting. I licked my lips, leaning forward.

"I learned to drive here," she continued. "I broke my heart here..."

Who the fuck broke her heart?

My hands were in fists before I realized.

"I lived in a house until Crowne Hall, and now I have a home."

Disbelief froze my tongue, washing over my face. "You actually *like* it here?"

I just assumed everyone hated it. I know my siblings did. I *know* my mother did. My grandfather only showed up on holidays he hated it so much. How could servants like it here? The thought didn't even compute.

"The only thing wrong with Crowne Hall are the Crownes. We are like ghosts to you, but you? You are monsters to us. We tiptoe around you and pray we never wake you."

I leaned closer, until I could smell her. "No one ever talks like this to me."

I'd spent a good thirty minutes talking with Lottie today.

She wasn't mad at me anymore. She wasn't...anything with me. But worse, I kept waiting for that *pop* that happened every time I was with Snitch, and it never came.

We talked about the weather, about the music, respectable things that people like us should talk about.

Lust.

That's all it was.

I'd loved Lottie for years.

She peered at me. "Do you have any real friends, Grayson?"

No.

I laughed. "You have to be insane to keep talking to me like this."

"Maybe. My mom told me what happens at night doesn't count. The stars blind our judgment, and night hides our fear. What she really meant was it's easier to steal at night...easier for men to leave their wives..." She shook her head. "I'm sorry, I didn't—I'll shut up now."

"Tell me more."

Her lips parted. "For my seventh birthday my mom taught me how to lie to the police. By my thirteenth my mom had already shown me how to use my body to get or keep a man's attention. I guess what I'm saying is I get it. It sucks when your childhood is stolen."

I know what it's like to have the world on your shoulders and have no one see the weight.

What could someone like you know about me?

I was such an asshole.

"What did you mean earlier?" I asked. "About loneliness."

She lay on her side, head propped on her hand, looking up at me. Something twisted in my chest at that image. It wasn't casual. It was...comfortable. And I liked that.

"Well, the way I see it," she said. "No matter how many friends or family or just *people* surround us, we all have that

thing we can't tell somebody, a jagged shard of glass cutting our soul. You know?"

Shit, yeah. I did. Too well.

"So we bleed silently. Alone." She sighed. "But...if you're lucky, you might find someone who has a similar piece of glass to your own. So then you don't bleed alone. That's what's so addicting about loneliness. The hope against everything that maybe one day you won't be alone."

A heaviness weighed her lids, and she messed with her springy curls still wet from her shower, as if distracting herself. What was the jagged piece poking Snitch? The thing she felt she couldn't tell anyone?

"Have you found someone, Snitch?"

She rolled her lips, uncharacteristically silent. When she finally spoke, her husky voice was barely louder than the crash of waves.

"Are you bleeding, Grayson?" she asked.

I met her eyes, voice rough. "I don't know. Am I, Snitch?"

Snitch got to her knees, sliding between the open space in my legs. I could barely think on that before I was wrapped in a hug. I went stiff. Suspicion and uncertainty froze my muscles.

"What are you doing?" My words were stiffer than my body.

"Hugging you," she said.

"I know that. Why?"

"Because for this moment I'm Story, and you're Gray, and right now it's okay."

I couldn't remember the last time I was hugged. Probably when I was five, before Grandfather put a stop to "such nonsense." I didn't know how to react, so I stayed frozen.

She smelled like marshmallows, and warmth suffused through my body.

She pulled away too soon, head tilted. "Sorry, I didn't mean to make you uncomfortable."

I itched to drag her back, crush her against my body, close my thighs so she couldn't leave.

Fuck. She was sliding into my bloodstream.

My voice was hoarse. "What am I going to do with you when the sun comes up?"

She fell back to the floor on an exhale, pulling the blanket I'd given her back over her body.

"When the sun comes up, I'll go back to being Snitch, and you'll go back to being Mr. Crowne."

I opened and closed my fist, trying to steady the throbbing. I didn't fucking like that.

I wanted to stay like this.

Bleeding together.

"Get up here," I grated.

There was an audible pause before she said, "Like, on your bed?"

STORY

I swallowed and said again, "On your *bed*?"

"I can hear you rolling around all night, and I can't fucking sleep."

"I'm fine, really."

"You need somewhere better to sleep."

"I don't!"

He exhaled. "Story, what the fuck did we just talk about? When you need something, you tell me."

Story. He called me *Story.* Shivers like slowly melting snow dripped down my spine.

"Um, I...guess...I wouldn't mind....sleeping on a bed..."

I climbed up but made sure to stay on the edge. Still, I was only a few inches from being shoulder to shoulder in Grayson Crowne's bed.

With Grayson Crowne.

I focused on breathing.

Grayson lifted his arms over his head. I snuck a glance at him. His black sleeve had ridden up past carved biceps and triceps. The moonlight outlined the pout in his lips, the concentration in his jaw.

I wondered what he was thinking. He always acted like he didn't care, that his thoughts only grazed the surface, but then why didn't he ever sleep? Why did he stay up, staring at the ceiling?

"Does Lottie know she's the reason you have a sucker habit?" He shot me a look, the one that said I was poking in things I shouldn't be. Still, I pressed on. "I think she'd like to know."

He made a noise in his throat but said nothing.

"Are you upset that I messed things up with her...again?"

His jaw twerked. "I should be."

"You're not?"

He ignored me, and I rolled over on my side, watching him. I think I must have really been insane to keep asking him questions, but occasionally he answered them, and I was addicted to that.

It was worth the burn when he didn't.

The night wrapped around us like a blanket, and I remembered my mother's words. Even if she'd been talking about stealing, her words never felt truer than now. In the dark with nothing but the lullaby of waves, my fear was stolen.

"Why do you love Lottie?" I asked.

He looked at me out of the corner of his eye. "Nosy."

"Just with you."

A wrinkle formed in his brow and he shifted, like something had poked his back. He turned onto his shoulder, and then we were eye to eye. All my breath vanished. Up close, I could see the ridges of his nose. Sadness lurked along the silver striations of his blue irises.

I trailed my fingers along the grooves of his broken nose.

His eyes popped, then narrowed. "You have a death wish, Snitch."

I can't stop myself with him. All of my self-preservation flies out the fucking window.

No friends.

No home.

No family.

One chance at love that I stole.

A horde of admirers, and no one. *Lonely*. That must be so lonely.

I kept trailing my fingers along the crooked ridges of his nose. "You get into a lot of fights."

His hand covered mine as if he was going to take it off, but then it just stayed. Covering mine, engulfing my fingers with his heat.

"My grandpa broke my nose when I was fourteen," he said.

My fingers froze on the bridge.

"He found me crying. Over Lottie...ironically...said he would give me something to cry about."

"Grayson..."

His eyes met mine, burning, but a small crooked smile quirked his lips. "I didn't get it fixed out of spite. He wanted the perfect son Dad never was. Every time he looks at me he has to see his imperfection."

Grayson dragged my hand down from his nose, across his lips, to his jaw, holding me there. Holding my *hand* with his, a look in his eyes that I was too afraid to decipher.

I swallowed. "Am I the only one who knows the truth about you? Not even your best friends?"

"After all you know now, you think I'd tell anyone? My 'best friends' Alaric Carmichael and Geoff Black have sold every word I've ever told them."

Tell me who sent you and I might let you live...The Carmichaels? The Blacks?

The very first night with Grayson slammed into me. Oh my God. He thought his best friends had sent me?

He tried to shrug it off like it was no big deal. "You learn early to keep shit to yourself."

"Because they can't take what they can't find," I said. "You can talk to me. I know I'm not supposed to have this secret. It's not mine. But you can talk to me."

Another look I was afraid to decipher, then his eyes fell to my lips.

"You have witchcraft on your lips," he said quietly, reverently.

"*Henry V*," I whispered.

His eyebrows lifted ever so slightly at my words; then he yanked me to him by the waist, separating my thighs with his knee, hiking me up against his thigh. I had no panties on, and my naked flesh pressed against his. I knew the moment he figured it out, because he grinned.

"Dirty little nun," he said, voice rocky. "Do you always sleep without panties?"

He hiked his thigh against my aching core and a sound fell from my lips, but before it could fully fall, he gripped my jaw, tilting it. Ripping my face closer. Locked on my lips. Jaw so tight I could see the muscle quirking.

"Have you ever come on someone's hand, Snitch?" he asked, still fixed on my mouth. His free hand floated from my hip to the naked skin at the back of my thigh, just below my ass.

I swallowed, throat thick. "No."

He groaned. "Do you want to?" His self-control is so fucking intense. I can feel his cock throbbing at my hip, but he just stared at my mouth.

Even as I lay spread on his thigh, he didn't try to force anything more. His hand only held me tight to him. Oddly and surprisingly, he seemed to respect my boundaries. And yet that made it worse, because Grayson Crowne dripped sexuality. He wasn't the threat...*I* was.

Maybe it was just in my head, but was he leaning closer to me? Millimeters of air that were nothing on the outside but in this moment, may as well have been miles.

His lip slowly curved, hooking right, arrogant. "Your answer is all over my leg."

His smile was arrogant, but his tone wasn't. It was almost sweet. *Wondrous.*

Our eyes collided and the breath rushed out of me. A bit of the mask dropped. Gone. Raw. A glimpse of Olympia. *Grayson.*

I felt like he was a second from pouncing on me.

And...I wanted that.

"I want to know what your face looks like when you

stretch around my dick," he said. "The sounds you make taking me in."

"What about Lottie?" I whispered.

Something flickered in his eyes. Guilt?

His jaw tensed. "Maybe I've started rooting for you to fail."

My eyes popped.

His own narrowed, like he'd realized what he'd let slip. In the same instant, he dropped my wrist, dropped *me*, and rolled back, staring at the ceiling.

"Get on the floor," he said.

NINETEEN

STORY

For days after Grayson let me into his bed, he ignored me. I woke up and he was gone, and that was the pattern for the next few days. He made sure to not look at me, not acknowledge me, never be alone with me. There was no party save the looming Fourth of July tomorrow, so I stayed in his wing. Tiptoeing like the ghost I was.

I don't know why I expected anything different.

This day, instead of sitting in his wing waiting for him, I'd taken a shower, gone to town, and taken a much-needed break from Grayson. From the Crownes. The entire time I kept waiting for Grayson to pop up and tell me I'd broken some rule. I didn't *get* to leave.

But now, as the sun sat high in the sky, I was back, and he wasn't there. My fear was for naught. I twirled the green pen I'd bought on a whim, feeling like a fool.

Tomorrow was the Fourth of July, and the Crowne Fourth of July party was the biggest nightmare—I mean

party—of the year. To the world it was a spectacular, exclusive event. To us, it was months catering to the Crownes' insane whims. Fireworks shaped like various Crowne family members, or sand that shimmered gold in the night, to name a few.

I counted at least a hundred servants outside; they looked like a murder of crows on the pristine white beach.

The morning after the Fourth of July, the Crownes were to go on a European family vacation that would start in France and end in Switzerland. It was always our—meaning the servants'—little unofficial vacation, too. We still worked at the Hall, but it was a respite from the Crownes themselves. Now I wondered, would I be going with him?

"Story."

I sat up at my uncle's voice. He would have finished cleaning Grayson's room hour's ago. Yet he watched me.

"You've been avoiding me."

"No I haven't!" I hadn't been avoiding him, but I haven't been seeking him out. I had nothing good to tell him, nothing that could make this okay.

Red rimmed his lids. "I can't leave you until I know you're going to be safe and taken care of, Story."

"Leave? What do you mean?"

The ocean crashed behind us as my uncle's silence stretched.

"Are you going on vacation?" I tested, already knowing the answer.

Woodson Hale didn't go on vacation; he didn't retire. He'd once told me he would die here, and we'd come close. When he looked away, fear rose like acid heartburn.

"Is it back?" I swallowed, unable to say the word *cancer*.

When he looked back, his face was stone. "Of course

not. I'm the healthiest I've ever been. I came here to tell you one thing, Story. If you don't end it, I will."

At that moment—the worst moment—Grayson came back.

Grayson slapped my uncle's shoulder. "Woodsy! Late in the day to be cleaning."

My uncle's glare was trained on me. I waited, heart pounding, for my uncle to go through with his threat, but then slowly he turned his attention to Grayson.

"A job well done knows no time limit, but I'm finished now." He gave me a knowing look, then left.

For the first time in days I was alone with Grayson. The words he'd spoken had played on a loop over and over in my head.

Maybe I've started rooting for you to fail.

I waited for him to say something, *anything*. There was a nondescript black bag in his hand. A bunch of scenarios ran through my head, ones I had no right to think. All of them included Lottie.

Maybe they went on a date. Maybe they spent the past couple of days together.

He touched her.

Kissed her.

"Were you with her?" I asked.

I actually sucked in a breath the minute the words left my mouth. I couldn't believe I'd said them aloud. I was getting bolder—*stupider*.

He arched a brow. "With who, Snitch?"

He was giving me an out. The whole point of me being

here was to give him back his happily ever after, not burn it further to the ground.

I pushed my canine with my tongue. He was never supposed to look back. He was never supposed to invite me into his bed. He was never supposed to touch me and smile at me, dammit.

He came closer to me, and fear strangled my throat. Fear that I would give in, and he would abandon me again.

"You're what everyone says you are," I said. "A callous, cold playboy. You were never supposed to touch me! Not unless I failed."

"Fucking predictable." He laughed, but his eyes were dead. "Turning in your fangirl card, Snitch?"

"Am I wrong? You don't let anyone in your wing, not even maids. Why? Do you think you're better than everyone? You force my unc—an old man to clean the entire place by himself. I read the magazines. I see all the girls you've ruined—"

"You think I keep my wing closed because I think I'm better than everyone?" He cut me off, grabbing my wrist. "I guess maids love to gossip, huh? But not about how they steal my shit or plant cameras in my fucking shower."

My lips parted, but no words came out. Maids had done that to him?

"The last girl I got even remotely close with? She was planning to tell the world Gray Crowne raped her the minute we had sex. The girl before that? Was hoping to sell our sex tape and get famous like a Kardashian. The girl before her—"

"Stop!"

"You don't like it, Snitch? Is it messing with your black-and-white view of me?" He pushed me off and I stumbled

back. "Whatever I said to you, forget it. I was sleep deprived. Lottie was there for me when my dad died. Lottie has been there and was *always* there. Until you stole her fucking spot."

He walked away, but stopped, looked slightly over his shoulder, and tossed the bag in his hands at my feet. Then he disappeared down the hall.

Against everything in my heart telling me not to look, I opened the bag.

Peanuts.

A bunch of different varieties from canned to bagged, unshelled to shelled, like he wasn't sure which brand to get.

My heart collapsed, as somewhere down the hall, a door slammed.

TWENTY

STORY

Hours later I was on the floor next to Grayson's bed, but I wasn't asleep, and I was pretty sure he was awake too. So I said the thing that had been haunting me.

"I'm sorry."

So many minutes passed I thought he actually *was* asleep.

"You know there's a reason why I haven't given it up all these years," he said, sounding annoyed.

"I figured it had something to do with the harem of girls who fucked you over...sorry. Again. For, you know, joining it."

I heard what sounded like a laugh, and I bit my lower lip, gut pancaking at the sound.

"Lottie and I were grade school sweethearts, and when we were fourteen we were gonna lose it together," he said.

I all but froze, holding my breath. Was Grayson Crowne actually opening up? To me?

"I came in my pants like a fucking...well, like a schoolboy."

"She cared?" I couldn't hide the shock in my voice.

"Nah. I was embarrassed. I was *Grayson Crowne*, and I was supposed to be perfect. The next day I expected my shit to be all over the halls, but she just...kept it to herself. She didn't have to be threatened or bribed. I pushed Lottie away, which was dumb, and after her, it was a revolving door of chicks who wanted my name, not me. You already know what happened with most of them. I got off other ways, got them off other ways. Once the first person lied about sleeping with me, others did it. Who wants to admit that they only got Grayson Crowne to eat them out? I got close a lot of times—" Suddenly he stopped. Only a few seconds later I knew why.

"Every time I'm with you, I tell you more than I have anyone my entire fucking life." He sounded so mad. Pissed at me. At himself.

But my heart thumped.

Even Lottie? I wondered a question I had no right to ask.

"It doesn't mean anything," I said, throat scratchy. "We're just connected by a secret I was never supposed to know."

I hated the silence. I couldn't see what he was feeling up on his bed. At least when he spoke, I could discern by his voice. He had the most telling voice, even though he tried to hide it through layers and layers of impassivity.

"I'm sorry I stole your happily ever after, Grayson."

Lottie and Grayson had a love story a decade in the making, and I had come along and thrown a massive wrench into it. Where she gave him lollipops to make his childhood sweeter, I was its bitter aftertaste.

I heard the blankets shift, the bed creak, and when I looked up, Grayson was on his knees before me. Some emotion burned and cracked in his eyes. But before I could wonder, he pulled me into a hug.

———————

GRAY

Story was stiff in my arms.

Then slowly, hesitantly, she snaked her arms around my waist. Her grasp was small and tender, hands warm.

It was just a hug. It meant nothing.

Friends hugged. So what if *my* friends don't hug? If my mother would recoil at the thought, if my grandfather would call me a pussy?

Normal people hugged.

"Get in my bed, Snitch." I spoke against the top of her head—it smelled like marshmallows. Is that why she always smelled so sweet? It didn't sound like my voice, but with Snitch, I was learning my voice was a raw and grated thing.

She pulled back, and my eyes dropped to her full lips.

Fuck, I wanted to kiss her. I came really close last night.

"Are you gonna kick me out again?" she asked.

I bit my cheek to keep from smiling. "Maybe."

Her jaw quirked, and I wanted her to say something. Talk back. She was the only one who did. But she only stood. I stayed on the ground as she did, catching a rare glimpse of her bare knees in her nun nightgown.

Only goddamn Snitch could get me hard over *knees,* like I was fucking Amish.

When she was settled in my bed, she threw me a

curious look. I stood up as well and went to the other side. I stopped, looking at her. Snitch had settled atop the covers again. She gave me that walnut-sized open eyed-stare.

"Get under the sheets," I grated.

She chewed her bottom lip for a few seconds, then slowly crawled under. I came in after her. I knew I should probably turn on my side and face the ocean. I was starting to like her in my bed too much.

I'd even made a rule last night: don't bring her up on the bed—and also keep my fucking mouth shut. But when she got it wrong, when she saw *me* the way everyone else saw me, it fucking twisted me up.

I lay on my side, face edging my pillow, and she did the same.

Nose to nose, her warming my sheets.

Fuck, I really liked this.

"Do you believe in soulmates?" she asked softly.

I arched a brow. "Like fate bullshit?"

"Like...maybe there's someone out there for us, someone we match with, someone whose soul fits our soul."

I paused, then said, "Nah."

"What about Lottie?"

I laughed. "Lottie is way too pure to be my soulmate."

She frowned at that, and I decided I really didn't like it when she frowned.

I tried to lighten the mood with another laugh. "Why, do you have a soulmate, Snitch?"

She rested her cheek on her palm and stared back at me, way too open and honest. "If I do, I don't think he's someone I'll end up with."

TWENTY-ONE

STORY

Grayson Crowne was asleep, and *I* was next to him. Me. Morning light bathed him, muscles lovingly chiseled by golden sunlight. I wanted to curl up closer to his naked chest. I wanted this to be something I was allowed.

I started off believing his lies. No one was worthy of him, and that was why he'd never had sex, never let anyone in his wing...But now I saw through it. He's been burned too many times, he can't trust anyone, he barely trusts himself.

What a lonely, heartbreaking existence.

Even if it wasn't meant for me, I'm the only one who knows his truth.

It makes me want him *more*. It makes *me* want it more. All the things I don't deserve, all the things that aren't mine, what I promised to fix and give back to his real love.

"You breathe like fucking Hannibal when you stare," Grayson said, stretching his long, lean arms over his head.

He opened his eyes, and then I couldn't hear over the blood in my ears.

A smile quirked his lips.

It hurt. It physically hurt how much I wanted to keep this.

His gaze lifted over me. "Hey, Woodsy."

My brows knitted, still embraced in the morning. *Woodsy?*

"Mr. Crowne." My uncle's voice shattered everything.

I couldn't turn over.

Torn.

Torn between the fact that I'd slept all night in Grayson's bed. He hadn't made me get on the floor. He hadn't kicked me out in the morning.

Torn between loving that and the all-out *terrifying, perilous fear* that was my uncle finding us in bed.

"I see you're getting close with my niece."

GRAY

A few moments passed, and I studied Snitch to see if what he'd said was true.

It was crazy.

Ridiculous.

She wasn't his fucking *niece.* I would know. I would *know.* But the look on her face, the abject shame and sorrow, told me the truth.

I jumped out of bed. Scrambled. The sheets wrapped around my ankles, and I nearly fell over.

"Niece?" My voice lifted with my shock, my fucking

horror.

The girl I'd had on her knees.

The only girl I'd put in my bed...

Was Woodsy's *niece*.

I was gonna throw up.

"I am particularly fond of her," Woodsy said, then looked at his watch. "I must finish." He shot us another look and headed up to the second floor.

"Hey, Woodsy!" I chased after the old man, almost tripping over my feet, ignoring the walnut eyes on my back. He acted like he couldn't hear me. "Stop, hold up." He kept walking, so I sprinted, cutting him off halfway down the stairs.

"Oh, Mr. Grayson, I didn't hear you." He tapped his hearing aid. "Must be on the fritz again."

Uh-huh, sure.

"She's your niece?"

I'd set up a trust fund for his niece years ago; most of it was Woodsy's money...but I'd thrown in a little extra.

"Yes."

I raked two hands through my hair. "You don't see the problem? You made it sound like she was ten or something. You never mentioned her working here."

"You owe me nothing, sir," he said.

"Woodsy—" I owed him everything.

"You owe me nothing, sir, but if you ever held any sort of affection for me, let her go. Whatever it is you're doing here, end it."

The idea of letting Snitch go shouldn't have twisted my chest. Lottie was my end goal.

Snitch had gotten out of bed, watching us at the head of the stairs.

I met her eyes when I spoke. "I will."

TWENTY-TWO

GRAY

"Will you talk to me?" Snitch asked for what must have been the hundredth time. "Are you mad?"

Ignoring her, I made my way past the beach to the docks. To most, the Fourth of July party was the one being held on the beach of Crowne Hall. With our famous glittering sand populated by assholes in tuxedos and bespoke dresses most women spent a year having designed.

For me and my sister Gemma, it was usually spent hopping from yacht to yacht, seeing who could get the most obliterated the quickest.

Snitch talked the whole goddamn way.

Where are we going?

Isn't the party that way?

She was getting way too fucking comfortable. I was letting her.

"Please don't hurt my uncle—"

I gripped her shoulders, and whatever she was about to say vanished.

"Be a good pet and stay." I placed her next to an ice sculpture of a dick. "Don't speak unless spoken to. You'll be gone soon enough, Snitch."

"Gone?" Her voice must have raised ten octaves. "What do you mean *gone*?"

Across the deck, Lottie leaned against the railing, wearing the sexiest fucking mini dress.

"Lottie!" I called out.

She lifted her head, smiling, waving me over.

"Shit, Lottie," I said when I reached her, giving her a long once-over. "Are you trying to give everyone a stroke?"

She laughed.

I put my elbows on the railing, crooking my head to look at her. "You're gonna fall if you keep leaning against the boat this way."

"Will you jump in to save me?" she teased.

"Nah," I said, shooting her a grin.

She shoved me. "You're always so mean."

I shrugged like *yeah*, and she smiled at me again, leaning forward until her shoulder touched mine. Fucking finally —progress.

"But that isn't who you really are, Grayson Crowne," she said softly, and our eyes locked.

"What do you know of it?" I asked, voice raw.

"I always thought I knew the parts of you everyone else didn't. The arrogant boy who secretly did everyone's homework."

So of course someone had to stumble over and ruin it.

"Lottieeeee."

Lottie blinked, turning to find her friend Aundi.

"I need a teammate for pong. Come play with me."

"I'm busy," she said.

"With Playboy Gray? I think he'll be fine without you." Aundi tugged on her wrist.

I looked away, over the ocean and to the beach, while they battled it out. Eventually Lottie shooed Aundi away, but the vibe was dead. Awkward. Stale.

"Did you ever consider dating me?" I asked after a moment. "You let me court you for a year, but the entire time you knew about the marriage. Were you ever once interested in *me*?"

Lottie bit her lip. "I mean...are you asking if I would have had I not known of the marriage?" She looked away.

Fuck.

Yeah, fuck this.

I pushed off the railing.

"But wait, Grayson!" She caught my arm. "You're *Playboy Gray*. I don't want to be with someone with a wandering heart. You don't *know*—you don't understand what that's like for me. What I've grown up in."

She looked close to tears, and why the fuck wouldn't she be? An entire year she was forced to entertain me, her worst goddamn nightmare.

I opened my mouth to contradict her but stopped. Why bother? At that exact moment, as if fucking fate knew, my eyes collided with Snitch. She knew my secret; she knew I didn't have a wandering eye.

Fucking worst of all, she asked questions.

But why *her*?

Why did it have to be *her*?

I gently removed Lottie's arm from mine. "Yeah, that would suck."

I looked around at the party pulsing with models, actresses, and princesses, and found the nearest two girls

dressed in only bikinis. I draped my arms around them. "Who wants to party with Playboy Gray?"

STORY

Be a good pet and stay.

Which I'd done. For the past hour. We were on the back of a small docked yacht, our view the glimmering Fourth of July party beach. I always thought the Crowne Fourth party was the most exclusive party in the world, but this was the *other side* of the other side. We were far enough away to be secret, close enough to still see the glittering sand and fireworks.

On the yacht, everyone was either dressed in their best, in the skimpiest bikinis known to man, or in absolutely nothing at all.

I couldn't have stood out worse.

I'd had to watch Grayson and Lottie flirt, see his sweet yet leonine smiles. Pretend it didn't bug me. Because that was the goal, right? Then all this would be over.

But I couldn't stop wondering, *Did he whisper dirty, cruel things like with me?*

Did it light her on fire, like it did me?

Now? Grayson leaned off the back of the yacht, his tuxedo jacket long tossed to some forgotten corner of the boat, his white dress shirt unbuttoned and showing the muscular planes of his chest. Two barely clothed models simultaneously poured champagne into his mouth, and it splashed past his lips, wet his chest, and soaked his shirt to his skin.

Grayson had barely looked at me since he'd discovered who my uncle was. I understood why he was ignoring me, but *why* is he ignoring Lottie?

He came up laughing and kissed one, then the other, before taking a drag of his cigarette. Once again I wondered how he could do this to Lottie. He was supposed to love her, and he'd left her alone to kiss random models.

"I upset him."

I jumped at the voice. Turning, I looked into the dark-brown eyes of Lottie du Lac. In a silk green minidress with diamond straps that hugged every curve and left little to the imagination, she was gorgeous.

I quickly looked at the shiny maple deck.

"I think we're past that."

I lifted my head, but her eyes were on Grayson.

"Any advice? What can I do to fix what I broke?" She turned to me. "You have a unique relationship with him, after all."

Have you ever come on someone's hand, Snitch?

The memory blasted through me.

"No. He just likes my uncle," I lied. Why? Why was I lying? "So I guess it runs in the family."

I was starting to feel like I was in over my head. Dirty. Icky.

Wrong.

"Maybe if you told him the truth, what was on your mind."

She laughed softly. "Du Lac women keep anything untoward to themselves." She spoke almost robotically, like they weren't her own words.

"Apologize?"

"Hmm...but I don't know what I did." She rolled her lips, eyes back on me. "Maids hear all our dirty secrets.

Why would Playboy Gray get mad when he hears his nickname?"

I lifted my eyes, stupidly, foolishly, to see Grayson watching us very intently. A cigarette in his hand glowed like a firefly in the night.

She shook her head. "Never mind! I don't know what I'm saying. Too much Cristal. Ignore me."

"Maybe it hurt his feelings," I said quietly.

"Grayson?" She laughed, the idea so ridiculous. Still, she watched him. For so long, I thought she might go to him.

But after a moment, she said, "It was nice talking to you again."

"Wait!"

I dug out the green pen I'd saved to give to Grayson. "Give him this."

Lottie and Grayson were always supposed to have the happily ever after.

She gave me an odd look but took it. "Thank you...?"

"Story."

"Thank you, Story." She smiled and left, going back to join her friends against the railing.

I don't know why I gave it to her. I don't know why I even saved it to give to him. But *she* should be the one to give it to him.

Not me.

Still, I couldn't help but notice she'd treated me like an equal. Couldn't help but be warmed by the realization.

And as if fate heard, moments later, a shoulder slammed into my back, and I stumbled forward, catching myself on a fake baby shark tank—wait, no—*real?* I shouldn't have been surprised. They were using diamonds as napkin weights, and I'd seen some guy open a beer with an iPhone.

I'd barely steadied myself when a hand ripped me away.

"It's the virgin servant girl." He was like everyone else here, suit rolled up, handsome yet someone I *wouldn't* want to be alone with. Perfectly handsome, no sign of imperfection in his bone structure or on his skin. Lips full, cheekbones sharp, eyes lazy, inky black hair soft, shiny, and messy.

He was Grayson's other friend, Geoff.

"You still got your cherry?" he asked.

"She's been with Grayson for more than two hours, so no," a voice from the crowd yelled, and laughter followed.

"Step the fuck off, Geoff," Gray called out, leaning forward, eyes glowing on me like a tiger through his champagne-wet hair.

The boat hushed.

"But we're all really damn curious about this snack you're bringing with you everywhere, Gray." Geoff tightened his grip on me, twisting me closer.

Gray eyed me. "She's nobody."

"A nobody you threatened our death with...okay. Is her pussy that good?" He raked his eyes over me. It didn't matter my clothes covered me from neck to wrist to toe.

I looked at Gray, praying he'd intervene. His eyes slimmed on me; then Gray shoved the model off his lap, and she fell awkwardly onto the yacht's leather seats.

"This is what separates people like me from you," Gray said. "I don't care if it's dog shit. If it's on my property, ask before you step on it."

I was dog shit in this scenario...

Cool.

Geoff wrapped his arm around me, thrusting me to him. "Not usually a fan of Gray's sloppy seconds, but I can make an exception."

Someone in the crowd laughed. "Your nickname at Rosey was Secondhand Gray."

"Fuck off," he said absently, before narrowing back on me. "I'm curious why Prince Gray stamped his name all over your pussy."

He closed his eyes, leaning forward, as if to kiss me. I leaned as far back as I could in his vise grip. His lips inched closer and closer, and I pulled away, back biting harshly into the table, jostling the diamond paperweights. I prepared for the worst.

Then Geoff was yanked back by his shoulder and *flew* —literally *flew*—against the yacht's white railing. It all happened so fast, I caught only the aftermath.

"What the *fuck*?" Geoff yelled, holding his nose as blood spurted between gaps in his fingers. "All I did was touch her."

Gray wrung out his hand, looking totally put out. "I think I made it pretty clear, if anyone so much looks in her direction, you die." In a split second, his cool demeanor vanished, and he gripped him by the collar. "Does your dad like working at Crowne Industries?"

"Uh..."

Gray's grip became a vise, pulling him closer. "How's that coke habit working for him? Probably not as good as his love of jailbait." Geoff's eyes widened. "Touch her again, see what happens."

Gray dropped Geoff with a slam to the deck. The dick ice sculpture jostled and fell, shattering into chunks of ice on the maple floor.

For the first time all night, Grayson looked at me.

I had to say something. "Thank you."

Gray stepped to me, forcing me against the railing he'd

just bloodied his friend on. Beyond him the ocean raged iron blue, brackish and unusually cold for summer.

"What are you doing?"

"Do you think I did that for you, Snitch?" he growled. "Do you think I give a single shit about you?"

He gripped my waist, pulling me close, and slid his palm along my back, over my ass, gripping.

"We're in public."

Maybe they couldn't hear what he was saying over the music, but his actions were crystal clear.

"Didn't stop you last night." His voice was cold against my ear. "I saw the look in your eyes this morning. You're like every other girl out there. You want me. You're brazen about it. If I stuck my hand between your thighs, you wouldn't stop me."

He probed me from behind, through the thick fabric of my pleated black skirt. I looked around us, along the massive yacht. At his peers just waiting for Grayson to confirm everything that Geoff thought I was: a *nobody* for these somebodies to use and play with.

Finally, I made eye contact.

His breath warmed my lips when he spoke. "You're disgusting."

Hurt slammed into my chest, but I wouldn't let him see. He took a step back, as if to leave me with that. Leave me to feel worthless.

"I feel sorry for you." I whispered my venom. "You don't have any friends. Not really. They think your favorite food is steak, and they've never seen the inside of your wing. Everyone wants a piece of you, but no one could give a shit who you are."

Anger, and something else, flashed. "What the fuck do you mean they *think* my favorite food is steak?"

Fear battled with adrenaline. I was calling Grayson Crowne out on his shit, and if he wanted to toss me over the ship, leave me to drown, none of these perfectly beautiful people would bat their eyelash extensions.

"You're afraid to tell the girl of your dreams you love her. I feel so, so sorry for you. You're so fucking lonely, Grayson Crowne, that friendship feels like a trap."

"Do you think you're my friend, Snitch? You're nothing to me in private; you don't exist to me in public."

"Liar," I breathed.

He froze, eyes hard.

I couldn't say all my words. That in private, behind closed doors, in the dark...he needed me. We'd started to need each other. It took all my strength just to look at him. So I settled on the one word I *could* get out.

My mouth was dry, my heart pounding.

I dragged my lip between my teeth to hide the tremble. Even though I wished I wasn't, I was scared. This world was harsh and cruel like an icy tundra, and no amount of living as a ghost around them had prepared me for when they would finally notice me.

Gray's hooded eyes dropped to my lips, then lazily, slowly, *so* slowly, he found my eyes. I knew I should look down. It was growing impossible not to look him in the eyes. Yet there was something smoldering in his stony blue eyes. A heat I knew was impossible—*insane*—because there was no way he wanted to kiss me.

Not after calling me disgusting.

After saying I was nothing.

But when I licked my lips, his jaw tensed, and he took the smallest step toward me.

Then a scream sounded, a splash following soon after.

"Lottie!" Aundi screamed. "Lottie just fell off the boat!"

Grayson jerked his head toward the scream.

"And?" The douche I recognized as Khalid, the one who'd tried to gamble for me, said. "Does she not know how to fucking swim?"

Across the boat, Khalid leaned forward on a table, doing a line of what looked like cocaine.

Without missing a beat, Grayson spun from me, pushing through the crowd to where Lottie had been. He stepped over the table where Khalid was, leaving a footprint in his cocaine, to the leather seat, until he stood atop the railing, wind whipping his blond hair.

He tore off what remained of his shirt, diving off the back of the boat. Disappearing after Lottie with a splash.

A few interested parties leaned over the edge, and some pulled out phones. The rest were on me, eyes glittering. The one shark stopping the others from eating me had just jumped off the boat.

TWENTY-THREE

STORY

There was a sea of people between me and the exit, and their expressions all held some kind of wicked promise. Geoff had somewhat cleaned up his nose, but the skin around his mouth and philtrum was stained strawberry, and his eyes were bruised, both the skin and the intent behind them.

I sank against the railing.

"Come on, I'll get you out of here."

I jumped at the voice, looking to my left. Westley du Lac smiled back at me. His tie hung loosely off his neck, and a few buttons were undone from his white dress shirt, showing a smooth, hazelnut chest.

I looked back at the sea of hate, preferring that to him.

"How long have you been here?"

"Long enough to see Grayson punch his best friend's face because he touched you." He leaned closer, full lips

grazing my ear. "Long enough to know if you don't come with me now, you're in deep shit."

I made a face. "I think I'll choose shit."

West laughed. Fuck. I all at once hated and missed that laugh. A full-bodied, confident, cocky thing that had ensnared me like bramble.

West entwined my arm with his and I stiffened, trying to pull mine out. "I don't want your help."

"You want his?" He raised a brow at Khalid. "Or hers?" He angled his chin at Aundi. My gut sank deeper and deeper. "Angel, this is my world. Take my help."

"Don't fucking call me that."

But I swallowed my pride and used West as a shield. I kept my eyes down as he pushed our way through the crowd. A den of hissing snakes barely kept at bay by Westley du Lac.

The minute we got to the ramp, I ripped my arm from his. Night sea air blew in my hair, and a few feet away, safely on the dock, were Lottie and Gray. Grayson pushed away Lottie's wet braids, and a smile lit up her face.

Ouch.

I didn't like her smile.

I didn't like him touching her.

I really didn't like that he'd left me alone, with my only option *West.*

I shook out of it, all but sprinting down the bouncy ramp, off the boat, and to the dock.

I should've been happy. The closer they get, the closer *I* get to my debt repaid. I was one step closer to ending this weird thing between us.

"That's it?" West called at my back, his heavy footfalls slamming into the ramp. "No thank you?"

"I'll send you a card," I muttered.

He laughed, running to catch up to me. "Are you going after him?"

"Stop following me," I said.

"Story, come on, let me explain."

I stopped, but only because Lottie and Gray looked about to kiss, and my heart was cracking like glass. I spun away from the image.

"Why now, West? Because for four years you haven't cared at all about me, and now suddenly I'm all you can think about."

He ran a knuckle down my cheek. "You've been all I can think about for four years. I tried contacting you, but you must have changed your number."

I definitely hadn't changed my number. Hadn't changed anything. Was still the same girl he'd once asked for a light, working in the same spot.

"I heard what you said about me," I said. "The maid whose V-card you got."

He dropped his hand. "What did you hear?"

"All of it."

"I was a different guy then, Story. It was a stupid bet."

Bet.

I didn't know that part of the story.

Everything was a bet. My virginity was just a bet. My *love* was just a bet. My heartbreak, confusion...

When we'd had sex, I wasn't ready. I didn't want it. But I didn't say no. I'd tried to make my intentions clear by pushing him away, by not kissing him back, by saying words like *wait* and *can we slow down* and *I don't think I'm ready*...but in the end...I didn't say no, and he didn't ask for my yes. I should've been mad, right? I should've hashtagged his ass or something, but I just kept hoping he would call me.

And it was all over a fucking *bet*.

"A bet." I repeated the words, the answer to the question that had haunted me for four years. Why did he leave? Why didn't he respond to my texts? It was all just a *bet*.

"What did you win?" My voice was dead, too low.

"Story..."

"Just wondering what I'm worth," I said, mouth thick and cottony. "I think you at least owe me that."

West rubbed the back of his head. "I don't know."

"Just tell me."

"Bragging rights."

I opened then closed my mouth. I wasn't sure there was any right answer to my question, but that was definitely the wrong one.

"Congratulations," I said, numb.

I turned to leave, but he grabbed my elbow, yanking me back.

GRAY

Lottie's emerald-green dress was soaked black, and she shivered. I gripped her forearms, rubbing, trying to get her warm.

"I'd give you my jacket," I said to Lottie. "But, uh..." I gestured at my shirtless body.

"You jumped in and saved me," Lottie said, eyes wide.

I paused, hands still on her forearms.

"Should we acknowledge the elephant in the room?" she whispered.

"I don't know if it's that big—"

Lottie rolled her eyes. "I hurt your feelings earlier."

I let her go, dragging a hand through my hair, getting the wet strands out of my eyes. I wasn't about to admit that, but I couldn't deny it, either, so I let the faded sounds of the yacht above us fill the silence.

"I didn't think Grayson Crowne had feelings," she said. "There's a lot of things I got wrong about you." She pushed the remaining wet strands of hair out of my face, palm lingering. "I want to know you. The real you. Is steak still your favorite food?"

They think your favorite food is steak, and they've never seen the inside of your wing. Everyone wants a piece of you, but no one could give a shit who you are.

Our eyes locked, when just beyond her, on the dock, I spotted two blurry figures. *West* talking with Story, going so far as to run a knuckle down her cheek. My stomach tightened at the action.

No one can touch her.

No one.

"Grayson?" Lottie asked, and I looked back. "Did you hear what I said?"

I rubbed my neck and shook my head.

She stepped toward me until our chests were practically touching. "I said I think our parents are going to push this wedding, whether we want it or not."

All my attention was back on her, voice firm. "I won't force you to marry me."

Even though I knew I had little, if any, power in this.

She smiled softly. "It could be worse..."

I brought her hands into mine. "I'll be a good husband, Lottie. I want to marry you. You've always been it for me."

She looked over her shoulder at what I'd been looking at, then back at me. "Are you sure?"

"Since that day at Rosey."

She worked her mouth. "We were babies then. What if you don't like me now? How can you be sure?"

"Lottie, I—"

I broke off. West grabbed Story, yanking her to his chest.

Was she fucking *kissing* that chode?

Fireworks popped overhead, sounding a bit too much like my angry, beating heart.

"We haven't kissed since that day, either," she said lightly.

"How does your brother know Snitch?" I snarled.

"Who?"

"Uh, my...maid."

Her eyes followed mine. "Oh...I don't know. I didn't know they knew each other." Her eyes narrowed on mine.

I dropped Lottie's hands and took a step back onto the dock. "We'll finish this later. Go get dry. I promise I won't force it, Lottie."

"I know..." She moved her mouth like she was trying to suppress more words, then said, "Where are you going?"

"Back to the party."

"You're going to go get her, the servant you're always with, the one you throw punches for."

I stopped, foot almost on the dock.

I scratched the back of my head.

"You should. My brother's an asshole."

She watched me as if she saw something I couldn't, then turned and walked toward the beach.

I stared a moment after her.

I suddenly couldn't think. Itchy.

I went to yank her out of West's hold, but she shoved him off first. Now I was behind Story, only an inch between us, her head just below mine. I felt like her protector. I liked

it too much. I itched to hit West for no other reason than the anger coming off her.

"You are all the same," Snitch's voice shook. What did this fucker do to make her voice shake? I tightened my fist, the barely scabbed knuckle breaking open.

West caught my eyes, glaring.

Well fucking bring it on. This asshole was the worst kind. The snake-in-the-grass kind. The assholes I hung out with? Total fuckers. But they wore their poison as stripes on their skin for everyone to see. You didn't kiss those frogs without knowing you were going to die.

Westley du Lac? He hid his poison beneath kind smiles and volunteer duty, while being worse than the rest of us. It was always a mystery how the du Lac family could make someone as sweet and pure as Charlotte, and then a dude like West.

"I'm not worth anything to you unless someone else looks at me first," Snitch continued. "You're all speculating on fool's gold. Gray might be cruel, but you're poison."

She spun, then stopped abruptly, almost slamming into me. In the split second she was shocked to see me, I saw all of her. The pain, the tears about to fall. My anger rose and rose.

I was ready to break his nose just for those unshed tears; then he smiled, vicious. Smug. The fuck did he have to be smug about? I fisted and unfisted my hand as West gave me the look like, *Let's fucking do it.*

Story quickly swiped her tears away and walked by me.

Fuck.

I went after her.

"Let's try this again. How do you know West du Lac?" I called to her back.

"Let's try *this* again. Why do you care?" she snapped. "Why?"

Our furious footsteps went *plunk plunk plunk* on the dock. Above us the sky was black, too many blinding lights.

"I don't need you fucking up my relationship again by fucking her brother."

"Are you jealous?"

I laughed.

No. Yes. Fuck.

"Jealous of West? He jacks off to the sound of his own voice."

I swear I heard her laugh, but it was impossible to be certain with the music from the yacht and beach clashing together.

"What was that?" I asked, chasing after her. "Don't give me bullshit about being friends."

She was silent, ignoring me.

That pissed me off.

"Did you love him?" I goaded at her back. "Was I just witnessing a lovers' quarrel?"

She stopped. "Yes."

That hit me like a fucking arrow to the gut.

Love? She fucking loved him?

I dragged my hands through my still-wet hair, salt burning my nose. Why the fuck did that upset me? Story started walking again, faster, almost at the beach.

Fuck this. I never chased after girls. After anyone.

Yet I ran for her.

"You lied about your uncle too," I said. "What other shit are you keeping hidden away?"

She tensed, then spun on me. "I didn't want you to hurt him!"

I scoffed. I would never fucking hurt Woodsy. Ever. I

never fucking did any of the shit I was accused of doing. People thought I got my guard deported because he looked me in the eyes. That dude saved my life and they thought I deported him? He was living out his dream of having an animal sanctuary somewhere in Brazil.

"So, what, you and West had some great fucking love affair? West du Lac?" I laughed. "You can look him in the eyes, but did he look back?"

Her glare sharpened. "You don't think someone like me can be with someone like West?"

"I thought you said you knew your place, Snitch?" I countered.

"I said I know my place. I didn't say that made you better than me." She took a step to me. "You were born above me. I was born below you. That's fact. Pretending it doesn't exist doesn't make you enlightened or woke. But it doesn't mean you're better than me." She looked away and said the next part so quietly I barely heard her. "That's the part everyone always forgets, anyway."

Sadness swamped her, stole her breath, her energy.

I knew I should be fucking livid. She lied about her uncle. There was something weird going on with her and West, the fucking brother of the chick I was trying to win back, but the abject look on her face made rational thought fly out the window.

I pulled her to me with one arm, anchoring her against my wet body.

She tensed. "What are you doing?"

"Right now...you're just Story, and I'm Gray."

Story stayed tense, like she wanted to pretend she was fine, but my body was cold with the ocean, and her hot tears branded my skin.

When I pulled back, she moved to completely separate,

but I kept her still. Our chests touching, my arm anchoring her shoulder blades, the other at her jaw, lifting her eyes to mine.

Her eyes were sad and hardened, a stone in the water. Then she sniffed, and fuck, my entire chest caved. Why is she the one I want to comfort? The one whose tears boil my blood?

I wanted to kiss her.

I wanted to kiss that trembling bottom lip she keeps trying to hide.

Why can't Lottie see me? Why does it have to be *her*? She's the one who hugs me. Who isn't afraid to ask me questions. Who isn't afraid to acknowledge my scars. Who looks at me like she understands them.

But she isn't the one I love.

She isn't the one I'm marrying.

Why her?

"Why you?" I growled, bruising her chin with my finger. "Why is it *you*?"

Her bright, pained eyes looked at me through thick lashes, and I dragged her closer. I wanted to taste the lips I knew I shouldn't. Kiss her until I swallowed all the salty tears on them. Until we both forgot the reasons we shouldn't.

"Why *you*?" I said softly, our mouths so close I could taste her breath.

Then the fireworks popped, and we separated.

TWENTY-FOUR

STORY

Why you?

Grayson said it over and over again with anger, then despair, and nearly kissed me after that sudden shocking hug. I know he did. The possessive, burning look in his stony blue eyes has left claw marks in my gut.

I keep ruminating on what it might mean, and coming up empty.

It was another night and a stiff tension between Grayson and me in the dark. I'd been mentally kicking myself for hours. First, for letting way too much slip. Second, for West. I'd fallen for the unattainable. A boy who only wanted to play a prank on the silly maid.

Was I doing the same thing? Doomed to make the same mistakes.

"I know you're awake, Snitch." Grayson's trademark bored grit wove into the darkness.

I understood why his fans were so obsessed with his

apathy. I'd had a taste of the other side of Grayson, of his depths of passion deeper and hotter than the earth's core. Now that I'd had a taste of it, I found myself wanting to do anything to hear it again.

The growl.

The heat.

The bite.

I knew it meant nothing. It's just, in a twisted way, I was the only one he can trust. Our truth bulwarked by deals, and more secrets, and contracts. It wasn't how it's supposed to go, but in Gray's life, it's insurance.

When I didn't immediately respond, he said, "Your thoughts are almost louder than your constant shifting."

"What did you mean earlier when you said I'll be gone soon?" I asked the dark.

He didn't respond.

I shifted again.

"What did you and Lottie talk about?" I tried instead. I had no right to ask, I never did, but the darkness peeled away our caste.

"What did you and her brother talk about?" he countered.

Silence pervaded.

I took a deep breath. I couldn't tell him everything...I just couldn't. But maybe if I opened up a little, he would share a glimpse of himself.

"He made me think he loved me and then ghosted me," I said. "As part of a bet."

I could physically feel the silence between us.

"Come up here." His cool voice drifted through the dark.

I know I shouldn't. I'm falling harder than I ever did with West, and the crash would obliterate me. There

won't be enough tape in the world to piece me back together.

"Snitch—"

"I can't come up there," I whispered. "I can't do it. I can't wake up in the morning and go back to being nothing."

The thunderous roar of waves amplified the silence. I figured he had dropped the matter, and I let my vision blur in the glimmering crystals of his art deco chandelier above.

Then he spoke. "I can't wake up tomorrow and not smell you in my sheets, Snitch."

My breath caught.

Silently, I crawled up, making sure to stay on top of the sheets.

This thing between us in the dark was more dangerous than anything that he did to me in the light. These moments we snuck in the dark felt like our little secrets from reality. I studied him, shirtless, arms folded behind his neck, making his biceps and triceps pop.

"Something on your mind, Snitch?" He slowly turned to me, a look in his eyes that said he knew I'd been watching.

This time, I didn't look away.

"I was wondering the same," I whispered.

His brow furrowed, but he said nothing.

"Did you always dream of being the CEO of Crowne Industries?" I asked.

Grayson laughed bitterly. "Did you always dream of being a servant?"

My heart pinched. "You can do anything. It's not the same."

He rolled his neck, staring back at the ceiling. "I've been working at Crowne Industries for as long as I can remember. For my seventh birthday, Grandpa had me fire an

employee before their forty-year anniversary, to teach me about the importance of losing deadweight. On my thirteenth birthday, Grandpa wouldn't let me go to bed until I'd secured the votes for a hostile takeover. From the time I was seventeen, Thanksgiving, Christmas, and New Year's were all dedicated to the Crowne."

He said it without any emotion, and that made it so much sadder to me.

I scooted closer, entranced. Until I could see how his knuckles were abraded—blood had crusted on the back of his hand.

From when he'd punched someone.

For *me*.

"What did you want to do?" I said quietly. "Before you had no choice?"

"Too young to remember." He turned his head, blue eyes catching mine. "What about you, Snitch?"

"I wanted to be a poet," I said. "I wanted to be remembered. I wanted to have a voice. I wanted to be seen."

His stony blue eyes cracked and filled with so much emotion that I had to look away, down at the silky black sheets that barely separated us.

Sheets he'd said he wanted to smell like me.

"I like you in the dark," I said quietly. "Away from everyone else. Why can't you always be like this?" The quiet engulfed us. "I'm starting to think we have more in common than either of us wants to admit," I whispered, looking up.

He arched a cocksure brow. "Oh yeah?"

"You're born to be seen, and because of that, you hide your heart. I was born to be forgotten, and because of that, I wear my heart on my sleeve. I don't think it's working out so well for either of us."

"Why do you keep fucking talking to me like this?" he asked. "Why is it only you?"

I sucked in a breath. "Everyone's too afraid."

"You're not?"

"I am."

Before I could blink, he was on top of me.

Grayson Crowne was on top of me. His arms caged me, holding his weight. A satin-pajama-clad knee separated my thighs, and his shirtless abdomen was a hot weight against my belly.

He traced my lips and every breath vanished. "These fucking lips...witchcraft."

It was too much to focus on. Grayson's hot, carved eight-pack only separated by my pajamas, his cock growing harder against my thigh. Caged by him, spelled by his dark, possessive eyes. The soft pad of his finger caught the ridges of my bottom lip, pulling, tugging.

"Please don't make me leave Crowne Point," I breathed against his finger.

His eyes softened. "You'll go back to your world, I'll go back to mine. That's all, Snitch."

Things must have gone well with Lottie then. I opened my mouth to ask, but he pushed the finger tracing my lips into my mouth, and all thoughts vanished. At my sharp inhale, his eyes flamed, then flashed down to my breasts, back up to me.

"I'm thinking I need to let you go, Snitch... There's just one problem." He dragged my lip out to expose my teeth, rubbing my gums. "I've also started thinking what happens at night doesn't count."

Then he slammed his lips against mine.

Grayson captured my face, biting and claiming my lips. I arched my back, and he freed a hand from my cheek, grasping the small of my back, sealing me against his body.

Every breath I took, he stole. Every movement, he corrupted.

It was like our first kiss, but darker, stronger.

More possessive.

"The bruises I'm going to give you, Snitch." He groaned. "I'm going to cover you in them. No one will know."

I gasped and he slanted his mouth, stealing it. I dragged my nails across his bare back. My heart pounded and ached and burned with his gentle kiss and brutal words.

I groaned his name.

"Fuck..." He dragged the fabric of my nightgown, exposing my shoulder, never leaving my mouth. "I'm going to make you scream that."

He was still calling me Snitch, and a weird, twisted, dark part of me liked it. It was humiliating and savage and cruel, and combined with his attention it made my stomach ache in ways I didn't know possible.

He bit my lip, and I tasted copper.

I hissed and he pulled back, watching me, waiting. I touched my lip, wet where he'd bitten.

"More."

His eyes darkened, a strangled sound in his throat. When he dragged me back to him this time the fervor was doubled. Frenzied. Fire.

But my throat filled with cotton.

"I'm not going to sleep with you when you love someone else," I gasped through kisses on my neck. "While you're practically *with* someone else. I won't be that person."

Don't make me *that person.*

He raked his fingers down my thighs, leaving a bruising trail, and with his ragged exhale, he stopped kissing me.

He lifted himself onto his elbows. "That's going to be a problem for me, Snitch."

Our eyes locked. Pulsating.

"You're starting to take up too much space inside me. I don't think there's any other way to get you out."

When he kissed me again, it was slow, gentle, languorous. My heart bled from the tenderness and the words I'd always wanted to hear, yet fate had given me a catch-22. His confession was wrapped inside barbed wire. Maybe he was starting to feel what I felt...but to him it was a tumor that needed to be ripped out.

Brutal kisses and gentle words, or gentle kisses and brutal words—I was learning there was no other way with Grayson. He never gave you both.

"I don't want this to end," I said against his lips. "I don't want to go back. I don't want you to forget me."

Use me to forget me. Why did they always do that? Why did I always let them?

Grayson froze and pulled back, lips red and swollen from kissing me. Eyes stone and impenetrable.

"Forgetting you would be..." He trailed off for so long, that same distant stony look in his eyes. I wished I could drag it back, the bleeding part of me.

"It would be impossible," he said at last, locking eyes with me, tone harder than diamond.

My heart cracked in uncertainty. Words I wanted to hear, but he looked so, so unhappy.

Then below us, the door slammed against the wall.

"Grayson!" his mother called.

TWENTY-FIVE

GRAY

My mother waited for me in my foyer, always dressed like she was about to host some luncheon for the queen, even at three in the morning.

"It's the middle of the fucking night," I whispered.

My mother smiled with glee—fucking glee. The last time I'd seen that look on her face we'd learned Gemma was betrothed to Horace.

At the ripe age of thirteen.

"This can't wait."

I tangled my blond hair in my fingers, nerves on edge. "What is it?"

She pressed her palms together. "Next Christmas."

Fucking *Mayday*.

"...Is another bullshit Crowne family holiday party?" I said, knowing it wasn't, knowing in my gut what she was about to tell me.

"Is your marriage, dear," she said lightly.

I walked away from her, to the desk pressed against the ocean window, and tore open the drawer that held my suckers. I grasped for a lemon one, ripping off the plastic and shoving it into my mouth.

"What happened to the 'end of summer'?"

"We were worried you were getting too...distracted with extracurricular activities."

My mother kept a warm tone, but her words were sharp.

I knew she wasn't talking about fucking tennis.

I don't want to go back. I don't want you to forget me.

I could sense my mother at my back, her soft ivory hands no doubt clasped at her waist, waiting for my perfect response. The kind that she'd come to expect from me, the perfect son. For the first time, I didn't want to give it. I wanted to pull an Abigail and revolt.

A loud crash sounded outside the door.

Snitch.

I turned to see Mother's face instantly twisted in suspicion.

I jabbed the lemon sucker into my cheek. "Does Charlotte du Lac know about this?" I asked, quickly shifting her attention. "When I last spoke to her, she seemed pretty certain that the marriage was still just a possibility."

My mother looked away, silence speaking volumes. I shut the door so Snitch couldn't hear the rest of the conversation and gently guided my mother to sit on one of the couches in my foyer.

"Great. I can't wait to wed a woman who can't lift her veil because then everyone would see the running mascara."

Mom laughed. "Give Charlotte some credit." She

narrowed her eyes. "We all thought you'd be happy. You've been in love with her since grade school."

I narrowed my eyes on the shut door, dragging my hands down my face. "Call me old-fashioned for wanting her to like me."

"That's not old-fashioned, Grayson. That's a bit progressive." She wrinkled her nose at the thought. "With Abigail's wedding happening at the end of this summer, we don't want yours to outshine, as it would inevitably. We'll wait until Thanksgiving to announce, and then you and Charlotte can prep for a full year of media touring."

"A year."

"You're Grayson Crowne. Your wedding isn't an event; it's history."

This is what I should want.

So why the *fuck* can't I get Snitch out of my head? Her soft, eager mouth. Her teasing body. Her *insane* honesty.

More.

I crushed my teeth against the sucker, splintering the candy like glass. It was like she'd been made for me, and someone switched up the shipping labels.

My mother stood, following my eyes to the door. "A mistress or two is fine, but don't make the same mistake your father did."

Parting words from my mother.

Tansy Crowne didn't miss a thing. I'm sure the minute she saw Story, she knew something was up. Hell, the day my grandfather saw her in my bedroom, he probably ran a fucking background check on her. I dragged two hands down my face. My father had taken a mistress and "like a fucking idiot"—Grandpa's words—fallen in love. So when she got pregnant, he didn't "take care of it."

The same mistake as my father, in their eyes, was

keeping the babies. In mine, it was keeping a mistress in the first place.

None of this was how it should be.

Snitch should be gone.

Lottie should be the girl in my bed.

I never wanted to be my father.

TWENTY-SIX

STORY

I froze when Grayson opened the double doors, nervous that he would be upset with what I was doing. But he was in a trance. He walked to the center of the room, grabbed a vase that must have been worth thousands, and chucked it at the wall.

It shattered into thousands of gilded white porcelain pieces and then we descended back into silence. Thorny, leaded silence. Gray stared at the spot now scratched on his matte white wall where the vase had shattered, breathing heavy. His shoulders strained, his jaw even tighter.

My Atlas.

In him I saw me—not Story, but Storybook—the little girl forced to seal secrets to keep her mother's world afloat.

Then his eyes found me, and they turned to ice. "What are you doing?"

I looked at the small mountain of clothes in my hands. "Packing."

"No shit, why?"

"I succeeded. Lottie wants you, right? You're getting married."

He stalked to me like a predator about to eat its prey. I stepped back, hitting the back of the couch. Like the first time I'd come to him, my things started to tumble off my little mountain.

"Should we talk about how you know that?" Grayson growled. "You really have a knack for hearing shit you shouldn't."

I attempted to ignore him, tried to pick up what had fallen, when he grabbed my wrist so tight I opened my hand and the cotton shirt fluttered down.

"We were in the middle of something."

This was never going to end any other way. With Grayson Crowne marrying the love of his life, and me forgotten. The stupid thing was I had been starting to forget. Pretend maybe things could be different.

"Deal's finished. I'm out." I broke off, voice disappearing down my throat as his knee separated my thigh, his hand slammed above my head.

He quirked his head, eyes narrow. "I thought you didn't want this to end?"

"You're getting married," I said, keeping my voice even.

"That's not what I asked."

"Are you asking me to be your mistress, Mr. Crowne?"

My chest hurt, but I wouldn't let him see the pain.

The second choice. The girl behind the girl. Good enough, but not worthy. My mother's daughter, after all.

His eyes flashed. "Why are you calling me that?"

"That's who you are to me. Who we are to each other."

I could've sworn I saw hurt flicker in his blue gaze, but it was so quickly replaced with contempt, I couldn't be sure.

"How much is a Snitch's cherry worth?" He raked his blue gaze over me. "Ten seems fair."

I sputtered. "Ten thousand? I'm not having sex for ten—"

He rolled his eyes like I was an impudent child, letting go of my wrist so I fell. Once again, my little mountain of personal items scattered at my feet.

Grayson stood straight, towering above me with folded arms like a god. "Million."

TWENTY-SEVEN

STORY

All the breath rushed out of me.

That kind of money would change my life, and he knew it.

"Why would you want to ruin everything we've been working toward?" I asked. "You're getting married to her. I saw the way she looked at you on the dock."

Unless...could he? Was he maybe feeling it too?

You're starting to take up too much space inside me.

Words he'd whispered against my lips that had made hope sprout unwanted in my chest.

His eyes narrowed. "Don't get butterflies in your stomach or hearts in your eyes. You're an itch I need to scratch, Snitch. You're mold on my soul, a growing infestation. I'm not going to end up like my father and grandfather, in a marriage with a mistress on the side."

I blinked at the rare bit of honesty.

Mold. Infestation. An itch.

This is where I should tell the truth.

Tell him I'm not a virgin. Everything was built on a lie meant to save myself from another rich boy who only wanted to use me. Instead, I'd put myself back in the same fucking position.

West only ever wanted me because I was a virgin. He used me to get that part of me. I stared at Gray, wondering if he was the same.

"What if I wasn't a virgin?" I tested. "Would you still want me?"

He arched a brow. "Think you'll get out of it if you lie?" He laughed; then his face went dark, dangerous, and he leaned forward until I could taste the truth on his hot lips. "I don't give a shit if you've had the entire New York Giants starting lineup in your cunt. I can't be with her until I know what you feel like coming on my cock. I've been going about this wrong. I'm a Crowne. I take. I'm given. I'm *owed*. So name your price. I'll pay it."

Of everything Gray has said to me, those words hurt the most, because I'd always wanted to hear them. To West my virginity had been the only worthwhile thing about me, worth so much he'd betray me for *bragging rights*. I wanted to hear someone say my virginity was nothing, that the only thing that mattered was *me*, Story. *So badly*. In the end, I'd heard the words, but only because I *didn't* matter.

Not at all.

He just wanted to use me to get another girl.

I swallowed the thickness in my throat and ducked under his arm, straightening my spine. "You could pay me a billion dollars and I won't have sex with you."

"I'll turn you into a published poet," he added. "A famous one. Shit, everyone will know the name Story Hale."

I wasn't sure what hurt more. The fact that he remembered my once biggest dream, or that he was now *using it* to try to make my nightmare a reality.

"I don't want that," I said, voice weak. "Not anymore."

A crooked, knowing grin speared his cheek as he saw right through me. "Lottie du Lac's family owns every publishing house on the East Coast, runs every major magazine." *They do?* "When we're married, one phone call and you can choose where you go. Do you want a Pulitzer? I'll get you a Pulitzer."

It was so, so tempting. But... "I don't want to do it this way."

He grinned, like he knew he had me on the line. "Snitch, this is the *only* way to do it."

My poetry had once been how I was seen and heard. If I do it this way, what kind of voice would I have? Would it even be mine?

"Don't fucking find me again," I said. "From now on, I'll never look you in the eyes."

"Offer stands until morning," he said.

———

I slammed the door to Grayson's bedroom behind me. Could he hear the desperation in my voice? The fear trickling like a leaking dam?

This isn't about Lottie anymore.

I'm too close to giving him all of myself when he doesn't even want pieces. Fuck his money. Fuck the thing throbbing in my chest to stay close. I need to get out. I ran out of the wing, past his guards, down to the servants' quarters.

Most everyone would be asleep at this time of night,

and the very quarters themselves were dark and hushed. Only the humming sound of pipes.

Home.

Mildewy, cramped, *home*.

A tiny part of me felt...empty. Missing. I ached for black and gold, for bare walls and barer insides, and a looming, lonely presence that wandered its halls like a ghost.

I quickly shook my head. I pushed open the door to one of the girls' dormitories. Early morning ocean air drifted in through cracks in the walls, salty and cold. In a few hours Grayson would leave for his trip.

It would end, this knotty, wrong thing between us.

Ellie's straight, dark-brown hair was visible on one of the cot-like beds. I launched myself at her like I used to.

She gasped and I said, "Ellie belly, it's me." She froze, and didn't grab my arms and tug me tighter like usual. "Ellie?"

"Shouldn't you be sucking Grayson Crowne off?" she whispered.

I froze, then sat back. She slowly sat up, sitting against the iron bedpost.

"I thought you believed me?" I asked after a minute.

"That was before he threatened everyone in broad fucking daylight over you, before he punched his best friend *because* of you." She narrowed her eyes on me.

"That doesn't mean anything."

It *didn't*. He told me over and over again I was worth nothing.

"I'm not mad that you're with him, Story. I don't know how you managed to get Gray Crowne to fuck you when he doesn't so much look in the direction of the maids. I just wish you weren't so damn fake about it."

"I didn't—I wasn't—we never..."

She rolled her eyes and slid back down into the small twin bed, pulling a plaid cotton duvet higher. I climbed off her bed, staring at Ellie a moment longer, at the home I'd built crumbling in my fingers.

It was nearly two in the morning, but Uncle was a night owl like me. We used to share hot chocolate at this hour and talk poetry or the weird things poets did. Like how Mary Shelley kept her husband's heart in a locket, or Byron's mistresses would send him pubic hair as a keepsake.

My uncle was fond of reminding me that we weren't any less depraved back then; we just didn't have the internet.

I tapped on his dark wood door. Maybe now I was back, things could return to normal and he would talk to me.

"Uncle?" The door was a feather's distance ajar, so I pushed it with my finger, and it creaked open. "Uncle?" I said again.

My uncle was awake, and when he spotted me, he jumped. "Story, my God, knock first."

On the bed behind him were pill bottles of all kinds, and flashbacks to the last time I'd seen Uncle with so many temporarily seized me.

"I did," I said, staring at the pills on the bed. "What's going on?"

He exhaled. "I didn't want to tell you like this."

"Tell me what?" The blood in me was hot. Boiling.

Silence built as jagged spikes between us.

"It's back, isn't it?" I whispered.

"It's only stage one. A snip here, a snip there, I'll be fine."

"But what if you're not? Is that why you've been ignoring me?" The second thing that came to my mind almost as soon as I'd spoken: "How are you paying for it?"

He nearly went bankrupt the first time. I suspected he was still paying off the bills, but he wouldn't tell me. He wanted me to put all my money toward getting out of this place, toward my dream. Not toward "an already old and dying man"—his words. The Crownes provide decent health care, but at the end of the day, we're still servants living in a country with pay-to-play health care.

"Hey." He tapped my shoulder. "Don't worry about me, Storybook."

"But..."

"I'm tired," he said, cutting me off. "We can talk more about this later."

My uncle gently ushered me out of his room, shutting the door, until the very last inch of light was snuffed and I was standing in the dark in the hallway.

Deep down, I knew I had only one choice here.

One devil to sell my soul to.

I took a deep breath—and one last look at my home. I was pretty sure when this was over, there was no coming back.

TWENTY-EIGHT

GRAY

Dawn was rising and the Crowne family jet was on the tarmac, ready for our annual summer holiday, when there was a soft knock on the door. I bit back the smile curving my lips.

Fucking called it.

"Come in."

The door unlatched, followed by quiet. I focused on the book in my hand, refusing to look up. I wouldn't let her see she affected me, that for the past couple of hours, I'd been staring at the same page, wondering if she really would come back.

Wondering what the fuck I was going to do if she didn't.

"I'll do it," she said after a moment, voice quiet and husky—addicting.

Still without looking up, I reached for the coffee table, grabbing a stack of papers. I threw them in her direction.

"What's this?" Not a moment later she said, "*Another*

contract? You already had this made? You were so certain I was going to come back?"

"Ten million is hard to turn down." Even for someone like Snitch, who I'd started to think was different. It was a cruel temptation to want her back, and also never want to see her again, so that my hope was right—she wasn't like everyone else.

She didn't just want *the* Grayson Crowne.

"I don't want your money," she spat.

I looked up before I could stop myself. She wrinkled the contract in one hand. Somehow when she glared, it made her eyes fucking *bigger*.

"My uncle gets it all," she continued, "and he *never* finds out."

My brow furrowed. What game was she playing? Did she think if she tried to act like some innocent altruist I would give her more money?

As if I hadn't seen that before.

Silence passed between us, her glare stone.

"Why are you here, Story?" I asked against my better judgment.

She glowered. "To sleep with you, get ten million, and never see you again."

I don't know why that response fucked me up inside.

So I shook it off with a grin. "You didn't read the contract. Again."

She shot an uncertain glance at the papers. "Can't we just seal it with another secret?"

"Maybe," I said. "If you let me choose your secret."

Discomfort colored her cheeks, and a wrinkle formed on her lips, but she said, "Okay."

I set my book down. "Why do you like me, Story Hale? What is it about me that caught your eye?" It was a

dangerous question to ask, because no matter the answer, the outcome was the same.

I marry Lottie, the girl I've loved for almost a decade.

I forget the girl who stole her way into my thoughts and heart.

She swallowed. "You're Grayson Crowne. What's not to like?"

I wasn't expecting to feel a stabbing pain in my chest at her response. Something flickered in her eyes—regret? Like she could see my thoughts. So I quickly plastered a smile on my face. I was starting to be too transparent with Snitch. Not a good sign.

"Now you," she said.

I shook my head. "Sign the contract. I've been playing by your rules. Now we play by mine, Snitch."

"So why ask me a secret at all?" She dropped her hands, desperation trickling from her words.

I shrugged. "Bored."

Her mouth dropped. "You're horrible."

"The worst. Now read it."

She swallowed, shooting me one last burning glare, before looking at the contract. At the first line item, a deep groove formed between her brows.

"No kissing?"

I stared at her lips.

I can't stop thinking about her fucking lips. Can't stop replaying our kisses over and over again in my fucking head. She's black tar heroin, seeping through my lips and corrupting the very essence of me.

I want more.

Need more.

I shrugged. "You suck at it."

Her pretty hazelnut cheeks reddened, but she just read more of the contract.

"I can't tell anyone...I can't *talk* to anyone?" She stared at me, and I shrugged. "How is that going to work?"

My jealousy—my *possessiveness*—had grown into a green, ugly monster that I had no right to feed. I should have killed it and buried it.

Instead I'd put it in ink and used ten million dollars to buy it the best fucking food on the planet.

"Standard NDA," I said. "Keep your mouth shut."

"I have to do whatever you say. If I need something, I have to ask you for it. I have to sleep in your bed." She listed rule after rule, growing more indignant with each one. "No *hugs?*"

"I only want one thing from you, Snitch." When she hugged me, I tended to forget that.

She ground her jaw, looking back at the list. "No lies?"

I don't know what possessed me to add that rule. A hungry need deep in my chest was starting to form, and her brazen honesty fed it.

"P-Pick..." She stumbled over the second to last item. "Pick a safe word. Why?"

"That's the most important one," I said. "I've been holding back. I'm not doing that anymore. I'm not asking for permission."

She stared at me, lips slightly parted, bottom one wet and begging to be sucked and bruised.

Fuck.

She quickly shook out of it, finishing reading.

"I have to do this until Christmas," she finished. "So you can ruin my favorite holiday. Great. If I fail I don't get the money and...what is this about property?"

"Just another reminder that whatever you see, discover, find, or fucking *hear* on my property is mine."

"Terms to remain in effect in perpetuity. So even after Christmas?" Her eyes popped. "What the hell?"

"Keep reading, Snitch. It's only the NDA and the part about my property. You think I'm going to let you steal my shit and run your mouth once you run off with my money?"

The furrow in her brow deepened. "This is an insane list of rules, and it doesn't mention sex anywhere."

I grinned. "Doesn't need to. You'll give it up."

She scoffed. "Awfully confident."

"The only reason you haven't given it up, Snitch, is because I haven't wanted to take it."

"My mistake," she grumbled. "Arrogant..." She whispered the last part so I couldn't hear it, but I'm pretty certain it wasn't kind.

And shit.

I really liked that.

I needed to fuck this girl fast. Get her out of my veins.

She lifted her head at the last item. "If I leave Crowne Point, this entire thing is void?"

I smiled. "Except the parts that remain in perpetuity, yeah. Consider it your escape clause. You're welcome."

She bit her bottom lip in what was probably frustration but just served as another fucking reminder to what that lip tasted like.

"So..." she continued. "I just have to stay with you until Christmas and follow these rules? Even if I don't sleep with you, you'll give me ten million?" She narrowed her eyes, suspicious.

"There you go again thinking we'll be doing any sleeping," I said.

She met my eyes, raising her chin. "I've slept in your

bed on and off for over a month. That's all we've *been* doing."

I gripped her chin, dragging her lips a breeze away from mine. "The minute you sign those papers, you're mine. All that legal jargon says one thing: I own you. Mind, body, what you eat for dinner, what you want for Christmas. You're fucking mine." The last bit came out on a growl. "I get to use you. Break you. Own you."

I could feel her suck in a breath. She practically stole my own. "You might own my body, you'll never own my mind."

A slow grin spread. "Sign the papers, Snitch."

I held her a half second longer, then dropped her. She swallowed a shuddery breath, placed the papers on a nearby table, bending over to sign.

"Before the fucking plane takes off would be nice."

"A plane?" she scrambled. "Why?" A second later she answered her own question. "The vacation...but I can't leave. Not now."

I quirked my head. "Then stay. But if you sign the contract, Snitch, you do what I say. You go where I go."

She twisted her face in determination, and it was too fucking cute the way her brow furrowed. "Can I at least say goodbye?" she asked. "What about my clothes? I haven't packed."

"I've got everything you need."

She was wearing another nun outfit. A simple white cotton dress with quilted flowers on the top.

I wanted to get it fucked up, dirty.

I came behind her, pushing aside her hair, leaning over so my lips brushed her ear.

"The minute your name hits that paper, I'm going to

make you come so hard your pussy will only ever come for me."

Her hand shook with the pen. "I want to add one."

I raised a brow.

"No falling in love."

I grinned, running a hand down her spine. "Good luck with that, Snitch."

She scribbled *No falling in love* into the margins to be added later, then signed her initials on each page before doing a cute, loopy Story Hale on the last. "Done."

She hadn't even set down the pen before I grasped her wrist, spinning her to me.

"Now it's inked in pen." My voice didn't sound like mine, warbled and raw. "You're my girl, Story. I can do whatever the fuck I want to you."

Her breath was rocky, her breast straining against the white cotton she wore.

I didn't have long until I had to be outside for the trip, but fuck if I'm not going to touch her now. I might not be able to taste her lips, but I can taste every other fucking inch. And I will.

I reached behind her, caging her with my arms, pressing her back against the table, and swiping the contract off it in one motion.

She swallowed. "Now?"

"Now."

"But—"

"Starting today, I own you, Story Hale. What's your safe word?"

———

STORY

. . .

"What's your safe word?" he asked, eyes dark.

I paused, then said, "Mr. Crowne." A wrinkle formed between his golden brows, and he leaned back a fraction.

I chose the one word that wouldn't only stop him, but myself. Put distance between us and remind me who I really was in this equation: just his servant, his nothing.

"Come, Snitch."

His eyes burned, waiting for me to do as he said. My heart hammered. The ink was barely dry on the pages. I don't know if I was ready for this. Somehow I felt like I was more of a virgin than Grayson. Nervous, skittish. He'd warned me when all of this began that the things he'd seen and done would wreck me.

I should've believed him then.

When I didn't do anything for a minute, he arched a brow.

Do whatever he says.

I could use my safe word, but a twisted part of me *liked* doing what he told me to do. Liked the rush and the way his eyes hardened. It felt like power, power over one of the most powerful people in the world.

I'd barely taken a step to him when he ripped me to him by the small of my waist. His other hand tangled in my hair, yanking my head to the side.

"Fuck," he said, lips at my neck. "Which part do I eat first."

Delicious tingles spread along my skin at his words. His nose ran along my neck, goose bumps following in his wake. His hands slid from my hair, to my waist, and along my body, feeling every inch of me, like he couldn't do it fast enough, before tangling back in my curls.

Deliriously, I found the zipper of my dress, but his hand overtook mine. Stopping me.

"I'm going to ruin your white dress, Snitch. Ruin you. Until you're all fucked up from me."

His words were a jagged growl, and my heart pounded and ached from them. I was drunk, I was needy. He vibrated in my soul and clouded the air.

Grayson pushed up my dress and bruised the inside of my bare thigh. I thought he would rip at my panties, fuck me, and get it over with. My first time with West had been like that. Quick, dirty, efficient.

All Gray did was rub my thighs. I wanted him inside, *deeper*, but he rubbed me over the fabric, an excruciatingly teasing rhythm. I tried to push myself into his hand, and he smiled against my neck.

"Ask for it, Snitch," he said, breath hot on my flesh. "Beg."

I wanted him to bite me like he did before, but I couldn't be the one to say it, so I held on to him tighter. The coarse fabric of his jeans rubbed against my bare legs, his shirt silk beneath my nails.

"Please," I whispered.

Grayson pushed aside my panties, swallowing what sounded like a groan. "You're so fucking wet."

With two fingers he rubbed a delicious, *aching* friction that made me throb. I don't know if I was breathing. I only knew *him*. Making me throb, ache. Up and down, but not going inside me.

Then he gently spread me, and our eyes collided.

A small sound escaped my lips, and I dug into his shoulders. His eyes blazed, his jaw feathered. Since that night, we'd skirted crossing the line. Tiptoeing up to it, stepping a little over, then always hopping back. With his fingers almost inside me and his eyes locked on mine, that *thing* between us more than popped.

It exploded.

This felt like something meaningful. Something important. Something *more*.

"You are perfect," he groaned. "Fucking divine."

This is why I can't rip the tether out, why I can't let this go. There's more to him than cruelty. He uses it like armor. I'm addicted to these stolen moments. These gentle touches and soft words and softer moments.

No...not addicted. I'm strung out.

"You are *mine*," his voice warbled, so low it was like chimney smoke. "Fuck. Say it."

He spread me further with his fingers, yet still not inside me, and I arched, begging him with my body for what I couldn't with words, just to go *deeper*. Deeper, more, inside, *please*.

"Say it," he said, voice gravel. "Fucking say it."

I couldn't say those words. Because even though they're true, he would never be *mine*.

With his free hand, he ripped my hands off his shoulder, holding them above my head.

"Don't touch me," he said, eyes going dark. "Don't fucking look at me, Snitch. Nothing's changed."

And then he finally thrust his fingers inside me.

I gasped at the intrusion. Grayson Crowne was *inside* me. Was this what it felt like to be touched by a god? A lightning strike of pain shot through me at the same time a bolt of pleasure wove its way through my body.

Don't look at him.

Nothing's changed, he said.

Except he's *inside* me. Pleasing me. Paying attention to what I like, what I *need*. Any slight change in breath he followed, chased, trapped, and captured.

I don't want to enjoy this.

Don't enjoy this.

"More," I breathed.

"More?" His soft lips quirked to the side, making his jaw that much sharper. He pressed lightly on my clit, and pleasure fluttered from the tips of my toes to tingles in my teeth. I was melting. Aching. Jagged pleasure cut me.

Stop.

Don't stop.

Something wicked was happening, twisting and growing. I was almost at the brink, but he's back to being a blurry Polaroid. He slid another finger inside me, and I bowed.

"Should I fuck you now, Snitch?" Grayson asked, voice cutting and low. "Would you like that? Will you take my cock as eagerly as you do my fingers?"

I get to use you, he'd said. *Break you. Own you.*

You've been doing that.

My lids burned as pleasure climbed and climbed inside me. With sadness? With pleasure? I clawed at the wall, trying not to come, as he still kept my wrists in a vise.

I couldn't come this way.

But my abdomen muscles hurt with the force of me trying to push the orgasm back.

"Did you forget your first day of training, Snitch?" he growled.

My eyes found his, and my breath left me.

Was this why I can't meet Gray in the eyes? I'd read a story about a mythological creature that killed with a single look. It was said if you looked into their eyes, you would see the soul, and knowing such dark secrets was a death sentence.

Gray's blue eyes pinched, and for a moment, I thought maybe I *can* see into his soul. My teeth ache and knees go weak when he looks at me like that. I forget everything. Forget the pain. The heartache.

Then anger flashed.

He gripped my chin and forced my head away, to stare at the door.

"When I say come, you *come*." He breathed his words against my cheek, his words a possessive, hot kiss. Then he pressed down on my clit and I arched my back, bit my lip to keep from crying out.

I *came*.

I wondered if I'd ever come before. I came with his grip on my jaw so tight I wondered if I'd bruise. I came with his lips on my cheek, not kissing but searing his possession. I came with the look in his eyes still blazing in my mind, setting fire to the pleasure coursing through my body, until I was left ashes.

I fell apart.

I absolutely fell apart.

His name a whisper on my lips.

My insides ripped and shredded, floating in the wind like ash.

The moment I finished, he tore his fingers from my body, as if he couldn't wait to be done with me.

"I, um..." I blinked. Blinked away the tears. Quickly swiping my face so he couldn't see. Except the feeling lingered, in my chest, and in the warbled way I spoke. "I thought that you wanted to...you know..."

I couldn't look at him.

I stared at the door.

I was in so over my head.

I don't understand how someone could hate me so much, but also look at me like I'm the answer to all his problems. I *want* to be his answer. For a moment, I swear he looked like he wanted me to be it too.

"I'm Grayson Crowne," he said. "I'm not taking your V-

card. You're going to give it to me. Beg me to take it."

Oh, right, he still thinks I'm a virgin. That lie between us, growing like an untamable weed.

"I'll never do that," I rasped, staring at the door.

He grasped my chin, ripping open my mouth, thrusting his fingers into it. Forcing me to taste them.

With his fingers gagging me, breath hot against my ear, he said, "You're a pretty good beggar, Snitch." Then he dropped me, my head banging against the floor.

TWENTY-NINE

STORY

No falling in love.

I repeated it to myself, a mantra I tried to wrap around myself like steel, as we made our way to the Crowne family jet. Grayson was a few steps ahead and hadn't said a word since he'd obliterated me. It meant nothing to him.

It couldn't mean a thing to me.

In fitted dark-blue jeans, blond hair whipping his cheekbones as we got closer to the jet, he looked like something out of a high-fashion magazine. He threw a look over his shoulder, and I glanced down.

The Crowne jet was more famous than Air Force One, and bigger than it too. I've packed many things for Crownes who go on the family trip, but of course I'd never been on the jet. My experience with it was through gilded windows and itemized lists. Now I was staring up at the doors as a salty sea breeze whipped tendrils of hair around my forehead.

Tansy Crowne stood next to the stairs leading up to the open plane door. Grayson said nothing, taking the stairs, as Tansy spoke.

"Oh, dear, you know we have all the help we need on these trips."

I froze, stuck on the stair directly parallel to her. Despite her carefully manufactured neutral tone, tension hung in the air.

"The help needs all the *help* they can get," Grayson said.

He kept walking and I scurried after him. Though she spoke kindly with her son, her displeasure was like rotten food.

"I think this is a bad idea," I whispered. "Your mom—"

I stopped, freezing on my words, staring into the jet. It was bigger than the whole servants' quarters. Luxurious, as I would expect. With *hallways* leading into more rooms. Multiple televisions, a fucking *fireplace*.

Grayson plopped down on a couch, turning on the TV, bored as always.

"Sit, Snitch."

I did.

I looked around the plane. It had freshly cut flowers, multiple couches, and a bar. That was just what I could see.

"Close your mouth," Gray said.

I did, feeling caught.

Gemma stumbled in a few minutes after us, looking hungover from the night before, her fiancé, Horace, at her heels. The rumble of the plane engine starting up vibrated, but still no Abigail. Gray kicked up his feet, playing some kind of video game.

Abigail barely made it on the plane, her bodyguard

Theo with her. Tansy followed after, looking pissed. Well, as mad as Tansy could look.

We lifted off.

My mind wouldn't shut up.

I'd be gone from Uncle, and during that time he'd be getting cancer treatment. And what would my uncle think of me if he knew *what* I was doing?

I swallowed, glancing at Grayson from the corner of my eye. If what we'd done earlier had affected him, he didn't show it.

Grayson Crowne is the harmless crush you know you can never have. It doesn't matter if he's wrong for you in every way, because he's unobtainable. Rock stars, book boyfriends, and movie villains all fall into the same category.

So what happens when the unobtainable becomes in reach?

How do you deal with that?

How do you *stop* looking at him?

"I heard you say *I love you!*" Abigail yelled, pulling me out of my internal monologue. "You can't trick me on this, Theo."

Both Gray and I paused, looking in their direction. Was something going on with Abigail and her bodyguard? Gray threw his remote, and it landed on my lap with a thud.

"Okay, this is way more interesting than demolishing eleven-year-olds," he said, crossing his arms overhead.

The remote vibrated in my lap and kept vibrating. I shifted, but that made it worse, igniting that forbidden and wrong need inside me. I shifted. Did he *know*? With his arms still over his head, he shot me a clandestine look. Tongue at his canine, eyes hooded. All male satisfaction.

Oh, he knew.

Abigail left.

"Stop, no, come back," Gray said lazily, and he took the remote from my lap. He ever so slightly squeezed the inside of my thigh. I sucked in a breath, and just like that, I couldn't think. Remembering the way he touched me. The promise he made. My thighs still vibrating.

Whatever was happening between Abigail and her bodyguard had me hooked. They were on the other side of the plane, whispering furiously.

Abigail brought Theo into Crowne Hall. He was never a servant, but he'd lived in the servants' quarters with us. He was always just Abigail's. Then one day he was gone, a bodyguard for Mr. Beryl Crowne.

It had been everyone's favorite rumor. We all knew Abigail Crowne had no future with some random street orphan, so who was he to her? I swallowed, forcing myself not to look at Gray. Maybe Theo had been nothing at all.

Like me.

Abigail reappeared, sitting next to Gray, tea in her hand. He glanced at Abigail before going back to his video game. Theo stared daggers at us.

"I knew we couldn't be together," Theo said.

Abigail looked up from her tea, surprise written across her features.

"A guy like me, with someone like you, Abigail? I was your dog. I was only good enough to sleep at the foot of your bed."

"Yup," Gray said, without taking his eyes off his video game.

I swallowed against the pain of another scratch on my heart.

"Theo—"

"You weren't just my best friend, Abs," Theo said,

cutting her off. "You were the best thing that ever happened to me. I couldn't lose you... but if I loved you, I would. Every day with you I got closer to telling you the truth and ruining everything. When you kissed me?"

My heart was pounding and pounding. Whatever was going on between them, it obviously wasn't meant for us, but I couldn't stop listening. It *felt* like I was supposed to hear it. Nothing had ever been more relevant.

Was that what Grayson Crowne had become? My friend? After years of loneliness, of hiding, I had someone to talk to, a confidant. Someone to share my soul with. Even when he ignored me, I felt like he was watching me, seeing me, the real me.

I felt sick.

No.

I barely glanced at him, but his steely blue eyes were already on mine. I didn't hear what Theo said next, because I was lost in Grayson. Then he looked away, back to his video game.

I don't know how many minutes passed in silence, but I watched him play a few games. When Gemma came into our part of the plane, heading toward the cockpit, the silence shattered like glass.

"Why is Story with you?" Abigail suddenly snapped.

"Who?" Gray asked, and my chest hurt, even if he was pretending.

"My *servant*."

Gray barely glanced at me, but Abigail stared at me. I wasn't used to having the attention of all the Crownes.

"You took her from me. She doesn't belong to you."

Gray shrugged, eyes back on his video game. "Tell me her favorite food, and you can have her back."

My heart leaped but I forced myself to stare at my hands. Did he really remember it was Italian?

How are you going to convince her you love her when you don't even care enough to learn her favorite food?

Abigail sputtered. "Are you kidding? Can you name any of your servants' favorite *food*?"

Gray shook his head, a smile twitching his lips.

"This is so. Fucking. Ridiculous," Abigail practically screamed. She stood up, but her eyes were on Gemma, and it felt like that was where her anger was really directed.

Don't ask. Don't ask. Don't ask.

Gray didn't remember anything about me. He didn't care about me, and thinking any other way was foolish.

"What's my favorite food?" I asked.

Gray rolled his eyes. "Who cares?"

Something inside me dropped and shattered, cutting the soles of my feet. At the cockpit, Gemma and Abigail were fighting, Theo was trying to break it apart.

He glanced at me. "Oh, did you think I actually remembered? That I cared?"

I ground my teeth. "No."

The plane shook and I fell forward, but Grayson caught me, his grip on me tight.

His breath ghosted my lips. "You sure about that, Snitch?"

When he spoke, it wasn't cruel, his question weighted with something else, something I wanted to answer, if only he would lift the barbs on his heart long enough for me to enter.

"Can we have one flight without—"

Tansy's voice was an electric wire to my spine. In pajamas and a dark, silky green sleep mask around her neck,

she was clearly on her way to the Abigail-Gemma fight, but she froze upon seeing us.

I tried to pull myself out of Gray's grasp, and his grip tightened, almost *possessively*. Abigail yelled, and Tansy tore her eyes in the direction of the cockpit. She gave us one last look, then headed over there.

Gray gently dragged my face to him, rubbing my lip. It was so tender. So sweet.

I should've known the words that followed would be cutting.

"I don't give a shit about your favorite food," he said softly. "I only care about eating *you*. When we land, I'm going to eat your pussy until you tap out; then I'm going to keep going till you pass out." He let me go, absently saying, "Let's see where else you taste like lemons."

My eyes shot up, meeting his.

Lemons?

Had he been thinking about *me* that night?

Another shout from the cockpit, and this time the captain yelled he would be making an emergency landing.

"Looks like we'll be landing soon, Snitch."

We weren't more than a few feet past Grayson's towering guards when he yanked my wrist, spinning me around until I faced the wall. I barely planted my hands on the wall in time to keep my cheek from slamming into it.

In the time it had taken us to land, the sun had risen high in the sky, and hazy midafternoon sun set his hallway aglow.

"What are you doing?" I asked, eyeing the guards.

His palms gripped my waist, spanning down to my ass. "I think I made that clear earlier."

I looked over my shoulder, trying to see him. He couldn't be serious. Not *here*.

"Don't fucking look at me," he said, and I stared at the backs of his guards. Forced to only *feel*. Feel as his soft, forceful touch drifted below my knees, to the hem of my skirt.

"What's your safe word?" he demanded.

"W-What about your bedroom?" I asked.

He hiked my skirt up even higher. "Can't wait."

"But..."

"Hold this." He handed me the bunched fabric of my white skirt, and I did, catching a glimpse over my shoulder of him on his knees, face to my ass.

"Spread your legs," he said, voice rocky.

I swallowed a lump of nerves, spreading my legs. He palmed my ass over my panties, gripped it, and my head fell forward as waves of pleasure made me weak.

"I own this wing," he said. "Someday I'll own Crowne Hall and the town it's in. The only people in this wing are my guards, but it wouldn't matter if the entire town was here, because I own *you*, Story Hale. What's your fucking safe word?"

"Mr. Crowne," I said.

His grip lingered on the hem of my panties. "Are you using it?"

I hesitated but shook my head. "No."

He ripped my panties down, my ass bare in his hallway, and then his lips were on me, hot and sure and igniting a need I wasn't sure could be quenched.

I held on to the wall for dear life.

"Fuck," he groaned. "You taste so fucking good."

Teeth. Tongue.

Grayson Crowne was wicked with his mouth and teeth. He bit my thigh hard, then returned to my lips, sucking, twisting wicking spirals of heat into my gut, bleeding down into my thighs. My vision warped. My forehead fell against the carved flowers molded into the wall.

"You need bruises on your thighs," he said. "You need them on your cunt. You need to see who fucking owns you."

His words vibrated with possession, and I wanted that. I wanted to be owned, even though I shouldn't. Even though I knew he didn't want to keep me.

"Someday I'm gonna eat your little ass, but today..." He trailed off, sucking on my clit, hard enough to draw a sharp gasp. His groan vibrated against my flesh and it was too much, too much pleasure.

"Come for me, Story."

Story.

Millions of butterflies fluttered and exploded in my gut.

He was using my *name*, breathing it against my pussy as he sucked and tongued and bit me into a pleasure coma. I couldn't stand. I slipped, and he wrapped his arm around my thigh, keeping me upright.

"Grayson," I breathed, impending orgasm blurring my vision.

"Yes, *fuck*," he groaned, tongue diving deeper. "That's it, that's my girl. Come on my fucking tongue, Story."

"Gray?" a faint voice called into the hallway.

Grayson stopped, and my dream shattered. I knew the voice but didn't want to think about the person it belonged to. Not with her fiancé tonguing me into oblivion. With my name on his lips, breathing it hot against my pussy, as he bit me and marked me.

"Gray, I can't get into your wing..." Lottie called out. "They won't let me. But I need to talk to you."

And like it meant nothing, Grayson stood up. Fixed the back of my dress. Then he wiped me off with the back of his hand and went to find his real girl, Lottie.

THIRTY

GRAY

Lottie stared down the hallway of my wing, a wrinkle between her brows. "Do you want to talk in your room?"

"Here's fine," I said.

"You still don't let anyone in there?" She kept fucking staring.

Had we been too loud?

Shit, I'll never get the sound of Snitch coming out of my head.

"Shouldn't you be in Asia?" I asked, changing subjects.

Every summer, like we traveled around Europe, Lottie went to the Maldives.

"This year I'll be in France."

I raised my brows. "That's a first. Which part?"

My family always went to the Riviera, spent our time on a little island that we had to sneak off if we wanted to do anything other than fossilize on the sand.

Lottie rubbed her shoulder. "Our parents want to start

taking pictures, building the narrative this has been an ongoing thing. We're supposed to take selfies at Unknown."

Unknown was the most exclusive club in the French Riviera, one my sister Gemma and I frequented each year. One most *everyone* in our circle frequented. Like everything else, Charlotte had always been the exception.

Only a few knew its location and how to get there. It was as much a tradition to party there every year as it was for Mother to force us on the island for "family time." You needed a boat to access it and power to know its location.

I dragged my hands through my hair. What a fucking mess.

"Charlotte, I can get you out of this. You don't have to marry me, not if you don't want to."

Lottie looked at the floor, working her mouth. When she finally met my gaze, there were fucking tears in her eyes.

"Lottie..." I went to her, thumbing the tears out of her eyes. "This is fucked. I'm *not* going to force you into this. Is there someone else?"

Her mouth dropped. "No one. There's no one. That's not it." She swallowed, looking away.

"Whatever it is, we'll fix it," I said. "You don't have to marry—"

Lottie seized my face between her palms. Her hands were colder than Snitch's, I thought absently, before realizing what the fuck was happening. The way she stared at my lips with a determined look on her face.

She crushed her lips against mine.

With *Snitch* still on my lips, she kissed me.

Why the fuck did it feel wrong? Why couldn't I stop thinking of Snitch. Lottie's kiss was too light, too tender.

Not the gasping, breathy, desperate thing that Snitch gave me.

I'd been waiting for this fucking moment for years, and Snitch was still between us. So I pulled away, but our foreheads were still pressed together. She blinked up at me, her eyes dark and bright.

"That was...unexpected," I said.

"I really want to make this work," she said quietly.

Of course she would. Charlotte du Lac was the epitome of high society. She would never not do as she was told. Never not face her impending nuptials with anything save class. Even if it was to the man of her nightmares.

She arched a brow. "But am I too late?"

Immediately Story's face popped into my head.

"No," I said instantly. "Fuck no."

Charlotte smiled, a beautiful, bright Charlotte du Lac smile. The kind that had brought all the boys at Rosey to their knees.

"What about the servant?" Lottie asked, breath ghosting my lips.

Story, something in my chest yelled. Her name is Story.

"No one."

I pressed Lottie against the wall, determined to exorcise Snitch from my thoughts and taste buds. I kissed Lottie until she gasped, until she fisted my shirt. I dragged her lip out, biting, punishing—

"Ow!" Lottie gasped, and I stepped off.

I tangled a hand in my hair. "Sorry. Shit."

Lottie pressed fingers to her wounded, parted mouth. "It's okay."

It *wasn't* okay. This was everything I'd always wanted, but my chest ripped and pounded.

It was wrong. The kiss. This moment.

"I guess I'm your fiancée now. Even if we can't announce it yet," Lottie said, obviously trying to move past it, dropping her fingers with a smile. "A dirty secret. I've never had one."

Seal it with a secret.

"A Christmas wedding," I said, clearing my throat. "At least you love Christmas."

Her brow furrowed. "I *hate* Christmas, Grayson."

I could've sworn I'd heard her say she loved it. Before she could see the frown forming on my lips, I shot her a smile.

"Whatever fucking wedding you want, Lottie. We'll get married on the moon if you want."

She grinned, but just as quickly, it fell. "As long as you *really* don't have anyone. I can't go through with this if you have someone."

I thought of Snitch.

There was something forming between us. Not just friendship, a tether in my soul.

At night, I wait for her.

I grabbed Lottie by the waist, pulling her to me, eliciting a small squeal.

"It's always been you," I said against her lips.

THIRTY-ONE

STORY

I was in France.

I was in France, on a private island, and *miserable*. Gray hasn't said a word to me since Lottie visited. He was with her for hours, and when she left, he didn't come back to the wing. He only came to get me in the morning to get back on the plane.

And that was the most he'd spoken to me.

I don't know what they talked about. For all I know, they spent the night together. It's not like I can ask.

After all, I'm nothing to him.

We spent all day on the beach. I sat on warm white sand, staring out at a mesmerizing aquamarine ocean, wondering how hell could look like paradise.

That's it.

The moments before Lottie had interrupted us played in my head like a broken record, over and over again. Scratching and pausing at the worst moment, while I'd

stared at Grayson's shirtless, sun-kissed muscles, strung-out for some kind of attention.

That's my girl.

Any kind.

Cruel.

Kind.

Come on my fucking tongue, Story.

Hopeless and pathetic and needy.

I used to think Gray's attention was the worst thing to ever happen to me, but I was so wrong. It was like the sun had turned off.

"Your family is starting to wonder about me," I said when we got back to his room. "What are you going to tell them?"

At the beach, Abigail had stared at me, Theo had stared at me. I felt his mother's narrow gaze on my back. When Gray had needled Abigail, Abigail had questioned why he wasn't having *me* do anything.

I was his servant, after all, right?

Gray popped the buttons on his jeans, exposing a slice of his cut lower abs, the sharp V that hinted at so much more. Again I was blasted with the memory.

That's it. That's my girl.

He went into the next room and slammed the door.

"Ass." I whispered to myself.

Out the window the Mediterranean Sea glimmered like topaz in the sun. I wasn't surprised we were on a private island—as if the Crownes were the kind of people to stay in hotels unless they *had* to. They'd once bought—as in, *purchased*—a five-star hotel because they'd booked a last minute trip during the Olympics, and all the rooms were full.

They'd kicked everyone out.

I still remember the press, the way they managed to spin the story and make themselves the victim.

Gray came out of the adjacent room, and it looked like he was going to leave me without another word, but then he froze at the door.

"Do you think I owe you an explanation, Snitch? Do you think I owe you anything?"

Yes.

No.

This was a trap. There was a razor edge to his words I could cut myself on.

"Well," I swallowed. "My uncle has always taught me to live with dignity, and now I've basically said, fuck it, time to be an ignominious slut. So maybe I do. Maybe I feel entitled to something more than silence."

Grayson spun, blond brows pulled high into his forehead.

Something was happening between us. Was I really the only one who felt it?

"You're entitled to exactly what I choose to tell you."

So choose to tell me something! I wanted to yell it.

Scream it.

Make him bleed it.

But I wasn't going to say that. I wasn't going to be the only one offering my heart up for sacrifice.

So I steeled my eyes. "Of course not, Mr. Grayson."

Something flickered in his stony blue eyes, but he said nothing. He left, shutting the door, leaving me alone in his wing of the palatial French villa.

GRAY

· · ·

Hours after I left Snitch, I was once again back on our island.

Fucking shit, the island was way too small.

But Snitch's glare followed me everywhere. So brazen, like everything else about her. I knew every thought, every curse she wasn't hurling at me, just by her hardened hazel eyes.

Ignominious slut.

Who the fuck talked like that?

"What's that you've got in your hands, Grayson?"

I stopped at my mother's voice.

I looked at the bag. "Food."

I kept walking, hoping that would be the end of it. The hallway was long and marked by open sandstone arches on either side, the sun fading into a tapestry of periwinkle and orange.

"You used the private jet to get that food," she said to my back. "Was dinner so not to your liking you had to go all the way to Italy?"

I exhaled, turning to see her red-brown eyes narrowed.

"I'm not going to sit back and watch you make the same mistake your father did."

I rubbed an eye.

There it is.

"I am nothing like him."

"You're right," she said lightly. "At least your father gave me the honeymoon."

I knew my mother was manipulating me. It was her fucking go-to. The surprising thing was that it was *working*. I couldn't stop picturing Lottie, the sweetest, purest person I knew, as Tansy Crowne. My mother wasn't born black

hearted. Her heart was left out like an apple, to rot and decay.

"I see the signs," she continued. "Living in your wing. Bringing her to parties and on vacation. A mistress or two is fine, but you're forgetting the most important rule."

A mistress always comes second.

I clenched my jaw. "I won't have a mistress. I won't even fuck another woman when I'm married."

She smiled thinly. "You can't be with her twenty-four seven, Grayson."

Ice filled my veins. "Are you threatening her?"

My mother smiled, a warmth that didn't reach her eyes. With no more words, she walked down the hallway, leaving me in the fading sunset's shadows.

I'd planned on leaving Story alone tonight. I had to meet Lottie at Unknown. We were supposed to take pictures for our upcoming *wedding*, after promising I didn't have anyone. Abigail had fucking demanded we take her with us, threatened to tell on us to Mom like we were teenagers again. So tonight the boat was already going to be filled with Gemma, Abigail, and Abigail's dog.

Unknown was dangerous for a person like Story, someone who hadn't grown up in my world. Forget your average everyday date raper. Unknown is filled with sex traffickers and traders—the insidious kind. The ones that promise to put you on the cover of magazines, the ones that get you in so deep you don't even realize you've sold yourself until you're famous.

The kind that live in Hollywood.

But I couldn't fucking leave Snitch, not with my mother all but saying she'd ship her off to Russia.

I tangled my hands in my hair.

"Fuck."

STORY

Gray was gone so long the sun dropped below the ocean, stars appearing one by one like diamonds stabbed into a dark-velvet blanket.

I tried calling my uncle to check in, but he didn't pick up my call. I tried like twenty times. Each went to voicemail. The only way I knew he was okay was by calling the servants' quarters and speaking with Ms. Barn. *Busy,* she'd said. I knew what busy meant.

Uncle was avoiding me.

Why?

The door slammed open, Gray following with it. He dropped a bag into my lap seconds later.

It smelled *amazing.*

"Spaghetti?" I asked, caution lacing my tongue. Did he bring me spaghetti?

"You should really try the seafood while we're on the fucking Riviera," he gritted.

I made a face. Gross. I hate seafood. Something was...off with him, but I couldn't be sure. After all, it wasn't like he was talking to me.

I fished around the bag, watching him warily. "Where did you get this?"

"Italy," he deadpanned.

"Like...the country?" I stared at the spaghetti, then slowly lifted my head. "You went to Italy?"

I stared at him, my jaw about to drop off its hinges. He said he didn't remember my favorite food, but not only did

224 MARY CATHERINE GEBHARD

he come back with it, it was from the *country*. He took hours out of his day to fly there and back.

He'd utterly ignored me, but then he did something like this, and I didn't know what to think.

I think he misinterpreted my silence, because Grayson grabbed the bag like he was going to throw it in the trash. I ran and grabbed his arm, wrapping one around his bicep, reaching across his chest for the bag.

"Wait!" I said.

He turned his head, and our lips were so close. I could smell sugar on them. He'd been chewing suckers.

Something was on his mind.

His eyes dropped to mine, the air thick.

"I'll eat it," I said quietly. "Thank you."

His eyes slowly found mine, and then I saw, saw what distance had hid. He was all kinds of twisted. His hair was a mess, as if he'd been running his hands through it over and over again.

So I did the insane thing. I pushed the wild messy hair off his face.

"My father cheated on my mother," he blurted. "Kept a mistress and had three kids with her. They go to the same boarding school I did, and we've seen them every Thanksgiving and Christmas for as long as I can remember."

I knew that. Everyone knew about the bastard Crownes. They came for the holidays with all the others.

But I waited, breath pulled.

"I don't know if my mom was ever a human, but I'm sure being reminded every family holiday that she was only there because he *had* to keep her there didn't help. I always told myself I wouldn't be anything like him, nothing like my grandfather. I would be loyal." His eyes slowly found mine, burning with anguish.

Keeping me, a mistress.

I fiddled with the rose gold strand of hair I'd pushed above his forehead, taking a breath.

A secret for a secret.

"I never wanted to be like my parents either," I whispered. "The only thing my mom taught me was how to lie. Even though I promised I would tell the truth always...it was really easy to lie to myself."

"Why the fuck did you kiss me?" The pain strangling his voice choked my heart. Wrapped it in razor wire, cutting and bleeding.

"Grayson—" I started, but he cut me off.

"When I decide to let you come again," he growled. "Know it wasn't for you; it was for *her*."

He dropped me like fire, stepping away so quickly I fell forward onto my hands and knees. I stared at my shadowy reflection in the glossy floor, trying to regulate my breathing, as he walked out of the suite.

"Finish your fucking food. You're going out tonight."

He dropped the bag of spaghetti next to me a moment later.

Grayson Crowne pretended nothing mattered, but I was starting to suspect the opposite. He would do anything for the one he loved. Move the earth. *Destroy* the earth.

Destroy me...

So long as it meant he got the one he loved.

THIRTY-TWO

STORY

The minute we got off the boat, Grayson grabbed my wrist. Behind him, his siblings exited the boat one by one as a man dressed in white—a *servant*—gave them a hand.

"Tonight you don't know me, and I don't know you," Gray said.

I gawked. "But I don't know anyone here!"

"Exactly. If you so much as look in their direction, I'll start another poker game. And I'll lose."

My mouth dropped, but he spun from me, only to stop an instant later and look over his shoulder. "Don't talk to anyone. Don't look at anyone."

"I don't know anyone, remember?"

Grayson stared at me, a look on his face I'd only ever seen when he thought no one was looking—concern. But it quickly vanished, shook off with his devil-may-care smile, as he continued on his way to find Lottie.

I leaned against the rock, blowing a stray curl from my eye.

This place was the craziest thing I've ever seen. Girls dancing inside rock, a DJ surrounded by glowing water, *mermaids* swimming in it. Grayson had to maneuver the boat through a secret tunnel, too, until we reached this cliff-side grotto encased by shimmering rock on three sides.

I recognized a lot of the people here, either from serving them at parties or by their faces on magazines. One of them, Khalid, the dude who'd tried to bet on me, seemed to be walking toward me until he abruptly changed directions.

I settled deeper against the rock, counting time by the change of electro-pop songs.

Why even bring me along if my only job was to become one with the rock?

"So you're not from around here."

I didn't know he was talking to me until he touched my shoulder.

I looked up into the greenest eyes I'd ever seen.

Holy shit.

I knew this guy—*everyone* knew this guy. His movies always hit number one at the box office.

I swallowed a cough. "How did you know?"

He shrugged. "Everyone kind of knows everyone here."

"Oh..."

"So." He leaned forward, smiling. "Where did you come from, new girl?"

I glanced at Gray, who'd been flirting with Lottie for the past hour. Don't talk to anyone, he'd said...but a fucking *movie star* was talking to me. I'd seen actors and actresses at Crowne parties, at Crowne Point, even, but always from a distance. They never looked at me. Never *smiled* at me.

"Around," I said.

I was breaking Grayson's rules. I wasn't sure if the thrill racing up my spine came from that knowledge or the fact that a movie star just laughed at what I said.

"All right. *Around*. Never seen you here, though."

"I don't know anything about this place," I admitted.

"It's *Unknown*. It's only open for one week out of the year, so for this week, everyone who's anyone is dancing on the stages built into the rock or swimming in the water that surrounds the DJ...or fucking in the rooms built into the rock," he added with a low voice.

I snapped my eyes to the floor.

Did he really just say that to me?

"But the coolest part of Unknown is actually *unknown*, though," he continued easily. "Want to see?"

I glanced at Grayson. Flirting with Lottie. Kissing her cheek. I could stay here, heart aching. Or...I could go flirt with the guy who had just sold out theaters everywhere.

I smiled at him. "Sure."

GRAY

When I found Lottie, she was sitting with her feet in the grotto. The water glowed with LED lights, shades of fuchsia and violet and all colors of the rainbow.

"Here you are," I said, taking a seat next to her.

Lottie lifted her head at my voice, smiling. "This is my first time at Unknown since Rosey. It hasn't changed much."

I rubbed the back of my neck, eyes wandering again to the wall. Khalid headed for Snitch. I caught his eye with a

glare. He raised his hands, walking backward, a coughing laugh I could hear in my fucking head.

Fucking shit, these places were incestuous.

I pulled out a sucker, ripped the plastic off, and shoved it into my mouth. Something to distract myself.

"Yeah, still a bunch of douches trying to get laid, and a DJ with a boner for dubstep." We were so close to him too. Only a few feet away, spinning on a dais in the middle of the grotto.

Lottie laughed. "I mean it's pretty. The water is beautiful and the view..." She looked out over the cliff to the view of the twinkling ocean.

Girls swam in the grotto, wearing mermaid fins and nothing else. Occasionally someone dove off the stages, splashing us. I swiped my forehead.

Fuck.

I hated this place.

"Do you remember the first time we came here?" Lottie asked. "I was fifteen, you were sixteen. Geoff and Alaric were high on coke or something."

"Sounds about right," I said, trying not to roll my eyes.

She played with the fabric of her dress, working the sheer black material between her fingers.

"Someone spilled their cocktail all over my white dress," she said. "You gave me your shirt and told me not to tell anyone."

My brows drew. "You remember that?"

"I remember everything about you." She lifted her head, and our eyes locked. "I can't stop thinking about our kiss... I've been looking at your orchid every night."

"The one next to your bed?" I arched a brow, throwing her a half smile. She didn't return my joke. She looked up at me through her thick, dark lashes.

"Yes."

Fuck.

I reached into my pocket for a blunt—I needed more than a fucking lollipop to distract myself. I lit it and inhaled, trying to get my fucking mind focused on the beautiful girl beside me.

"I have a present," she said suddenly.

I leaned back on my elbows as she reached into a glittery purse, pulling out a green pen. It wasn't anything fancy, not some Montblanc or S.T. Dupont bullshit. It looked like something you'd get at a gas station.

She handed it to me.

"I meant to give it to you a while ago, but things kept getting in the way."

"Why did you get this for me?"

Lottie blinked, looking like a kid with their hand in the cookie jar. "Don't you like it?"

"Yeah, babe, just wondering how that mind works."

She blushed, which should've driven me wild. Instead I looked for Snitch. She was still settled against the wall, looking bored.

Lottie doesn't deserve this. Doesn't deserve someone like me, whose heart is halved.

Why the fuck did Snitch have to be the one I grabbed? Why wasn't Lottie in that fucking room?

Some dildo movie star wandered up to Snitch. My eyes sharpened on him. That guy had a reputation for taking pictures of girls who were too "sleepy" to know better.

"I don't know," Lottie said. "I just had a feeling."

Snitch looked like a missionary among the heathens. Her eyes were wide, starstruck, as the dildo leaned forward to brush something off her shoulder. She laughed. Who the fuck is vampire boy and where does he get off touching her?

"Gray? Do you want to get a drink or something?"

I tried to shake out of it, give my attention back to Lottie, but Snitch lifted off the rock as if to follow the asshole. I stood up quickly, tossing my blunt into the water. Some mermaid in the process of dumping her margarita yelled at me for littering.

"Where are you going?" Lottie asked.

I squeezed her shoulder. "Need some air. I'll be right back."

STORY

Hollywood guy wound his fingers in mine, leading me through the crowd. "It's just beyond here."

It felt wrong to hold his hand, wrong and dangerous, but I let him. I let him weave us through the crowd, past skimpy dresses and bikinis that shone like dragon scales. Above us, I even caught a glimpse of Abigail dancing on one of the stages, until we were at the edge of the club, over-looking the black sea.

Technically Grayson hadn't said anything about holding hands with others.

"Do you know what's inside these rocks?" Hollywood asked.

"Shouldn't you be deep-throating the Academy?"
Grayson.

Grayson, with a twinkling sea of dancing at his back.

Hollywood heartthrob stared at me a moment longer, then slowly lifted his bright-green eyes.

"Nice to see you, too, Crowne," he said easily.

Grayson didn't look at me, but I knew better now than to think his attention wasn't laser focused on me.

"This one belongs to me."

Hollywood eyed me. "Didn't see your name on her."

Grayson stepped forward and grabbed my elbow, his grip surprisingly gentle. "It's not on me they don't teach you to read in Hollywood."

Grayson didn't wait for his response, dragging me away.

"Talk to you later, new girl..." Hollywood's voice drifted over my shoulder. Grayson's grip tightened at his voice. It excited me—it shouldn't have, but it did.

My heart pounded. At Hollywood's attention, at Grayson's tight grip, at being talked about like I was little more than dirt once more.

Grayson shoved me into a room built into the rock and slammed the door.

"Am I not giving you enough attention?" he asked, tone deadly impassive. "Did you forget what you signed already?"

"Don't talk to anyone," I mumbled. "But that's an *insane* request, and I won't fucking follow it. And he came up to *me*."

A pause followed, the thumping beat pounding against the rock like it wanted to get in.

"Why do you care?" I asked.

He laughed. "I don't give a shit."

"Liar," I yelled. "You act like nothing matters, like you're just as corrupt and depraved as the rest of them, but I see you, Gray."

He stepped closer, voice a low snarl. "What do you think you see?"

I stuttered. "I—I—"

"Tell me, Snitch. What do you see?" He cornered me

against the wall, shoulders wide and head bent. Forcing me to crane my neck back to see into his eyes. "You must have painted a pretty fucking picture in your head. I wonder if you can outdo my stans—their pictures are pretty goddamn perfect."

"It's not pretty," I whispered at last.

He reeled, and even in the low light, I saw the surprise, the furrowed brow.

Then he slammed his hands on either side of my head. "I should get it over with, right? Fuck you. Get you out of my system." His hands came to my dress, hiking up the fabric. "The girl I've always wanted finally wants to make it work, but the girl I never wanted won't get out of my fucking head."

"I..." My word dripped off on a gasp, or was it a sigh? As his hands fisted my dress higher, his body pressing hot into mine. "That's not what I meant," I managed.

"What's your safe word."

I met his eyes. "Mr. Crowne."

He leaned down, forehead pressed against mine, and shoved the fabric of my dress into my hand. He forced me to hold it up for him, keeping me open and bare for him. He caressed the inside of my thighs with one hand, ghosting bruises on my flesh, the ones he'd given me just days before. I couldn't stop my shiver.

"Do you want me to kiss you, Snitch?" he asked lightly, his breath teasing my lips.

"You said no kissing..."

His laugh feathered my lips.

"Want me to say your name?" His touch rose higher, over my panties.

Yes.

I shouldn't.

But, God, *yes*.

His eyes locked with mine, ripping, piercing.

Maybe I should look away, but I couldn't.

"Know I know it's *you* I'm kissing?"

His lips were *so close* now, I could taste the warmth, taste the lollipops on his breath.

He pushed aside my panties, sliding inside me, and I sucked in a breath. In and out, slow, easy, *torturous*. His thumb slid around my clit but never touched it. My heart was a traitor, beating too fast. My skin prickled and my gut tightened. My only reprieve knowing he can't read my thoughts.

"Know I want to kiss you." The only way I knew I'd slightly affected him was the grit in his voice.

He pressed against my clit just as he pressed his lips to mine.

"I don't want you," he whispered, as I shattered against his fingers. His lips were warm, wet, but barely touching me. Just enough so I could feel the vibration of his cruel, cruel words.

I was too far gone to stop it. Too far gone to push him away, to stop the wave of pleasure. I grasped his shoulders, coming undone.

He didn't stop massaging my clit or pumping inside me. Didn't stop forcing me to come as his words echoed within me.

I don't want you.

His words dripped inside me, mixing with the taste of him, the want I couldn't suppress, until I could barely stand.

When I finished, he licked my upper lip, slow, easy, until flames threatened to burn me to the ground.

Then he stood back.

He eyed me from down his crookedly beautiful nose. "I could never want you."

I fell to the floor, tears burning the corners of my eyes, but thank fuck they didn't fall. I stared at my knees, knobby, bruised.

I could never want you.

I knew he'd opened the door by the sudden rush of sound. Of laughter and music.

"Who was that for?" his cold voice drifted back.

"What?" I blinked through my tears.

Suddenly my hair was in his fist and he yanked my stare to his. "*Who* was that for?"

It dawned on me what he meant, and then I couldn't stop the tears from falling.

"Lottie," I rasped.

He dropped me.

I put my head in my hands as the door slammed shut.

I had only one fucking rule, and here I was breaking it, falling for the cruel prince once more.

THIRTY-THREE

STORY

I could never want you.

I promised myself I wouldn't cry, but back on the island, through the open window the Riviera skyline was a blurry, twinkling treasure through my tears.

I stayed in that room until Grayson came and got me. Silently ordered me to follow him back to the boat. Grayson had spent the rest of the time at the club with Lottie, and now back home, I don't know where he was, but I didn't care.

I pretended to be asleep.

But I cried.

Messy tears I refused to let him see.

I heard the subtle, muted creak of a door opening. A moment later, Gray's cold voice followed. "Why aren't you in bed?"

I didn't respond, hoping he'd think I was asleep. My chest couldn't take it.

"Get up here, Snitch." Grayson bent down, blocking the open sea window, and placed one careful finger below my chin, lifting it so I met his eyes. "Or have I broken you already?"

Grayson Crowne was the cruelest person in the world.

Cutting, ice-blue eyes. A nose slightly broken. Plush pink lips. Blond hair that was constantly falling out of his coif, messy like his personality, messy like his soul, messy like the way he'd kissed me when he'd woven my love irrevocably with his hate.

He lifted me up into his arms without another word and settled us into bed together, cradling my head on his bare chest. I noticed he'd taken off his shirt and had changed into sweats.

"What's your safe word?" he asked.

"Mr. Crowne," I croaked. When he made me choose one, I thought it was because we were going to be doing some kinky whipping and paddling Fifty Shades of Grayson shit. Not ripping apart my soul.

"Remember to use it," he said, chest rumbling.

He stroked my hair. My back. Tears fell in a constant, hot stream down my cheek. I decided his sweet side was worse than his cruel side. Like the way the twinkling Riviera blurred with my tears, it blurred my picture of him.

"Why don't you want to be a poet anymore?" he asked softly.

I wasn't prepared for the question.

"Someone needs to take care of my uncle," I said even more quietly.

"You can write while taking care of him."

"Yeah," was all I gave him.

I don't know how many minutes passed as I lay on his hard chest. I kept telling myself to get up, to yell at him, to

not let him get away with it. But he was warm, and his fingers were soft and loving, and I was weak.

"I received a really thoughtful gift from my fiancée today," Gray said. "A green pen."

"Oh," was all I managed.

"I keep wondering how the fuck she knew to give it to me."

"She's your fiancée. You love her. She *should* give that to you."

I sat up, angry.

Angry that he had the audacity to ask me such personal questions. To be sweet to me. To act like what he did to me never happened.

"What do you see in me, Story Hale?" His words were jagged and cutting, like the look in his eyes.

This is where I should tell him *nothing*.

After what he did to me, after all he said to me, I should tell him I see nothing in him. I couldn't lie, but I couldn't tell him the truth—it was too damning. An Atlas carrying a world of expectations and responsibilities. A lonely prince who pretends he doesn't care but cares so much he's isolated.

I see the only person who sees me back.

So I stroked the broken ridges of his nose, because it was the closest to a confession I could get.

His eyes burned and broke and cracked. "Everyone who gets close to me, who gets close to the real Grayson Crowne, never likes what they see."

"I see you," I said brokenly. Hating myself for not hating him.

"Trust me, Snitch, I've only ever been good at making people hate me. At the end of this, you'll hate me too."

He pulled my fingers into his mouth. His tongue

twirled around them, hot, demanding, reminding me how he'd done it to my pussy.

I groaned. "Gray."

"Tell me more, Snitch. Tell me to keep going." He dragged me back to him, wrapping his body around mine, pulling me against his hard cock, sliding a hand beneath my panties.

It felt like an apology, a surrender.

Like what he was really asking was for me to say it was okay, what had happened before was okay. And the thing was...I was so close to it, so close to giving in.

"Fuck you're wet." He bit my ear at the same time he thrust. The pain and pleasure colliding. "God I love your pussy."

He grasped my breast harshly, not giving me a chance to respond. I sighed as his lips found my neck, then my ear, biting and pulling on the lobe. Leaving marks only he and I would know about. Ripping a gasp from me.

So close to giving in once more...but I shoved him off.

Breaths heavy between us.

"No."

He arched a brow.

"You take and take and take."

Both eyebrows popped up. "You weren't saying that when you were screaming *more*, thighs digging into my head."

My face was hot, and I prayed it was too dark to see my embarrassment.

"No kissing," I said. "No looking into your eyes. *Who* was my orgasm for, Gray?" Something flickered in his eyes, but it was gone before I could see. "You take but pretend you're giving."

He stretched his neck, raising chiseled golden arms. "If you want my cock, just ask for it, Snitch."

I know what he's doing. I'm starting to see through it. He thinks if he's crude and brash it will scare me away. Because then no one gets close to Grayson Crowne. Grayson Crowne holds the key to his heart, his soul, and if you happen to stumble too close to the gate, he throws the key in the fucking sewer and acts like it never existed.

"Would you really give it to me?" I rubbed over his sweats, along the hard, tapered outline of his cock. "I think you won't."

"Go for it," he said, sounding choked.

"What if I said I wanted you inside me? Isn't that what you're waiting for?"

His back was rigid against the bed, but his eyes were locked on mine, burning. Searing. Jaw clenched so tight.

I slid my fingers beneath the waistband, grasping hot flesh. He wasn't wearing any underwear, and my fingers barely fit around his girth.

"You don't want me to look you in the eyes. You don't want me to kiss you. You don't want *me*."

I climbed down his chest, further down until I was at his jutting hips, his hard cock.

"I see through you, Grayson Crowne. You're not ashamed. You're not saving yourself for someone better. You're scared."

His eyes sharpened on a glare, but then I lowered his sweats a fraction of an inch, and he released a rocky breath.

"You were the little boy whose nose was broken because he dared to care; now you're the man who refuses to let that happen to his heart. I understand what my uncle meant now. You have the biggest heart of anyone, so you wrap it in thorns."

"You think I care about you?" he gritted. "Don't read into this, Story. I'm just another person in your life who doesn't want you."

His words ripped into my chest, tore jagged, irreparable lines down my soul. But I wouldn't let him see that. He'd already taken too much.

I stared back, unflinching. "The thorns make you bleed the most."

His eyes burned raw emotion.

There he was again, my Grayson.

I tore down his pants, exposing his iron-hard cock.

"Can I look you in the eyes like this?" I asked, finding his eyes. "Can I kiss you like this?" I wrapped my lips around his cock.

"*Fuck.*" He threw his head against the carved wood headboard, still watching me.

I followed his lead, swallowed, sucked, licked him, anything to get his jaw tighter, the look in his eyes burning darker. He pulled the hair out of my face, fisting it, like he wanted a clearer look at me.

I think two kisses shouldn't be enough for me to love him. I kept thinking that, even as the days wove into weeks. I kept waiting for something inside me to snap. I'd worked for the Crownes for years. I knew humiliation. But the thing inside me grew.

Maybe it isn't love.

Maybe it's obsession. Maybe I'm *obsessed*.

"I'm going to come," he gritted. "Stop right now if you don't want me in your fucking mouth."

I kept going. Going until hot, wet spurts laved my tongue and hit the back of my throat while he groaned my name. *My* name.

Story.

His eyes burned with something that looked a lot like love.

Moments afterward were still. Unaffected. Tender.

"Get up here," he growled.

I crawled up him, and when I was in reach he dragged me the rest of the way by the waist. He stroked his thumb across my lip, pushing the rest of his come in my mouth. Then he kissed my jaw. He kissed my chin, my nose, my cheek, my forehead. Everywhere but my lips.

I pushed him away, a knot in my chest.

He still won't kiss me.

Because I don't mean anything.

He dragged me back.

"Mr. Crowne," I whispered.

He rolled off me. I was cold, *so* cold.

Grayson Crowne is the cruelest person in the world, and I'm hopelessly in love with him, but his love only bloomed in the dark.

THIRTY-FOUR

STORY

The rest of the trip passed with Grayson barely acknowl-edging my existence. I couldn't believe it was almost August, that the summer was almost over, and this thing between Grayson and I was getting closer to the end.

I kept telling myself he was marrying Lottie, and I needed to get used to being invisible again. My heart hurt, was breaking each second he kept choosing her, each second I *let him* keep choosing her. Until one moment it cracked in two, when everything changed, the night of Abigail Crowne's engagement party.

I heard rumors about her fiancé.

Abigail was supposedly marrying a horrible, abusive man. I think it bothered Gray...he acted like it didn't, refused to let the world see anything save his perfect mask. I tried to tell myself I had no right to wonder, let alone ask.

He had a constant frown, his shoulders were slumped,

and anytime he left me to go spend time with Abigail's fiancé, he looked ready to throw something.

The day of the engagement party he stopped talking to me completely.

He lounged on a dark-leather couch overlooking his private beach, one leg propped on a glass table, scrolling through his Instagram feed.

"I'm going to visit my uncle," I declared, both telling him and testing to see if he would try to stop me. A little spark in my gut hoped he would. I don't know *why* I liked it. I was a servant. I shouldn't like being told what to do.

But I *missed it*.

He didn't come for me at night anymore, didn't acknowledge me in the day, and for the thousandth time I wondered why he kept me around.

I took a step toward the door, and when he didn't so much as lift his head from his phone, I kept walking.

The house was buzzing with energy for Abigail Crowne's engagement party. Servants cutting and preparing fresh flowers, a multistory ladder erected so they could shine the sparkling two-ton chandelier that hung from the domed ballroom. Paparazzi being escorted into the press room. I paused when I saw Ellie, hoping she would say something...but no one looked at me, not even to glare.

I was afforded the same treatment as a Crowne, or a Crowne's guest. Yet I was not a Crowne. I was in an in-between world. Not belonging below, not belonging above. As a result, I was the loneliest I'd ever been.

When I reached the servants' quarters, my uncle's heavy black door was already open. Silver was piled high on his bed, and he lay against the headrest, polishing.

"Uncle?" I asked, eyeing the silver.

"Story." He smiled when he saw me. "Good to see you."

"How are you feeling? You haven't been responding to any of my phone calls, texts, or emails."

He waved a hand, going back to polishing. "You know how things get around here. I'm fit as a fiddle with a clean bill of health. I told you it was nothing to worry about."

Again, I eyed the silver. You don't take silver down to the quarters. You don't move it from its spot, period. You shine it where it is.

"You're doing better? Really?"

He smiled. "Would I lie?"

Woodson Hale was the most stringent, rule-abiding person I'd ever known. If he saw a servant so much as move a piece of silver to the left, that servant would get a talking-to. My uncle wouldn't sit with a pile of it for no reason.

"You can tell me, Uncle," I said softly. "I'm not a child anymore."

He set down the silverware. "With you gone we've had to make some concessions. It would take too long to go around and polish these. Much faster to do it all at once."

Guilt slammed into my chest. "I've missed you."

He picked up the chalice. "Missing me one place?"

"Search another..."

He smiled softly. "Walt Whitman. Do you remember when I first read that to you?"

"The anniversary of Mom's death."

Some people were sung lullabies or read bedtime stories, my uncle read me poetry. I was a little too old for bedtime stories anyway, but I never *got* bedtime stories, and Uncle always said with poetry, for a moment, you could fix the unfixable.

There were so many things in my life that needed fixing.

"I might have time in my schedule for a poetry reading."

He winked. "After this engagement dies down. I do miss your poetry, Story," he added, eyes bright, waiting.

The Crowne phone buzzed on the wall and saved me from answering. Still I watched him a moment longer. It had been so long since we'd done a poetry reading. Since we'd just sat and talked.

I paused as I was about to exit. In the corner of his room was a toppling mountain of shoes, what looked like Grayson Crowne's sneakers. The ones he wore once and then never again.

"What are these?"

Uncle was too busy on the phone, but I looked closer. They were labeled *donations*. Why did Grayson Crowne always act like he cared the least, when he cared the most?

I gently shut the door behind me as I left.

Abigail's engagement party was starting soon. I had no idea if Grayson was going to want me there. For every event since the vacation, he'd had me stay in his room. Still, I hurried.

You can write while taking care of him.

Grayson's words echoed in my head as I walked back to his wing. It was getting late, the light waning in long, gaunt shadows along Crowne Hall.

I could. I can write anywhere. But every time I put pen to paper, I froze. I've hidden for so long I didn't know how to show my soul.

What if people see me, and they don't like what they see?

When I got back to Grayson's wing, shouting stopped me short in the hallway.

"One fucking thing, Mom," Grayson's voice bounced off the walls.

I paused a few feet down from the door to Grayson's bedroom, his yelling echoing in the barren halls.

"Grayson, dear," Tansy Crowne's tinkling voice drifted like a breath of winter wind. "You know how these things work."

"He hits her. He's a fucking psychopath."

"His father's company will be quite the addition, and we both know Abigail isn't the most...attractive investment."

I looked back down the hall, thinking I should leave, when the *click-clack* of heels stopped my heart. I turned, finding Tansy Crowne. We both froze as I stared her straight in her red-brown eyes—eyes so similar to her *least attractive investment's*. Then sanity returned and I quickly looked at the floor.

Her approaching footsteps were the only sound; then she stopped exactly parallel to me. I stared hard at her polished, nude heels, my heartbeat thunder. The minute dragged on like nails against a chalkboard.

"How much?" she asked, voice low.

"What?"

"How much?" she repeated. "I've paid off every girl who thought she loved my son. You all have a price. Name it."

The shock of that statement had me looking up and into Tansy Crowne's eyes.

"You've paid off every girl interested in Grayson? Does he know?"

Her red-brown eyes slimmed. "Do I tell him about the girls who wanted his money?"

"I don't want his money," I said, though I had to look away. Because what was I even doing here? I'd signed my name on a dotted line for cash. All this was *only* for money.

Tansy kept walking, and I let out a breath.

When I got to Grayson's room, he was on the edge of a couch, legs spread and head in his hands, already in a tux for the party. He looked every bit the lonely, broken prince I knew him to be, crushed beneath the weight of expectations. I struggled with the decision to leave him alone or go to him.

I wanted to take the weight off his shoulders as no one had done for me when I was a kid, but I knew that was impossible, because no one could take that weight away. Sometimes problems are just unfixable.

So I said the one thing I wished someone had said to me.

"It's not fair."

He lifted his head at my voice. It was the infamous *Playboy Gray* with his tangled, messy hair—all to hide the deep-blue eyes beneath. The iconic messy image of Grayson Crowne, the boy who doesn't care, but in reality, it's because he cares *too* much.

"Whatever this weight is on your shoulders, you shouldn't have it..." I looked down, unable to stare into his burning eyes, fiddling with my thumbs. "Your shoulders will get stronger, though."

Silence stretched until his choked voice called to me. "Come here."

My heart was already close to shattering, but I couldn't say no to him. Not because he didn't give me a choice, but because my heart was wrapped around a wire, and he held the leash. When I was within distance, he grasped my wrist, tugging me into his lap.

He stroked the back of my neck, looking beyond, like he wasn't aware I was even there.

"I had *one* fucking thing," he said, still staring ahead, like he wasn't talking to me. "When my father died, I filled

the shoes as the patriarch, became the beam of support for my mother. I became a son for my grandfather...all I asked for was one fucking thing."

He stopped talking, brow furrowed in thought, and cautiously I pushed the hair off his forehead.

"My mother, my grandfather, my sisters, this fucking house," he continued. "Everyone needs a piece of Grayson Crowne. Fine, whatever, I just wanted one goddamn thing. Don't marry my sisters off to assholes. Don't let them marry someone like me. Which, admittedly, is like fishing for minnows in a sea of sharks." He dragged his free hand down his face.

"Marrying someone like you wouldn't be so bad," I said.

His heavy eyes found mine, a look in them that strangled my soul.

"Yeah, Snitch, you'd marry someone like me?" He had a sardonic, self-deprecating tone, but I saw beneath that. To the hurt. The hope. And I knew I should lie, change the subject, to put *some* kind of frail armor around my already cracking heart.

"I would," I whispered.

Pain splintered his blue eyes.

I've missed you, I almost said, *missed these small moments where you trusted me enough to pull away your thorns...*

But I stopped myself.

"Why do you share these things with me?" I asked instead. "Why don't you let everyone know who you are?"

He paused, then said quietly, "I felt it shelter to speak to you."

I frowned. Why did that sound familiar? Then—"Emily Dickinson!"

A small smile broke his lips, and the soft, tender way he watched me wrecked me more than anything.

"You know a lot of poetry for someone who claims to hate it," I said.

"Someone once told me I could fix the unfixable with poetry."

My heart stopped, lips parted. He was talking about Uncle! Grayson gently lifted me off him, placing me back on the couch. He stood up, adjusting his bow tie.

He looked at his phone. "We have a funeral to get to." He then eyed me. "You need to get dressed."

"Get dressed?"

"There are only so many formal functions I can take you to dressed like a Vatican escapee. It's hanging in my closet."

I followed him to his closet. Inside, amid suits and jeans and jackets worth more than house payments, a dress hung, its silver embellishments catching the light.

It was...beautiful.

It was also somehow so *me*.

"Did you buy this for me?" I asked, stunned.

"No," he said.

My heart dropped.

"I had it made."

And just like that I couldn't breathe.

"It should fit perfectly." His fingers lightly grazed my spine, trailing down until his hand rested right above my ass. "Silver will look beautiful on you."

I also knew enough to know a dress like this would require assistance to put on, but at the moment all I could think about was his hand at the small of my back, eyes blazing into mine.

"It will show your collarbone," he mused.

I licked my lips, and his eyes dropped to them. "That's okay."

"It wasn't you I was worried about."

There was a knock on his door, and we separated. He went to one side, tangling his hands through his hair, and I went to the other.

"She'll help you get dressed."

"You let someone come here? Wait, who—" I broke off, spotting Ellie.

"Your foot, miss," Ellie said.

"I'm not a *miss*," I tried for what must have been the thousandth time. "I'm *me*, Ellie." Ellie said nothing, holding the dress out for me. With a sigh I stepped into it.

She buttoned up the back, and I stared into the mirror at the stranger in silver. It was an A-line, long-sleeved gown that covered my shoulders in patterns of sheer silver that shone like liquid in the light.

It was also airy enough for summer.

"Anything else, miss?" Ellie asked, once she'd finished. Her eyes were on the floor.

My shoulders fell. "Ellie, *please*. Please talk to me. I miss you."

"If that's all, I need to get back down for Ms. Abigail's engagement." She bowed her head and left. Tears filled my throat. Of joy. Of confusion. Of fear. I loved myself in this dress, and I hated myself in it.

When I came out, Grayson was leaning against the wall next to the double doors, on his phone. When he saw me, his phone slipped from his hand with a clang to the hardwood, eyes steel.

"What?" I looked at the dress, thinking I'd somehow already managed to spill something.

"Nothing," he said, voice choked. He bent down to pick up his phone, and that was all we spoke.

I followed him downstairs, my nerves growing with the orchestra's music the closer we got to the ballroom. A voice in my head kept whispering: *You're not supposed to be here. You're not supposed to be dressed like this. This isn't where you belong.*

I was flying too close to the sun.

THIRTY-FIVE

STORY

Grayson hasn't stopped staring at me.

I shifted on the soles of my feet, more and more insecure. "What? Is it my dress?"

Grayson gripped his drink just as a hush overcame the crowd. The double doors opened above us, and Abigail Crowne emerged with her fiancé. Grayson tensed, then turned from me, eyes on them.

The ballroom was beautiful, the freshly cleaned chandelier dripping from the domed ceiling. It was Tansy's pride, vintage and imported from some long-fallen monarchy—many speculated the Romanovs. It shimmered like the sun.

I was grateful I could again blend in. I wondered if that was why he bought the dress. Did Grayson know how important that was to me?

Abigail descended looking beautiful, ethereal, and so, so

sad. Theo was at her back, walking down the stairs like a dead man. Her fiancé? Couldn't have looked more smug.

Before Grayson, when I was just a servant, I'd thought these people the worst kind of entitled. They had everything, and yet they dared be angry and miserable. Now I saw them for what they really were: trapped.

"Champagne, miss?" I turned to find a server dressed in the black-and-white uniform, staring at the floor. Andrew.

"Andrew, I—" I stopped, remembering Ellie. I wanted to yell at him. *Andrew, it's me, Story.* But I was in a silver gown, and he would never look me in the eyes, not here. Maybe not ever again.

I looked around at all the servers.

When this was all over, I couldn't go back to them.

When this was over...

I glanced at Gray, standing ahead of me, because I was still not his equal.

"What is my place here, Grayson?" I whispered to his back.

Grayson turned around, his eyes locking with mine.

"Why am I still here?" I pressed.

I waited for him to say something like *because I own you until Christmas.* But a silver thin thread of hope needled. *Tell me it means more. Tell me I'm not just a tool, something to use and get over.*

My heart pounded, and my lips suddenly felt so dry. I darted my tongue out to wet them.

His gaze dropped to them. "Come with me."

The room faded away, the concerto disappeared, the laughter died. All that was left were his tight jaw and the burning look in his eyes. The one that made me forget all the reasons why I shouldn't feel this way.

"Don't you need to stay?" I asked quietly.

A slight smile quirked his jaw. "Who says we're going anywhere?"

Grayson held out his hand, and I knew I shouldn't take it. I should put distance between us.

I placed my hand in his.

"Are you allowed to hold my hand?" I asked as I noticed what must have been the fifteenth person stare.

"You have a bad habit of forgetting who I am, Snitch," Grayson said easily. "There's nothing on earth Grayson Crowne can't do."

Still, my stomach churned uneasily. We were buoyed on all sides by stares. They couldn't tell who I was, not in my silver gown, but *I* knew.

"Where are we going?"

He ignored me, dragging me until we were on the edge of the ballroom, almost against the gilded latticed floor-to-ceiling windows.

"The way the ballroom is designed, from this spot, you can see everything and everyone, but you're obscured by these two pillars."

He motioned to the Grecian columns with his two pointer fingers, and I followed Grayson's stare out to the ballroom. He was right.

"I used to come here with my dad," he said. "No...I used to follow him, hide over there"—he pointed to a spot near the stage—"then wait for him to find me and force me back to the party."

I studied his wistful face. "You never talk about your dad."

"We're not supposed to speak ill of the dead." He shot

me a grin, but it was sad. Darkness lurked in his stony eyes, and I wished we were different. I wished I could hug him.

"Abigail has stars in her eyes because she was too young to remember him. But he was an asshole. He loved his real family more than us."

Grayson stared off into the party. I followed his line of sight to where Abigail stood next to her fiancé. She was a real princess in her lace-up, flowing white dress. Beautiful.

Beautiful and sad.

It should be the official motto for the Crownes.

"When my dad died, I told my mom I wouldn't let anything happen to this family," Grayson continued. "I said we would always be together. I swore it as she cried on his fucking grave. We're together. We just hate each other."

"You don't hate each other," I said instantly, but even I could hear the lie.

"Tell me something about you," Grayson said, turning to me, eyes earnest. "Something I don't know."

Immediately, I knew the thing he didn't know about me. The dirtiest part. The part I wanted to keep hidden.

"My mother and I stole a lot," I said quietly. "The worst thing my mother stole was happily ever afters. I lost track of how many families she ruined."

I waited for him to recoil, but he watched me eagerly.

"Like, I never really knew my dad," I continued. "I have a pretty good idea who he is, because he stuck around the longest. But he was married, so he didn't stay. And I don't blame him...because my mom didn't love him. He was just another man in a long line of men we fooled and ruined. She taught me how to use my perceived innocence to trap men. That was her go-to scam. Sometimes it was guys she'd slept with once a while ago. I'd tell them I was their daugh-

ter. They'd pay us off not to ruin their family. Other times it was darker..."

I looked away.

I couldn't talk anymore.

I couldn't go down this road.

"If you never wanted to be your father...I never wanted to be my mom."

"What would our wedding look like, Snitch?" he asked.

My eyes snapped to his. Why would he ask that? He took a step closer, forcing me to take one back, until my back was almost pressed against the glass window.

"Tell me."

My brows caved with my lungs. *"Why?"*

"I need to fucking know." His voice was raw, shredded.

A part of me yelled to lie. Tell him I hadn't thought about it at all.

"It would be small," I said softly. "Not a ridiculous Crowne party. Intimate. So all we had to worry about was each other."

"You'd like that?" The hope in his voice splintered my heart.

"You'd like that."

A sad, barely there smile flickered and died on his pink lips. When he spoke, his voice was rough, like he'd inhaled a year's worth of smoke. "Yeah."

God, these moments with Grayson were so addicting. I should hate him, right? But how could I when he let me see the broken, lonely prince beneath all the thorns?

"In the winter," I continued, getting sucked into his eyes, into a fantasy that would never be. "So snowflakes frosted the glass like glitter. And you'd wear something just for me."

"Oh yeah?" He reached out, caressing his knuckle down my cheek. "Like what?"

"A pocket square..." I closed my eyes, drowning in his touch, goose bumps shivering along my heart. "M-Maybe something green."

He took a deep, jagged breath.

"I've got you fooled," he eventually said, throat thick with tension.

I opened my eyes. "I'm the only one you don't have fooled, Grayson. You let your sisters think you don't like them. You let the world think you're a playboy. But you care *so much*."

Something flickered beneath the deep blue of his eyes. His hand slipped from my cheek, to the back of my neck, locking me in place. His jaw clenched, gaze focused on my lips, dark and possessive.

I put a hand to his chest, but I couldn't quite shove him off, so it just lingered.

This isn't something to do for a servant. These aren't things you say for someone you're going to abandon in two months.

"Why are you doing this?" I begged. "Why? Why can't you be like this always? Do you remember what you said to me, what you *did* to me, back in France?"

"Why are you giving my fiancée green pens?" he countered, grip on my neck harsh. "Why are you telling her what I like?"

"So you're happy. You deserve to be happy."

His jaw clenched. "No one has ever accused Grayson Crowne of deserving happiness."

I fisted the fabric of his white dress shirt before he spoke again.

"I tell you my deep secrets, my dirty pieces of me. I can

breathe when I talk to you. With you I have no weight on my shoulders. I...I fucking trust you, Story Hale." He said it like he couldn't believe it—and also hated me for allowing the trust to blossom.

I looked away. "Lottie is waiting for you."

"And?" he demanded.

"And she's your *fiancée*."

"You're fucking ripping me apart, Story."

I snapped back to him. "*I'm* ripping you apart?" Was he fucking serious?

"For the first time in my life I can see myself throwing everything away, Snitch." He pushed me against the window, cold glass biting through my dress. "And it's not for the love of my life. It's for the girl who stole it."

My wrist on his chest bent backward. He pinned me with his eyes.

Me. He was talking about *me.*

"Grayson?"

I jerked my head at the voice, heart pounding for a new reason. Charlotte du Lac approached him in a pale-pink ball gown with intricate flowers embroidered in the thin tulle. The skirt was so big it looked like an overturned teacup. Her long black hair was pulled back, curls falling in waves down her back.

It was exquisite.

She was exquisite.

Grayson was still looking at me—*still pinning me.*

Then slowly he turned to see who had come.

"I had a feeling I'd find you here..." she said, brows knitted on me.

Find him here.

He'd brought *her* here. I don't know why that cut me so sharply. It wasn't like I was special.

"I know we're supposed to be keeping everything somewhat on the DL, but what about one dance?" Her spaghetti strap bodice pushed her breasts up every time she spoke.

"Uh..." He took a step back, allowing space to breathe between us. He frowned at me, though, almost like he wanted me to say something. What? What could I say? That was his *fiancée*. Even if it wasn't announced yet.

Me? I was...well, I wasn't really anything. I was just the girl stealing their happily ever after.

This is why it couldn't work.

This is why we were wrong.

I was a dirty secret.

When I said nothing, Gray took her hand, leading her to the dance floor, her arm intertwined with his.

STORY

Off to the side of the ballroom, against the wall, I watched Grayson dance with Lottie. They looked good together. Right.

"Showing your shoulders. Sort of."

My spine stiffened at the voice. *West.*

I didn't bother acknowledging him, or even turning to face him.

"Nice dress," West continued. "Must have cost a fortune."

His obvious implication hung like a guillotine.

Lottie placed her head on Gray's shoulder and smiled at something he said. Then Gray's eyes met mine. My heart stopped, the room disappeared. He was once again

saying something to me in a language I still hadn't learned.

Then he looked back at her, smiling. She snuggled closer to him. My heart shriveled up.

"They look good together."

I turned away from both him and the sight that was tearing my insides to ribbons, staring off into the crowd until they blurred into one glittery blob.

"Do you think he loves you?" I clenched my jaw and he laughed. "Holy shit, you do."

"I don't."

I can see myself throwing everything away.

"He's going to marry my sister. You could have the greatest fucking love story of all time, but he's still going to marry her. You didn't grow up in this world, Angel. That dopey look in your eyes means you're on track for one thing, a broken heart."

"I don't love him," I repeated, queasy.

"Want to know what I can offer you that he can't? Kids and a place by my side."

My lips parted at his offer, but no words came out.

"Crownes don't have children with their mistresses. The bastards his father had saw to that. Us? Not so much. My father and grandfather have more bastards than I can count. Our mistresses are just as important to us as our wives. Some even more so."

I felt like I was going to be sick.

Like mother, like daughter? Chasing other women's men. Too busy loving someone she had no right to love to love her own daughter. The girl behind the girl, invisible and unloved forever.

I glared. How did I ever think I loved West? "Is that all I am to you?"

262 MARY CATHERINE GEBHARD

"That's all you can ever be to any of us." He shrugged like it was no big deal, picking out the cherry from his cocktail and tossing it to the floor.

I eyed it.

A servant would clean that up later.

Someone like me.

I gritted my teeth. "I'm not going to be anyone's mistress."

West laughed again. "You already are."

It hit me like a gong to my chest. Is that what I'd become? Wearing the pretty dresses, sleeping in his bed. The in-between world where you're given respect, but not respected, acknowledged, or seen.

"There will be a time when you realize it, Angel. When he offers you everything and gives you nothing. When that happens, I'll be there."

I clenched my jaw. "I don't want anything from any of you."

West tilted my chin up with his knuckle, gaze softening. For a moment he looked like the boy who'd stolen my heart and shattered it. "I was stupid, Angel. I was a teenager. Give me another chance."

"To be your mistress," I said, hollow.

He thumbed my chin. "To be the love of my life."

My brow furrowed, and West dropped me, stepping back with his arms up in surrender.

"I'm just giving her options, Grayson. Seems like you're not being honest with her."

I looked over my shoulder, finding Grayson, hands fisted, a look in his eye I wasn't sure I'd ever seen before. Unhinged. Ready to kill.

Lottie stood feet behind him on the dance floor, face twisted like he'd left her there in the middle of a dance.

"Do you have a fucking death wish, du Lac?" Gray gritted.

West smiled at me. "Think about it, Angel."

West walked away, laughing, in on a joke that felt an awful lot like I was the punch line. Gray watched West walk away, eyes zeroed and sharp like a predator, until he was completely out of view. Then they landed on me with the same intensity.

He gripped my wrist, dragging me to the arched doors of the ballroom.

I looked over my shoulder at Lottie's caving brow. "Grayson..."

People were definitely watching.

Staring, even.

But he either didn't notice or didn't care.

He pulled us out of the ballroom, a few feet down the hallway, before opening a door. It was a small closet used by the servants for spare linens. It smelled clean and soft. The light dark, but soft, like the muted string music.

"Grayson," I started again, when he slammed his hands on either side of my head, eyes furious and searching. By the fiery look in his glare, I was certain he was going to punish me.

I swallowed.

"Grayson. You can't bring me to events and expect me not to talk to people. It's insane and—"

"Snitch," he cut me off, voice rocky. I sucked in a breath, expecting the worse. "Shut up."

He dove for my neck, biting and sucking.

THIRTY-SIX

STORY

He'd leave marks.

Visible marks.

"Grayson," I breathed. I grasped his shoulders for support as his lips found my collarbone, kissing, sucking, biting.

"I fucking love my name on your lips."

My knees weakened, and he slid his hand from the wall, grasping the small of my back, hiking me up against him and the wall, his hands under my ass.

He hiked me harder against his thigh, his dick iron against my stomach.

"Y-You'll leave marks."

He looked up at me, sultry and heavy lidded, then grazed his teeth along my collarbone. Goose bumps followed after them, tingling in my teeth. Between my thighs ached and throbbed. I threw my head back and sucked in a sharp breath.

"Yeah, give me those sounds," he said. His voice was rough like sandpaper, abrading my blood and making me squirm. He bit harder, and this time I gasped. "Fuck, those are *mine*. You don't make those noises for anyone else."

Another bite, this one at the juncture between my neck and collarbone. A whimper escaped as my vision twirled into a kaleidoscope of pleasure.

"You like that. Fuck." He groaned. "Of course you do."

The room became only him. *Grayson. Tongue. Teeth. Hands.*

"Your dresses are perfect," he said. "My little nun. Do you wear them just for me?" He pulled a bit of the giving material aside, biting my shoulder, then laving his tongue over the wound. "A taunting, teasing, torturous nun."

He tugged on the sheer neckline, exposing my cleavage, paused. His blue eyes searched mine, waiting for me to tell him to stop. I licked my lips, his eyes dropped to them, then he tugged harder, exposing my breast.

I was exposed.

My heart must have pounded at three times the speed.

Obscene.

Raw.

That was how I felt.

It was a tight fit, the material barely had enough give, and my breast pushed out farther. The dress dug into my ribs. Gray's jaw clenched so tight the muscle twerked, and his eyes hardened.

"I don't like sharing you, Story," he said, voice rocky and deep. "Any part of you."

He took my nipple into his mouth. I arched my back. Swam in a sea of new sensations. Tongue, lips, sparks shooting and catching fire in my abdomen, lighting a blaze in my gut.

Teeth.

I gasped, opening my eyes and catching his at the same time. A hot, burning question in them. He took my nipple between his teeth, and I grasped the collar of his shirt, his bow tie, anything, and he bit harder. I was wickedly burning, a pain twisted and set fires inside me I couldn't ever hope to put out.

Then I saw just beneath my thumb, a lipstick stain, a pale plum color.

I don't like sharing you...

"I don't like him talking to you." His lips vibrated against my flesh. "I really don't like him touching you."

He stood up, pressing his clothed chest to my half-naked one. My nipple was bruised and marked. And so was he.

Just not by me.

He grasped my chin, pulling my eyes to his. "This is mine." He pressed down my chin for emphasis. My eyes wandered again, to his collar.

Pale plum.

A pretty color that matched Lottie's dress so well.

Grayson kissed my chin, his top lip barely grazing my bottom one, before pulling back to thumb my lips. "*These* are mine."

He leaned in like he was going to kiss me, but I turned my head at the last second.

Pale plum.

It paired so well with her skin, and the matte made her lips look plumper.

"Kiss me," Grayson growled.

"You said no kissing," I breathed.

He gripped my shoulders, dragging me closer, fingers bruising. He was hard and throbbing against my hips, and

every time I breathed, I breathed in *Grayson*. I could all but feel his heart pounding.

"Fuck what I said, give me your mouth." His teeth scraped against my chin, dragging along my neck, before following the same path with his lips.

"The contract—"

"Is that *really* all this is to you?" He dropped me and slammed his hands beside me in one motion. "A contract?" His blue gaze flitted left and right, searching mine.

No, I need you.

No, I love you.

My eyes landed on his collar, where the purple truth lay smudged on his white shirt. Marked, because Lottie *could* mark him. She *could* kiss him. She had the right. Me?

This dark closet was suddenly too fucking dark.

This was *my* right.

Darkness.

He'll marry her, leave me behind. If I'm lucky, I get holidays.

"Yes," I whispered.

Coldness swept his face and sucked away my breath like a winter wind. He stepped away, eyeing me with that Grayson Crowne apathy and disgust.

"Don't leave this room, Snitch."

He opened the door, slammed it, and left me in the dark.

I was alone for maybe ten minutes before I heard them. I had only fifteen seconds' warning. Her soft giggles. His dark, cocky laughter. There was nowhere to run, so I had to hide, but a linen closet didn't afford many places. I looked

268 MARY CATHERINE GEBHARD

left and right, and dove behind a stack of unopened boxes as the door opened, two bodies falling through it.

"Grayson, stop, people could walk in," Charlotte laughed. Light flooded the room, then snuffed out, slammed shut.

"Can't wait to feel your pussy," Grayson said, pushing her past the boxes, to me. Her back hit the wall beside me, and I crawled to hide, to not be seen. I shrank between two piles of linen, drawing one over my body, hoping to disappear.

Lottie laughed. "You're dirty."

I could see them through my flimsy sheet. They were fuzzy through cotton, but I saw him kiss her and saw her kiss him back. I couldn't help but think of the one year I went trick-or-treating and my mom had just grabbed a sheet and cut holes in it.

I'd wanted to be some princess or something.

She'd made me a ghost. It was easier.

"This dress is too fucking big," Grayson said.

Lottie turned around, bending over and hiking up her dress to give him easier access.

I lowered the sheet a few inches, exposing my eyes but covering my nose. I needed to see the crash, needed to see for certain the moment my heart cracked in two.

He ripped down her panties, then prowled over her, thrusting his fingers inside her.

I wished for numbness, but my wish wasn't granted. I was an exposed nerve forced to feel everything.

"Do you like that, little nun?" Grayson groaned.

"Nun?" Lottie's delirious voice questioned. He never answered her, but by the way she gasped, he did something to make her stop questioning.

Hot tears streamed down my cheeks, but I made sure to stay quiet.

Grayson's eyes opened, locking with mine as he kissed her neck and made her moan against the wall where he'd just done the same to me.

While I was behind her.

Then he closed his eyes.

She cried out, hitting her peak while I could still feel his lips, my breast throbbing from his kisses. Bruises would sprout.

I can't breathe.

I can't *breathe*.

Is this what a panic attack feels like?

I didn't even realize she'd righted herself. That they were ready to go, until Grayson spoke.

"Come on, Lottie."

He shut the door once again, leaving me in the black.

THIRTY-SEVEN

GRAY

Lottie hadn't stopped grinning since the linen closet, and I felt like fucking slime. This was it. I was finally the Grayson Crowne everyone had always said I was, a callous playboy. The engagement party was over. Only a few shit-blasted men in wrinkled tuxes remained with their poor dates trying to keep them upright, and I ran my hands through my hair for probably the hundredth time. A few hours before, my sister had wandered into the ballroom in a ripped gown and running makeup.

And with that, the party had ended.

There was *still* no sign of Snitch. She should've come out by now. Was she seriously still sitting in there?

Her teary eyes slammed into me like a bullet.

Fuck.

"You could come spend the night at my place," Lottie said, dragging my attention back. "It's always empty. You know how it is."

I did. We were raised without parents, but with more responsibility than anyone.

I smiled softly. "Maybe another time."

Lottie's smile wavered but didn't fall. "I understand."

Fucking. Slime.

I walked Lottie out to the curving driveway, where her driver was waiting and opened the door for her. She hesitated a moment before getting in, looking left and right like she was trying to work up the courage for something. She kissed me swiftly on the cheek, then hopped into the car, slamming the door shut.

I stared after the sleek black town car, bile rising in my gut.

On my way back to my wing I thought of what I would say to Story. I don't know if I've ever apologized in my life.

A Crowne doesn't apologize, because they are never wrong. Everyone else is mistaken.

My grandfather's voice echoed in my head.

I know what Grandfather would do. He wouldn't even acknowledge what happened. Shit, Grandfather wouldn't have let Story get away with a third of what I had.

But I felt...wrong.

On paper, we weren't anything to each other. I didn't owe her an apology. It's not like we meant anything to one another. Lottie was who I was supposed to be with. Snitch made that fucking clear.

But those words were starting to feel hollow. A bell to ring when I needed to distract myself. The truth was what she'd said to me earlier, when she was on my lap before the party.

I cared.

I cared most for the one person I wasn't supposed to care about. I cared when she was sad. I cared when she was

angry. I cared when West du Lac looked at her. I fucking cared. I was starting to think she cared too.

"Is that really all this is to you?"

"Yes."

The memory slammed into me. I'd fucked up. I'd reacted. Another person who'd stolen their way into Gray Crowne's heart just to rip it out. I opened and closed my fists, wishing I had something to punch, when obnoxious laughter echoed down the hall.

Abigail's fiancé was laughing with two assholes I vaguely recognized.

Perfect.

Whatever had happened to Abigail, this fucker had something to do with it. I wasn't a good big brother. I was a fucking asshole, but I could be a dick to my sister, because she was *my* sister.

I pushed the two assholes out of the way and gripped Abigail's fiancé by the collar with one hand, dragging him to my face. They made a move to intervene, but I shot them a look, and suddenly they were very interested in something on the opposite side of the hall.

"The fuck did you do to my sister?"

He laughed. "Oh, like you fucking care."

I twisted the material at his throat until his face reddened.

"I didn't do *shit*, Crowne," he coughed.

I wanted to punch him. I wanted to let go of all my anger until his pretty boy face was raw and bleeding. This kid had always been a fucker, even back at boarding school. All he ever wanted was to be part of us. He used to follow us around, and we'd let him, only so we had a fall guy.

"She ditched me for her dog," he choked out. "Check your fucking phone."

Keeping his collar gripped tight beneath my fist, I fished around my pocket for my phone. The Finsta hashtag *abbyslostdog* had apparently been trending for hours, a photo of my sister Gemma kissing Abigail's dog, Theo.

I glared at him a second longer, then tossed him to the side, making him stumble backward.

"I'm in, Crowne," he yelled at my back. "I'm finally in."

Fuck him.

Fuck that dog.

Fuck this family.

I pounded down the hallway until his choking laugh dissipated. He was like Story, like everyone else, a user. I stopped short a few halls away from my wing. That *wasn't* Story.

Fuck.

Story wasn't that asshole. She wasn't malicious. Story wasn't conniving. She would set herself on fire to keep someone warm. Which meant my brutally honest nun had lied.

I tangled my hands in my hair again, catching a glimpse of myself in a mirror. My blond hair was wild, unkempt. My bow tie was undone, hanging askew off one side. Lipstick stained my shirt from when Lottie had rested her head on my shoulder while dancing.

"I'm sorry," I said aloud to my reflection.

It sounded weak.

"I'm sorry?" I tried again.

Worse.

I worked my hands through my hair viciously, walking back and forth.

"I didn't really mean to get her off—it just happened," I laughed weakly. "She fell on my fingers."

This is a fucking joke. There's nothing I can say to her

to make up for what I'd done. I tried to prove to myself that I'd be fine without her. That I didn't need her. And instead all I fucking did was prove the opposite.

I dropped my hands on a sigh. "I want you a lot more than I should, and I don't know what the fuck I'm gonna do come Christmas."

"What are you doing?"

"Fuck." I jumped at Gemma's voice, finding my oldest sister with her arms folded. She'd changed out of her ball gown into sweat pants and an oversized sweatshirt but her rose gold hair, so similar to mine, was still done up for the party.

"What does it look like?" I snapped.

"Uh...it looks like you're apologizing to yourself. And complimenting yourself. You really take narcissism to the next level. Be sure to avoid open pools of water."

"Saw the Finsta hashtag," I said. "Pretty gross, even for you. Didn't think you fucked dogs."

She glared. "You don't know what the fuck you're talking about."

I don't know a lot about what goes on between my sisters. There are three Crowne children, and two pedestals. My mom gave me one, and pitted Gemma and Abigail against each other for the other. The dirty secret? My mom already gave it to Gemma.

"You live in the World of Grayson. You don't know what happens outside of it."

I laughed. "And *you* are so empathetic to others?"

"I know that Abigail loves her dog, and he loves her. I know that her fiancé is a total psycho."

"Anyone with two eyes can see that."

"I know she was considering leaving him, leaving *us*, until tonight."

Gemma kept walking, giving me no space to respond.

Give up everything. Not only disinherited but *excommunicated*. Could I do that? I wondered as I walked past my ever-present guards, into my lonely wing. Abigail was abandoning ship, but for me, it wouldn't just be jumping overboard.

They counted on me to plug the leaks. To steer the ship. To hoist the sails. Without me, the boat would sink.

With an even messier head than when I'd left Lottie, I arrived at my room.

"Story, I'm—" I stopped completely, finding Story with a teetering mountain of items in her arms, like the first time she'd come to me. "Where are you going?"

"Back to Ms. Abigail. If she'll still have me. If any of them will..."

She plopped the last cherry on top of her mountain, then attempted to walk past me. I grabbed her arm, spinning her until she faced my chest. Her mountain fell. Still, she refused to look at me.

"You think I'm done with you?"

She stared at my chest. I gripped her chin, forcing her stare, and she closed her eyes.

"You're doing that again?" I gritted.

"This is who I am. Who *we* are." She shoved me off. "You won. Let me out of my contract. She wants you. You're kissing her. You're doing...with..." She swallowed. "You're getting married. *Why am I here?*"

If she would just fucking admit there was something between us. Give me something to grab on to before I jumped off the cliff. Before I destroyed everything. My family. My company. Everything I'd built.

"Because I own you until Christmas," I said.

"In a few months you start your official engagement

tour. Am I supposed to stay with you and your *fiancée* the entire time?"

"Why? Would that bother you, Snitch? Is there a reason you can't do it?"

Just fucking say it.

"How is this going to work?" she yelled. "Why keep me around? *How* are you going to keep me around?" Her eyes found mine. "Or is it like father, like son?"

"What about you, like mother, like daughter?"

She shoved me again. "I didn't ask for this. I just wanted to—"

"Disappear into nothing, hide away forever, hope no one ever saw you because if you don't dream you can't fail, if you don't love your heart can't break? You found me that night. You stole what didn't belong to you. You started this. Finish it, Snitch."

Her eyes found mine, locking. "*You* finish it."

"Fine."

I grabbed her by the waist, thrusting her against my chest, crashing my lips against hers.

THIRTY-EIGHT

STORY

Bruising. Furious. Consuming.

His kiss was cruel, forcing my surrender. I shoved him off, but he just gripped my wrists and shoved me against the wall with more lips, more teeth, more tongue. I kissed him back even though I knew I shouldn't. To punish him. To beg him. I wasn't sure.

"I'm not going to stick around and watch you fuck her," I said against his rose petal lips, biting the lower one, bruising it back. "I don't care what you do. I don't care about damages. *I don't care.*"

I felt his fingers at my bodice at the same time I heard the rip, then cool air on my flesh, knowing he'd torn the pretty silver dress. He palmed my breast, tugging at my nipple, tweaking the bruise he'd just given me. Sparks of pain ignited pleasure.

I threw my head back on a gasp.

"Sure about that, Snitch?" he growled against my neck.

"That sounds an awful lot like *caring.*"

Awareness froze the marrow in my bones. Because I do care.

Too much.

I shoved him with both hands, and he stumbled back. Hair wild. Eyes ravenous.

"I can't fucking *do this anymore.*" Tears welled and undulated, made my view blurry. "Don't do this to me. Let me go!"

He slammed both hands on either side of my head. "This is all just a contract to you!" he yelled.

The raise in his voice shocked me.

I haven't ever heard him yell. He's always so nonchalant.

"Tell me why you can't do this anymore," he said. "I'll let you go. If this is all just a fucking contract to you, but first tell me why it's so damn hard?"

I couldn't lie, but I couldn't tell the truth, either, so tears fell down my face. Weak, cowardly tears. Tears I'd promised myself I would keep inside.

He thumbed them with the savage curiosity of a wolf finding an injured deer.

"What is it? What has you crying?"

"I don't like seeing you with her, okay?"

"Why?" He stepped closer, his thigh separating mine. "Why? Fucking say it, Snitch."

I looked away, and he threaded his fingers into my hair, yanking my gaze back to his.

"You don't like sharing me?" I glared at his beautiful sideways face. "I don't like sharing *you.*"

The moment that followed my confession was too quiet. A snow globe shattered, glass everywhere, cutting the soles of my feet. He gave me *nothing.* No look. Nothing. My

heart pounded for him to say something. *Anything*. But he just stared at me silently.

So I shoved him off.

"Let's just do it. We can do it now, and then you can let me go. Get it out of our systems. Why don't you just fuck me and get it over with?"

He pulled me by my hair and my scalp burned. "You think I won't?"

He spun me around, forcing my palms flat against the wall. Then his hand was on me, palming my pussy. I tried not to think about *who* he'd been touching only hours before. It lanced. It hurt. And going into that dark place would shred me.

"Are you gonna let me go once I fuck you, Snitch?" His voice grated my neck. "Will I be out of your head?"

He kissed my neck, my ear, and I arched back.

"Will you forget how I feel sliding inside your cunt?" Harsh words from such sinfully soft lips. I heard the rasp of a zipper; then I felt it. *Him*. Just the tip, but it stretched me deliciously.

"This was how it was supposed to be," I said on a breath. "A secret that disappears and dies with us."

He tangled his grip in my hair, pulling my head back on a painful arch, until I could see his piercing blue eyes and the addictive sheen of sweat on his sharp-as-glass jaw.

"So you want me to finish it?" he asked, sliding a little bit more inside.

My mouth opened to form words, but he bit my shoulder, and all I could do was gasp. Next came his free hand, sliding between my thighs, finding my clit. A shaky, jagged groan slipped from my lips.

Sparks. Butterflies.

"So fucking wet," he groaned.

He had me speared, spread, but only enough to tease, to madden. I tried to push back, and his other hand slipped from my clit, holding my inner thigh in a vise grip. His self-control was such an aphrodisiac. Every muscle in his body was strained, and I had to imagine he wanted to plunge in.

Had to.

He'd been waiting so long.

He thumbed me again. I scythed my nails into the wall. It was like the butterflies in my stomach were sparking, electrified from that one perfect spot between my thighs. But it wasn't enough. I needed more.

It had never felt like this with West.

I never knew it *could* feel like this.

"God, fuck, yes. Come apart on my dick, Story."

I groaned as he slid another torturous millimeter inside of me.

"Fuck me," I begged, stupidly, wantonly, high on the little doses he'd allowed me.

He froze, fingers digging into my hip.

I should've taken the out.

"Please," I said, finding his eyes. "Fuck me."

His blue eyes burned. "You want more?"

I nodded fast.

"I don't have a condom with me, Story," he said, sounding suspicious, but more than that, *greedy*.

"What about the one in your wallet you've had since you were twelve?" I asked. "You know, just in case you got lucky?"

Something dark flashed in his eyes, and I was sure I was dead.

"Jokes?" He growled, pushing more. "You're fucking joking?" But he didn't sound mad. He sounded as desperate as I was.

I should've pushed him off right then. I wasn't on birth control, after all. "More."

He groaned, a broken, rocky sound.

"When I fuck you, Story—really fuck you—you're *mine*." His voice was rough, darker than anything I'd ever heard. "I'm not letting you go. Ever."

"What?" I gasped, face contracting. "But...that wasn't... you said you would *let me go*."

He shoved me off. My legs were weak, and I stumbled into the wall, letting myself fall to the floor. He towered above me, looking every bit the mythical man magazines and blogs made him out to be. His dick jutted out from his tuxedo pants, thick, veiny, beautiful. Loosely unbuttoned dress shirt giving me a view of abs carved with slick sweat.

The boy. The legend. The god.

Through it all, his eyes blazed—on *me*. Darting back and forth from my face to between my legs. I moved to close my thighs, but a single twerk of his jaw stopped me.

I must have looked a mess, clothes ripped and naked, but the way he watched me had me feeling like a goddess. He bent down between my legs with that casual, entitled grace I'd come to expect from Grayson.

Close your legs, idiot, some distant self-preservation screamed in my head.

"You said you would let me go...You said all you needed was sex. You *said*—"

I broke off on a jagged, rocky sound, as he pressed two fingers between my legs, cleaning up all the wetness, all of *us*. His eyes focused on mine. Then he stood.

Licked his fingers. "Game's changed."

He left, leaving me to ruminate on the fact that he'd said not *if* I fuck you, but *when*.

THIRTY-NINE

STORY

I'd always read that soulmates were beautiful, pretty things. They fixed you, made you whole. But that doesn't make sense to me. Souls are ugly, twisted, and dark.

It makes sense when you finally found yours, the torture is equal to what lurks inside.

"Storybook," my uncle's voice lifted me from the floor, the very same spot I haven't moved from since last night. In a panic, I scrambled to find clothes and change out of the dress Grayson had ripped and ruined.

"Storybook, are you still here?" His voice grew closer.

"I...uh...yeah, one second." I grabbed one of Grayson's sweatshirts and a pair of sweats, hoping he didn't notice, hoping I could change before Grayson got back. I wasn't sure where Grayson was, but he wasn't there when I woke, and he didn't come to me in the night.

"There you are." My uncle's bright, smiling face

appeared. In his one-toned gray suit and closely cropped white curls. "Want to help me clean? Like old times?"

"Sure..." His kindness was off-putting. He's been sure to be cold, like everyone else. To let me know how little he approves of what I'm doing.

We cleaned in silence, dusting Grayson's sparse furniture, polishing what needed to be polished. I keep waiting for a lecture, *something*.

We headed up to the second floor, and my heart beat faster. I took one corner of the sheets, and my uncle took another as we removed them to put on a fresh pair of linens.

"I've found you a place," my uncle said casually.

I paused. "What do you mean?"

"I mean, you need somewhere to work. I found you somewhere to work. You can't work here anymore. You must know how the servants view you."

"Well, yes, I do."

"I don't know what you're thinking, Story. I know you're smarter than this. I have to assume something else happened, more than simply looking him in the eyes. I've found you somewhere to work, an estate in Scotland."

Scotland.

I looked at the linens in my hand and back again to his bed that I've slept in, where I've done *more* than sleep. We've whispered secrets, we've shared pieces of our soul, but when it comes down to it, this is who I am.

I change his sheets.

Gray always said the contract wasn't about sex, because I would give it to him. If I could just last until Christmas, I'd have enough money to set Uncle up for life, but I don't know anymore. There was one escape clause—leave Crowne Point forever.

I never thought I'd even consider it.

But I *can't* be my mother.

Now Uncle was giving me a place to escape *to*.

A crash pulled me out of my thoughts. Uncle dropped his side of the sheets, falling into Grayson's night table, pushing the lamp off, shattering on the floor.

"Uncle?" Fear strangled my throat. "Uncle!" He was awake, but cross eyed and loose limbed, barely held up by the nightstand against his thighs. I ran to him, grappling with his body, sliding my arms under his as his body weight transferred to mine. We both slid down, when suddenly the weight lifted.

Grayson.

My heart pounded with his arrival. I'd started to expect his hardened voice. His shadowy presence whenever things were starting to go south. That was wrong. That wasn't good. Because I knew without a shadow of a doubt there would come a day when Grayson wouldn't be there.

When I would have to carry the weight on my shoulders alone, once more.

I looked up at him, wide eyed. If he noticed my stunned reaction, he didn't show it. Grayson lifted Uncle up, putting one arm over his shoulder as I did the same, and silently put Uncle to bed—in *his* bed. My heart lurched. The Grayson the world knew would never do something like this.

The Grayson I knew? I wouldn't doubt it.

So why was he always trying to show me the lie?

Grayson ripped out his phone, muttering fast, furious words into the receiver. I caught *ambulance, doctor, paramedic*. Meanwhile I stared at my uncle's passed-out, white-as-a-sheet face, the truth I didn't want to acknowledge staring back at me.

Grayson turned to me, furious. "What the hell is happening?"

"Cancer," I croaked, barely above a whisper. I swallowed, saying more clearly, "He has cancer."

And apparently wouldn't fucking stop lying about it, either.

"It's back? How long have you known?"

"I mean, since right after the Fourth, but he said...he said he was getting better."

He turned from me on a curse.

A thought popped into my head, and a new fear bubbled up my throat. I grabbed Grayson's wrist, trying to get him to face me.

"Please don't tell anyone, Grayson. Please. If word gets out, he'll lose his job."

Grayson's eyes narrowed. "We don't fire people for having cancer."

I rolled my eyes. "And you call me naïve."

An awkward silence bloomed.

I let go of his wrist, realizing I was still holding it.

"That's why you agreed to do this. The contract. All of it. Because of him."

I couldn't exactly deny it. It was the truth, after all. Somewhere along the way, though, I'd stopped thinking about it.

Grayson rubbed the ninety-degree angle at his jaw, and I noticed it looked like he hadn't shaved.

A strange look crossed his face. Guilt? That couldn't be right.

"Please, Grayson," was all I said.

Raw hurt bled from his face. "You really think I'd do that?"

I didn't know *what* he'd do.

"Grayson!" The voice ripped both of our attention away.

"Lottie, what? How did you get in—" Lottie jumped into Grayson's arms, kissing him hard. He looked into my eyes, until I tore my eyes away, back to Uncle.

When it rains, it pours most people said.

My mom always said when you bleed, you're a cut away from bleeding out.

She was fucked like that.

"Oh, what..." Lottie's enthusiasm drained, spotting Uncle. "What's going on?"

As if in answer, a horde of paramedics rushed his room, taking the stairs two at a time. Lottie grasped Grayson's hand as paramedics strapped my uncle to a board, carrying him down the stairs.

"I better—" I started.

"Yeah," Grayson finished.

GRAY

"That was intense," Lottie said, a few minutes after everyone had cleared out.

I still stared at my bedroom door, picturing Story's confused, hurt face. She'd only agreed to this for Woodsy. Somehow that was so much worse than if she'd just wanted to use me for money.

In no way, shape, or form had she ever wanted to be involved.

Fuck.

Before I'd felt like slime; now I was slime.

I fell back onto my couch, head in my hands. Woodsy's cancer was back. We barely beat it the last time, and the

stubborn old man refused to let me pay for any of it. Fuck that. Not this time.

How bad was it?

I needed to call the hospital, call the doctors like last time. Get him the best—

Lottie entwined her hand with mine. When had she sat beside me?

"It's really sweet how you help your servants," she said.

Servant.

I really fucking hate that word.

"I was a little scared when I saw her in your room...but now I see she was just cleaning."

Just cleaning. She wasn't just cleaning—she fucking belonged here. In my bed. In my veins.

I didn't like leaving her, letting her go to deal with her uncle on her own. She was afraid, and I wanted to be there.

I glanced at the hand in mine, itchy inside my skin, itchy in my blood.

"I'm sorry for just showing up. I really wanted to continue what we started last night. I guess I snuck in."

Lottie wove her hands in my hair, dragging me for a kiss. Soft kisses. Teasing kisses. Gentle kisses that weren't bad but weren't fucking *Story*.

Why couldn't I let her go? So many mistakes at every turn...bringing her to my wing.

Letting her stay.

The deal.

The contract.

Lies I'd said were to get the girl I finally had in my arms, against my lips, but were really to keep Story around.

Lottie trailed a hand down my chest, to the outside of my pants, rubbing my cock. Biology had me hard. It felt good, and Lottie's soft kisses didn't feel bad.

Do it. Fucking do it. Get it over with. Lose the thing that's become like a damn anchor. I've given it too much control, given *them* too much control, and Grandpa always said you don't give control without losing power. So just fucking *do it* with the girl who is supposed to be my soul mate.

I tore Lottie's hands off, standing off the couch, putting distance between us.

"I...fuck. I can't. Lottie, I can't do this to you."

What the ever-loving fuck is *WRONG WITH ME?*

Why can't I just do it?

I'm everything my grandfather says I am.

A pussy.

A fucking coward.

Lottie chewed her full, glossy lip. "It's because of her, right? The servant?"

I pushed my hands through my hair. Outside the sun was bright through the wispy, foggy marine layer. Was this because of Story Hale?

The more I touched Story, the deeper she sank. She was ink in the water of my soul, spreading, changing the color and make of me. I wanted to kiss her so fucking bad. So goddamn bad. Taste *me* on her. I ground my jaw until the grinding echoed in my skull.

My self-control was a wire-thin thread that frayed every second I was with her. I was beginning to think the minute I plunged my cock inside her wouldn't remove me but seal myself inside her permanently. The problem was, I wasn't sure what I wanted anymore.

Even if she couldn't acknowledge what we were, I couldn't ignore it any longer.

"What did last night mean to you?" Lottie asked, no

longer waiting for me to respond. Fear of my answer made her voice needle thin.

"I was using you," I answered honestly. "She was in the room. And after...I was with her—"

Her palm collided with my cheek, her slap harsh and stinging, but the tears in her eyes branded much worse.

"I hate you," she said with a trembling voice.

I sat on the edge of my bed, dragging my hands through my hair.

"You don't like me," I said, finding Lottie's eyes. "You're only trying to make it work because you have to."

"I *do*. I *do* like you. I thought by turning you down I was saving myself from my fate. I told myself I wasn't going to do this," Lottie said. "I wasn't going to be like my grand-mother and mother and sister. I wasn't going to end up in a marriage with a man with a wandering heart. And you're *Playboy Gray*, the boy whose heart only knows how to wander."

I never really understood the term *knock me over with a feather* until now. She *liked me*?

"I like you, Grayson," she said quietly. "You were always my Prince Charming, and I've always wanted to be your princess. From the very first day we met, to that day at Rosey, to now. I was afraid, and I thought pushing you away would make it better. That it would hurt less when you didn't like me back. It didn't. It made it worse. I *really* like you, Grayson."

We stared at one another, the same realization shad-owing our faces. If only we'd been honest from the start, maybe when we fell in love, it would have been at the same time.

"It was always supposed to be you," I said quietly,

taking her hand. Tears glittered in her eyes. "I'm sorry, Lottie. She's inside me. *Shit*. I can't fucking let her go."

"It's my fault," she mumbled, numb. "You gave me every opportunity to love you, and I was too afraid."

She swallowed and straightened her back; then the Lottie I knew returned. "So we do what everyone else does, a marriage in name only."

"I don't want that kind of marriage," I gritted.

"Are you going to cancel?" Wonder spread across her face, knowing what that meant.

"No."

And just like that wonder shattered into misery. "So she's going to keep staying with you."

Obviously I couldn't do that anymore. I rubbed my forehead, unsure of what to do. I can't let her go. I can't keep hurting Lottie.

Fuck.

"I don't know," I admitted.

Lottie rolled her lips. "Is it love? Do you love her?"

Her laugh. Her smile. Her brazen honesty. Her death-wish questions. The way she glared. The way she challenged me. Those eyes, how they see into my soul.

Is that love?

It can't be, because I can't *be* in love.

I shrugged. "Nah."

"Okay. Just get it out of your system before the wedding. In the end, it doesn't really matter who we love. You'll still be my husband, and I'll still be your wife."

FORTY

STORY

I spent days with my uncle at the clinic. It provided a pretty decent distraction from what I'd had to leave behind. Now today was Abigail's birthday, I thought absently. I'd memorized her calendar ages ago, and days popped out and poked me like pin needles. *End of July, Ms. Abigail's birthday, don't forget to steam her towels and prep her tea each morning...*

But that was all before.

Now, as Uncle was seen by the doctor, I was in the billing department, ready to beg the surly woman behind the desk for a payment plan. My mind kept drifting back to what I'd left behind.

Lottie kissing Grayson. Lottie in his *bedroom.*

"Excuse me," the woman snapped. *"Name."*

"Oh, excuse me." I shook the image out of my head. "I'm here to see if I can set up a payment plan for my uncle Woodson Hale."

She typed his name into her computer, and my mind wandered again.

Grayson never allowed anyone in his bedroom...except me. How foolish was it to think that I could be the only girl when he had a real girl?

Did they sleep together?

"It's all paid for."

I stared, stunned, at the billing woman. "What do you mean it's all paid for? By who?"

She didn't even look up from her computer. "We can't give that information out."

"But..."

She slowly looked up at me, giving me the coldest glare. "Do you have more business?"

"I mean, no, I suppose not..."

When I got back to my uncle, he was eating a red Popsicle and sitting upright in a teal hospital chair. He had his trademark smile on, even in the face of death, but fear knotted my throat.

"Who is paying for your treatment?" I asked.

He slowly lowered his Popsicle. "I can't tell you that, Story."

A look crossed his face.

Shame.

I'd never seen the look on my uncle's face before.

That told me everything I needed to know. Instead of clarifying, it made things murkier. Of course I meant nothing to Gray. It was only because he had a relationship with my uncle.

"I can pay," I said. "It's different now. We don't have to take his money."

You don't.

"I'd like to leave you with something, Story," he said,

patting my hand.

Leave me.

I took a seat on a free chair beside him, mustering the courage to ask a question I really didn't want the answer to.

"How long do you have? Really? Don't lie to me."

He exhaled. "A year, maybe two."

A year.

The answer ricocheted inside me. I was thankful I'd already sat down. A year left with my uncle. A year with the only real family I'd ever known.

He grabbed my hand, and I found his eyes, trying to keep my own from watering. It wasn't his fault; he shouldn't have to see me hysterical.

"Miss me one place?" he said.

"Find you another..."

GRAY

"Did you pay for my uncle's treatment?" Story's husky, angry voice stopped me in my tracks.

I rubbed my eye. "I don't see how that's any of your fucking business."

Story ran after me, running in front of me, cutting me off. "Did you even notice I was gone?"

Yes.

Every fucking night I went to bed with nothing save the sound of waves. I couldn't sleep without her. My eyes ached from it. I wondered every moment how Woodsy was doing. I wanted to go check on him, as it had been days since I'd seen Story, but while she cared for her uncle, my

family combusted, self-destructed, and I played an integral part.

Hours had passed since my sister Abigail's birthday party. Another shitshow. Abigail had cut Gemma's long, trademark hair and screamed something about her taking the damn dog, Theo.

More fucking family drama.

Albeit...a little funny.

I pushed her aside. "Not really."

Hurt slashed her eyes, and her jaw quirked. I pushed past her, not quite sure where I was headed. I'd just left the library and was in the heart of the house. A few feet in one direction was my mother's favorite room, the sunroom. I could also go left, or right, and be in either Gemma or Abigail's wing.

"You have the biggest heart of anyone I know, so why do you keep acting like you don't?" Story yelled.

"Because everyone I've ever known just wants to rip it out." I spun, yelling so my voice echoed across the halls and towering ceilings. "Until you," I added quietly.

Her eyes grew.

"Grayson?" my mother's voice called out from the sunroom. "Is that you?"

Fuck.

Not a great spot to have this conversation.

I closed the distance, dragging Story by the wrist into Gemma's wing. Last I heard, she was out getting her hair fixed.

"Gemma's wing?" she whispered. "Won't we get in trouble?"

Gemma had fewer security measures than me. Her hallways weren't guarded, but her bedroom was watched like the fucking White House. She always whined and said it

was because Grandfather didn't care about who came in—
he cared about if she got *out*.

I slammed my arm above Story's head, caging her.

"I don't have a heart. Stop looking at me like I do, stop
expecting it. Do you want to know what I was doing while
you were in the clinic with your sick uncle? I was meeting
with the dog that broke Abby's heart, getting bribed by the
last of his money, so I could throw her birthday party."

"But that's nice—" she started before I interrupted.

"And I only did it so I could burn that twenty grand."

She sucked in a sharp inhale.

So many sins that were *nothing* in the grand scheme of
things but weighed like an anchor, because Story won't stop
fucking looking at me like I'm decent.

I'm not fucking decent.

I wonder what it would feel like to apologize to my
sisters. Weird. Just the thought made my stomach twist.
They'd think I had a tumor. If they apologized to me...I'd
think the same.

Some cracks are too wide to fix.

Her brows pinched. "Why?"

"Why do you think I'm capable of anything else?" I
growled.

I ripped her palm away, but she grabbed me, dragged
me back. "You must have a reason for it all."

Maybe it was revenge for him breaking my sister's heart.

Maybe I knew my mother wouldn't throw any kind of
decent party for Abby.

I ran a knuckle down her face. "No, little nun, I don't."

"You're not going to scare me away," she said. "I'm here.
Even after she was in your room. Even after you slept with
her."

Anger choked her words.

I knew I should let her believe I had. Prop up some kind of distance. Story didn't want me. She didn't even want my money. I was getting sucked into someone who wouldn't just take a piece of me—they could take all of me.

"I didn't sleep with her," I said, hoarse. "I didn't fuck her."

"You didn't?" She lifted her head, eyes locking with mine.

"I couldn't. You're inside me, Story."

STORY

He pressed me deeper against the wall, one arm still over my head.

"I can't stop thinking about you, Snitch. I keep trying, but you're on my mind when I wake up, when I sleep, in my dreams."

"What you taste like." His lips fluttered against the flesh of my ear.

"What you *sound* like." He pressed his knee against my core, and a whimper fell from my lips. He pulled back, his forehead pressed to mine. It created a shadow, a secret just for us. His eyes locked on my lips, hooded and burning, jaw squared so tight.

"She's my fiancée," he said, voice thick. "She's the girl I've always wanted. She's *perfect* for me. I should want to marry her, but every fucking minute I see you."

It wasn't *I want you. I choose you over her.* It wasn't a promise. It wasn't an apology. It was a thousand miles below what I deserved, and yet I would've taken even less.

"I'm not going to be the girl you cheat with," I whispered. "I'm not going to be that girl, Grayson."

"I'm not going to be that guy," he growled.

Then what is this?

His jaw was clenched so tight, and he was so close, I could see the pain cracking in his blue eyes.

"You're the only friend I have, Story. With you, I don't have to lie. You see me. I can't lose that. I can't lose *you*."

"You're the only person with whom I've *ever had to lie*." The words tumbled and fell with the tears I'd been trying to hide.

He froze. "What?"

I shook my head, as if I could swallow the words, seal the hole I'd just punched in my heart.

He gripped my chin, trying to force my gaze to his. "Why, Snitch? Why are you lying?"

I exhaled, defeated. I was tired of lying, tired of pretending.

I met his eyes. "Because from that very first moment we kissed, I knew if I didn't watch out, you could destroy me."

His fingers turned bruising. "More."

"Because I like you. I more than like you, but if I stop lying, if I tell you the truth, if I tell you everything—" I broke off. "But I don't have any reason to stay. I don't need your money."

"I guess it's a good thing I had you sign a fucking contract this time," he growled.

"Is that what's keeping me here?" I asked.

"Is it?" he demanded.

A moment passed like forever. Grayson still hadn't told me he loved me. He hadn't really given me *anything*. But someone had to be honest.

"No," I confessed. "I lo—"

"Why is *she* with you?" Ms. Abigail's trembling, out-of-control voice cut me off. It sliced through the moment like a guillotine, and I glanced to my left, finding her pointing at me. "She's *my* girl."

Gray curled his fist into the wall above me, jaw clenched tight, eyes burning. Why was Abigail even *in* Gemma's wing? They hated each other.

He stared at me a moment longer, then pushed off the wall.

I wasn't sure if I'd been saved.

"She's *my* girl now," he said, and stepped in front of me.

For a moment I couldn't hear over the rushing of blood in my ears. It was different than the times before, the thorns lifted, letting me in, cocooning me in his dark, tender possession.

His girl...I really liked the sound of that.

Ms. Abigail reeled. "What? Why?"

"I don't really think that's any of your fucking business, Abby."

Ms. Abigail ignored him, holding her hand out to me. "Do you want to come back?"

Gray's neck muscles bunched, his upper back tense. This was the moment I could end it all. I'd been waiting for this, right? I could go back to her, back to where I should have been from the very beginning. No need for Scotland. It was a perfect out.

This twisted, savage, ruinous thing between us that never should have been—ended.

I rolled my lips, then shook my head. "No, Ms. Crowne."

Gray moved to turn back to me, but Ms. Abigail grabbed him, pulling him back. She fell apart, yelling at him, screaming at him, words that clearly weren't meant for

him. It felt like it lasted forever, her cries filling the hallway like an omen.

When it was over, Gray blinked, then shook his head. "Yeah, I don't think that was meant for me."

Gray waved a hand over his shoulder, motioning for me to follow.

I gave Abigail one last look. Forgetting for a moment I was a servant and she was a Crowne. She was on the floor. All that had happened in the months I was away utterly ruined her. As my mistress, she'd been entitled and demanding, but no one deserved to have that much despair on their face.

Not being with her love, forced to marry someone else...

I looked at the floor, following Gray.

We'd barely made it out of Gemma's wing when Gray stopped and gripped my face, dragging me to him. Our location rushed over me. We were in the no-man's-land between Gemma and Abigail's wings, a few feet away from the room where all of it began.

Gray gripped my face. "Say it. Say what you were going to say."

"Why?" I fought to keep my voice even, steady. "It's not going to change anything."

His eyes were hard. "Say it, Story. Don't make me rip it out of those beautiful lips."

His eyes darted from my lips back to my eyes. He throbbed with a need I could feel all the way to my marrow.

"I love you, Grayson Crowne—"

The words hadn't left my lips before his were on mine.

FORTY-ONE

STORY

Devouring. Sucking. *Stealing.* Gray tangled his hands in my hair, pulling me closer, bruising our lips together. Hot and wet, his groans melding with my sighs. He dragged me by our kiss, through the halls, pushing open the door to the antique room with his back.

When I broke for air, he bit my bottom lip, never disconnected.

I put my hand out, trying to push him away, put distance between us.

"It doesn't matter!" I said, breathing heavy. "You still have to marry her."

He looked crazed, focused on my lips, a man with a single mission. He gripped me by the waist, dragging me back to him, eyes still locked on my mouth. I pressed my palm to his chest, but it was weak, like my resolve.

"Grayson..."

"I won't," he gritted.

It wasn't so easy, was it? We'd just watched his sister attempt the same thing and *fail*. Her cries were still fading from my ears.

"But—"

He captured my mouth, shutting me up with furious lips. Sucking my top, then bottom one.

"I knew from the moment we kissed in this room you'd be trouble. Wicked, tempting trouble. Knew I'd have to watch myself around your lips. Do you know how hard it was not to kiss you?"

I couldn't have responded if I wanted to. His words were a confession against my mouth, spoken as he devoured and bit. He pressed me so close to him I felt every hard pack of muscle, every rigid piece of him, just like that fateful night, but now the lights were on, and I could see him clearly.

"Every goddamn minute." Another searing kiss. "Of every fucking day." Another bite. "I wanted this." A swipe of his tongue. "I wanted you." Until I couldn't think. Until I was Jello-O.

His fingers trailed the buttons at the back of my dress, up my spine, pressing cool metal into my flesh and leaving a burning trail of goose bumps.

"Fuck, Story. I'm going to undo each button." He popped the one at my neck. "Unravel you like the dirty Victorian nun you are."

Somewhere a part of me was saying this isn't right.

He was still engaged, no matter what he tells me. His sister's tear-stricken face was fresh in my mind, a portent of what's to come. For me? Or for him? Or maybe...for both of us. Or maybe, it was screaming, when we have sex, this is all over.

"Grayson..." I started, then trailed off when he took my

hand, pressing it against his cock. Thoughts fractured. All I could focus on was the hard iron throbbing beneath my fingers. *How is that going to fit inside me?*

Inside me.

Is that where we're finally headed? After months of teasing, is it finally happening?

"Rub my cock, little nun." His lips were on mine again, his tongue plundering, hot and wet.

Pop.

Another button and I couldn't think. An onslaught of lips and tongue. I did as he told me, palming his thick, iron cock over his pants. His belly-flipping groan was my reward, dripping down through my throat like warm whiskey.

Pop. Pop.

His soft fingers slid inside my newly exposed back, edging my shoulder blade.

I rubbed harder, faster, anything to hear his groan again.

"Fuck." His hiss was hot and warm against my lips. "I'll come in my pants, Snitch."

I smiled against his lips. "Well, you're a virgin. Isn't that what you're supposed to do?"

He shoved me against the wall, biting my neck so hard my vision blacked. "Always with the jokes."

His tongue swirled over his bite mark, stoking fire. Another three *pops* and my shirt was only hanging on by my shoulders, my back entirely exposed.

"Unzip me."

It was real. It was happening.

I froze. "Here?"

Amid the antique paintings and white clothed statues, where I'd stolen his love, where I'd rewritten all our fates.

He wanted to do it *here?*

He gripped my face between his palms, demanding I look into his eyes. "I see you now, Story Hale."

He kissed me, deep and searching, until my legs were jelly and all that held me up was Grayson's palms on my cheeks. I think my heart stopped beating, or at least, when it started again the rhythm was completely irregular—new.

Rewritten according to Grayson, a rhythm that only beat for him.

He came to my shoulders, finding the fabric of my shirt, and I let him pull it down. Inch by inch, exposing me. His jaw was harder than stone, eyes gleaming.

I wanted him to touch me, bruise me, bring me back into a kiss.

So when he turned away, to the opposite side of the room, my chest bottomed out. Intrusive thoughts spiraled.

He's done with me. It's a prank. This was all to torture me.

From the wall he grabbed an ornate rug that must have been worth millions, tossing it to the floor. He threw satin pillows, jewel toned and looking like they belonged in a Russian czar's palace, not on the floor in this storage room.

"Lie down," he said.

"I'll ruin them," I said.

He grinned, wolfish. "Good."

When I hesitated, he grabbed my wrist, pushing me atop the plush pile. I felt vulnerable again as Grayson Crowne towered over me. It didn't help that he watched me like a lion.

"Take off your skirt," he said, voice rough.

I slowly undid the zipper at my side, nerves blossoming into wild butterflies in my chest as he unbuttoned his shirt at the same time. I was stuck on the way he watched me.

When we finished, his shirt hung open, betraying the most unfair glimpses of his rigid abs. *Lickable* abs.

Seconds ticked on, too long, marked by the waves and wind. Nerves clawed at my neck. I was naked in front of Grayson Crowne. Naked, and he was giving *nothing* away. No words, nothing but the tightness in his muscles and pinch in his eyes.

Then he fell to his knees—his *knees*.

"Fucking perfect," he groaned, crawling up to my legs. I gasped at the sudden warmth of his lips, on the curve of my knee, my inner thigh. His hands dragged and gripped my flesh.

He just kept saying that over and over again—*fucking perfect*.

He raised his head, looking up at me from between my thighs. My heart rate stuttered and spazzed.

"You've waited so long...don't you want it to be special?" I whispered. "I'm not going to be good."

"We're both virgins—it's not supposed to be *good*, Story." He kissed the inside of my groin, never taking his eyes from mine. "But it won't be bad. It can't be."

My breath caught on the realization I was still lying. I should tell him. *This* was the time to tell him.

He climbed atop me, until his lips were so close I could see the gloss of our earlier kiss, and he said something that stole all my words.

"I never wanted to share this with anyone until you. It was always just another thing to dread, another piece of control I was going to have to give up, power that they would hold over *the Grayson Crowne*. But you? I don't fucking care if you have it. I *want* you to have it. Take it. Own it."

"But Lottie...How?" Abigail's tear-stricken face was still too fresh in my mind.

"That's tomorrow's problem. I'm Grayson Crowne, Story. The world only turns because I allow it." He pressed deep into me. I sucked in a breath at the hard pressure on my sensitive flesh. "Right now, I want to fuck you."

"Don't you need to like..." I licked my lips. "To get naked first?" I was stunningly aware of the disparity in our clothing situation. He was rock hard and pressing against me, but he still had pants on. Even his shirt was still on his arms.

Still between my thighs, he slowly got back up on his knees. Eyes never leaving mine, a small smile playing on his lips, he stripped. It was slow, languorous, dripping intent.

My breath sped up, and I shifted, the ache between my thighs growing.

This was the Grayson Crowne in the bedtime dreams of millions of girls, and he was staring at *me*. Like he wanted to devour me. Consume me. The attention was intoxicating.

He caught my wrist and dragged me to him, flesh to flesh. I still couldn't believe this was real. This was happening. Pressed against his rigid abs, I felt unworthy. Like Leda and Zeus, a god coming down to a mortal.

I looked away because I needed to breathe, his stare stealing my oxygen.

He tilted my chin to his perfect thick eyelashes and blue eyes, the kind you should only see in oil paintings of Greek gods. I could see the worry in his eyes. I wasn't sure how to tell him I was fine...just so nervous I wouldn't live up to a god.

Then he smiled.

"Hey," he said, tone soft and gentle. "Right now, you're Story, and I'm just Gray."

Then he kissed me. Soft at first, coaxing almost, then hard—demanding. Like he couldn't stop himself. His fingers flexed against my flesh, pulling me closer with each breath.

Mine fumbled for his pants, the button, then the zipper. He groaned when I met his cock over his silky, tight boxer briefs.

In the outside world, I hid beneath layers. I lowered my eyes. When I was with Grayson, I became someone different. Someone who reached without reserve into his pants, stroking the ridges and veins of his powerful abs, needing to go deeper, needing—

"*More,*" I breathed the word, an incantation, a spell, inside me whenever I was around him.

More. More. More.

Because with Grayson, I *needed* to. I *needed* to feel his silky, hard flesh, needed to sate the unbearable ache in my stomach. He sucked in a breath when my fingers met his hot flesh. His kiss turned aggressive, biting.

He thrust me back against the blankets, still tangled in my hair, kissing me viciously and violently until I tasted copper. I rubbed my thumb on the tip of his cock, smearing wetness, grinding on his thigh.

Anything to sate that deep, growing *ache.*

He pulled away, stood up.

"Fuck," he hissed, raking his hand through messy rose gold hair.

I got on my elbows, dazed. "What?" What did I do?

"You really are fucking trouble." Grayson eyed me, rubbing his cock, up and down. "Little nun almost made me come with her hand."

His cock was so, so hard, and I sucked in a breath now that I could see it all. Seven inches? Eight? I don't know. I'd never had to, you know, measure something like that. It was long and thick, veins like delicate vines throbbing up to a glistening head.

I looked up and realized Grayson was watching me, a soft, satisfied smile on his face that made my stomach tighten painfully. He reached for his discarded jeans, finding a condom, and rolling it over the head.

"Tell me to stop," he said.

Some stupid joke about expired condoms flitted through my brain but died as the condom reached the base of his cock. Because I just wanted *more*. Inside me.

I opened my legs.

His eyes darkened and he crawled between them, putting his weight on his elbows. The head touched me, and I sucked in a breath, arching, aching. It wasn't enough, barely a kiss. He gripped my face in his hands, thumbs spanning my jaw.

"I want to be inside you, Story Hale," he said. "I've wanted to be inside you since the day you turned my life upside down. I can't stop thinking about it. What you'd feel like coming on my cock. The sounds you'll make."

His voice was strangled, thumbs digging into my cheekbones.

"So what are you waiting for?" I whispered.

He raked his gaze along my body like a man who'd spent years at sea and just found land, finishing where my thighs were spread for him, and all he needed to do was slide in.

When he came back up, his eyes throbbed with a dark need.

"I wasn't supposed to fall for you."

My heart lurched at the words.

"Before if I fucked it up, the worst that could happen is you spread some bullshit rumor. Now?" He shook his head, then his eyes softened. "I don't want to hurt you. I don't want to mess this up for you."

He was getting lost in his mind. In the thorny places he didn't want others to follow. I arched up, pushing him in that first few millimeters.

His eyes flashed to mine.

"Don't think about that," I said softly. "Don't think about anything. Just...just the tip." I smiled and was rewarded with a rare Grayson grin. He leaned forward, teeth grazing my ear, igniting a flurry of goose bumps that left no part of me untouched, even tingling in my teeth.

"I can't promise I won't come fast, but it is not over." He bit down on the lobe and I gasped. "I want to fuck you until you fall apart. Until your soul is bruised with me. I've got way too much I want to do to you, Story. Understand?"

He lifted up, pinning me with his stare.

I nodded, and he gave me another crooked smile. "There's my girl."

He pushed in a little more, and I gasped.

"You tell me when it hurts, and we stop." His voice was strained.

He *was* big, and maybe it hurt, but it hurt in a right way. That gnawing, dripping ache was satiated by the pain.

"More." I grasped his shoulders, urging him into action. Dragging my hands down his muscled back, begging for more. I could tell he wanted to go further, but something was stopping him.

I shifted, trying to urge him. His neck was corded, and his biceps were so strained I could see muscles I didn't even know how to name.

"You sure?" He frowned at me.

"I want to feel you all the way in me, please." I kissed him, begging him with my lips. "Please," I asked against his lips. There was a mental block in him. Maybe he didn't want to hurt me, I don't know. But he was still torturously barely inside me, so I took his bottom lip between my teeth and bit. Hard.

He slammed into me on a groan. I gasped out of the bite as my breath disappeared into stars of pleasure. His lips came to my neck. It was a lot. It was pain. I couldn't see. Couldn't breathe.

But oh my God.

It was perfect.

"Story?" Grayson's worry filtered in through my fog of pleasure. "Was that too much?"

"It wasn't enough," I rasped.

"Fucking perfect," he groaned, head falling to my shoulder.

And then he pumped, in and out, a slow rhythm that had me feeling every inch and ridge of his cock. Over his shoulders, I could see the muscles in his back work, the dimples of his golden ass.

Grayson Crowne was on top of me, *inside me*, and I'd never felt anything so amazing. I didn't think I could come this way. After West, I never dreamed I could, but oh my *God*.

I shifted, rolled my hips, starting to feel it, go with it— and he stilled.

"Fuck," Gray said. "Oh *fuck*."

I felt him tense, and I realized he was coming, his lips pressed to my neck, and the guttural sounds he made sounded a *lot* like my name.

He rolled back, staring at the ceiling, throwing one

sinfully carved arm on his forehead. The condom was still on, and his cock was still so big, even if it wasn't hard. He just stared at the ceiling.

One minute passed.

Two...

Insecurity crawled hot up my spine.

Was it really so terrible?

Another minute passed as he just *stared at the fucking ceiling*.

When it was over with West, he did the same. Rolled off me, grabbed his phone. Then he got out of bed and threw my clothes at me. I couldn't have that happen again. Couldn't have my clothes tossed at my face. So I sat up, reaching for them.

Grayson grabbed my wrist, ripping me back to his body, flipping me beneath him in the same instant.

"The fuck are you doing?"

"I, um... I don't know. Going? You were quiet. I figured you were done with me."

A painful, open look in his blue eyes—then he crushed his lips to mine. Kissed me savage. Senseless. Raw. Until my lips throbbed even when he'd stopped.

"I was really hoping to avoid that whole virgin cliché of coming quick, but your fucking pussy. Shit."

He laughed and kissed me again.

"You blew my fucking mind, Snitch. You got magic in that pussy or what?"

I giggled, then admitted, "It was amazing."

He barked a laugh, caressing a line down my face with his pointer finger. "You didn't come, little nun."

"You still felt really good."

He groaned, kissing my throat slow, laving the muscles. "I can't wait to mark you. Cover you in bruises and bites.

Out here where everyone can see. But inside..." He palmed my pussy, finger sliding inside. "Only you'll feel it."

Just like that I was worked up again.

Hot.

Needy.

"I want to know everything that makes you scream." He bit at my shoulder, pumping harder, faster. "Learn what makes your eyes roll back."

With the silky pillows at my back, and the open window breathing a salty, cool air that hadn't changed for millennia, it felt like I'd stumbled back in time. The servant who shouldn't be with the master.

But love always broke the rules.

"Unless you're done?" He paused his assault, and the sudden stop in sensation was brutal. I didn't realize how far I'd bowed my back, how I'd shifted my hips to him, until he'd stopped.

"I want you inside me." I dragged my nails across his shoulders, down his back, to his ass, all but begging.

"Fuck, say that again. Where do you want me?" He tossed the used condom to the side and reached for another.

"Again?" I wondered. How many did he keep on him?

He dragged me on top of his body and I let out a squeal I couldn't keep inside. Now he was on his back, and I was on him, thighs spread around his chest. His cock was at my ass. His eyes settled between my thighs with a rumbling noise in his chest I felt in my core. He dragged a finger up and down my center.

I dug my nails into his chest, a small whimper escaping me.

"Where do you want me, little nun?" His voice was rough.

"Inside me..."

He shook his head. "In your pussy? In your ass?"

I clenched my thighs at his dirty words. My ass? Did he really want that? And...why did it make my gut tighten?

"My p-pussy," I breathed.

"So what are you waiting for?" He grinned, throwing my words back at me.

I tensed, suddenly nervous. All the control was in my hands, and I'd never *had* any control. But the look in his eyes, the hot, half-lidded look, gave me courage. I chewed my lip, slowly lifting myself, sliding onto his cock.

He groaned, jaw clenched, nostrils flared. That spurred me on, until I was filled with him. Until I couldn't breathe with the fullness. Grayson was somehow even *more* in this position.

The minute he was totally inside me, Grayson yanked me to him, dragged me so we were both sitting up, and kissed me brutally. Tongue lashing and possessive, stealing my air.

"Your pussy is mine," he said against my lips, thrusting up and forcing a strangled sound from me. He bit my lip as I cried out.

His words were a dark, forbidden poetry sliding inside my veins and lighting me on fire. I gripped his shoulders, the position forcing him deeper inside me.

"Fuck, you like it dirty. I can feel it on my cock."

Oh God, I've never felt this. I can feel everything. Every molecule. I was already at the precipice, but his kisses, bites, and words...I'm about to shatter.

"Come all over my dick, Story," he groaned.

"Bite me," I gasped.

He let out a strangled sound, and then his teeth were on me, just above my breast. I arched into it, into his teeth, into

the feeling strangling my core, and let go. I let go and gave in for the first time in my life.

But Grayson's arms anchored me, and his hot whispers were on my neck, my lips, urging me on.

Fucking beautiful.

You're so goddamn perfect when you come.

Because even as I tumbled into oblivion, he wouldn't let me go alone. My thorny, cruel boy was too sweet.

When it was over, when I came back down, he was already watching me. A softness tinged the serious look in his eyes, like a foggy night. I'd wondered before what it would be like to sleep with Grayson Crowne, and now I had my answer.

Untamed, yes, but not how I'd imagined. Not destructive. He was a forest untouched by man, so beautifully raw.

A smile curved his lips. "Goddamn, Snitch. I'm never letting you go now."

FORTY-TWO

GRAY

I'd dragged Snitch's thigh across my lower abs, stroking her from hip to knee, knee to hip. I couldn't take my hands off her—something about her flesh eased a tension in my chest. I never wanted to let her go. The floor was hard as fuck, though. Some imported Italian marble my mother *had* to have, so I pulled her across my body, ignoring the twinge in my shoulder blades. Her breasts pressed against my pecs, and her thighs spread across mine. Fuck. I was already getting hard again.

She blinked at me. "Am I too heavy?"

I laughed at that and pulled her closer, gripping her ass. Goose bumps dotted her flesh, so I asked, "You cold?"

"A little," she admitted.

I reached for my discarded bomber jacket, draping it over her back.

"Grayson Crowne is very kind," she mused, playing

with the golden strands of hair covering my eyes. "And attentive. And most certainly not a playboy."

"Good thing no one will believe you."

She giggled, pressing her lips between my pecs, trying to hide it. I swallowed a groan—fuck, that noise was almost as addicting as her moans.

"Are you upset I joked about your virginity?" she asked quietly after a moment. "I didn't mean to make you feel..."

"Like some pussy?"

She coughed. "I wouldn't ever say that."

"I fucking love it, Snitch. Never stop joking with me. The world puts so much weight on the thing. It's so serious for whatever stupid fucking reason. You were the only one to laugh with me."

After a moment, she settled her hands on my chest, her chin on them, watching me with those big soul-searing mossy eyes. I think they're my favorite part of her, because like her, they betrayed so much. Strength. Vulnerability. Fear. Courage. Right now, they're slightly pinched, like she wanted to say something.

"Speak, Snitch."

"The sun is coming up," she said quietly.

I glanced out the window, where the day smudged the night a blue gray.

"And?"

She looked down, tracing circles on my bare skin. I gripped her chin, lifting her gaze back to mine. I'd gotten so fucking addicted to her stare. Big as walnuts, deeper than the ocean.

"I can't be forgotten," she said. "I can't be left behind again."

I swiped my thumb back and forth across her softly

pointed chin. "Not gonna happen, little nun. That would be like forgetting the moon."

She furrowed her brow, like what I'd said bothered her, but she didn't say anything.

"You are the only one in my life I can trust. The only one who has actually been honest with me. I'm never letting you go, Story."

Her brows caved. "I'm no different than those girls who lied to you."

She was light-years away from them, from *everyone* I'd ever known. She's honest. She's quiet but strong. She doesn't hide from her darkness.

I knew in my fucking bones this was it. Story is my girl. She's it.

I love her. Fuck. I've *been* in love with her.

I pulled her by the wrist back against my chest, holding her tightly. "You're the only person in my life who's ever been honest with me, Story."

She tensed.

"There were times I had no choice but to give up parts of myself, so it was really important I never gave anything to those who didn't deserve to have it. What I'm trying to say is, I thought everyone wanted a piece of me, and I had no choice but to hand the pieces over, but you showed me..." *What it's like to* give *someone a piece.*

"You showed me differently," was all I said.

She slid off me, pulling her knees up to cover her naked chest. There were tears in her eyes, and alarm pounded in my chest.

"Why are you crying?"

"Because I'm a liar," she said. "I have so many secrets, Grayson. You wouldn't look at me the same if you knew."

"Try me."

Her brow knitted further, and it must have been minutes before she actually said anything. "You know my mom had her demons. You know I did bad things."

I remembered what she'd told me. *We stole a lot. She taught me how to use my perceived innocence to trap men. Other times it was darker...*

"You don't have to tell me, Story."

"I want to. I've been...holding it in."

I waited.

"She'd get these guys involved with her, and once they stopped giving her what she wanted, whether it was affection, time, money, that's when I came in. She'd have me lie, say I'd go to the cops and tell them they raped me."

A stale silence followed her confession. Story buried her face in her knobby, hazelnut knees, as if trying to hide.

"It wasn't your fault," I said lamely.

"It was..." she said. "But I paid for it."

I pulled her back, forced her head down on my pec. "Go to sleep, Snitch. I'll be here in the morning."

STORY

I knew many hours had passed by the time I woke, because the room was warm and bright. I could hear the caw of seagulls, then the crush of waves, and a strip of bright sunshine heated my right arm. I stretched my arms, fulfilled.

Then it hit me. I was alone.

Every horrible thought slammed into my head at once. It was like video I'd watched of an escalator breaking down.

Hundreds of people falling into one another, crammed to one position. Those were my thoughts.

Worthless. Useless. Good for one thing.

"Good. You're awake."

I gasped at the voice. Tansy fucking Crowne leaned in the doorway in a light Chanel suit, watching me. How long had she been watching?

This is a nightmare. I haven't woken up.

I scrambled to cover myself. My clothing was still where we'd left it by the door, so I could only reach for Grayson's bomber.

She gave me a tight smile. "If I see something new, I'll tell you."

Still I held his jacket tighter.

"What...where..."

"Where is my son?" she asked with a bright smile. "Oh, well, he's with his family of course."

I chewed on my bottom lip, piercing it with my top two teeth. He promised not to leave me. Promised.

I told him I loved him, but he never said it back. And the realization sat like a hot lead.

That would be like forgetting the moon.

I stared out the window at the bright, sunny day.

We do forget the moon. For a good twelve hours, it's as if the moon never existed.

I stared at her shoes and she sighed. "Oh, I think we've moved far past that."

I lifted my eyes, staring Tansy Crowne in her red-brown ones. I had to remind myself to breathe.

"I'm late, you know. I've been waiting for you to wake up."

I bit my tongue, fighting the urge to ask her what the

hell she wanted. I knew looking Tansy Crowne in the eyes wasn't a promotion—it was a sentencing.

"I've been thinking about it." She smiled thinly, rubbing her lip like her son. "If I pay you off, he'll go searching for you. If I threaten your uncle, it will only last until he dies..." She tsked her tongue like *what a shame, too,* and I sucked in air. How fucking easy it was to say something so cold.

"You're lucky, Story."

Lucky.

She bent down, pushing messy curls out of my face. I was never more aware the difference between us than at that moment. On the floor, naked, alone, while Tansy Crowne, in her bespoke suit and cream leather heels, told me I was *lucky.*

"We women don't get much leverage, but when we do, it sticks. You get to be the mistress. You get to look me in the eyes. You get to *stay.* Because he decided he liked having you in bed. So all I need from you is to learn. No more dressing like you went dumpster diving outside of Goodwill. You're not a servant anymore. Even our mistresses must wear the weight of the Crowne."

"I don't want that," I blurted. She arched a surprised brow. "I don't want to be the mistress."

She laughed—a cold, tinkling sound. "Oh, darling, you don't get a choice."

I'd heard the saying "kill them with kindness," but it was never more appropriate than with Tansy Crowne, who wielded kindness like a dagger. She never yelled at the servants; in fact, we'd grown to shiver when she added words like *darling.* It generally meant someone was getting deported.

I think the only time I'd witnessed her mask falter was with her daughter, Abigail.

She stood up, giving me a saccharine smile. "I suggest you get dressed, Story Hale. I have to go. I'm late, remember? Late to deal with the repercussions the last person in your position left me. Do you know what happened to him?"

I swallowed.

Theo, Abigail's love, her bodyguard.

He was...gone.

She smiled. "You do. Good."

FORTY-THREE

STORY

I spent a week accompanying my uncle to appointments at the hospital, trying to avoid everything Crowne, while secretly hoping Grayson would reach out.

He never did.

Now, on the small square TV in the corner of the wall, I watched him and all the Crownes at the pier at Crowne Beach. Abigail wore the Crowne family tiara, an heirloom that supposedly went back centuries. Her fiancé had his arm around her, and she looked absolutely miserable. Blurred in the background were Gemma and Gray.

Always blurry...

I exhaled a sigh.

"Story?" my uncle asked.

"Humm?"

"The Popsicle."

"Oh!" I handed it to him, though now it had melted down my wrist.

I stared at the TV. Was that what was so fucking important he had to leave without a word? Some family function at the pier? I'd been trying to work it out for a week, trying to understand his silence. Hoping it wasn't the truth that hung ugly in the air.

I'd been used by Grayson Crowne.

It bit like tiny insect bites into my chest. Because what if it *was* important. Still, I had to be in the shadows.

I *get* to be his mistress. That was how his mother had worded it. More and more I felt like I was running a marathon, and once I got to the finish, I'd have to face the truth. Grayson and I could only end one way.

He came into focus a little bit more, and I saw he wore the jacket I'd held to my chest days ago. A sharp pang hit me.

Had he come back for me?

Uncle and I talked for an hour or two about nothing until he was hungry again, and I had to go on a food hunt. He looked so bright and happy, and I could forget the black cloud inside my chest, because Uncle was getting better.

The hospital was beautiful, paid for by Crowne money, and was set close enough to the beach to have a view of the ocean. Summer was basically over. The leaves would turn soon, and in a few more months the year would end.

Christmas.

There was only one vending machine on his floor, and apparently it ate quarters.

I kicked it.

"Stupid machine." I kicked it again.

"Did you try paying?"

What was Grayson doing *here*?

I fought every nerve and need in my body and bones to

turn around, instead walking down the sterile hallway, fast. I was gripped by the wrist, spun around. I stared at his chest, at another white T-shirt that cost more than college tuition.

"Let me go," I said.

"Look at me, Story."

I did. I glared at him, at his beautiful blue eyes partially obscured by his constantly untamed blond hair.

"How did you know where I was?" I gritted.

He shrugged with one shoulder. "We have eyes everywhere. But I wouldn't need them to know you were visiting Woodsy."

I glared harder. "Not everywhere." His smile dropped.

It was hidden by fog now, only the very top of the decrepit Ferris wheel that marked the one place the Crownes didn't touch in Crowne Point: the underworld. Once Crowne Park, now known as Horsemen's Wharf, it was run by the four eponymous boys known as the Horsemen.

"You don't fucking go there, ever," Gray growled.

I ripped my wrist out of his. "You *left* me."

For a week, my throat choked.

You didn't just leave me in the morning, you left me alone for a week.

To wonder.

To fight back tears.

His jaw clenched. "Something happened."

"You had a week. A *week*. I don't care what you have to say."

I shoved him, but he gripped my forearms, forcing me still. "I didn't have a fucking choice." I tried to shove him off, but his grip was steel.

"My mother was planning to ship Abigail off to her new

family. Was gonna lock her up or some fairy tale villain shit."

I swallowed a gasp, freezing completely.

"I came for you the minute I could," he said gently. "I came here for you and Woodsy. I haven't even seen the guy since I got the news."

His eyes ached, and I believed him. Believed he'd been pulled in every direction, had bricks upon bricks piled on his shoulders.

"I left you a note." His eyes found mine. "I waited for you to text me or call me."

"I didn't get it. Your, um, your mother found me that morning." I'd planned on being so angry when I told him, angry for abandoning me and leaving me to be found alone by Tansy Crowne.

Now I couldn't, not when he looked at me with such open, honest eyes.

Grayson grimaced. "What did she say to you?"

Oh, darling, you don't get a choice.

I looked away. "Nothing. She said something about sleeping in her house..." I quickly looked for something to change the subject. "Which I take to mean you didn't tell her. You didn't tell any of them. I'm still your mistress."

He gripped my shoulders. "I'm going to tell her."

"I'm not going to be the girl you cheat with. I'm not going to be that girl, Grayson. What we did...it can't happen again. Not until you break it off."

"I'm not going to be that guy," he growled. "I'll tell her."

That didn't fill me with any happiness, any sort of reassurance. I'd heard a revolving door of men tell my mother that for years.

I'll tell her tomorrow.

It's not that simple.

By the weekend we'll be together.

I'm leaving her.

I'd even fallen for it once, with Westley, when he promised to love me.

He grasped my face. "Why don't you look happy?"

"You're going to tell everyone, just like that?" I asked. "It didn't work so well for Ms. Abigail."

Storm clouds were forming outside the windows, darkening the sunny day into monochrome. Gray sand, iron waves, and chilly air. He grasped my waist, pulling me close. I knew I should push him away, but I missed him. I ached for him.

"I don't want to fuck you in secret," he said. "I want to fuck you in my bed. I want to wake up next to you, Story. Smell you in my sheets."

He trailed his nose along my neck.

"You've corrupted my soul completely." He pulled back, forcing me to feel the earnestness in his soul. "I don't feel without you." He ran his nose up and down my neck, voice warbled, raw. "Let me say sorry to you. Let me say sorry to you over and over again until you say I've fixed it." He stoked fire with his fingers, up and down my arm, along the inside of my waist, short and quick and debilitating.

When he lifted his head, his blue eyes pulsed. "I won't let you go, Story Hale."

But that was what I'm afraid of...and the consequences hung ready to pop like the rain about to fall.

He stepped back, giving me his hand. "You hungry?"

FORTY-FOUR

GRAYSON

"When I said yes, I thought you meant like...down the street," Story said, eyes wide. "Not out of the country!"

I shrugged. "You're hungry, you like Italian."

"Yeah, but *Italy?*"

She needed a break. We both needed a break, and after visiting Woodsy and taking him back to Crowne Hall, the doctor assured me nothing would happen over the weekend.

Still, I had someone watching him.

Snitch hadn't stopped staring out the window, nose pressed to the glass, and I hadn't stopped watching her. Her wonder was mesmerizing. When we'd taken my family trip, not once had she been like this. Because then she'd been restrained.

Uncertain.

Hiding parts of herself.

I never wanted to go back to before.

Honesty, *always*, between us.

I captured her chin, bringing her face back to mine. I stroked her chin softly, thumb to jaw. "It's nothing, Story. I'm Gray Crowne. I can make the world stop turning."

"If the world stops turning, it ends," she whispered, a darkness clouding her gaze. Something was off, and I had a feeling it had to do with whatever my mother said.

"So fucking what? I'll move the earth for you, Story. I'll make the sky fall."

She touched my chest, my beating heart. "And you would be the one cut by the jagged blue pieces."

What kind of fucking torture is it to wait years to fuck, to wait until you've found someone who won't rip you to shreds, to *finally* find that girl, and then not be able to have her?

"I don't fucking care." I gripped her closer.

She twisted her lips into an adorable pout. Anytime she had that fucking pout on her lips it just made me want to bite them, which was pretty fucking distracting, considering I'd just promised to obey the boundaries we'd set.

"Tell me where you want to go first," I said, voice rough.

She took a deep breath, then exhaled a blinding smile. "Can we get spaghetti?"

I laughed. "Yeah, Snitch, we can get all the spaghetti."

Five different restaurants and I don't know how many bowls of spaghetti later, we were back at the Crowne Hotel penthouse.

"I'm full," Story said, clutching her stomach as she flopped onto a plush rug on the ground. The penthouse had a three-sixty view of downtown Rome, and St. Peter's Basilica was aglow atop the twinkling lights.

I arched a brow. "I didn't think it was possible."

She stretched her arms above her head. The white blouse she was wearing came loose from her dark skirt, exposing a thin stretch of skin. She was so unaware of her effect on me. Of how sexy she looked, just lying on the rug.

I got to my knees, crawling beside her.

She rolled on her stomach, smiling. "It's possible. It just takes a few bowls of spaghetti."

I slid a hand under the thick cotton material of her skirt. For a moment I felt I was back in fucking boarding school, sliding my hands beneath those pleated skirts—but even the skirts at Rosey were shorter than this.

She gasped. "Y-You said we wouldn't do it again."

I loved her stutter almost as much as I love the raspy voice it came from.

I slid my hands farther up her thigh, just beneath the swell of her ass. "We're in a different country."

She laughed, burrowing her face into the rug. "Is this an episode of *Friends*? The rules still count."

"Do they?"

I rounded the swell of her ass with my palm, bruising the tender flesh before gripping and spreading her. She sighed and I kissed her shoulder, kissed the fabric there.

"Once we get back, I'll call it off."

"Well...then..." She arched as I slid a finger between her cheeks. "When that happens...we can..."

"Fuck, Story." I groaned. "I'm going to mark you everywhere. Would you like that?"

She nodded, letting me use a finger to probe the hole.

"You want me inside your tight ass?"

She groaned into the furry fibers of the rug.

"Let me fuck you in the ass. Even the Catholic church says it doesn't count."

She giggled.

That fucking *giggle*.

"I don't think that's true," she said, voice so fucking husky.

I pressed gently, just enough for her to feel the pressure, and her sharp inhale had me rigid, rock hard.

"Shouldn't you take it slow, Mr. Grayson?" she asked. "You did just lose your virginity. I don't want you to pull a muscle."

She twisted, head on her shoulder, so I could see her bright grin. I loved her smile. Seeing it has only made me realize how bereft I've been without it. I'd do anything to keep it on her lips.

In one motion I was on top of her, caging her. "Oh, you got more jokes now?"

Still she smiled, eyes bright on me.

"What about a kiss? It doesn't count if it's not on the lips, right?" I kissed her neck, her jaw.

"Or what about here? Does it count if it's over the shirt?" I palmed her tit, and her lips found my jaw, soft and wet and hot.

"What if it's under the shirt?" she asked, unbuttoning the first few buttons, leaving her breast exposed.

I groaned, palming, bruising, gripping her breast.

"Dirty nun." I bit her jaw, her ear. "So fucking dirty."

"Grayson..."

"Fuck, say it again. Love my name on your lips."

But then my eyes found hers, swirling with fear. I stopped, lifted myself up enough to give her space.

I traced my knuckles down her jaw. "What, little nun?"

"I don't want us to be something that only exists in the dark, in the cracks, in the places people don't want to look or talk about."

Her tit was out and all I wanted to do was suck it, take it into my mouth, fuck her until her voice was hoarse from screaming my name.

I stood up, running my hand through my hair, getting my fucking cock under control.

"I'm sorry—"

"Don't fucking apologize," I said, spinning. "Don't ever apologize for saying no." I closed the distance, getting down on my knees.

"I didn't say no."

"You may as well have."

A small smile speared her lips, then dropped. "Aren't you mad? You looked upset."

"I'm not mad." I grinned and pushed the hair out of her face. "It's just torture to stay in a room alone with you."

"So what do we do?" she asked.

"We have Italy to explore."

STORY

"Closed till *February* of *next year*?"

I turned around, lips pushed in a pout. His eyes dropped to them, dark. Dark like earlier when we'd almost broken rules that hadn't even had a chance to dry.

I shifted. "What?"

"Nothing." His voice was hoarse. "So, you wanna see the Sistine Chapel?"

"It's closed." I threw a thumb over my shoulder at the sign.

He arched a brow, then rolled his eyes, grabbing my

hand and dragging me from what I learned was a public entrance *cough* peasant's entrance *cough*. Because all it took for Grayson to get us in was an expertly placed wad of cash in the hands of someone with the right key. I didn't even try to count how many bills, but the denominations were high.

"What if we get caught?" I whispered, looking over my shoulder, where the Rome night silhouetted the man counting his new cash.

"That's what the rest of the cash is for."

My eyes bugged, and he laughed. "Come on, little nun. Let's go." He tugged me harder, forcing my eyes forward.

I stopped short, tilting my head back, frozen in awe. So many colors, so many scenes, it would take months, maybe years, to decipher them all. The murals were bathed in a warm glow. Somehow, it felt even more secret, more special.

"Wow," I finally managed.

Grayson wrapped his arms around my waist, pulling me flush against his chest. I pulled his hand, tracing his ring finger, staring at the most beautiful thing I'd ever seen.

"Do you know why engagement rings are worn on the ring finger?" I felt him shake his head. "Ancient Greeks thought that finger contained the *vena amoris*, or the 'vein of love' that ran straight to the heart."

His voice grated when he spoke. "I always thought engagement rings were a bit too ephemeral."

"So you'd want, like, a tattoo?"

"Something like that...Did you know Michelangelo hated painting this so much he wrote a poem?"

I gasped. "What? No!"

His smile warmed my cheek. "I think the first line went something like...*I've already grown a goiter from this torture.*"

I laughed, then focused again on the masterpiece above

me. Torture. It had been torture for him, but wow, people traveled from all over the world to see it.

It was in history books.

"Hmm...I guess some good things come from torture."

He pulled me tighter, resting his chin on my shoulder. "Anything else you want? Would you like to sneak into the Colosseum? Whatever you want, I'll get it for you."

My stomach did a pancake at his words.

"What if I wanted the moon?"

He sighed. "I'd at least like a challenge, Story."

I laughed and he groaned into my neck.

"Are you..." I trailed off. I could feel him hard against my back. "I only laughed!"

He buried his face into my neck. "I want to kiss you. I want to taste you until my taste buds groan." His lips moved against my neck with his words, so close to a kiss, but not quite right. Goose bumps rose along my skin.

"I want to eat you until your voice is broken from screaming." His breath heated my skin, a whisper, a promise, lips not kissing but the promise sending tingles.

"I want to fuck you until you can't walk."

He slid his hand under my jacket, on the bare skin, just beneath my breast.

Skirting a dangerous line that I wanted to cross.

He spun me around, so I stared into his earnest eyes. "Let me hold you tonight. Just hold you, nothing more. I promise."

I nodded, unable to speak.

He gave me a wicked, curling grin. I couldn't stop staring. It was so beautiful. So bright. Like the sun had come out after a year of unrelenting storms. This was Grayson Crowne, the rose without the thorns, the boy without the heavy armor, Atlas freed.

He arched a brow. "You're staring."

"I don't think I've ever seen you smile. Not really."

He closed his lips, but the smile stayed, and the warmth in his eyes. The softness. I wanted to kiss him. I wanted this moment to be different, for us to not be strangled by circumstance.

"This has been the most amazing, magical dream of my life," I said. "I don't want to wake up."

He pushed the hair behind my ear, hand staying. "You don't have to."

I woke to a pair of pants in the face.

"We have to go," Grayson said.

He tossed more clothes at me, some of them not mine. I looked outside. It was still dark. Only a few hours, if even that, had passed. Grayson scrambled around the penthouse, dimly lit by one desk light and the glittering sea outside.

"What's going on?" I asked.

"The Crowne papers came out," he said absently.

"They have that in Italy?" I wondered.

Gray made a face. "I get them delivered everywhere I go. If you don't own them, know them..." He said the last part absently, almost like they weren't his own words.

He dropped the papers on the foot of the bed, reaching for phones I didn't even know he'd brought. He must've had five cell phones, and they were all going off. Grayson looked like he'd been hit with a bomb. I wondered what could have been so terrible. A terrorist attack? Something with Crowne Industries?

While Gray frantically buttoned up his shirt, a cell phone on either shoulder, I reached for the paper.

ABIGAIL CROWNE ELOPES WITH MYSTERY BODYGUARD.

"You let her fucking leave?" Gray said into one phone, then snapped into the other phone, "Don't. They aren't related."

When the calls ended, Gray sat down on the edge of the bed, his tie undone. "What the fuck is she thinking?"

"She loved him."

He lifted his head at my voice, staring out at the inky Roman morning. "I always thought he was a dog who wanted to use her. Who wanted her money."

"People would probably think the same about me," I said lightly.

He tensed.

"You were protecting her."

He made a noise like *yeah right*. It was so hard for Grayson to admit he cared. So hard. Grayson Crowne, who said he hated his sisters, who pretended he couldn't give a shit what happened to either one, so painfully obviously grieved the loss of her.

"Now?" I hedged. "What do you think about him now?"

He dragged two hands through his hair. "I don't know. She's gonna lose everything."

"Can you help?"

"Are you trying to make me a good guy, Story Hale?"

"You already are a good guy."

Another scoff, disbelief evident in the way he refused to look at me and simply stared out the window.

"I've decided you care about your family," I said.

"Oh, you've *decided*."

"Yep."

He laughed, dark, unamused.

"You're just doing that Gray thing where you care so much about something that instead of admit you care, you do the opposite. You're cruel. Because if you lose it, it might not hurt as much."

"That 'Gray thing.'" He shook his head on another scoff, and for a minute I was certain he was going to push me away again, but then he looked over his shoulder, locking eyes. Voice too thick, eyes too raw, bleeding, cutting. "How do you know?"

Because maybe that's what he does with me...

I chewed my lip, looking away.

"Just a guess," I whispered.

For the rest of the trip home Gray didn't look at me, nor I him.

FORTY-FIVE

STORY

We weren't even off the plane before Grayson was pulled in all directions. He was dragged from the steps by an army of people in suits as his mother orbited.

I slowly finished the descent alone. Grayson kept whipping his head from one person to the next. I wondered if his neck would ache.

Abigail Crowne had left Crowne Hall, left her fiancé, left her *family*. She'd chosen her love, but now she was excommunicated. It was like the universe knew I was starting to hope and dream, and they threw a meteor-sized reminder back at me.

Grayson Crowne was Atlas, and if he left, the world around him would shatter. The company would fall apart, people would lose their jobs, his family would crumble.

But for these few days it was nice to pretend.

Grayson lifted his head, rose gold hair silky and shimmering against the thundering sky, searching for something.

His eyes landed on me.

He pushed aside his mother and grandfather. Pushed through the small army of people. Until he was before me.

"What are you doing?"

He grabbed me by the waist, ripping me to him, planting a furious breath-and-mind stealing kiss.

"I'm telling her," he said, breaking our kiss. I blinked, dazed. I'd fisted my hands in his shirt. "This doesn't change shit, Snitch. Go visit Woodsy or something. But don't go anywhere. Wait for me."

He planted another kiss on my lips, then let me go—not before tossing me a bone-melting grin.

He regrouped with the army of suits, and then my eyes connected with Tansy, right before she turned and followed her son into Crowne Hall.

The route felt like an ancient one I hadn't traveled in years. I ran my fingers along the intricate fleur-de-lis molding until it stopped—the servants' quarters.

"Uncle?" I called out.

His room was empty.

"You're not supposed to be down here, Ms. Hale."

I jumped—Ms. Barn's baritone voice still able to startle me.

"It's *Story*, Ms. Barn. Where is Uncle?" When I turned to face her, her eyes were downcast. I knew the other servants weren't looking me in the eye, but *Ms. Barn?*

"Woodson Hale is in the hospital."

"Back in the hospital?" I looked at his empty room, like it would give me answers. "How long?"

"He wasn't feeling well this morning and fainted. He was rushed over. That's all I know."

"And no one thought to fucking *tell me*?" Anger rushed out of me, untamed. I rarely yelled, much less at *superiors*. But what the fuck? Seriously?

"It's proper protocol to alert a Crowne before the mistress. If you'll excuse me, Ms. Hale, I have much to attend to."

"I'm not—"

I broke off, finding the doorway empty.

Hospital. Have to get to the hospital.

Those were the only words in my mind when I left Crowne Hall, and they propelled me to the only hospital within miles of Crowne Point, the one Uncle had been seen at previously. They kept me from collapsing, and they carried my feet through the doors, up to the information desk, until I was face-to-face with a cheerful looking woman.

"I'm looking for Uncle, um"—I shook my head, trying to speak clearly—"I'm looking for my uncle, Woodson Hale. I think he was brought in?"

She smiled and said something I didn't catch, returning to her computer. It felt slow and languorous. I realized only a minute had passed, but it was *too much time*.

Finally she told me where to find him, and I dashed off in that direction.

He was asleep in the hospital bed when I found him, so I took a seat opposite it. His round face was sunken, his bright hazelnut skin sallow, his lips chapped. When we had first faced cancer, he'd had to go in for treatment, but they

let him come home afterward. He never collapsed. He never had to stay.

I was told a doctor would be in to talk with me shortly, but it was maybe thirty minutes after I arrived when a tall, older man in a white coat came in.

"He needs ChapStick," I said.

The doctor blinked, then said, "Are you his next of kin?"

"Yes," I said, still watching Uncle in bed.

"Good. We've been needing to talk to someone. Your..." He trailed off, waiting for me to supply my connection to Uncle.

"Uncle."

"Your uncle hasn't given us anyone to contact. We've done all we can do here. Now he'll need round-the-clock care. We can suggest some good hospices, or if you have the means, in-home providers."

Rushing. Like the waves outside Grayson's window. Or the blood in my ears when he touches me.

"Miss?"

"What are you saying?"

"Your uncle is dying."

I read somewhere that doctors have to say it that way, have to be horribly blunt, so we accept it. So it feels real.

I still didn't believe it.

"But he said he had two years, maybe more."

The doctor made a face. "He has a few months, *maybe*, if he decides to continue treatment, but I don't think he will. If you want to be there with him—"

"I *do*." I said. "I do."

"Don't make any travel arrangements."

340 MARY CATHERINE GEBHARD

GRAY

At the end of my hellish day, I waited for Story. Grayson fucking Crowne doesn't wait, but I waited for Story, pacing back and forth like an idiot.

Some bullshit party was happening to distract everyone about Abigail. I looked at myself in the mirror, in my stupid fucking tux.

Where the fuck was she?

I wasn't going to wait through another party to find out what happened to her, and I could think of only one place to find her. Halfway to the servant's quarters, I collided with a body.

My mother.

"Where are you going?" she asked.

"Nowhere."

I skirted around her, continuing.

"She's most likely gone," my mother said to my back. "Let her go."

I paused.

"What did you do?" I didn't turn around.

"Only told her what she needed to know, what you refused to tell her," my mother said simply. "She's a mistress, Grayson. You're marrying Charlotte. Those are facts."

In that moment, resolution steeled my spine.

Before I saw Story again, there was something I needed to do.

I turned from the quarters, pulling out my phone.

All day I'd cleaned up the mess Abigail had left behind, reassuring board members with my grandfather, keeping

our stock from plummeting. All the while my grandfather's voice had been in my ear, *Thank fuck for the du Lacs.*

My mother followed me to her favorite room, the sunroom, just as my grandfather answered the call.

"I'm out. Wedding is off."

FORTY-SIX

GRAY

Silence followed my proclamation.

Then Grandpa exploded. "It hasn't even been a day since your sister pulled this shit!"

"This joke was unfunny when Abigail tried it; it is even less funny from your lips," Mother hissed.

"Do you know what happens if you refuse to marry Lottie?" My grandfather's yell was so loud it crackled through the speakers.

"Crowne Industries will be fine," I said. "This isn't like when Father died. We aren't on the verge of collapse. Our stock is fine. We don't *need* to keep fucking marrying people."

Grandfather was a greedy fucking asshole, is the truth.

My mother scrambled up from her chaise, wrestling the phone from my hands.

"He's joking," she said with a smile.

"I'm not joking."

Mom pounded the mute button, breathing fire through her nostrils. "You saw what happened with Abigail. He will cut you out. He will give all of your birthright to the bastards."

"I don't give a shit."

"You promised to me on your father's deathbed you wouldn't let anything happen to this family."

"I was *seven*."

"Do you know how much damn damage control we had to do after Abigail's rushed engagement fell through?" My grandfather yelled through the speaker. "It's sloppy. Fucking sloppy."

Of course I knew.

Damage to his reputation. Damage in the public eye. Suddenly the Crowne was a little rusty.

It was a moment before my grandfather spoke. When he did his voice was calm, cold. "I don't want to rush a marriage, but I will."

"You'll break Lottie's heart," my mother tried. "You'll break my heart. And you will break *her* heart. You can't have it, Grayson. You would ruin this family for your selfish desires."

My mom placed her palm on my cheek, eyes warm in the way I knew meant her next words would be about her desires.

Her wants.

"You should have the marriage of the century, Grayson," she said. "You're a king."

I pulled away and stabbed the button again to unmute the phone.

"I will happily continue my role in this family, but I'm

not marrying her. Your greed will destroy our family faster than ending any fucking marriage."

I ended the call and left the room, hearing my mother scrambling to smooth things with Grandfather.

Time to get my fucking girl.

STORY

I must have walked in a daze back to Crowne Hall. I hadn't wanted to leave him, but they didn't have any clothes for him to come home in. I guess he'd soiled the ones he'd come to the hospital in.

He still hadn't woken up when I left.

I read and reread my hospice options, each more expensive than the last. All the while my brain spitting out the same thing: Does. Not. Compute.

When Uncle died, who would I have left? No one. Officially, *no one.* It was such a selfish thing to think after someone gives you that news. *What happens to me?* Not, oh that must be horrifying, scary, terrible, for them. But *What happens to me?*

I went through Crowne Hall's servants' entrance, passing by rushing servants, until I found Uncle's room. His clothing consisted of suits and slacks and the occasional turtleneck. I grabbed a bundle of the most comfortable clothes I could find, still dazed.

I ascended the stairs, taking all the winding lefts and rights, heading back for the exit.

It wasn't like he can die here. He would like that, though. This was his home.

All he knows.

Like me.

"Story?"

I stopped short. Grayson stood before me, dressed to kill in a dark tux that fit every sinful muscle. I looked around me in a daze. The world glittered and gleamed—piano music rushed into my ears.

I was crashing a party. Oh *shit*. I'd taken a wrong turn.

"You weren't there when I got back." He scratched the back of his neck. "I realize, I don't even have your number or anything. I guess...I guess I never needed it."

I'd always been at his beck and call. I'd barely even used my phone the past few months.

Like a good little mistress.

"Wait—what's going on? Are you leaving?" His voice lowered a dangerous octave.

I stared bemused at the lump of clothes in my arms.

"What's this party about?"

"Some bullshit foundation we're using to launder our reputation after Abigail. Story, *what's wrong?*" He gripped my chin, dragging my gaze to his earnest blue ones.

"Was I invited?" I wondered aloud, and like that, he dropped me.

He scratched the back of his neck harder, and that was when I spotted Lottie.

"I wasn't invited," I said.

We were gaining an audience. It looked like everyone had come to this party. Lottie and her friends, Aundi and Pipa. Grayson's friends Geoff and Alaric. People I didn't know were watching. All wondering why Grayson Crowne was talking to the servant with a pile of clothes in her hands.

"They probably don't invite mistresses to these things,

right?" I stared into his blue eyes, numbness creeping into my veins, slowing my heart.

His brow furrowed. "What are you talking about?"

"I'll go," I whispered.

I sprinted away from him, on the verge of tears, and really not wanting him to see.

"Story—" Grayson called to my back.

I'd just made it around the corner of the ballroom.

"Oh look." Aundi stepped in my path. "It's the social-climbing whore."

"I was just leaving," I said.

Aundi knocked the clothes out of my hand. I scrambled to pick them up as others grabbed them faster than I could.

"Please just give them back."

"Isn't this a little manly, even for you?" Pipa asked, tossing an item to Geoff, who tossed it to Alaric.

"Just give them back."

They were playing keep-away, and I was the one in the middle. I had no reserves left to pretend it didn't bother me. These were my uncle's clothes, and I needed them.

I fell to my knees. "Just give them back."

They all suddenly stopped laughing, stopped throwing my things. I knew before he'd spoken, knew before I felt him behind me. The icy chill of anger lifted the hair off the back of my neck.

"I seriously fucking hate people touching my shit," Grayson growled.

One by one my stolen clothes landed in a pile at my knees. I still couldn't look up, utterly humiliated. Couldn't even take the clothes back. I just sat there, willing it all to end. Until Uncle's sweater was lifted from the pile and passed to me by a strong, veiny hand.

"This is Woodsy's, yeah?" Grayson asked quietly.

"Yes," I mumbled, taking it.

"Why are you *always* defending her?" Pipa snapped.

"Seriously, what the fuck?" Alaric added.

"It's like you're legit into her or something." Aundi laughed, and then everyone laughed at the ludicrous idea. Someone like Grayson Crowne being into *me*.

I held the clothes tighter to my body.

"I am," Grayson said, and the laughter came to a crashing halt. "I am into her. She's mine. If you hurt her, you hurt me. If you fuck with her, you fuck with me. This is the last goddamn warning I give."

Awkward laughter trickled out, a few eyes wandering to Lottie, then back to us. Lottie gazed into her drink, a look on her face like she wished it could drown her.

"Geoff, you already *got* a warning. I don't want to see your fucking face. Your dad, fired. You, out."

I don't know if Grayson snapped his fingers or simply gave a look, but two guards appeared and dragged Geoff out.

"Aundi and Pipa..."

At their names, their eyes went wide.

"Be really fucking grateful Lottie likes you. For whatever reason."

Silence. Everyone stared at me with uncertainty, disdain, begrudging respect.

He wrapped his arm around my waist, lifting me off the floor, carting me out of the room.

GRAY

. . .

We were barely out of there when Story yanked herself away and shoved me in the chest.

"Uh, you're welcome."

"Thank you?" She looked away on a laugh, a breathy, indignant sound. "You want a *thank you*? What the hell are you doing?"

"Being romantic, doing the right thing."

"You just confirmed all of their suspicions. Grayson Crowne is fucking his maid. His maid is his mistress."

"I...shit..." I rubbed the back of my neck. "I didn't look at it that way."

"Do you want to know what your mother really said to me before Italy? She told me I was your mistress. She said I was *lucky*. Now I had leverage. She all but welcomed me into the Crowne family!"

She threw up her hands and turned from me, facing the wall.

"Story." I placed my hand on her shoulder, and she flinched. "Story, look at me."

I turned her by the shoulder and found her eyes red, tears running. Fuck.

"What happened? Where were you today?"

All I wanted to do was tell her what happened between my mother and grandfather.

I'd told them.

The wedding was off.

But I'd never seen her this way. I've seen her cry, yeah, but she was unhinged. Hysterical. And it was freaking me the fuck out. I want someone to punch. Need someone to hurt.

She swiped at her tears, snot. "I'm beginning to think she's right. This only ends one way."

"Shut up." I gripped her chin. "Tell me the truth. Where were you today?"

She wiped her eyes. "I'm going to see my uncle. You should go back to Lottie. After all she is your fiancée, right?"

She didn't wait for me to respond, turning to leave.

FORTY-SEVEN

GRAY

It was a goddamn sleepless night waiting for Story. I should've told her I broke off my engagement hours ago, but it didn't seem like the right moment, with her on the verge of tears and all.

At around five in the morning, I said fuck it and got up to go get her.

I walked the winding steps to the servants' quarters and knocked on the dark oak door that marked Woodsy's room. He was already sitting up in bed, and made a *shh* motion with his finger, pointing to a corner.

Story was asleep on the chair.

I came in, shutting the door lightly behind me.

I came for Abigail, but there was so much I needed to say to him.

"You promised I could die first," I said quietly.

He shrugged with a smile. "Seven-year-olds are easy to trick."

Fuck.

Fuck fuck fuck.

I bit the skin at my thumb, hating this.

"Whatever you want. You can have it. The best doctors, anything."

He shook his hand. "I'd like to spend my last hours here."

"You can be buried in the family plot."

He laughed, then coughed. "Don't promise the moon."

"But you're family."

"All I need to know is when I die, she'll be taken care of."

"She'll have all the money—"

"Not with money." He pinned me. "She's disappearing, Grayson."

We both looked at her, asleep in the corner, neck at an odd angle.

"You and I both know you can't take someone like her as a wife."

I ground my jaw. "Maybe I can."

"Your father tried that."

A yawn drew our attention, and we both turned to see Story stretching awake.

"You're awake." Story smiled at Woodsy, but the smile dropped when she saw me. She straightened in the chair and said, "I'll go get you breakfast."

I followed her out of the room. "This is where you slept last night?"

"Yeah," she said without turning around.

Distance. Growing like a weed. I wanted to pull it out at the roots.

I grabbed her elbow, stopping her. "You sleep in *my* bed."

She stared forward.

Only my grip on her biceps keeping her from walking away.

"Anything else, Mr. Grayson?"

I wanted to teach her a lesson for that obvious disobedience. Put her on her knees. Fuck her. Bite her.

Really, I wanted to pull her into a hug and comfort her.

Fuck, she'd be the death of me.

"Be in my room by five," I said, voice strangled.

"Of course, Mr. Grayson."

My grip tightened, and then I let her go.

STORY

Grayson paused when he came to his room, finding me on my knees and my eyes down.

"There's a dress hanging up for you in my closet."

I stood. "Sure, Mr. Grayson."

"Call me that again, see what happens," he growled at my back.

I swallowed but ignored the goose bumps on my skin.

Grayson hadn't chosen me—over and over again he hadn't chosen me.

I nearly lost my breath when I saw what was hanging in his closet.

Once again it was like Gray knew me down to my marrow. The dress was *me*. It went all the way up to my neck and down to my wrists, but the sleeves and neck were a sheer material embroidered with hundreds of little blue

dots. I was covered, and uncovered, at the same time. It was a gorgeous cornflower blue that looked great with my dark skin, and the skirt flounced along with the neckline. I felt like I belonged in a fairy tale, as a nutcracker princess.

When Gray saw me, he swallowed a noise in his throat, and my belly twisted into knots. He stood off the couch and came to me, dressed to kill in a perfectly tailored black suit that somehow looked both disheveled and intentional.

"I'm regretting this dress," he said, twisting my lip between his fingers. Though he dragged my lip between his thumb and forefinger, his eyes hadn't strayed from my body. Soaking me up. Swallowing me whole.

"Why?" I croaked.

Slowly his eyes found mine, burning. "I was getting used to keeping you all to myself."

Ice water doused my veins. I'd gotten lost in him again, lost in what his touch promised but his actions never kept. I took a step back, eyes finding the floor.

"Anything else, Mr. Grayson?"

"The fuck did I say about calling me that?"

"Why, what are you going to do, Mr. Grayson?" I met his eyes, goading him, suddenly overwhelmed with emotion.

Sadness, sorrow, from my uncle.

Anger, from being strung along.

"Mr. Grayson," I said, tears fire in my eyes. "Mr. Grayson—"

His eyes flamed, and I thought he was going to punish me, but he pulled me into a hug, so tight I couldn't breathe. Suffocated in his suit, in the dreamy smell of him that felt too much like home.

And I fell to pieces, getting snot all over his nice suit.

He gripped the back of my head tight. "Fucking hell, Story."

"He's *dying*." I sobbed, over and over again.

He gripped me tighter, and for a moment I let myself give in to his comfort.

But he was *still marrying her*.

This didn't belong to me. I was stealing him. I was doing everything my mother taught me to do.

I pushed him off, swiping my eyes and staring at the floor.

"Look at me," he demanded.

I changed the subject. "Why am I dressed like this?"

"I thought you could use a distraction. And I needed a date."

"As your mistress," I said glumly.

"As my lover, as my girlfriend, as the girl I want by my side, as the girl I want everyone to know belongs to Grayson Crowne."

My heart jumped at his words, but still, "You promised to tell Lottie. I'm not going to do this anymore. I can't."

Yet I'd still put on the dress.

I'd still come to the room.

Who of us was I lying to?

"I'm *not* marrying Lottie," he said.

Even more hope, even more pounding in my chest. "You've said that before, Mr. Grayson."

"I spoke with my grandfather and my mother. I'll tell Lottie tonight."

It ricocheted through me. He'd told them. Had he really told them? I slowly lifted my eyes, meeting his earnest ones.

"And they just accepted it?"

"I *made* them accept it."

I couldn't believe it. I just couldn't. It was too much like a happily ever after, too much like a dream come true.

He gripped my hands. "I need a date tonight, Story."

"You're *really* not marrying her?"

"There will be a lot of paparazzi, tonight, Snitch. The whole world will see who I really want. Can you handle that?"

FORTY-EIGHT

STORY

He wasn't kidding when he said there would be paparazzi. Outside the town car, I couldn't see beyond them. A sea of white-hot lights was barely muted by the black-tinted window. Beyond them, rows and rows of stone stairs led up to hulking columns, lit up at the base by lights, looking somehow more giant, haunting, and regal. Embossed in the stone were the words *Du Lac Library for Rare Books and Scripts*.

A hand slid along my thigh, and Grayson's lips found my ear, warm. "Second-guessing?"

I swallowed and shook my head, just as the door opened.

Grayson got out first, and the paparazzi swarmed him like piranhas. He paused, then turned around, giving me his hand.

I sucked in a breath and took his hand. They were *everywhere*. Overwhelmingly so. A machine-gun fire of

flashbulbs and questions. Grayson pulled me tight to his side, arm wrapped around my waist.

Grayson!

Who is she?

Grayson, over here!

Through it all, his grip on my waist remained secure, and I felt sheltered by him. He never looked more in his element than right here, with the flashing white light silhouetting his angular jaw. His trademark crooked, cocky smile as he easily navigated choppy waters. He spoke with the paparazzi like old friends.

When I imagined the life of Grayson Crowne, this was what I'd always conjured up. Glamorous parties every night, schmoozing the paparazzi. Not the lonely prince I knew to be true...but *this*. Even now, I saw through his smile, saw the weight on his shoulders.

Then all eyes were on me, and I realized someone had asked me a question.

He leaned down, lips whispering against my ear. "What's your name, Snitch?"

"I, um, Story."

Flash. Flash. Flash.

I blinked a trillion times in what must have produced the worst photograph in the history of magazines, because *ow!* Are they taking a picture or trying to *blind me*?

"She's my date," Grayson supplied easily.

Date.

I'm his *date*.

Everyone went crazy taking more photos.

How did you tie him down?

How did you meet?

My throat closed. The flashes were bright and hot. Grayson slipped his hand from my waist, sliding it

between my fingers. He said something to them I didn't catch, spellbound by our joined hands in public. My heart pounded as we ascended the red carpeted steps, floating higher. The paparazzi flanked us on either side. What world had I fallen into? I was a movie star. I was in a fairy tale.

Inside the library, the lights were dimmed, and a glow and faint sound of big band music filtered out from some-place unseen. Yet he stopped, gripping my shoulders.

"Breathe," he said.

I sucked in a breath and exhaled, suddenly realizing I *hadn't* been breathing. At my big breath, Grayson smiled softly.

"This is a lot," I admitted.

He shrugged. "This is my life."

He thumbed my lip, a dark, possessive look consuming his features. He pulled me forward, crashing his lips against mine.

Lips still pressed to mine, he said, "I'll never get enough of your lips, Story Hale."

Then he gripped my hand in his, and we entered.

Multiple stories of leather-bound books flanked by towering Grecian columns. It was beautiful, ancient, intimidating.

I spotted Tansy Crowne and instinctively tensed. A little way away from her, Lottie du Lac smiled with her friends, the same ones who had so very recently tormented me. Grayson's friends, if he still called them that, leaned against a column, looking bored. Everyone in this room was dressed in the finest silks and satins, but all I saw were sharks.

I might be dolled, Grayson might have told the paparazzi I was his date, but I did not belong here.

Tansy gestured for Grayson to come with a crook of her finger.

"If I don't go now, it will be a thousand times worse for us later." He looked at me, worry creasing lines in his smooth forehead.

"Go," I said. "I'll be fine."

GRAY

On my way to my mother I was stopped by Lottie's yell.

"You brought *her* here? How could you do that?"

Tears glimmered in her eyes. Around us, partygoers turned to watch, eager for gossip.

"Shit, Lottie, this isn't how I wanted to do this." I caught her elbow, dragging her someplace more private. "I was going to talk to you later."

I caught Snitch's eye before we disappeared, concern and question writ across her usually smooth face.

Lottie's shoulders dropped. "You're taking her as a mistress."

"No, fuck no. I can't go through with it"

"You're canceling it?" Lottie's face crumpled. *"Tonight?"* Lottie was the perfect high society woman. She didn't show emotion. She didn't lose face. She didn't start scenes.

So seeing her cry in *public* was a shock and made me feel like fucking shit.

"That's good. That's...good." She sniffed, covering her mouth and wiping away a stray tear. Back to the picture of perfection.

Still, she looked so broken and beat down. I'd loved Lottie and I'd never intended to fall out of love with her.

"Lottie..."

I didn't know what words to say to make this better.

To fix it.

"I said get it out of your system...I just didn't think you'd call it off. I'm a little shocked. I shouldn't want to be married to someone who doesn't want me, right? I even tried so hard to convince my father," she said. "I told my brother and my father I didn't want to marry you anymore, but...you know. It doesn't matter. You're canceling it. I'm sorry. I didn't have the guts." Her shining eyes met mine. "I'm sorry I realized it too late. It was always you for me, too, Grayson." She smiled weakly. "I hope you're happy with her."

"Lottie, shit." I messed up my hair. "You're perfect. You'll find someone so much better than me."

She looked into her champagne. "When will you tell them?"

My mother's gaze had shifted from me to Snitch. She set down her glass of champagne, and I could see the wheels turning.

"No, I *canceled* it," I said. "It's done."

Her brow collapsed, and her head shot up. "But tonight—"

"Can we finish this later?"

"Of course, Grayson."

STORY

Grayson has been gone for ten minutes, and the last time I saw him he was with Lottie.

I keep telling myself he chose me.

He chose *me*.

I have nothing to worry about.

But that doesn't calm my nerves.

At least my dress is the best camouflage. People would never expect Story Hale to be here, dressed the way I am. So far I've blended in beautifully next to a row of books.

I eavesdropped on the conversations like back when I was a servant, and, still, the things the rich and famous say are quite...dull.

There is no truth to their words.

Honesty. Bloody, raw, jagged truth.

I shivered at the memory.

"Story?" West du Lac's voice made me freeze. I stared straight ahead, hoping he would think he was mistaken.

"Story, I know that's you."

Shit.

West grabbed my arm, turning me to face him. "What are you doing here?"

"What are..." I stopped. *Du Lac* was on the freaking building.

"I'm Grayson's date."

"His date?" West laughed, but more to himself than to me. It was bitter, caustic, cutting. My high from before eviscerated by his cutting laugh. "So it's because of you."

I narrowed my eyes. "What do you mean 'because of me'?"

But he didn't respond to my question.

"What is it, Story?" he asked. "Why are you with him? I didn't pay high enough?"

I imagined pouring champagne on his head or throwing

cake in his face. Instead, as years' worth of feelings I'd repressed came bubbling to the surface, I spoke the truth.

The bloody, raw, jagged truth.

"If you recall, *West*"—I bit his name off—"*you* didn't call *me* back."

He looked away, but only for the briefest second. "I apologized. I want another chance."

"I thought you were the one, West," I said. "I cried about you. I cried about you, and you didn't even care to text me back. You didn't even care enough to ask if I wanted to lose my virginity in the first place. I told you I wanted to wait. I said I wanted to slow down, but you didn't care enough to listen. And *now* you don't care to listen when I'm telling you I don't want to give you a second chance."

He reeled. "What are you implying, Story? You didn't say no."

"Just because I didn't say no doesn't mean I said yes," I whispered.

He glared. "I'm West du Lac. I can have anyone I want. What *are you implying*?" His voice raised, and a few people looked over. I chewed my lip.

I hadn't wanted to get into this.

I never wanted to talk about it again.

But he kept coming around, poking me, prodding at the wound that wouldn't heal.

"This always happens," West scoffed. "You don't call the chick back and suddenly it's rape. Is that what you're saying?"

"I..." I stared into his eyes. Yes. *YES*. "No..."

My mom used the word *rape* as a weapon, and I never wanted to be her. Besides, if he did...do that...then that meant I wanted my rapist to call me back. I *cried* when he

didn't. And he still broke my heart. So what does that say about me?

"Are you looking for money?" he asked. "Is that it? You heard my dad's company is doing well and wanted in on it? Heard I was about to take over?"

"No..." My shoulders sank further and I felt like sludge.

"You're willing to fuck Gray while he's about to marry my sister—so how much is he paying you?"

My eyes flashed. "They're not getting married."

"They sped up the wedding because of you, Angel."

Sped up the wedding? "What the fuck are you talking about?"

"What do you think this is?"

My heart beat faster and faster. "A benefit for books. I don't know."

"Oh." His eyes popped, and I saw actual pity behind them, concern. "Angel..."

For the first time since we'd arrived, I allowed myself to look beyond the Gray bubble. We were at a du Lac building, Lottie was here and dressed beautifully...but she *always* looked beautiful, right? It wasn't strange her family was here, because it was a du Lac building.

So what? So what if there was enough press for a royal engagement?

There were diamonds on all the cakes, glittering and cascading like waterfalls. Atop them rings sat...one could even say they'd been designed to emulate engagement rings...but I'd been to enough Crowne parties to know they always go all out. The Fourth of July party had four-karat gold in the sand.

When West took a step to me, thumbing my jaw, I was too shell-shocked to stop him.

"Angel, those are my parents. You see his parents. You see the engagement rings."

"Stop calling me that!"

Fear ripped through me.

The cake. The parents.

"Give me one more fucking chance, Angel. It was a mistake I made years ago. I messed up. I shouldn't have taken your virginity that way. I shouldn't have ghosted you. You're a dream I can't stop reliving."

He thumbed my jaw, and this time I swatted his hand away.

"Well, you were my worst fucking nightmare."

"Goddamn, West," Gray said, appearing at the best or worst time—I couldn't decide. His hand found my lower back. "Stop bothering my date. I'd hate to have to knock you out at your own party."

"*My* party?" West laughed.

I spun away from Gray, away from them both, needing air. To get out of the room filled with books and diamonds and lies, somewhere dark, somewhere I couldn't be seen, somewhere I could disappear.

"Yeah, *your* party, dickhead—Story, wait!" He caught up to me just as I was about to leave the library and grabbed my shoulders. "Where are you going?"

I don't know how much Gray had overheard. Maybe he'd learned I was lying about my virginity. I should probably be worried about that, worried the small lie that had grown into a massive monster was about to devastate us.

But in this moment it didn't matter.

"Where am I right now?" I demanded. "What is this?"

"Some benefit." He shrugged. "I don't know."

"Please tell me you didn't bring me to your engagement party. Please tell me you didn't. *Please.*"

FORTY-NINE

GRAY

"Of course not." The smile on my face lingered, even as dread wove its way into my gut. I was still high on the night, when I believed I could have it all without consequences, but the tears in her eyes told me the truth.

My mother had been way too fucking nice about me bringing Story.

She'd said she looked *lovely*.

"I called off the wedding," I said, more to myself, like it would make it true.

"Champagne, sir." A server appeared with a tray of golden liquid in a thin flute of crystal.

I waved him away.

Worst fucking timing.

"I called off the wedding, Story," I repeated.

She shook her head.

The silencing tapping of crystal filled the air like wind

chimes, and we both looked to see my mother and Lottie in the center of the room.

"Toast!" my mother said cheerfully, raising her glass.

The dread grew and knotted.

I closed my eyes.

Fuck.

"To a Christmas wedding," Mrs. du Lac said.

Fuck. Fuck. Fuck.

"To the future Mr. and Mrs. Grayson Crowne."

Cheers rang out, crystal clanked, and everyone shouted for me and Lottie—my future wife. I briefly caught Lottie's eyes, miserable and broken.

"This is so fucked up," Story whispered.

My mother's eyes locked with mine, a tight, satisfied smile on her lips.

Why hadn't I seen it coming? It was classic Tansy Crowne, vintage Beryl. They don't give in that easily. They never declared check-mate. They would throw the board out and place their pawns exactly where they needed them to be.

When I looked back, Story was halfway to the door.

"Story, wait!"

I ran after her, grabbing her.

"You have to believe me," I said. "I didn't do this."

"I can't keep watching you choose her," Story cried. "I can't do it anymore. I can't keep being the girl behind the girl."

"Let me prove it to you."

I shoved cake off one of the tables. Million-dollar rings that would go home as party favors clacked to the ground. Diamonds skittered across the marble floor. And the room went silent. I climbed atop the table, shoes smashing into frosting. Then I bent down, giving Story my hand.

"What are you doing?" Her eyes were wide, darting around the room.

"Choosing you."

I didn't give her a choice this time, ripping her up on the table with me. I pressed her against my body, anchoring her lower waist.

"Everyone came here for an announcement?" I yelled.

Tansy's nostrils flared, the only sign of displeasure she'd show in public. Lottie sank into the book stacks, putting a hand over her face. I hated doing this to her, hated that our parents had left me with no choice. We were puppets to them, and they were trying to cast our strings in steel.

"Looks like you got the wrong information. Weird." I glared at my mother. "*She's* who I choose. When I get married, it'll be to *her*."

I gripped Story's face between my palms, then whispered against her lips so only she could hear.

"I want to kiss you, Story. I want the whole fucking world to know you're mine. I want it cast in stone."

"What are you waiting for?"

I slammed my lips against hers. Apologizing with a gentle tongue, demanding her forgiveness with bruising teeth and lips.

Atop a table of broken cakes and promises, at an engagement party that never should have been, surrounded by the bright flash of paparazzi, I kissed my real love, my true love.

We broke apart, foreheads pressed, and I grinned against her lips. "Forever and always, I choose you, Story."

FIFTY

GRAY

Story asleep in my bed, on my chest, this was something I could get used to. I traced small patterns on her shoulder blade, thinking of the night before.

I shouldn't have taken your virginity that way. I shouldn't have ghosted you.

I should be mad. From the very beginning, I'd only asked for one thing, not to lie, and she'd lied about being a virgin. But that...didn't feel like a truth I was owed. It was one I wanted to earn.

That was the truth between her and West. He was a fucker, a cockhead, who'd ghosted her after taking her virginity.

So I'm not mad, I'm...hurt? Hurt she couldn't trust me?

Fuck.

My phone buzzed on the nightstand to my left, and my grandfather's name popped up.

I'm downstairs. Come now, or I'll go upstairs and wake her.

I slid out of bed, making sure Story stayed asleep, and descended the stairs, finding him in my study. He was behind a desk I rarely, if ever, used, facing a large, golden-latticed window with a view of my private beach.

"You really shouldn't sleep with the bride before the wedding," he said coldly.

"I'm sure you've seen the papers by now."

"I have," he nodded, turning around. "Have you? The great thing about marrying a du Lac is we get to decide what they say..."

I folded my arms over my naked chest, glowering.

"I'm not marrying Charlotte du Lac," I said. "Sorry if my message last night wasn't clear enough."

My grandfather's jaw twitched. "Bad joke, Grayson."

"I'm marrying Story Hale. She's a servant—"

"I know who she is!" he all but screamed.

I shut the door behind me, hoping I hadn't woken Story. Rarely had I seen my grandfather lose his composure. He was stone, even when facing the potential collapse of Crowne Industries.

"I've been thinking about it," I said. "You can't excommunicate me like you did with Uncle and Abigail. Who will run the company? Who will give you heirs?"

"You're just like your fucking father," he hissed under-breath. "Always thinking with your dick."

"I am *nothing* like him. He didn't have the balls to say no to you."

"Just like him, you'll listen when I say you are not special because you came from your mother's twat. Who will give me heirs? Your sister? The bastards? The nieces and nephews? Who will run the company?" Grandfather

placed his hands on the desk, leaning forward. "There are two bastard twins in boarding school who spend every summer and vacation at the company. You know how it goes."

I'd been prepared for this eventuality the moment I chose Story.

"So kick me out. I don't give a shit. Destroy me. Destroy everything. I'm done being your monkey."

"And that's what will happen. You must realize how untenable your situation is, Grayson. Without your inheritance, who is going to pay for her uncle's medical bills?"

I ground my jaw. I hadn't thought of that.

Grandpa stood back up, suddenly the picture of composure. "Where will he live without you *allowing* him to stay?"

"We'll find somewhere." Though a niggle of doubt sewed my words together.

"Stop thinking with your cock. Don't make the same mistake as your sister. Don't give everything up for someone who doesn't care about you."

I laughed. "What do you know about it? That girl asleep in my bed is the only one who has ever given a damn about me."

My grandfather put a finger to his mouth, nodding, as if really thinking about my words. I knew better. I knew he was only formulating his next argument.

"Really? That *girl up there* is a user, Grayson. Her mommy taught her how to lie for years, threatening honest men with rape. What's stopping her from saying you did the same? When this goes south, will you be a rapist too?"

She'd lie, have me lie, say I'd go to the cops and tell them they raped me.

It was. But I paid for it.

I saw fucking red.

I slammed my fists on the table. "Shut your fucking mouth. You don't know what the fuck you're talking about."

My grandfather's face curled in a sneer. "Spoiled fucking brats!" He stood up, slamming his hands next to mine on the table, until we were both eye to eye.

"I gave you *everything*," he shouted. "This is how you repay me? Your sister fucks off with a guard and now you want to marry a servant? I couldn't stop Abigail. I won't fucking let it happen to you. You won't ruin my name. You won't ruin a family I spent years building."

His hair fell across his eyes in his anger, face red. It was such a rare occurrence to see Beryl Crowne undone, like seeing my mother anything but placid.

He fixed his hair, sat back down, like he hadn't just combusted.

"I don't know what I'm talking about?" he asked lightly. "I know false accusations are taken seriously by the police, as is blackmail and stealing. She could get into a lot of trouble for the lies she's told."

I'd tell them I was their daughter. They'd pay us off not to ruin their family. Other times it was darker...

"She was a child. No one will prosecute that."

He laughed. "District Attorney Millard owes me more favors than he can count. I'd say, fifteen years' worth, at least."

I made a fist so tight my nails dug into my palm.

For years I'd carried the weight of this asshole's greed.

I wasn't surprised by his threat. I was pissed at myself for not seeing it coming.

"We have a very generous mistress package, Grayson. I don't give a shit what happens to her so long as you marry du Lac. Keep her as your mistress, deport her to

Switzerland—whatever, just make sure she doesn't get pregnant."

I wouldn't, I *couldn't*, keep her as a mistress. Even if she got hit on the head and decided she wanted to be mine.

Which meant Story and I were finished.

"I'll send her back to the servants," I said.

My grandfather froze. "That's funny. So she can tell them Cinderella stories? No. She needs an official title as mistress, and we can start the damage control."

"And if she doesn't want to be my mistress?" I hedged.

"She is done living here. Though, I would hurry and decide..." Grandfather said absently. "I think Lottie is arriving soon."

STORY

I woke up alone in Grayson's bed, and for a soft, cottony moment, was happy. Then I opened my eyes and saw the person at the foot of the bed. I scrambled to pull the sheets against my chest.

"Were you expecting someone else?" Tansy asked.

She smiled warmly at me, looking so elegant in her white dress and blood-red shoes.

My face flamed. "I...no..."

"Grayson is preparing for the arrival of his fiancée."

There was a song we sang in elementary school to annoy our teachers. The song that never ends...it just goes on and on again. As Tansy smiled down at me from the foot of the bed, all I could think was, *This is the nightmare that never ends...it goes on and on again.*

"He told everyone last night. He loves me. He wants to marry me."

"Oh, dear." Tansy smiled, but it was vicious. Her pretty smile dripped oil. "History is written by those who own the pen, and *we* own the pen."

She tossed a few papers at me.

Playboy Gray Has Eyes Only for His Future Wife.

Grayson Crowne Smitten with Charlotte du Lac.

"In the end, all that matters is who he marries. As I've said before, we have a very competitive mistress package. A house. A monthly stipend. Holidays. For someone like you, it's more than generous."

Mistress.

I couldn't breathe. I mashed my lips together and stared at the sheets.

"We simply expect birth control and abortion, if necessary. Oh, and keep your mouth *shut*." Anger bit off the last word.

"I don't want to be a mistress," I croaked.

"I didn't want three ungrateful children and a philandering husband, but fate doesn't take bribes." She stepped on the sheets hanging off the bed, forcing me to grapple with them so I wasn't exposed. "He isn't Abigail. He has responsibilities. This ends no other way for you."

Threat hung heavy and dark.

Then all at once she stepped off the sheets. "Oh, Lottie dear, perfect timing!"

I followed her eyes to where Lottie stood at the top of the stairs, with her two-toned cream-and-camel luggage behind her, hurt stamping her face. Tears in her eyes.

Our eyes locked. She looked just as surprised to see me as I her.

"It's time to have a frank discussion," Tansy said. "Which is, *frankly*, overdue."

I'd never felt more like the other woman than at this moment, naked, stuck in his bed, as his future wife waited to move in.

"Ideally, the mistress and the wife should be on speaking terms. As the wife, you can set your own rules of order for her to follow."

I stared at the sheets.

"Lottie?" Tansy probed.

"Yes?" Lottie croaked.

"Do you have any rules you'd like her to follow?"

"I...I need to sit down." Lottie wobbled over to a couch, falling on it instantly.

"Of course, dear, you have time to think on them." Tansy's inflection was so easy, like we were discussing what we would get for lunch.

I couldn't breathe.

Lottie looked like she was going to pass out.

Footfalls sounded, pounding, heavy things that echoed and boomed. A moment later, Grayson appeared on the stairs. His eyes darted around, taking in Tansy, Lottie, me, and doing it in reverse.

"What the fuck is happening?"

"Lottie is moving in," Tansy said easily. "We're discussing your mistress arrangements."

A tear fell down Lottie's cheek.

I loved Grayson. I'd been in love with him, but we could *never* be together.

What was I doing here?

I scrambled to get as much of the sheets as I could to cover myself, climbing off the bed and tripping as I did so.

"Story, wait," Grayson started. "Let me..."

My eyes were stuck on Lottie. "I'm sorry, Lottie, I—"

I ran down the stairs.

I only made it to the hallway before I collapsed into a heap of tears. The marble floor seeped through the thin silk sheets, cold, abrasive. I wasn't sure how long I sat like that, the sound of the waves outside muffled by the glass.

When suddenly *thwack*.

A thick stack of cash hit my thigh.

Thwack. Thwack. Thwack.

More cash landed on me, between my thighs, on my shin, pelting me, covering me. More cash than I'd ever seen in my life, flying at me. I looked up, finding Grayson.

"What are you doing?"

"It's twenty million dollars," he said. "Get the fuck out and go. Never come back."

I stared up at Grayson, speechless. He'd painted me in green, my only armor his sheets. It took a moment to swallow the tears in my throat, to speak through the hurt. He'd just thrown cash at me like I was nothing.

Like I was less than nothing.

"So that's it?" I said, voice hoarse. "It's really true? You're marrying her and leaving me in the dust."

His eyes were red but brutal.

"You promised you wouldn't do this to me," I said quietly. "Now not just everyone in Crowne Hall knows we're together, but everyone in the fucking *world*. But they also know you're marrying Charlotte. You didn't take us out of the dark. You just shoved me deeper into the shadows. You made me your public mistress. You made me your dirty secret. You made me your lie. *Why?*"

He clenched his jaw. "Just *go*."

"You're a coward, Grayson Crowne. Afraid to show your insides. Afraid to be truly vulnerable. Afraid."

"Me?"

He grasped my sheet, tearing me up until my back bent, and I was face-to-face with him. "How long have you been hiding, Story? Do you even remember what the real you looks like beneath all your armor?"

"You made me the mistress," I spat. "You made me the liar. Why, why did you do this to us?"

His eyes fractured, and for a moment I saw *Grayson*. I thought maybe he would let me in, tell me how we got from last night to here.

Then his grip tightened. "I'll give you double this, no, fucking quadruple it. Whatever you want, five hundred million dollars right now to get out of my fucking life."

Five *hundred* million dollars.

I couldn't breathe by the amount.

"I-I can't."

"Why the fuck not?"

"You *know why*. There's only one person in Crowne Hall who would let my uncle stay here. Only one person who gives a damn to let a dying man stay when he has no labor to offer."

His grip tightened a fraction; then he shoved me away. I clasped at the sheets so they didn't fall off me.

"Am I supposed to leave him and let him die here on his own?"

"You can visit him."

"When? Crowne Hall has never been very open to *visitors*. I can't imagine your family allowing *me* to visit whenever the hell I want."

"I'll make it happen," he gritted.

"What if he gets worse while I'm away? Or dies? Of anyone you should know how important family is. You act like you don't care, but you do. You know why I can't leave him."

He slammed his hands on either side of me. "You're only here because *I* allow it."

A rush of cold iced my spine.

Grayson *Crowne*.

Apathetic and entitled...cruel. Not the boy I'd fallen in love with.

"What aren't you telling me?" I punched his chest, but he didn't so much as stumble. "Why is everything different? Stop it. Stop it. Stop *ruining* everything." I shoved his chest again. "I thought we were past this. I thought you were letting me in."

I went to shove him again, and he gripped my wrists. My sheet fell to the floor exposing me, but his eyes were on me, and nothing save apathy stared back.

"Like you let me in? Like you promised you wouldn't lie?" he whispered viciously. "You're a virgin, huh?"

My mouth dropped.

"That's..." Blood rushed through my ears. "It was before everything. It was before the contract."

"How many other lies have you told, Snitch?"

"What if you thought less of me? What if—"

"You think that's what this is about?" he boomed. "You think that's why I cared? You think I want some shiny, untouched toy? How fucking little do you really think of me, Snitch? I thought you understood. I thought you got me."

"I do," I cried.

"If you did, you wouldn't have lied about this."

"When I started, I thought it was just a crush and it would go away—"

"So you were fine with hurting me?"

"You were fine with hurting me! I was looking out for myself, same as you. It was clumsy and ugly. I was trying to protect myself from you, who I thought you were, who I'd heard you were, who I'd *only* ever experienced you as."

He dropped me, turning to leave without another word.

I grabbed him. "Wait. Wait. Then I got to know you, and...you're so much more than I should ever deserve. I didn't realize how much my lie would hurt until it was too late."

"Were you ever going to tell me?" he asked.

"I don't know," I answered honestly. A vicious look flashed across his face that only pissed me off. "Just look what you're doing to me! You all want my heart, but no one wants to protect it."

"Are you comparing me to him?" It came out on a growl.

I raised my chin, eyes burning. "How are you different? You keep me in the dark. You take pieces of me to build yourself up. You're all the same. I'm sorry the lie hurt, but I'm not sorry I lied." I slowly stood. "At some point this becomes about survival. You wrapped your heart in thorns, and I buried mine in secrets."

His eyes softened, and for a moment I thought he understood.

Then he looked me up and down like dirt. "You're just like every other whore looking for a piece of me."

"It's not about you. You don't get those pieces of me!" I screamed, throat and lungs and *soul* hoarse with the effort.

He slammed his hands on either side of me. "I get *all* pieces of you," he growled.

He pressed me back against the wall, pressing his

clothed body into my naked one. The molding bit into my back, and his silky sleep pajamas rubbed against my thighs. His eyes searched mine, furious, and something else...a dark, hidden need.

"Is that why you're doing this?" I whispered. "Because I lied?"

Something flickered across his brow; then he stepped back, saying coldly, "Yes."

It didn't feel right.

None of this did.

"I don't believe you," I whispered.

It was his turn to shoot me an uncertain look.

He wiped it away with his apathetic mask. But I *saw through that* now. Something was wrong. Something he wasn't telling me. There was something weighing his shoulders to the point of collapse.

"The contract is void," he said coldly. "But I have the girl, so I'm feeling fucking generous. The rest of the money will be in your account tomorrow. Your job is done. Get out of Crowne Hall. Never come back."

"You know I can't leave!" I yelled at his back. "My uncle is *dying*."

He paused. "You have no place here, Snitch. The cooks won't take you. The maids won't take you. Do you expect free room and board? There's only one way you stay."

With each second that passed, the brittle wire protecting my heart snapped. I saw what he was implying, the ugly expectation.

"No," I whispered. "Don't say it. I'd sooner rip out my heart, but...I'll leave. I will. Just let me stay until Uncle p-passes. You won't even notice me. I'll live in my old room."

"That room is taken now."

"I'll stay with my uncle. I'll sleep on the floor."

He shook his head.

"Please, any other way. Please."

He rubbed his sinful, plump bottom lip, pulling it out. It was like I was begging at the feet of the devil.

"Lottie needs a girl."

My heart plummeted. "Even you aren't that cruel."

Lottie's words echoed in my head, the ones she'd spoken when she'd discovered us. *This is cruel, even for you.*

So, so similar.

"Do you have any other option?" he asked, bored, lazy. "You need somewhere to work, right? I mean, it's either work for her or keep working beside me. And that would raise questions, right?"

"Do you know what you're asking me?" Tears had entirely blurred my vision. "You want me to be a mistress or work beside your wife?"

Hide forever. Keep it a dirty secret.

"You *know* what the girl has to do on the wedding night."

His eyes flashed at my words.

The Crownes have wedding rituals dating back centuries, before they even came to America, and the thought of what I'd have to do...see...made me want to vomit.

"I know what you're doing," I whispered. "You're doing the thing. The Grayson thing. You don't think I'll last a day as Lottie's girl, let alone months. You're hoping you can push me away. Push us away. That I'll grow to hate you. And then it won't hurt me when you have to marry her. It won't work."

I didn't see him bend down until my chin was in his hand, grip vicious. "Oh, you see me so well, Snitch." His words were cutting, mocking, cruel.

Then he tossed me back to the ground like trash. I threw out my hands to keep from hitting the floor.

"You think you've figured me out?"

"I see you, Grayson Crowne," I said through tears. "I see you. Don't let this ruin everything. You can't rip us out. You can't make it disappear. I love you. That doesn't just go away because you want it to."

The pause he took to speak was so long I thought he'd left.

"Me or Lottie, Snitch."

I swallowed. "Lottie."

"Then you're welcome. Lottie only pays a little bit less than us."

FIFTY-ONE

GRAYSON

You wrapped your heart in thorns, and I buried mine in secrets.

By the time I made it back to my wing, Lottie was curled up on my couch, head on her knees, staring out at the ocean.

She must have heard me come in, because she said, "So this sucks."

I laughed. "Yeah."

Awkwardness swamped us. Lottie or my mother had opened the doors to the beach, and chilly fall air numbed the room. But it was better—better than lingering in the stale sadness.

"You never allowed anyone in here," she said musingly, "but you let her in here, and even now I'm forced upon you. I think they're hoping by forcing us in close proximity we'll have no choice but to like each other."

I came around to see her, and her eyes were swollen from crying. In her red eyes I saw Woodsy's words.

Your father tried that.

I'd loved two girls.

I'd ruined them both.

"I want to hate you," she said quietly.

I looked up. "You don't?"

"I do...Because I love you," she whispered. "I hate you for making me love you, and then changing your mind. I hate you for choosing her."

I rubbed the back of my neck. "Lottie..."

"I hate that you chose her...and I hate that I'm happy it didn't count. I hate that I'm turning into this person. A vicious person. A greedy person. Someone who's willing to take what doesn't belong to them anymore."

"It's my fault," I said.

"It's *my* fault. I thought maybe when you started liking someone else, my dad would stop trying to force me on you, but when I told him, he called your grandpa."

It all made so much fucking sense now.

I shook my head. "Nah, it's my fault. I had a thing for you, I pursued you. You have no blame, Lottie. It's my fault we're in this."

More silence, the melancholy sound of cold ocean waves. The whole place was muted by the overcast sky. There was one more thing I had to take from Lottie. One more thing I had no right to ask

"I need to ask one more thing from you."

Her dark-brown eyes found mine.

"I need you to take her on as your girl."

"You want her as my *girl*?" Lottie's face caved. "The rumors, Grayson. People are already talking. After what you did at our engagement party...We may have stopped

print, but you know we can't silence the internet. Not for long. Do you know what they say about her? About me? I'm a laughing stock. No, worse. I'm pitied. You turned me into everything I was trying to avoid."

"It won't last," I said. "She won't last a week."

"I can't think of one reason why I should do it."

"I can't give you any," I said.

She pursed her lips. "I have a feeling the reason you're doing this isn't out of cruelty."

Maybe. Maybe Snitch hit the nail on the head, and I was trying to push her away. Make it easier for her. Make her hate me.

Or maybe I just couldn't fucking look at her anymore. It was selfish.

Lottie sighed, a broken sound. "Just promise me you won't sleep with her. Ever again. As long as we're together. Please. I know what I said before. I know I said you could get it out before marriage, but please don't even look at her."

"I won't."

She put her cheek on her knees, like the weight of her emotions was too much. "We'll be married before the month ends. Does she know?"

I shook my head. "She'll be gone before the month."

"What if she isn't?"

FIFTY-TWO

STORY

As the month passed, though I kept my head down, whispers surrounded me like thick fog.

I was Grayson Crowne's mistress.

I was his wife's new girl.

Strange how I could be Grayson Crowne's mistress, when for a month Grayson hadn't so much as looked in my direction. Each time I saw him in the halls and he walked by me like I was air, another piece of my heart crumbled. I was a ghost again.

August had flown by, and we were now in September, the leaves changing. Soon they would dot a colorful mosaic on the white sand beach. The Crownes' annual opulent Labor Day was just around the corner, and I was back on the side I belonged: servant.

At least Lottie was a lot easier to work with than Abigail had been, though it was more than awkward. Dressing her for public dates with Grayson. Getting her prettied for

photo ops. All the while not acknowledging the elephant in the room.

They'd separated his massive wing, so Lottie had one side of it and Grayson the other. Two bedrooms and bathrooms for Lottie, and two for Grayson. It was about the same size as Abigail's now.

"I've drawn your bath, Ms. du Lac," I said. The water was a subdued aquamarine with floating roses, only candles to light the bathroom.

"Will you stay?" she whispered.

We rarely said anything to one another. So when she asked me to stay, I nearly did a double take.

"Uh...Of course."

Candlelight flickered against the matte white walls, and her shadow was superimposed against them. She placed her chin in her hands, head out of the tub. I tried not to gawk at her naked body, but she reminded me of the goddesses depicted in oil paintings. She was beautiful, so much more perfect than me.

"Grayson Crowne was my first kiss, and I was his first kiss. We were twelve, I think. Maybe younger." She scrunched her eyes, as if remembering. "He was always a good kisser, even when we didn't know what we were doing. Is he still a good kisser?"

Yes. He was the most perfect, heart-scarring kisser. Passionate. Gentle. Tender. Biting. He kissed with his entire soul. Lips that branded and hands that bruised. Every kiss was an occasion, a memory, a phenomenon.

And he'd been my first kiss too. How messed up is that?

My throat closed up.

"I—you—you haven't kissed him?"

She shook her head. "We fooled around that night..." She met my eyes, and I immediately knew *what night* she

meant. "He didn't kiss me. Now that I think about it...I've been kissing him."

Tears fell like perfect pearls down her cheeks, so silent I didn't notice at first. When I saw, I immediately grabbed a cotton handkerchief, bending before her and blotting her eyes.

"I'm so, so sorry Ms. du Lac." I kept repeating it over and over, like it could wash away the stain.

"Lottie, call me Lottie," she rasped.

Eventually her tears stopped, and I sat back.

"Crowne Hall is huge, and I don't have any friends here," she said. "Back home I had friends, and the servants look us in the eyes, and it's just...warm. Here it's so cold." Her pretty dark-chocolate eyes wandered to the window, to the dark night.

"I can be your friend," I blurted, before realizing how absurd that was. Of all people in the world Lottie would want to be friends with, I was probably the last.

Her gaze snapped to mine. "Even after my friends treated you so badly?"

"I haven't been a very good friend either."

We balanced on such a precarious needle.

"I'm sorry," I said, saying the thing that had been weighing on me every time I did her hair or helped her into a dress. "I wasn't supposed to be in that room. It should have been *you*. None of this should have ever happened. It's all my fault."

She chewed her lip, looking distant. "Maybe. Or maybe it was fate."

"But you love him," I said.

"I do," she agreed. "I love him more than I thought I could. As much as I know it hurts you, I can't wait to be his

wife. I can't wait for the wedding night. I can't wait for him to be mine."

Our eyes locked. Remorse rippled in her dark irises, but she wasn't sorry. It was the same way, though I was sorry I'd stolen him, I wasn't sorry for loving him, the same way I wouldn't be sorry if I could trade places with her.

We were only sorry that our love had to hurt each other.

"But my grandma always said our fates aren't a mistake."

She placed her head against her shoulder, staring out the window.

FIFTY-THREE

STORY

My uncle's condition was stable though not great. He was fading every time I visited him, and I kept wondering if each visit was the last. He kept talking about where he wanted to be buried. Here. At the grounds. I think he was starting to lose his mind, and it worried me. No servant had ever been buried at Crowne Hall. That was reserved for the Crownes.

Lottie was too beautiful, too kind—it was impossible to hate her. She let me visit my uncle whenever I wanted. So today I went down to see him with his favorite treat of cookies, but I froze outside the door, a laugh stopping me.

Grayson's laugh.

I didn't realize how much I'd missed it until it snuck into the cracks and crevices his absence weathered.

"My niece is starting to think I've lost my mind, Mr. Grayson."

"You can tell her you'll have a nice big plot of land, with

a view of the ocean. Shit, we'll get you a fucking mausoleum if you want."

"I have. She looks at me with pity. Pity for the old man dying of cancer, who's losing his wits." Grayson laughed again and my uncle said, "Who am I supposed to say is making this happen?"

Grayson exhaled, and I imagined him stretching his long arms over his head. "My mother, of course."

They both laughed.

My heart cracked, crumbled, disappeared into the wind.

I stayed outside the room, holding the tin of cookies, for thirty minutes, maybe an hour. Just listening to him talk with my uncle, at the happiness in my uncle's voice and the ease in Grayson's. I hadn't realized a smile had found its way to my lips until the sound of a chair scraping against the floor wiped it off.

"See you tomorrow, Woodsy."

Tomorrow? How often did he come?

Seconds later, Grayson walked out of my uncle's room. It was only the back of him, but it was enough to send my heart into shock. In a brown leather jacket that brought out the gold in his messy hair. Grayson with dark-blue jeans that hugged his ass too well. Grayson with his big, messy heart.

He kept walking, hadn't noticed me or didn't care. But I couldn't leave it be. I set the tin of cookies down to come back to later.

"Are you ever going to talk to me?" I asked his back.

Gray froze, two heartbeats marking the hope I had that he would turn around; then he kept walking, heading for the stairs.

"You promised!" I yelled. "You *promised* you wouldn't ignore me. You *promised* you wouldn't just disappear."

I followed him like the ghost I was, up the winding staircase the led out of the servants' quarters.

"I spend all day listening to how much your future wife loves you. How much of a good kisser you are. How much she can't wait for her wedding night. I almost threw up."

We wound and wound, me at his back—all that was missing was a fucking candle in my hand.

"You know what sucks the most? I can't hate her. She's too kind. Too beautiful. Too pure."

I slumped against the wall, falling down to the stairs.

"Was I just a game to you too?"

I put my head in my hands. Things I didn't want to acknowledge surfaced, riding a merry-go-round in my head. *A bet. Bragging rights.*

My hands were pried from my face, and I was staring into Grayson's deep pools of blue. He held on to my hands, soft.

I missed the way he held me. I missed the way his kisses consumed me. I missed the secrets he whispered in the dark.

"I miss you," I whispered, weak. "Your bruises have faded, Mr. Grayson."

For a single, shining second, Grayson was back.

My Grayson.

I don't know why he's doing this. I don't know why we're apart, but I see the crushing weight on his shoulders. I pried my hand from his, pressing it to his cheek.

"My Atlas," I whispered. "If your heart is stone, does it crack and weather?"

His eyes cracked, and I saw everything, every emotion I thought I'd dreamed up.

Then he dropped my hand, jaw hard, eyes harder. "I'll never be able to give you anything else but this, Story." He reached into his back pocket, pulling out a golden, heart-shaped locket.

"What's inside?" I asked as he dropped it into my palm.

He grinned a crooked, cruel smile. "My heart."

"You were supposed to die first," I mumbled.

I guess, in a way, our love did.

I went to open it, and he put his hand over mine, stopping me.

"Don't open it unless I've been an unredeemable jackass."

"So wait a few minutes..."

Another grin, sliding a tongue across his sharp canines. From my angle on the floor, it made his jaw sharper.

"Yeah," he said eventually, voice hoarse. "Wait a few minutes."

Grayson stood as if he was going to leave. Leave without another word. Leave me with a token of our love as some kind of parting gift.

I quickly scrambled to follow.

"Why are you doing this?" I grabbed his arm. "I know you're in there. I *know* it."

Grayson covered my hand with his, and urgency became heartburn.

"Either allow me to love you or leave me to hate you!" I exclaimed, chucking the locket to the ground.

He froze as it skittered along the stone, into the shadows.

"I don't want your metal, useless heart," I whispered. "Don't keep doing this to me."

Filling me with false hope and promises. Reminding me *why* I can't hate you.

A month of silence. Of trying to hate him and failing.

And then *this*?

His blue eyes softened for a fraction of a second. Then one by one he peeled my fingers off his biceps. Without so much as another glance in my direction, Grayson walked out of the servants' quarters.

The golden locket glimmered in the shadows.

It didn't feel like an apology or moving forward. It felt like an ending.

FIFTY-FOUR

STORY

All of Crowne Hall in preparation. It was early September, which meant the *holidays* and dreaded mass migration of Crownes were not yet upon us. I assumed they were readying for the great Crowne Labor Day party, but that was usually on the weekend, and today was a weekday.

I was walking back to Lottie from visiting Uncle, and I caught sight of Ellie. She carried a tray of fresh fish to bring to the cooks, so I grabbed her.

"Is there something going on today?"

She looked at the floor. Still no one looked me in the eyes, but I wasn't his mistress. I was just her *girl*. Just a few more months—maybe even less—I had to put up with this, and then I could leave, I thought morbidly. Dismally.

"Never mind," I uttered, letting her go.

She scurried away.

When I got back to Lottie, the sound of glass breaking met me.

"Ms. du Lac?"

A vase broke against the wall, narrowly missing my head. I froze as Lottie screamed and grabbed a porcelain lamp, chucking it at another wall. I'd never seen Lottie like this—she was always so demure. She reached for something else, a crystal votive, and I ran to her, grabbing her arm before she could chuck it.

Heavy breaths wracked her body, tension in every viscera.

"What's going on?" I hedged.

She jerked her head to the side, furious gaze colliding with mine. Then she shoved me off.

"Why don't you leave?" she yelled. "You think you're the only one who knows the unseen sides of him? I was the one who held him when his dad died. It used to only be *me*. Why are you still here? Are you hoping to seduce him back to you?"

I blinked, stunned.

"N-No! My uncle is here. He's...dying."

Her face collapsed. "That's why you visit him so much."

Tension drained from her limbs, and in its place sadness filled, sluggish, defeated.

"Why not anywhere else? The kitchens? Work as a maid? Why does it have to be *me*?"

When you're out, you're out. The servants have excommunicated me. I can't work in the kitchens. I can't even work cleaning the bathrooms. I mean, if Grayson still cared, maybe he could try to force them...but their revenge would make sure I never saw my uncle.

"I can't work for the Crownes anymore," I said simply. "I understand if you don't want me as your girl. I..." *Fuck.* "I understand," I ended lamely.

I don't know where I'd go.

But I wouldn't keep doing this to her.

Lottie looked at her perfect, nude manicure. "Of course I don't want you as my girl. I don't even want to see your face," she whispered. "I don't want to think about you. I wish you didn't exist."

When her eyes met mine, they glistened with unshed tears.

Instinctively I grabbed a silk handkerchief embroidered with the Crowne seal, dabbing her eyes so as not to ruin her makeup.

She slapped my hand away, and the handkerchief flew across the room. I got to my knees to fetch it, and she got to the floor with me.

"I'm sorry," she said. "I'm so sorry. This isn't me. I'm not this person. I just..." She exhaled. "I can't do this anymore."

"You don't have to apologize, Ms. du Lac."

"Call me Lottie!" she screamed.

We both sat back on our asses. Lottie pulled her face into her knees, sobbing.

"Once my uncle...once he..." I couldn't even get the words out. "I'll leave."

I don't know where I'll go. My *life* is here. I didn't want to be so pathetic as to say aloud that this was my home. My home, a place that had rejected me, had tormented me, had barely acknowledged me. I didn't want that to be me, but it was true.

This was my home.

So when it all inevitably ended—because it *would* end, the clock was ticking—I would have to leave, and I'd be without a home again.

"If the fates were fair..." she sniffed.

A box lay open with a pretty dress. I figured she needed to get dressed for whatever the hell was

happening downstairs, and I looked for anything to avoid this.

"Let's just get you dressed." I lifted the dress from the box. "This dress looks pretty."

She lifted swollen eyes. "You have no idea what today is, do you?"

It was something important, based on the number of paparazzi being ushered through the house, the increased security.

"Labor Day?" I guessed.

Lottie slowly got to her feet, defeat weighing her shoulders as she made her way to her bedroom. Pain strangled her eyes, and she looked at me like she couldn't decide if she wanted to throw something at me or hug me.

"That dress isn't for me; it's for *you*."

She slammed the door. I picked up the card discarded from the box. Written in green were the words, *For my little nun.*

The garment was an elegant, yet simple A-line dress with an off-the-shoulder neckline and lacy bodice that gave way to a pure snow skirt. It was perfect for their extravagant Labor Day celebration and reminded me of something Grace Kelly would wear.

It was gorgeous.

What did it *mean*?

Was he trying to say sorry?

I went to Lottie's door, gently knocking. "Lottie?" I said softly.

"You are the last person she wants to see today."

A cold, melodic voice straightened my spine, and I

spun, finding a tall, slender woman who looked a lot like Lottie. She had the same creamy milk chocolate complexion and that inexplicably soft aura.

Class, the first word that came to my mind. Unlike the Crownes', hers was subdued and somehow more intimidating. She wore supple white leather gloves that disappeared up the elbow, into a belted, sandy wool coat. She eyed me with nothing save coldness.

"I thought the servants at Crowne Hall didn't meet the eye," she mused, tilting her chin.

I quickly stared at the floor.

"I'm Mrs. du Lac, Charlotte's mother, and you're in my way."

I quickly stepped to the side, still staring at the floor.

"Lottie, sweet pea?" Mrs. du Lac knocked lightly. "It's me."

"Is everything okay?" I wondered aloud.

Charlotte's mother tensed at my question; then her wide, brown eyes landed on my neck.

"That's a very beautiful locket."

I slapped a hand over it. "I...it's..." Why was I stammering? It meant nothing. It *was* nothing.

So why couldn't I take it off?

"I'm sure you can busy yourself somewhere else for the next hour. I need to have a conversation with my daughter that you don't need to hear."

"Of course."

She eyed the card in my hand. "That card may have your name on it, but you will *never* wear that dress."

I felt caught, like I'd stolen something, even though she was right. It did have my name on it. I wanted to hide it behind my back. Instead, I just stared at the floor.

Mrs. du Lac tested the knob, voice gentle now. "Lottie? I'm coming in."

She opened and closed the door, and Lottie's sobs echoed even through the thick wood. Dread spread like smoke in my body, faint but choking. The dress still lay in its box on the table, and I couldn't help but wonder if Grayson wanted me to wear it tonight.

A Cinderella fantasy played out in my head before I could stop it. Maybe Lottie was crying because he broke up with her, maybe her mom was here to take her home, maybe this dress would take me to the party...

Maybe I was an awful, terrible human.

I looked at the dress again, shaking my head. I wasn't going to play his game.

I slid out of Grayson's wing, "busying myself" looking for answers as to what was going on tonight, and maybe a slice of pizza. I hated eating leftover fancy food.

Crowne Hall was even busier than when I'd left it. Double the servants on the floor, double the security, and more paparazzi getting walked through to the press room. A servant rushed by me, someone I didn't recognize. They'd hired *more* help for whatever was happening.

"What's going on?" I asked him, hoping he didn't know enough about me to ignore me.

He paused, looking at the floor. "It's taking place in the antique room."

My heart squeezed at the idea of returning there, but still I wandered into the antique room.

Artificial snowflakes dusted the black windows like glitter. That was the first sign, when I should've turned around and run. But I stepped farther inside, my toes crushing an aisle of white rose petals, and, I was sure, real diamonds that

cut the room in two. I was flanked by rows and rows of chairs.

Down the aisle was an arch, a backdrop, dripping with more flowers than I'd ever seen in my life. Hundreds of roses and calla lilies and orchids dotted with diamonds. At the helm was a boy. With messy spun rose gold hair, cutting blue eyes, and a suit so dark emerald it could be black...and an emerald pocket square to match.

That was when it hit me.

In my darkest, deepest nightmares I couldn't have dreamed this up.

It wasn't the Labor Day party. He wasn't saying sorry.

I grasped a chair to keep from stumbling. This was *our wedding.*

But it wasn't for us.

FIFTY-FIVE

STORY

My breath left me in gasps as I tried to suck in more air. I stumbled again, falling into one of the elegantly decorated chairs and knocking it over. Heads turned, including Grayson's. His eyes zeroed on me.

There'd been a time when that piercing blue gaze made my knees weak; now it just made my lungs collapse.

He took strides down the aisle, and I backed away, knocking into more chairs. He was too fast, and I was too out of control.

More people were looking. I backed away farther, tripping over some kind of lace or tulle decoration, bringing down a few chairs with me. I landed with a *thwack*, ass throbbing, head ringing when the back of a chair slammed into my face.

But still, for a minute, I was safely shrouded under their protection. My vision was obscured. I was safe in shadows,

and I prayed for the earth to open up and swallow me whole.

Then Grayson reached in and gripped my wrist, tearing me from the mess of tulle and flowers and chairs.

"You've made quite an entrance."

"You're marrying her?" I shoved him off, and he grabbed my biceps instead. Probably for the best, as I was still unsteady, trembling.

"That's how fiancés work," he responded with a bored tone that cut me.

"Ass." I tried to rip myself away to no avail. "You know what I mean. I thought the wedding wasn't until next Christmas."

Grayson didn't answer, but his grip on my bicep tightened painfully.

This was why Lottie was so upset.

You have no idea what today is, do you?

Why did he send a dress, a *white* dress?

I thought we had time. I thought *I* had time. None of it felt real. Until...until now.

"Why are you doing this?" I searched his eyes.

Do you not love me?

Did you ever?

"Next year, today, doesn't make any fucking difference." He sighed deeply—I was a chore. I'd become a chore again..

"What aren't you telling me?"

I punched his chest, but he didn't so much as stumble. A few servants turned our way, but when Grayson shot them looks, they busied themselves with the decorating.

"Why did you give me that dress?" I yelled, so loud everyone couldn't help but look, all turning to watch Story explode into whatever pieces remained.

He dragged me out of the room, back into the halls.

This time I managed to yank my arm out of his hold. We stared at one another in silence, the bustle of his wedding preparations around us our ugly melody. I wanted to yell and scream at him.

I wanted him to hug me and tell me it was wrong, this was wrong, he wasn't marrying her.

I wanted to go back in time and have never kissed him.

His tux was perfectly tailored. A deep and intoxicating green, and when the satin emerald lapels caught the light, he was heart-stopping. Everything from his bowtie to the watch on his wrist was so perfectly put together. Meanwhile I was coming apart at the seams.

"That wasn't *your* dress. You're Lottie's girl—a servant must have addressed it to you." He checked his watch. "The wedding starts soon." He lowered his wrist, arching a brow in the direction of his wing. "She probably needs help with *her* wedding dress."

"I hate you, Grayson Crowne."

He paused at my words, eyes pinched.

Maybe. Maybe he would say something, make sense of all this.

He turned on his heel, taking long strides back to the altar, never once looking back.

FIFTY-SIX

STORY

I knocked on the door before I entered. Now that I knew *why* Lottie was so upset, I felt like a bug begging to sit on her food when I came back.

"Come in," Lottie croaked.

Lottie was sitting with her spine straight, staring into the mirror of her vanity. She was calmer, and her mother was nowhere to be seen.

She caught my eyes in the mirror. "Oh, it's...you."

Tension bubbled between us.

"I was told you needed help with your wedding gown, Ms. du Lac."

She stared back at the mirror with a sigh. "I'm sure you know now I'm soon to be Mrs. Grayson Crowne."

I was certain she didn't say it as a jab to me, because there was too much sorrow in her voice. She stared at her face in the mirror blankly. Sometime while I'd been gone,

hair and makeup had stopped by. She reminded me of a statue.

I went to the window, where her dress hung, my heart aching when I knelt before her with it, and she took an elegant step inside.

"You know that's all I ever wanted," she said as I pulled the dress up her body, "since we were little kids and we shared our first bumbling kiss. I thought, I've found my Prince Charming. But then he became Playboy Gray, and I was too afraid. I couldn't see beyond it. Because I've watched my mom's heart break over and over again as she loved my dad, who loved everyone but her."

As she spoke, I swallowed my tears, adjusting the thick strip of satin off-the-shoulder trim. I tried to numb myself to what I was doing, tried to focus only on fabric. Not that I was helping the woman who would marry the man I loved into her wedding gown. My fingers trembled, my chest cracked.

Where did it all go wrong?

"It's all my fault. All of this."

I got to my knees, adjusting the snow-white A-line hem that just barely touched the floor. She was barefoot. She would need shoes. I repeated it over and over, looking for shoes, until I found the pair of glittering silver-and-glass Jimmy Choos that matched the dress.

Why did it have to be *glass*?

I slid one of her feet into them, then the other. I stood up, finished. She looked like a princess in her white dress. All that was missing was a tiara.

"I'm going to be his wife," she said, rubbing the lace that clung just above her elbows.

"And I'll still be your girl."

We let the unsaid words linger between us like carbon monoxide. Invisible. Choking.

She's going to be his wife. I'm going to be her girl, and I slept with her husband.

I *loved* her husband.

I still do, even though I should hate him.

Tears edged the ridges of her lids, and I reached for the nearest handkerchief on her vanity.

"Don't cry on your wedding day, Ms. du Lac," I teased without humor.

"Call me Lottie," she said absently, then sighed. "I'm marrying a man who loves someone else...do you think fate hears what you want, and so she decides to give it to you, but in, like, the most fucked-up way possible?"

I laughed darkly.

Maybe.

"He chose you," I said, heart breaking. "He loves *you*. This has always been about one thing, *you*. I was just..." I took a rocky breath that cut me all the way down to my lungs. "I was a thief. I stole him, and now I'm giving him back. This was the way it was supposed to be."

It was a wedding, but it felt like a funeral.

Lottie du Lac was always the princess, and I was always the thief. I could never look so *right* as she did in this moment.

She frowned at me in the mirror, touching her ears. "They forgot to put in my pearls."

I set down the handkerchief, searching for the pearls. When I found them, I had to stand on my tiptoes to reach her. She was a bit taller than me. Add in the heels, and it meant I was stretching.

"I hate you a little bit, Story," she said quietly, and I swallowed, trying to focus on putting in her earring. "I hate

you because I know he's going to be thinking of you tonight."

The earrings fell from my hand with a clang so loud compared to her soft voice, clattering, disappearing into shadows I couldn't see. I didn't move away, close enough to smell her light, floral perfume, to see the resigned sadness in her dark eyes.

"The same way, maybe, you hate me," she whispered. "Because after tonight, he'll be mine."

I swallowed.

Yeah.

"I think maybe..." she continued at a normal volume, and I realized I was still standing way too close, so I cleared my throat and took two steps back. "I've been thinking about it for a month now. How I can end this for both of us, *all* of us? I can't share him after my wedding, but maybe..." Lottie rubbed the lace along her dress again. "Can you do me a favor?" she asked after a moment.

"Of course, Ms. du Lac."

"Can you give Grayson something for me?"

I couldn't hide the pain and anguish from my face. I was hoping to avoid Gray as much as possible. Go back to before, when I was a ghost, and he was the monster I tiptoed around. So I would live in his house—it didn't mean I had to see him. I'd lived in his house for years without him noticing me. I just needed to survive a few months.

"Please don't make me see him. Please. I'll do anything else."

"He's not supposed to see the bride," she whispered.

Didn't I owe her this? After stealing him? After everything?

My shoulders fell. "What do you need me to give him?"

She rooted around the drawers of her vanity, pulling out

a sweetly scented letter. Where it opened, she signed it with her name, so that I couldn't sneak a peek.

"You have to wait for him to read it too," she added.

With another resigned exhale, I went to go find Grayson.

"One more thing, Story."

I turned back. Lottie faced me with a tense jaw, and if I saw right, fear in her eyes.

"I will forget everything that happens before he puts on the ring, but once we're married, if you fuck my husband, I don't care if your entire family is dying and this is the only place that can save them. I'll put you all on the streets. I'm not going to be my mother. Do you understand?"

"I won't be my mother, either, Ms. du Lac."

She frowned, not understanding what I meant, but maybe understanding my intention, because she nodded.

"Mr. Crowne?" I asked, voice like sandpaper.

My fingers trembled with the note in my hand. The paper was thick and silky, rich feeling. I stared at the rose petal floor, not daring to look him in the eyes.

"Mr. Crowne, your fiancée has sent me to give you something."

I could feel his eyes. I could feel the eyes of the crowd at my back. I saw his bow tie, his sharp angular jaw. His slight *Grayson frown* that served only to make his lips more luscious.

Back to being a blurry Polaroid

Then his hands were on mine, warm and strong, taking the letter.

Too brief.

Too swift.

His warmth gone.

I listened to the crinkle of paper as he opened the letter. His thick thumb grazed the edge of the silky paper.

I remembered too easily how his fingers felt on me.

In me.

It felt like forever that I stared at the rose-petal-dotted floor. The music was starting up, what sounded like a string trio playing popular songs as more people were being ushered inside. Then all at once Grayson crushed the piece of paper and tossed it to the floor. He grasped my wrist, pulling me away from the altar.

"What are you doing?" I gasped, throwing a look over my shoulder, at the quickly disappearing faces of the crowd.

He dragged me behind the flowery veil partitioning the antique room.

"You don't get to touch me!" I yanked myself free the minute we were hidden. "I just dressed your fiancée in her wedding dress. A dress you either sent to me or sent to *fuck with me*. It was written in *green*."

I couldn't cry. I *wouldn't* cry. But my lids burned fire.

Except as Grayson stood opposite me, he stared holes into me, a look that had been absent from his eyes, his face, for over a month. And it made me question again, question *everything*.

"I hate you," I said, but the words held no heat. "I hate you with everything I have."

My head was still down when Grayson took a step toward me, and lifted the locket from my collarbone with his pointer finger, raising my chin with it. His eyes throbbed with determination. "My honest little nun, lying really doesn't suit you."

We were barely hidden by our light-soaked flower wall,

and I wondered if the guests could see us, two shadows of a love that never should have been. The soft sound of a wedding about to begin drifted to us, guests chatting, the trio starting a song.

"Fine." I hung my head. "I can't say I don't love you."

Weak.

That's what I was: *weak.*

Or maybe this was the dignity my uncle spoke of. Not somehow avoiding shame but facing it. Shame for the heart that still beat for the man who broke it.

From the start, I've had an inexplicable, *inescapable,* connection with Grayson Crowne. *Why?* This boy *ruined* me. Treated me like fucking trash. That isn't a soul mate. It's pathetic.

"But I'll learn," I said, voice hoarse. "I'll learn to hate you, Grayson Crowne. I promise."

His grip on the locket tightened, and he yanked the necklace forward. It bit the skin of my neck, forcing me forward on a gasp. Until I was at his lips, tasting him, *breathing* him.

"Good," he growled, and crushed his lips against mine.

FIFTY-SEVEN

STORY

"Kiss me," Grayson growled when I tried to shove him off.

"What are you—" But before I could even get the word out, his lips were on mine again. Warm, firm, biting and sucking and so fucking *good*.

Lollipops and whiskey.

I sighed at the taste, arching into his kiss. He gripped my lower back, dragging me by the curve into his body, forcing me to bend more. He growled into my open mouth, devouring me. Anything I gave, he stole more.

Savage.

Wild.

The mask officially ripped off, tossed to the side.

I tore my mouth away to breathe, and he didn't stop. Kissing my neck, tearing down my collar to bite. I grasped his shoulders, and when I looked down, I caught him staring at me. Piercing blue eyes.

I looked away, and he dragged my stare back by the

chin.

"You're mine, Snitch," he growled, biting my neck, eyes glaring up at me from my exposed collarbone. "Say it."

I licked my lips, avoiding the thought blaring like a freshly carved tattoo.

I'm his.

His palms rounded my ass, lifting me, thrusting me up against the table, causing the items on it to rattle. I tried not to pay attention to the rattle of *what* was on the table. The marriage license, the gilded pens to sign their names.

Instead I focused on the ache in my groin as he spread my thighs around his hips.

"Fucking. Say. It." He punctuated each word against my skin with a sharp bite.

"I'm yours," I gasped, eliciting a groan of approval deep in his throat.

He tangled his hands in my hair, dragging my lips back to his. "Mine."

Because it was true. Even if he could never belong to me, I would always belong to him. Painfully, ruinously, irrevocably.

He broke from my lips and gripped the back of my neck with powerful hands. "I can't promise you anything. I can't promise you anything but this moment. After this...I'll leave you to hate me, Story."

Either allow me to love you or leave me to hate you.

Grayson thumbed tears out of my eyes. "So tell me to stop. Tell me your fucking safe word. Shit...don't say anything, and I'll let this be the end of it."

His eyes burned, willpower cracking in them like sky breaking through clouds. Months ago I could have ended this before the worst of it, if only I'd told him to stop when he'd given me the chance.

Say no, Snitch. Tell me to stop.

Then, I hadn't given him an answer. I'd hidden behind a lie out of fear of my desire. Now, I had the chance to right my wrong on the altar of his wedding. Do it all over again. Be the person I always thought I was. Good. Moral.

"I don't want you to stop," I said.

His eyes grew, but he didn't move. His body so tense and rigid, muscles coiled, like he wanted to grab me but was stopping himself, even after I'd said I didn't want him to. I tugged at his bow tie, loosening it until it lay crooked. I undid the top buttons of his dress shirt, and bit his exposed neck.

He let out a ragged sigh.

"Please don't stop, Grayson."

I was already in hell without him. What was one more sin?

I took his hand from my neck, placing it between my thighs.

He dropped his head to my shoulder on a groan. "You're already so fucking wet."

He pushed aside my panties, pressing one finger between my lips, but going no further. I arched, trying to force him in.

"You want this?" His voice was rough, sharp, jagged. "I don't have a condom, Story." He thrust his finger inside me, and my mouth opened on a silent gasp.

Outside, the music grew louder, a violent clash of strings.

"That's what happens when you only carry one around for ten years hoping to get lucky," I breathed out, arching into him.

He slammed his free hand on the wall behind me. "No jokes, little nun."

Still, he teased my clit with his thumb in slow, taunting circles. Watching me. Devouring me. His self-control evident by the muscle twitching in his neck.

His words cautioned, but his fingers pumping into me rough and hard belied what his lips would have me believe.

"I'm not on any birth control," I admitted.

"I don't give a shit. Tell me to stop. Tell me your safe word."

He fucked me with his fingers like it was his last time... and I guess...it was. He drank me in. I curled into the feeling, lost myself. He wanted words from me when all I could manage were whimpers.

He thumbed my clit. "What's the first rule of training?"

"When you say come..." I breathed, so close to hitting that spot.

He removed his hands *right when* I was about to come, leaving me dazed, buzzed, exhilarated.

"Tell me your safe word. Tell me your safe word, little nun, and I'll let you come."

His fingers ghosted across my clit, seizing my breath.

Everything about this was a bad idea. I knew it, but still, I craved him. I wanted him. Only moments ago he'd kissed me, and I missed his lips. It had been over a month since I'd had him inside me.

I reached for his pants, undoing them, reaching for his cock. "No. No safe word. I want you inside me."

He didn't stop me when I pulled out his cock, but he didn't help me either. He swallowed a noise low in his throat when I held him in my hand.

I spread my legs, wanting him, wishing him to just come to me.

His tongue darted out, wetting his full lower lip, nostrils flared.

"Is it because I could trap you with a baby?" I whispered my deep fear—of becoming my mother.

His harsh eyes softened, and he leaned forward, swallowing me in his arms, planting soft, intoxicating kisses along my neck. "You'd never trap me, little nun. But I could trap you. So say your fucking word."

He was hard at my entrance, so close to *being inside me*. "No."

He crooked his neck, jaw tense, nostrils flared. Then he slammed inside me.

"Fuck," he groaned into my shoulder, muffling the noise.

I grabbed his shoulders as he moved inside me, the marriage license rattling. I wrapped my legs around his, urging him farther. I buried my face in his neck, so I didn't see the flower wall, trying to scrub away the why and where of this moment in him. His warm neck, his strong arms, his intoxicating scent.

"Fuck," he groaned. "I want to fill you up until I leak down your thighs."

His dirty words sent shivers up and down my spine, and somehow had me aching, even as he was inside me. I wanted that too.

"Please," I whispered.

"Yeah?" his voice was hoarse. "Please what?"

He sped up faster, harder, holding the desk for balance as it rattled against the wall.

"I want you to come inside me."

"Fucking say it again."

"*Please* come inside me."

As I spoke, Pachelbel's Canon started. Lottie would make her appearance soon, but we were already too far gone.

"More," I whispered, delirious.

"That fucking word," Gray said, a delicious cocksure tease to his words. "More what?" He dragged out my lip with his teeth. The canon grew louder, masking his groans. I gripped his taut butt, flexing. He bit my shoulder, my neck, kissing my ear.

"More of your cock, more teeth, more—" Grayson slammed into me, and I broke off on a scream. He covered my mouth.

Because he had to.

Because his wife was walking down the aisle—to an *empty* altar.

Tears fell, and he grasped my face, kissing my cheeks, kissing away my tears, before finding my lips and consuming me in a long, soul-deep kiss. Sucking me. Consuming me.

For how wrong it was, but how much I wanted it.

His cock worked an evil, delirious rhythm inside me. I could feel every ridge, every throb, and he was hitting that perfect, amazing, addicting spot.

I scratched the wall behind me as pleasure started to hit too high, and he grabbed my wrist, putting my hand against his neck.

I blinked. "I'll hurt you."

"Do it," he growled.

"But—"

Grayson thrust, and I dug without thinking.

"Fucking *mark me*, Story."

I dug my nails into his neck.

"Harder," he demanded, voice like rock. I dug until I felt skin break, and his cock throbbed within me.

"Fuck yes," he groaned.

I lifted my hand, seeing four uneven lines down his

neck. I touched them, and he hissed, quirking his head to the side, but his eyes burned, and his cock throbbed harder inside me. Shivers ran all along my body, setting into my gut.

"Fuck, I can feel you coming." His hoarse voice was like whiskey against my lips. His grip tightened on my hips. "You were fucking made for me, Story. Your cunt is fucking magic, fucking *mine*. Fuck—fucking tell me your safe word."

"No," I said, tears wobbling my words. "Don't leave me alone. Don't make me be the only one."

The only person addicted, consumed, and lost to their wretched desires.

Tears streamed down my face as Pachelbel's Canon reached its crescendo, knowing Lottie had started her wedding march. I heard murmurs of the crowd, wondering where Gray was.

He gripped my face. "I won't. You aren't." He swallowed my lips, masking a soul-shattering groan as he came inside me.

For a moment I let myself forget this was an ending, our soundtrack my true love's wedding to another woman. Grayson pulled back, forehead pressed to mine, then grasped my hand, kissing my ring finger over and over again, before biting. So hard I let out a gasp.

"I love you, Story Hale," Gray said, voice so hoarse it sounded like sandpaper. "I'll never *stop* loving you, Story Hale."

My Atlas, *crushed*.

That was when he finally told me he loved me, when he was about to marry another woman.

More tears welled in my eyes, but he thumbed them away before pressing his thumbs to my jaw—*hard*—and

kissing me again. Sucking all my breath, my soul, bruising his lips.

I wanted to extend this moment forever.

But the song was almost over and Grayson...Grayson was back here, with me. The murmurs of the crowd were almost louder than the wedding march. How awful Lottie must feel.

"I think you need to go," I croaked, breaking our kiss.

"Story..."

"Goodbye, Mr. Crowne."

I used our safe word, throat dry and scratchy.

Grayson kept his forehead against mine for a moment, and I redirected my gaze to the floor.

He swallowed, then disentangled himself. I wished I could curl up in a ball and die, but I settled for closing my legs. Grayson buttoned his pants, fixed his shirt, retied his bow tie. He looked perfect, like he hadn't just shattered my world.

He watched me a moment, then took out the green pocket square, dabbing the tears I couldn't stop from my eyes. He let me take over after a moment.

I lifted it to give it back, but he raised a hand. "Keep it."

A pause.

"If you tell anyone—" he started, but I cut him off.

"Even if I did," I whispered.

A wrinkle formed between his brows, but it quickly disappeared, and he walked around the flower partition.

Back to his wedding.

Back to a fiancée and world where I would never belong. Because this is what happens in the real Cinderella story. The prince has to marry a princess, and people like us? We have to find peace in the ashes.

FIFTY-EIGHT

STORY

I folded and refolded the square Grayson had given me, stuck sitting behind the flowery partition as they said their vows. I was the girl behind the girl, literally.

"Do you, Charlotte du Lac, take Grayson Crowne to be your husband?" the minister asked.

I lifted my head, staring at the flowers that separated us, imagining her staring up at him from beneath her pretty veil, her even prettier dress.

"I do." Her soft, even voice drifted through.

"And do you, Grayson Crowne, take Charlotte du Lac to be your wife?"

A moment passed like a year as I waited for Grayson to answer.

"I do," he said.

"Ow," I gasped, all the breath leaving me like the time I'd had the wind knocked out of me.

I fell against the wall. I knew it was coming, so I didn't

think it would hurt as much, but it still felt like I'd been shot in the chest.

I gripped the square harder.

This was the only ending.

I knew when they kissed by the cheers.

When the music started up, I could imagine when they walked down the aisle, out the door, and presumably into a new life.

I sat in the dark for a while, thumbing the locket. I trailed the clasp with my thumb, sticking my nail into the groove. I wasn't sure I wanted to know what was inside Grayson Crowne's heart. I was afraid if I did, I couldn't hate him.

And I needed to hate him.

I waited until I was certain there was no one in the room to walk out from behind the partition. Walked in a daze through the halls, until the snap of fingers stopped me. I blinked and looked into the eyes of Ms. Barn.

"I've been looking everywhere for you. Where the hell have you been?"

"Around..."

Ms. Barn glared. "Mrs. Grayson Crowne will need her second, third, and fourth dress. You'll have to prepare her for the reception. Mrs. Tansy was *not* pleased with the size of the ceremony, so the reception is going to more than make up for it..."

Mrs. Grayson Crowne.

I blinked, stunned. I felt like I'd been shocked. *Mrs. Grayson Crowne.* The name thumped against my heart like someone stepping on a bruise.

"Story?" She peered at me.

"Right," I barely got out. "Of course. Wait, you're calling me Story again."

"You're no longer a part of the du Lac household. Welcome home." Ms. Barn smiled at me, but her expression carried something else.

Something darker.

I couldn't figure it out, but moments later, when I returned to the servants' quarters to change before refreshing Lottie's dresses, I got my answer.

It was my home.

Cramped, mildewy home.

And all my belongings were scattered on the floor, my clothes ripped and ruined.

"You really should've left, Story."

"Ellie?" I spun, finding her in the doorway. "Do you know what happened?"

She looked at me with almost pity. "Did you think because you fucked Grayson Crowne you wouldn't get the same treatment? Or maybe because your uncle has worked here longer than Jesus, we'd go soft on you?"

"I thought..." I looked back at my ruined belongings. "I've been back for over a month."

"You were a guest, working for Ms. du Lac. But now? Welcome *home*, Story."

Home.

I swished the word around in my mouth like stale soda when I got back to Grayson's wing and hung *Mrs. Grayson Crowne's* dresses up, each one more beautiful than the last. When I'd hung the last, I reached for the jewelry to accompany them.

It was time to forget about Grayson Crowne. I had bigger things to worry about. Like my uncle, or the fact that I had an entire palace of servants out for revenge.

But a bruise was already forming around my ring finger in the shape of his teeth.

The sound of the door creaking open behind me jarred me from my thoughts, and I turned, expecting and dreading to find Lottie—no, *Mrs. Grayson Crowne*. I all but dropped the diamond necklace I held when I saw who stood in the doorway.

"West?" I looked around, expecting Grayson's guards to storm in any minute. "How did you get in here?"

He shrugged with a smile. "I said I would be there, Angel."

FIFTY-NINE

GRAY

When Lottie and I were finally away from prying eyes, I lifted her veil. Mascara ran black down her soft cocoa cheeks.

I exhaled. "You can't bribe fate."

She swiped at her cheeks but only smeared the black. "It's nothing. I'm just really happy. Did you get my letter?"

I wiped her cheeks. "I did."

"Is that why you were late to the wedding?" I nodded. "Did it work..." She looked up at me through her runny eyes. "Is she *finally* out of your system?"

That's what I'd been trying to do for fucking months. This last month, I wanted to forever ruin that part of her that thought she could love me.

And I fucking failed.

Each taste, moment, second with Snitch just burrowed her deeper. I couldn't lie to Lottie, but I couldn't reassure her either.

Lottie fell to the bed, messing up the perfectly arranged roses, my silence speaking volumes.

"They think we're fucking in here." Lottie swiped at the roses. "I fucking hate roses. Especially white ones."

A small smile broke. "I don't know if I've ever heard Lottie du Lac use the f-word."

"There's a lot we don't know about each other."

I nodded. Yeah.

"I just really wanted my husband to love me. To think of me on our wedding night. And only me."

I touched my neck. Her scratches still burned. The way Story had come just hours before was fucking tattooed inside me forever.

How I came inside her.

A sick, twisted part of me wished for something I knew would only bring destruction to all of us.

"Are you going to be sleeping with her in this house?" Lottie asked. "People will talk."

"I know you don't know me very well, Lottie, but I wouldn't do that to you. Or her."

Her shoulders sagged; then her eyes shone again. "But... I'd understand if you need to say goodbye. If...if...tonight wasn't enough." More tears fell down her cheek, and she looked like saying the words had almost made her sick.

Music drifted in beneath the cracks in the door, floating around us. Downstairs, the real party was just getting started, my mother's revenge for forcing such a small wedding.

"I already said my goodbye. From this day on, I'm your husband."

TO BE CONTINUED.

ACKNOWLEDGMENTS

I always feel like I should keep this short and sweet, because I don't want anyone to skim! But it's impossible. My list keeps growing, because those I'm grateful to keeps growing. Those I'm forever thankful to for helping me bring *Stolen Soulmate* out into the world includes, but isn't limited to:

The readers! Every one of you who asked about Gray and Story, who wondered about their relationship, you helped bring this into the world!

My street team, The Diehardy Girls. You promo your asses off, but more importantly, you are a genuine sisterhood. I always know I can count on you. My favorite thing is to wake up and see our hilarious chats.

My reader group, GetHard. You continue to be a safe, inclusive, and welcoming place on the internet.

The bloggers, readers, and bookstagrammers.

You sign-up and devote your free time, your passion and dedication is unrivaled, and I'm so grateful to all of you.

The authors in this community. Those of you who build up instead of tear-down, who took their time to offer me sincere advice or friendship, you are gems in this community.

Aundi, Ellie, and Paramitra "Pipa." You are women who are very much *not* mean girls, and are some of the amazing people that make up this bookish community.

My dream team of PAs. Mel and Serena, you have my back, and, maybe more importantly, you keep my head on straight.

My betas. You read the raw versions of Story and Gray, and helped me turn it into something shiny. Sonal, Sarah, Rukaiya, Serena, Mel, your feedback was imperative, and your reactions when you realized this was a cliffhanger made me laugh way too hard.

Chelé. I am so, *so* thankful to you for doing a sensitivity reading! It was really important to me with writing this book that I didn't feed into any negative stereotypes.

My editors. James Gallagher of Evident Ink, Rumi, and Ellie with My Brother's Editor, you polished my story into something beautiful.

My cover designer. Hang Le, you once again perfectly depicted the insides of this book with a beautiful outside.

Sarah with Teasers by the Modern Belle. You continue to blow me away with your gorgeous graphics. #hotmesstwins

My promo team. Candi Kane, Give Me Books, this was my first time doing wide release and you were there every step of the way.

My husband, family, and my friends.

And to everyone and in-between...I love you!

If you've read my books before, you know I would love if you write your name in down here. Whether it's in ink in your paperback or a highlight on an ebook...

$$\longleftrightarrow$$

Because I am so grateful to **YOU** for helping me on this journey and continuing to support me.

BOOKS BY MARY CATHERINE GEBHARD

Crowne Point Universe (standalone)

Heartless Hero

Stolen Soulmate

Forbidden Fate

Gemma and Grim's book (coming soon)

The Hate Story Duet

Beast: A Hate Story, The Beginning

Beauty: A Hate Story, The End

Standalones

Dirty Law

Owned Series

You Own Me (Owned #1)

Let Me Go (Owned #2)

Tied (Owned #2.5)

Come To Me (Owned #3)

Patchwork House

Skater Boy (Patchwork House #1)

Patchwork House #2

Patchwork House #3

Patchwork House #4

www.PatchworkHouseSeries.com

Line editing by James Gallagher of Evident Ink
Proof Reading by Rumi and My Brother's Editor
Cover by Hang Le

Stolen Soulmate
ISBN-13: 978-1-7338510-6-0
An Unglued Books Publication
www.MaryGebhard.com

STOLEN SOULMATE

MARY CATHERINE GEBHARD